After a career in the Civil Service, Brenda Clarke began writing when her two children had left school. Since then she has written about twenty novels, many of which were published under her maiden name of Brenda Honeyman.

Brenda Clarke lives with her husband in Keynsham, Bristol.

THREE WOMEN

Brenda Clarke

CORGI BOOKS

THREE WOMEN
A CORGI BOOK 0 552 13260 8

Originally published in Great Britain by
Hutchinson & Co. (Publishers) Ltd.

PRINTING HISTORY
Hutchinson edition published 1985
Corgi edition published 1987

This book is set in 10/11 Melior

Corgi Books are published by Transworld Publishers
Ltd., 61–63 Uxbridge Road, Ealing, London W5 5SA, in
Australia by Transworld Publishers (Aust.) Pty. Ltd.,
15–23 Helles Avenue, Moorebank, NSW 2170, and in New
Zealand by Transworld Publishers (N.Z.) Ltd., Cnr. Moselle
and Waipareira Avenues, Henderson, Auckland.

Printed and bound in Great Britain by
Cox & Wyman Ltd., Reading, Berks.

. . . *the Monstrous Regiment of Women*
JOHN KNOX 1505 – 1572

Part One 1916 – 1920

Living from hand to mouth
Guillaume de Salluste 1544 – 1590

CHAPTER ONE

The Methodist chapel in Arley Street had never been completed. The red-brick and yellow-tile façade with its unstained glass windows, hid what had originally been intended for the Sunday School and Meeting Hall. The chapel proper was to have been built at the back, on a piece of land sloping towards the Arley Street canal, but the money had run out in the early 1860s. It was therefore decided to use the existing building for worship in all its various forms. The rostrum was, in fact, much too high for a pulpit, being almost on a level with the balcony which decorated three sides of the hall; but, fifty years later, people had grown so accustomed to this vagary that, in the eyes of the Arley Street congregation, it was the other chapels which appeared unusual. Elizabeth Evans, leaning her arms on the balcony's wooden balustrade this bright September Sunday in 1916, certainly saw nothing amiss with the building as she stared down into the body of the hall, where all the boys were sitting.

'Separating the sheep from the goats,' Jack Hennessey called it, knowing how the remark always irritated her.

'I suppose it's fair enough to call boys "goats",' Elizabeth would answer tartly, her fierce blue eyes sparkling with the light of battle, and toss her mane of reddish-brown hair. 'But I don't agree with segregating the sexes, not even for Sunday School. It's as though they're afraid the female sex will contaminate all you men.'

Jack, at sixteen, was too flattered by being described as a man to pursue the argument, which seemed to follow precisely the same conversational pattern each time the subject was raised. Also, although he would rarely admit it, he was a little in awe of Elizabeth, with her grammar school education and her rapier-sharp tongue. No matter how often he reminded himself that she was merely a girl, two years his junior, he could never quite rid himself of a sense of inferiority; particularly when Elizabeth scathingly referred to him as 'the son of an itinerant Paddy-whack'.

Jack Hennessey shuffled his feet in their shiny black Sunday shoes and scratched his left leg where the coarse brown woollen stocking made it itch. His knickerbockers and jacket were uncomfortably tight. He was growing out of them, but with three younger children to feed and clothe, his mother could not afford to buy him a bigger suit.

'That one'll have to last a bit longer, my sonny,' she had scolded only that morning, when he had dared to complain. 'I'm already in debt to Harrison's fer a shillin' a week. I can't afford more at the moment.'

Eileen Hennessey was local, and had been a plump, fresh-faced west-country girl when, seventeen years earlier, she had caught the eye of a young Irish labourer from Cork, helping to dig the Arley Street canal. In spite of the difference in religion, Padraic Hennessey had agreed to marry her when he discovered she was pregnant, and had stayed long enough to give her three more children, all girls, before finally irrevocably disappearing from Eileen's life one cold December morning, nine years previously. No one had seen him since, nor expected to hear from him again.

Eileen Hennessey had accepted her husband's

departure philosophically. She had not anticipated that Padraic would remain with her as long as he had, and by taking in washing, scrimping and saving, she had managed to scrape a living for herself, her son and her three daughters. She was a woman generally liked by all her neighbours; even by the Evanses, who lived next door, and had some pretensions to gentility on account of their connection with Joseph Gordon.

It was, in fact, the late arrival of young Helen Gordon which was delaying the start of the Sunday School service, and causing the Sunday School Superintendent to tap his fingers disapprovingly on the edge of the rostrum. Mr Pound did not dare begin without her, however, Joseph Gordon being too influential a man, both in civic and chapel affairs, to be upset. Gordon's Quality Chocolates had provided the district of Eastwood with the bulk of its employment for over a century; and although the family had long since moved to the more salubrious heights of Clifton, it was one of Joseph's conceits that his daughter should travel halfway across the city each Sunday afternoon to attend Sunday School at the chapel where she was christened.

'It's a sop to Uncle Joe's conscience,' Elizabeth had once remarked to Jack Hennessey. 'Sending Helen slumming every week is his way of propitiating God.'

It never occurred to her when she used big words that Jack did not always understand their meaning. He had left elementary school at the age of thirteen and gone to work for Harrison's Universal Clothing Company, Eastwood's other main source of jobs.

There was a bustle at the back of the hall, and all heads turned towards the entrance as Helen Gordon came in, accompanied by the Gordons' elderly, wartime chauffeur. The man removed his peaked cap and slipped silently into a pew, while Helen climbed the stairs to the gallery, her eyes searching anxiously for her cousin Elizabeth, who reluctantly made room

11

for her on the front bench. As she did so, the Superintendent cleared his throat and announced the first hymn.

Although Helen had recently celebrated her thirteenth birthday, she seemed much younger. The clustering fair curls, the wide-set blue eyes, the retroussé nose, the soft pastel colours in which her mother dresssed her, and above all her genuine air of candour, contributed to an impression of innocence which most people found irresistible.

'She'll break hearts,' Minna Gordon had prophesied years ago, dandling her dainty, fairy-like little daughter on her knee, and realizing that the gods had given Helen a nature as sweet and trusting as her face. Helen was everybody's darling and the apple of her father's eye.

The fact that Minna had presented him with a daughter, only to find that she was unable to have any more children, had long ago ceased to be a source of grievance to Joseph Gordon. At first, the discovery that he would never have a son to inherit the business had seemed like retribution for flouting his father's wishes; for marrying a girl so far beneath him, a girl from the factory floor. But as Helen grew more beautiful, day by day, year by year, Joseph no longer regretted the son he would never have, and ceased to remember his Aunt Harriet's accusation that his marriage had been the cause of his father's premature death. Helen became his world, his reason — apart from the factory — for living. Cosseted, protected, given anything she wanted, within reason, it was astonishing — everyone said so — that Helen remained so completely unspoiled.

The one person immune to Helen's charm was her cousin Elizabeth. But then, everyone knew that Elizabeth Evans was as hard as nails. Even her own parents and her elder sister called her 'strong-willed'. Only Jack Hennessey suspected that there was a soft core to Elizabeth's nature; that the abrasive shell was the protection for a vulnerable centre.

As the hymn drew to its close and they all sat down, bending heads into cupped hands for the Superintendent's opening prayer, Helen whispered: 'You haven't forgotten it's your Sunday for coming to tea, have you? I want you to see my new winter dress. It's ever such a pretty blue velvet.'

'Of course I haven't forgotten, silly! Don't we always come to tea on the third Sunday of the month?' Elizabeth snapped back. 'And I don't want to see your new dress, so don't bother getting it out to show me.'

Helen looked wounded, but as, at that moment, one of the Sunday School teachers hissed a warning 'Sssh!' she lapsed into silence. She was fond of Elizabeth — fonder than of her older cousin, Mary — and could never understand why her affection was not returned. The simple answer, that Elizabeth was jealous of her, never crossed Helen's mind. Having been denied nothing in her short life, she could not conceive of envy.

Nor was she old enough to realize that her father treated her Uncle William and Aunt Amy with a patronage bordering on insult. She saw only that Papa was perfectly pleasant and affable to them whenever they met; that Mama gave her aunt presents of money and cast-off clothing at birthdays and Christmas. She did not understand that generosity could be a cause of resentment.

It was sixteen years since Amy Evans, expecting her first baby, had asked if her younger, unmarried sister might be considered for the vacancy which her departure would cause at the chocolate factory. So the seventeen-year-old Minna Gould had gone to work, making the cream filling for one of Gordon's most famous products, and, within a fortnight, had captured the attention of young Joseph Gordon, nine years her senior, and just beginning to relieve his father of some of the pressures of overwork. Joseph, big, healthy, square-faced and beetle-browed, had never before seen anything as delicate and ethereal as Minna Gould. Her tiny waist, slender hands and feet, patrician features, were those of an aristocrat, not of a working-class girl from the tenements of Eastwood. He was completely bowled over by her charm. In the only quixotic gesture of his life, he proposed marriage.

Not all the threats of his father to disinherit him, nor all the tears and supplications of his aunt, nor the open disapproval of many of his friends, could alter his decision. He married his Minna in the Arley Street Methodist chapel and, contrary to all expectations, they were happy. And when, a few days after the wedding, Joseph's father died, without having had time to make a new will, it seemed that Fate herself had given the couple her blessing.

With his marriage, however, Joseph found that he had saddled himself with a sister- and brother-in-law who had none of Minna's looks and unlikely air of breeding to counteract their plebeian origins. Amy Evans was a homely, working-class girl who had married an equally homely, working-class man; a journeyman plasterer, who, in the uncertain times preceding the war, had managed to make just enough money to ensure the survival of himself, his wife and two daughters. Since the war, and the slump in the building trade, things had grown ever more difficult for him.

From the first, therefore, Joseph Gordon had made his position regarding his newly acquired in-laws quite clear.

'I shall do my Christian duty by them,' he had told Minna, shortly after the wedding, 'you can rely on that. I shall acknowledge the connection, however embarrassing it might be, and ensure that none of them ever starves. They can visit us once a month, as long as they know their place and don't encroach on my good

14

nature or yours. But that's as far as it goes. Your job now, my dear, is to learn to be a lady, so that you will be worthy of me and your new station in life.'

Minna, dazzled by her incredible good fortune, head over heels in love, had breathlessly agreed. She was fond of Amy, but shrewd enough to see that her sister's lowly situation in life would not enhance her own position. Over the years, she had salved a conscience which occasionally proved troublesome by gifts of money and clothing; gifts which William Evans would have preferred to refuse, but which his more practical wife insisted on taking.

'There's no point cutting off your nose to spite your face,' Amy would tell him. 'It would be stupid to give offence. One day we might need Joseph's assistance.'

William acknowledged the justice of her argument, but, along with his younger daughter, continued to resent his brother-in-law's patronage. Mary was more like her mother; a girl who saw no harm in getting what she could out of anyone. She had been suitably grateful when her uncle had recently obtained for her the position of under-kitchen-maid in the home of one of his friends. She had been annoyed when Elizabeth had told her: 'Domestic service is nothing but slavery. I'd rather work for Harrison's or go into the chocolate factory than that.'

'Well, of course you would! You're clever,' Mary had answered with asperity. 'Aunt Minna says Mrs Tennant is a very kind woman.'

Mary had always begrudged her younger sister her looks and brains. Elizabeth's superior intelligence had been obvious from her earliest years, when, at the age of five, she could easily do sums which Mary found impossible at seven. Mary, unlike her parents, had been neither pleased nor proud when Elizabeth had won a coveted place at Eastwood's Grammar School for Girls.

Elizabeth's promise of beauty had burgeoned more

15

recently. As both baby and child she had tended to be what her mother described as 'puddingy', inheriting her father's pugnacious jaw and Amy's plump cheeks. Now, suddenly, at fourteen, her face was thinning down, revealing the same aristocratic cast of countenance which distinguished Minna and Helen. Elizabeth would never be as pretty as her aunt and cousin, but she was already showing signs of being handsome in a way which would appeal to a more discerning eye.

Jack Hennessey had noticed Elizabeth's improving looks; a fact which only added to his secret but overwhelming burden of devotion. Glancing up briefly at the gallery, where he could see the cousins' faces, side by side, peering over the top of the rail, he thought Elizabeth infinitely better looking than Helen. He was aware that there were few boys present who would agree with him, but, like Elizabeth, he was impervious to the younger girl's more obvious charms.

The Sunday School proceeded. After the next hymn, boys and girls broke up into groups, each one gathering round its own Sunday School teacher. A Biblical text was discussed, or, more popularly, the teacher told a story from either the Old or New Testament. The former was generally preferred, its incidents and anecdotes being meatier and racier than the latter.

The service ended with a hymn and benediction. Then the Superintendent read out a list of the various evening activities for the coming week – Bible classes, Girls' Friendly Society, the Band of Hope — before everyone stood up with a sigh of relief and burst into speech. Within five minutes, the noise was deafening.

Helen tugged at her cousin's sleeve.

'Papa's given permission for you and Aunt Amy and Uncle Will to come back with me in the Daimler. He's given Hawken instructions to take us round to Springtime Grove to call for them. Isn't that exciting?

16

You'll be able to sit beside me in the car, instead of travelling by that rackety old tram.'

Springtime Grove, two rows of terraced houses, which in no way lived up to its name, had never seen anything so grand as Joseph Gordon's Daimler. Motor cars were not yet a common sight in Eastwood, and as Elizabeth climbed once again into the opulent, leather-smelling interior, followed this time by her mother and father, she was conscious of faces pressed to windows and the movement of curtains and blinds.

Amy smiled ingratiatingly at her niece. 'This is very kind of your Papa, Helen. It's such a journey by tram. The drivers are so slow. Old, I suppose. All the young men are away at the Front. What does your Papa think about these new tanks? Terrifying things, by all accounts, but perhaps they'll help beat the Kaiser and Little Willie. The war might be over by Christmas.'

Elizabeth glanced at her father, uncomfortable in his stiff, high-winged collar and Sunday suit, then looked away again. She guessed that he, like her, was wishing that her mother would be less eager to please. Her other feelings, however, were confused. Even while she jibbed at this unexpected gesture of her uncle's, hating to be under the slightest obligation, she was enjoying the sensation of riding in a car. It gave her a sense of superiority over all the pedestrians who glanced their way with as much respect as envy; filled her, like Toad, with the conviction that it was the only way to travel. The Daimler, with its rich, dark brown leather upholstery, represented the power of money and all the luxuries it could buy . . .

It was wrong to feel like that, Elizabeth admonished herself, ignoring Helen's endless chatter. Wrong, too, to resent the sense of obligation when she had made her parents promise to put themselves under an even greater one. She wanted to be a teacher, but could only go to college if Uncle Joseph could be persuaded to

17

lend her mother and father the money. She looked
covertly at them, both plainly ill at ease, but trying
desperately to hide it, and hoped that they would
remember their promise to approach Uncle Joseph this
afternoon. It was important she know as soon as
possible, so that a place could be reserved for her in the
sixth form of Eastwood Grammar.

As they got nearer Clifton the streets became wider
and tree-lined, the houses set well back from the road;
substantial Victorian mansions of brick and stone.
They were, Elizabeth reflected, a lot further away from
Springtime Grove than the distance they had actually
covered. The Daimler turned into a leafy side-street; a
cul-de-sac, where four big houses formed the shape of a
bow. The wrought-iron gates of the largest stood open,
giving a glimpse of the broad gravelled sweep beyond.
Towering dark green cupressus trees lined the railings,
a discouragement to prying eyes.

The car turned in through the gates and a maid, in
afternoon uniform of black poplin dress, frilled white
cap and apron, came down the steps to assist Helen to
alight. The rest of them had to manage on their own.
Elizabeth caught her father's eye again in a look which
spoke volumes.

'Follow me, please,' the girl said curtly. 'The Master
and Missus are waiting for you in the front drawing-
room.' Her voice softened. 'Master Charlie's here, Miss
Helen.'

'Charlie! How wonderful! I didn't know he was
coming to tea today.' Helen looked back at her cousin,
beaming with pleasure. 'Charlie's here. Did you hear
Smithson say?'

Elizabeth nodded sourly. If Charlie Harrison were
present then it meant that his parents were, too, and
that would make it more difficult for her mother to
speak to Uncle Joseph. As they were shown into the
hall cloakroom to take off their outdoor clothes, she
whispered to Amy: 'You will ask Uncle Joe about the

18

money, Mama, won't you? Miss Redditch wants to know first thing tomorrow morning.'

Amy Evans cast an anxious glance at her husband. 'I didn't think anyone else would be here today,' she protested. 'I can't say anything in front of the Harrisons.'

'Ask to see Joseph alone,' William advised. 'I'll do it if you'd rather not.'

Amy shook her head. 'No. He's my sister's husband. I don't think he'd be willing to listen to you.' But she looked unhappy.

A fire had been lit in the ornate, over-furnished drawing-room, even though the day was warm. Elizabeth noted that the general dearth of coal did not seem to affect her uncle. In spite of the war, nothing in this house ever appeared to be in short supply.

The room was stuffy and looked to be full of people, but this was mainly because Albert Harrison and his wife were so big and overpowering. Both were tall and fat, although May Harrison did have some pretensions to a figure. On the other hand, Albert, sole proprietor of Harrison's Universal Clothing Company, was simply obese. His face, with its receding hairline, was round and shiny, like an apple, his paunch enormous. Even his feet, in their grey spats and broad, gleaming, patent leather shoes, looked gross.

It was one of Nature's little jokes that this overweight couple should have produced two delicate, almost effeminate-looking boys with the features of startled fawns. Elizabeth despised the Harrison boys for no better reason than they were so obviously in awe of their parents. She could never understand Helen's deep affection for the elder son, Charles.

'Put a ribbon in his hair and he'd make a very passable girl,' she had once remarked, whereupon Helen had burst into tears and, for the first and only time in her life, rounded on her cousin.

'You're not to say things like that! You're cruel and

unfeeling. I love Charlie, and we're going to be married when we grow up.'

'Rather you than me!' Elizabeth had retorted, stung by the accusation of unkindness. 'Anyway, I don't believe you.'

But when she had scournfully repeated the conversation to her mother, Amy had said: 'Oh, I believe that's true. There are plans that Helen and Charlie will marry when they're older. Minna told me that it was her and Joseph's dearest wish. The Harrisons', too. It will join their two fortunes, you see.'

Elizabeth had exclaimed disgustedly: 'Who do Uncle Joe and Albert Harrison think they are! Behaving like a couple of medieval dynasts!'

She looked now at the occupants of the room, unconscious of the fact that her contempt for them all showed plainly in her sharp blue eyes.

'A madam,' Joseph Gordon mentally dubbed her. 'Too big for her boots. If she were mine I'd give her a taste of my belt. This is what comes of educating women.'

Helen was already sitting on his knee, winding her arms about his neck, fondly kissing his cheek. He asked: 'And what did you learn at Sunday School this afternoon, Puss?'

'We had the story of Abraham and Isaac and the ram in the thicket. And Mr Pound warned us about the sin of pride.'

'Very proper.' Joseph Gordon slid his daughter to the floor, as two maids came in, carrying tray-loads of sandwiches and cakes. He nodded complacently towards his friends. 'Well, Albert, May, fall to. You won't find much missing from my tea-table.' He laid a finger to his nose. 'My contacts don't often let me down.' He laughed. 'Money talks, eh? What? There isn't much we can't buy between us, is there, Albert?'

Yet again, he was aware of his niece's eye upon him. The word 'ironic' was not a familiar one in Joseph's vocabulary, or he might more easily have identified Elizabeth's expression. Even so, he knew that his younger niece made him feel uncomfortable. She was too pert and forward altogether, not a grateful, docile woman like her elder sister Mary, who knew her place, just as a woman, especially one who was a poor relation, should. He did not like Elizabeth. Clever females were freaks of nature. God, he was certain, had never intended women to have brains. He bit irritably into a slice of fruit cake and violently stirred his tea.

CHAPTER TWO

When the tea was cleared away, the company split naturally into three groups; men, women and children.

Joseph and Albert Harrison discussed the war; the new, so-called tanks, Lloyd George's visit to the Indian troops at the Front, and the entry of Rumania into the war on the Allied side. They spoke in loud, patriotic voices about 'death' and 'duty', 'King' and 'country', with all the comfortable assurance of men who would never have to leave their own firesides. Occasionally, William Evans made some more pertinent remark, but his voice was quiet and easily ignored by his companions.

The sisters and Mary Harrison chatted desultorily about food rationing and shortages, subjects which concerned Amy far more than the other two. None of them had, or was closely connected with, anyone involved in the fighting, and the carnage of the trenches meant little to all three. After a while, May Harrison began describing the new steam washing-machine which Albert had recently installed in place of the old, hand-operated one; and Minna, not to be outdone, indicated the new cabinet gramophone which had replaced the H M V with its convolvulus-shaped loud-speaker. Amy drifted into silence, wondering miserably if she dared interrupt Joseph.

Elizabeth, the two Harrison boys and Helen had been banished to the adjoining room, where the latter produced a box containing the Strand War Game, published by the Strand Magazine's proprietors, George Newnes.

'You're not allowed to play games on a Sunday!' Charlie Harrison protested, his brother, Stanley, nodding in horrified agreement. Even Elizabeth experienced a sense of shock.

Helen spread the board, depicting a map of western Europe, on the table.

'Papa says this game is all right because it's educational and helps you to learn about the war. And anyway, only two people can play. If you are afraid, Elizabeth won't mind playing with me, will you, Lizzie?'

Elizabeth answered as confidently as she was able: 'Of course not,' knowing full well that her father, in particular, would disapprove. But she was always avid for new experiences, and the *frisson* of wickedness she felt as Helen threw the dice was most exciting. It even compensated her for having to be the German army, with its yellow and black counters and squares.

Twenty minutes, however, was enough to bore her, especially as the rules proved too complicated for Helen to follow, in spite of Charlie Harrison's assistance. The clock on the mantelpiece pointed to a quarter-past five, and Elizabeth realized that if she and her parents were to be at Arley Street for the evening service, they must soon be moving. And her mother had not yet spoken to her uncle. Abruptly she got to her feet, ignoring her cousin's protests, and returned to the drawing-room. She laid a hand on her mother's shoulder.

Amy jumped and raised nervous eyes to Elizabeth, who whispered: 'Have you said anything to Uncle Joe?' even though she knew the answer.

Amy shook her head. 'I can't. Not with Mr and Mrs Harrison present.'

'But Miss Redditch must know tomorrow. Mama, you promised. You said you'd ask Uncle Joe today.'

There was a lull in the conversation, and her words fell clearly into the sudden silence. Joseph turned and looked curiously at his sister-in-law.

'What's all this then, Amy? What have you been promising the child to speak to me about?'

Amy cleared her throat. 'Nothing, Joe. I mean . . . it's just . . . What I mean is . . . Could I possibly have a few words with you in private?'

Joseph lay back in his armchair, fingers splayed over its fat, upholstered arms, enjoying his sister-in-law's discomfort. His sense of danger was alerted. Such uneasiness on Amy's part could mean only one thing: she and William wanted to borrow money, and the fact that they had never done so before in no way disposed him in their favour.

'You can say anything you have to say in front of May and Albert. I have no secrets from my oldest friends. Come along, woman! I'm not an ogre.' He laughed jocularly. Albert and May Harrison grinned.

Elizabeth, seeing Amy's hot cheeks, listening to her begin, then stammer into silence, hated her uncle more than she had ever done before. If the matter had not been so vital to her, she must have interrupted and put an end to Amy's misery. As it was, she could only stand and witness her mother's humiliation. To make it worse, Helen and the two boys had followed her in from the other room and were now ranged alongside their parents, their faces alight with curiosity.

'It's just . . . ' Amy knotted her hands together in her lap. 'It's Elizabeth. She's set her heart on being a teacher, you see, and that means she'll have to stay on in the sixth form at school and then go to college. It . . . it'll be expensive, and the thing is . . . Well, William and I don't have the money. Not to hand. What we . . . What I'm wondering, Joe, is if you'd be kind enough . . . be so obliging, that is, as to lend us what we'll need until such time as we can pay you back.'

She had got the request out somehow. She had done her duty by Lizzie, which was all that mattered. The colour ebbed from Amy's face, leaving it as pale as it had previously been red. The little tong-frizzed curls across her forehead clung damply to her skin. Her hands were shaking.

There was a moment's pause before Joseph Gordon gave a theatrical roar of laughter, in which Minna tentatively joined.

'Well, upon my word, that's rich,' he said, trying to appear amused, but merely succeeding in looking, and sounding, vindictive. 'When would you two ever have the money — that sort of money — to pay me back, I'd like to know?' He leaned forward, dropping all pretence of mirth and thumping the arms of his chair with a workmanlike pair of hands. 'You know my views on female education. A woman's place is in the home. Her proper function in life is to be a wife and mother. She should be taught to cook, clean and sew. Everything else is a waste of time! I accept that Elizabeth will have to earn her living until she gets herself a husband, but at least she will be earning money, not having it squandered on her, and there are plenty of useful jobs she can do while she's waiting. If Lizzie's as clever as you're always boasting she is, she can have a job in the office at Sebastopol Street. That should satisfy her grandiose notions. She won't be working on the factory floor. I hope I know my duty by my own wife's flesh and blood.' He snorted furiously. 'College education for women, indeed! It's money down the drain!' The veins were standing out like cords on his neck and his face was a turkey-red. 'I trust I've made myself clear.'

'Very clear, Albert, thank you,' William said quietly, 'and you may be sure that you have heard the last on this subject from us.' He got up. 'We must be going now if we're to be at Arley Street in time for the evening service. I'd be grateful if we could have our coats and hats.'

'But Dada!' Elizabeth turned to her father, hurt and reproachful. 'You can't let it drop, not just like that.'

'Ho!' Joseph placed his hands together across his paunch and glanced round at the others with an I-told-you-so air. 'This is what educating girls does for you. They get insubordinate, giving instructions to their parents. Helen would never speak to me like that, I can tell you. She'd get a good hiding if she did.'

Elizabeth ignored him. 'Dada,' she began again.

'That'll do, Lizzie,' her father answered in the same gentle tone; and to everyone's surprise, Elizabeth lapsed into silence. William Evans was a mild man, leaving discipline mostly to his wife, but there was a certain tone of voice which both his daughters recognized and never failed to obey.

Once they were in the omnibus, however, rattling downhill towards the city centre, where they would change into a tram, William leaned forward to the seat in front and touched Elizabeth on the shoulder.

'I'm sorry, Lizzie. But it wasn't going to be any use, you could see that for yourself. Your uncle isn't going to change his mind. Arguing with him would only have made him worse. I never thought there was much hope from the beginning, but your mother thought it was worth a try.' Elizabeth's head remained stubbornly turned away from him, as she stared out of the window at the shuttered shop-fronts and crowding roofs banked against the luminously fragile evening sky. Her shoulder stayed rigid beneath his hand, and William's grip tightened, but not urgently. 'Your mother was being insulted in the worst possible way; being made to look ridiculous and feel small in front of comparative strangers. Did you want her to suffer more on your account?' William gave his daughter a little shake. 'Answer me, Lizzie! Did you?'

Tears stung Elizabeth's eyes and she turned her

head. 'What's going to happen now?' she asked tremulously.

'About what?'

She twisted right round in her seat to face her parents. 'About my going to college,' she answered accusingly.

William and Amy looked guiltily at one another.

'You won't be able to go, I'm afraid,' her father said slowly, after a pause. 'I'm sorry, Lizzie, but we just can't afford it. We shouldn't have asked your uncle for the money if we could.'

'Couldn't you possibly ask him one more time? Catch him when he's in a better mood? Let me talk to him I might be able to make him change his mind.' Elizabeth knew it was a false hope, but in her desperation she was clutching at straws.

William's face was stern. 'That is the first and last time we ever ask your uncle for money. I refuse to let your mother be humiliated by him ever again. What he offers voluntarily is another matter. At least ... ' He broke off unhappily, then went on: 'I should prefer to take nothing from him, as you well know, but your mother thinks differently. Perhaps with reason. And it seems he is prepared to offer you an office job when you leave school, so your education will certainly not be wasted. You won't have to go into domestic service, like Mary.'

'I want to be a teacher,' Elizabeth said obstinately, her thin, mobile lips setting into an uncompromising line.

William sighed. He hated to deny his favourite child anything she had set her heart on, but this time Elizabeth would just have to make do with second best.

Elizabeth sang the familiar hymns for once indifferent to the sense of the words. The minister's sermon, too, flowed over her head unnoticed while she devised suitable punishments for her uncle and her parents.

27

She would die; go into a decline and pine away from a broken heart. That would make them all sorry that they had thwarted her. On second thoughts, however, it was too drastic a solution and denied her the opportunity of watching them suffer. Very well! She would somehow find the money to put herself through college and embark upon a brilliant academic career which would make them all ashamed and regretful that they had done nothing to assist her. But examination of her possible financial resources forced her into the realization that this proposition was no more practical than the first. There really was nothing that she could do.

Elizabeth sat down cupping her face in her hands for the final prayer. She would not be beaten. She would not! If the present outlook was bleak, there was always the future. She would make her uncle sorry that he had prevented her becoming a teacher. Moreover, she would prove to him that women were, mentally, the equals of men: perhaps even their superiors. She would go into business. She would make a lot of money. She would be far, far richer than the Gordons . . .

These schemes were interrupted by the closing benediction, which, in turn, gave way to the babel of sound as everyone started talking at once. The minister descended from the rostrum and hurried towards the door, ready to shake hands with each person as she or he departed. But, as always, no one was in a hurry to leave. People coalesced into groups, broke up, formed others. The noise was deafening. The place of worship had become the meeting-hall, the social club, the market-place; a legacy from the origins of Methodism, when the faithful used to congregate in the open air.

Jack Hennessey, who had arrived late and been forced to sit at the back instead of in his usual place beside Elizabeth, now fought his way to her side, catching her arm.

'You look like a thundercloud,' he observed. 'What's the matter?'

She threw off his hand petulantly. 'I'm not able to go to college, after all, that's what. Uncle Joseph refused to lend Mama and Dada the money.'

Jack breathed a sigh of relief. 'Is that all? I thought you were annoyed with me for not being here at the start of the service.'

Elizabeth whirled round to face him, her eyes blazing. Too late he realized that, as happened all too frequently, he had managed to provoke her to anger with his tactlessness.

'Yes, that's all!' she exclaimed furiously. 'Just my whole future gone up in smoke! But don't let it worry you! My *friends* might appreciate my loss, but why should you?'

'Don't say things like that,' he begged. 'I'm sorry. It was a thoughtless remark to make. You know I'm your friend. It's just that I'm selfish. I'm glad you won't be going away.'

Elizabeth was slightly mollified, but tried not to show it. 'If the war goes on another two years, you'll be the one who has to go away. You'll be conscripted.'

'Perhaps it won't come to that,' he said hopefully. 'Perhaps these new tanks will finish the Huns.' They were separated for a moment or two by a string of people pushing between them. When conversation was possible again, Jack went on: 'What I really wanted to say was that Mary came home this afternoon. She'd been given the half-day off unexpectedly, and forgot that it was your Sunday for Clifton. Ma invited her in and gave her a cup of tea and a piece of cake, but she couldn't stay long. She had to be back at Stapleton by five.'

'That's typical of Mary! She never stops to think!' Elizabeth, further irritated at having missed her sister, vented her spleen on the absent Mary's head. 'Sometimes she's so stupid I could throttle her!' She eyed Jack sharply. 'How is she? How did you think she looked?'

'We-ell . . . ' Jack seemed reluctant to give an opinion.

'Go on,' Elizabeth snapped impatiently, glancing towards her parents who at last seemed ready to leave.

'Ma and I didn't think she looked at all well. Pasty. And she kept coughing, like she had a bad cold. She told us she'd had the cough a while now, but didn't make anything of it. Nothing to worry about, was what she said. I don't know, though. It sounded pretty bad to me. She seemed miserable, too. When she'd gone, Ma said she didn't think your Mary was very happy.'

Mary slid her feet out of bed on to the freezing linoleum, then stood upright, the top of her head almost touching the sloping attic ceiling, her teeth chattering uncontrollably with the cold. The room was pitch dark, but in Mrs Tennant's household candles were forbidden in the servants' quarters, even at five-thirty on a bleak December morning.

As the raw air touched her lungs, Mary began to cough, waking Sarah Wilkins, the other maid-of-all-work who shared the attic with her. Sarah groaned and turned on her side, huddling the thin blankets around her shoulders.

'It can't be time t' get up yet,' she grumbled. 'We ain't been in bed five minutes.'

'Half-past five,' Mary answered. 'I heard the church clock strike it a few moments ago.' She was racked again by a bout of coughing and spit phlegm into a handkerchief. 'Best move, Sal. We'll never have everything shipshape by eight o'clock if you don't.'

Sarah gave another groan and rolled out of bed. 'Christ!' she exclaimed. 'It's like the bloody Arctic.'

Mary winced at the blasphemy and again at the swear-word. Bad language was something she had never encountered until pitchforked into the world

30

beyond her own circle. As children she and Elizabeth had attended the Wesleyan School in Eastwood's Canal Street; and in Springtime Grove itself, strong language, like strong drink, was forbidden. After more than a year. it was still painful for her to adjust to the ways of the other servants.

The Tennants, of course, were staunch Methodists; friends of Joseph Gordon. If any of the staff were overheard swearing it meant a fine of sixpence, docked from their already meagre wages. But even that was no deterrent. To most of them, blaspheming came as naturally as breathing.

Mary groped her way to the rickety washstand which stood in a corner of the room, and tried to pour water into the basin. But it had been so cold during the night that when she first up-ended the jug, nothing came out. She pushed her fist into the gaping neck and there was a tinkle, like the breaking of glass.

'Oh sod! Don't say the bleedin' water's frozen over again,' Sarah Wilkins moaned as she hunted under the bed for a missing stocking. She blew on her fingers which were refusing to do her bidding. 'Never think, would you, that last summer we couldn't sleep for the flamin' heat?'

'Attics are like that,' Mary answered philosophically, splashing cold water over her face and neck. It was so icy that it made her muscles ache, and started a bad tooth throbbing at the back of her lower jaw. She sat on the bed again, her eyes now accustomed to the gloom, and began to dress. She felt queer and light-headed, as though she were floating. Later, going down the back stairs to the kitchen, she stumbled and nearly fell. Sarah grabbed her from behind by the waistband of her apron.

''Ere! You all right?' she demanded in concern.

'Yes . . . Yes, thank you,' Mary answered.

And the odd thing was that she meant it. Her mind seemed divorced from her body. She could watch herself from an immeasurable distance as she knelt on the cold flags to light the back-boiler of the kitchen range. The wood was damp, and it needed all her and Sarah's efforts to get the fire burning. The water had to be hot by the time that Mrs Tennant, her husband and three children were awakened at half-past seven.

While Sarah filled the kettle from the scullery sink and made the morning tea ready for Cook and the housekeeper, Mrs Mabbutt, Mary began the daily chore of polishing the range. Using a small piece of blacking, she worked it all over the stove, making sure that no speck of the original metal colour was showing; then, with a brush, she buffed it to a shine and, finally, brought it to a high gloss with a big felt pad. By now the sweat was pouring down her body, but this morning it was not only the heat from the fire which caused it. She felt weak and her head was pounding.

'You sure you're all right?' Sarah Wilkins poured her a cup of tea. 'You look an awful funny colour.'

Mrs Mabbutt came in, tall and gaunt in her black serge dress with its high, starched collar.

'Come along you two,' she ordered briskly, 'less of this chattering and drinking tea. There are all the downstairs fires to be laid and lit. And Evans! Don't forget to polish the bars of the grates before you begin. The wire wool and oil are on the shelf by the window.'

Mary put down her cup with a clatter, slopping some liquid into the saucer. She seemed to have no control over her hands.

'I knew she was clumsy from the moment I first seed 'er,' Cook remarked, arriving just in time to witness the incident. She drew up a chair to the plain deal table and signed to Sarah to pour her a cup of tea. 'Them big, gangling girls are allus clumsy, I said to myself. Useless, that's what she'll be. An' I was right. Some o' that tea's gone on the table, me girl. This is a kitchen, not a pigsty. Mop it up. An' when you've finished layin' them fires, you can come back an' give it a scrub. An' I

32

want to see it spotless, d' you hear me?'

Mary forced herself to stand up. The intense heat of her body had now given place to cold and she could barely stop shivering. The other three women were a long way away.

Sarah Wilkins said: 'I don't think she's very well, Mrs Mabbutt. I'll do the downstairs fires this morning, on me own. I can manage. Mary can take the tea tray up to Missus.'

'She does look a bit peaky, I must say,' the house-keeper conceded reluctantly.

'It's that cough,' Cook said, going to the meat-safe and bringing out a pound of streaky bacon. She began frying breakfast for herself and Mrs Mabbutt. The two girls and the stable-lad would make do, as always, with bread and dripping. 'A reg'lar graveyard cough that is. Me sister-in-law 'ad one jus' like it, an' we buried 'er last Christmas twelvemonth.' She glanced around her. 'It's this kitchen. Damp. An' them attic ceilings are leakin'.'

The housekeeper nodded at Mary. 'Before you go upstairs with Mrs Tennant's tea, you can bring me my breakfast in my room.'

Mary barely heard her. The pleasant, floating sensation of the past half-hour had vanished, leaving her bilious. All she wanted was to go back to bed and never get up.

'I'll lay Mrs Mabutt's tray fer you,' Sarah offered generously, 'and the Missus's is over there, already done.' She indicated an elegant japanned tray, set with a delicate rose-patterned breakfast-service.

Cook came over with the housekeeper's laden plate which she banged down on the table.

'There's 'er 'ighness's breakfast then. All right fer some, retiring to their rooms. Can't eat in the kitchen with the rest of us. Too 'igh 'n mighty. Still, now she's out of the way, what d' you two say to a bit o' bacon? What the eye don't see . . . ' And she winked conspira-torially.

But her kindly meant offer was the last straw for Mary, who had just picked up the housekeeper's tray. As she fought down a rising tide of nausea, the kitchen spun dizzily around her in an arc of wavering lights and scattered shadows. The tray dropped with a resounding crash of broken china. Bacon and egg slid from the plate to lie in a rapidly congealing mess on the floor. As Mary's knees started to buckle, she flung out a hand to save herself but lost consciousness too soon, cracking her head on the edge of the table as she fell.

CHAPTER THREE

Mrs Tennant's equine features registered both surprise
and disapproval. When she had passed on a message,
through Joseph Gordon, that Evans was ill and should
be removed temporarily to her own home, she had
supposed that either one or both parents would arrive
to attend to the matter. She had certainly not expected
to be confronted by a child of fourteen; one, moreover,
who showed no sign of deference, only anger and
sisterly concern.

'I should like to see Mary at once,' Elizabeth said,
staring round the room to which she had been admitted.
There was the same comfort and luxury, the same over-
stuffed furniture and proliferation of little tables and
ornaments, which characterized the Gordon's houses
in Clifton. The popularity of Stapleton might be
waning, but there was still plenty of money there, as the
Tennants' style of life could amply testify.

'Have you any means of conveying your sister
home?' Mrs Tennant asked coldly.

'I've hired a pony and trap. I have a friend waiting
outside with it, now. He's taken time off from work to
come with me.'

'And have you done the same?' Mrs Tennant's tone
of voice implied that she suspected them both of
playing truant.

Elizabeth's roving eyes came back to rest coolly on her interrogator.

'I'm still at school. We've broken up for the Christmas holidays. Eastwood Grammar School for Girls,' she added, in answer to the woman's enquiring frown.

'Indeed!' Mrs Tennant's smile was dismissive. Her daughters, like herself, were products of Cheltenham Ladies' College. Education for women — upper-class women, naturally — was one of the few subjects on which she and Joseph Gordon failed to agree. 'You understand — er — I'm afraid I don't know your name.'

'You can call me Miss Evans,' was the pert retort, and a tide of red suffused Mrs Tennant's normally sallow cheeks.

Really! She had never encountered such impertinence, especially not from someone of this girl's age. But to lose her temper would be to play straight into the little termagant's hands.

'I hope your parents understand,' she continued, 'that Evans will not be paid for the period of her convalescence. My husband has already incurred considerable expense by having the doctor to her, and there is also the matter of some broken china. I have instructed Evans that she is to return to work as soon as she is fit. If there is one thing I will not tolerate, it's malingering.' Mrs Tennant rose and pulled the bell-rope beside the fireplace, maintaining an intimidating silence until the housekeeper sailed majestically in. 'This is Evans's sister, Mrs Mabbutt, come to take her home. See that she finds her, will you?'

Elizabeth unabashed, glanced once more around the room, then followed the housekeeper across the entrance hall and through a green baize door at the back. Once on the other side of this, she was aware of a dramatic change in temperature and surroundings. The cold here was almost palpable, striking up from the uncarpeted floor through the soles of even her stout shoes, and seeping in icy draughts under the ill-fitting doors. The housekeeper directed her down a badly lit staircase leading to the basement-kitchen; and the room in which Elizabeth eventually found herself was steamily hot, its walls running with water.

Part of the trouble, she saw at once, was condensation, a problem in every house in wintertime, particularly in kitchens, where the steam from constantly boiling kettles and saucepans formed into drops of water on window and walls. But the conditions here were made worse by an almost complete lack of ventilation, nearly four-fifths of the inadequate windows being blocked by an area wall. Elizabeth noticed large patches of mould on the ceiling.

The girl who had let her into the house now came forward, introducing herself as Sarah Wilkins.

'Mary's upstairs, packin',' she said. 'Don't s'pose she'll be long. Want a cup o' tea while you're waitin'?'

The cook who was making the pastry on the kitchen table, paused in her work to eye Elizabeth up and down.

'Not much like yer sister, are you?' she commented. 'Chalk and cheese, if you ask me.' She slapped the dough onto a marble slab and stood with floury arms akimbo. 'I 'ear you knocked on the front door, bold as brass. Don't suppose that pleased 'er ladyship.'

Sarah Wilkins giggled. 'I wondered 'oo the 'ell it was when I opened up. I nearly died when you said you was Evans's sister. Christ! I thought. Missus'll be mad as fire when she finds out you 'aven't used the servants' entrance.'

'I'm not a servant, so why should I?' Elizabeth answered curtly. She declined the proffered tea, adding: 'I'll go up and give Mary a hand, if you'll tell me the way.'

'Straight up the back stairs to the attics.' Sarah Wilkins wiped a runny nose on the back of her hand. 'Our room — Mary's and mine — is the second door on the right.'

Elizabeth retraced her steps to the stone-flagged passage, then mounted linoleum-covered stairs to the second floor, where, presumably, the housekeeper and cook had their bedrooms. From there, the staircase narrowed and boasted no covering at all, leading to an attic corridor which ran the length of the house. The second door on the right was ajar and Elizabeth could hear her sister moving about inside. She pushed the door wide and went in.

'What do you mean? You've told Mrs Tennant that Mary's not going back?' Amy stared in horror at her younger daughter. 'Lizzie! What on earth have you done?'

She had barely recovered from the shock of seeing Mary so white and thin, before Elizabeth had dropped her bombshell. Mary, huddled over the kitchen fire, still in her hat and coat, burst into noisy tears.

'It's true, Mama,' she sobbed. 'She's lost me my place. She told the Missus that she wasn't fit to have the care of pigs, let alone human beings. I heard her shouting. Everyone could hear her all over the house.'

Amy glanced imploringly at Jack Hennessey who had followed the two girls into the kitchen, where he deposited Mary's tortoiseshell-handled carpet-bag on the floor. 'It isn't true, is it, Jack? Lizzie didn't really say that to Mrs Tennant?'

'Well I was outside in the trap. But if Mary says so, then I'm sure it must be true, Mrs Evans.'

'Of course it's true,' Elizabeth chimed in impatiently. 'And if you'd seen that poky attic — two of them sleeping in it, mind! — you'd have done the same as I did, Mama. One blanket on the bed and the mattress as hard as a rock. No heating or lighting. And the kitchen so damp and steamy, it's a wonder all the servants haven't contracted pneumonia. Oh, stop sniffling, Mary! You make me cross. You know you were unhappy there. You told me so. Now you won't have to go back there again.'

'But I shan't be able to go anywhere else, either,' Mary wailed. 'Mrs Tennant wouldn't give me a reference. Mama, what am I going to do?'

She knew she was behaving unreasonably; that she should be grateful to her sister for freeing her from a situation she had loathed. But Elizabeth's high-handed ways had upset her, just as they had always done. The sister two years her junior had never been the soft and yielding playmate whom Mary could have loved. All her deep-rooted maternal instinct had had to be lavished on her dolls and, for a very brief period, on the baby brother who was now buried in the local cemetery. Mary had mourned little Edward unashamedly and had hated Elizabeth for her apparent indifference, when he had died at the age of six. Mary could not understand that Elizabeth deliberately concealed her feelings. What Mary felt she showed.

Her one ambition in life was to have her own home and family. She asked for nothing more. Indeed, everything else was simply marking time until the day when some, as yet, imaginary young man placed his ring upon her finger and led her down the aisle, a married woman. The trouble was, boys did not seem to find her attractive; and Cook and Mrs Mabbutt had had no hesitation in pronouncing her plain. The possibility of being an old maid kept Mary awake at nights far oftener than Mrs Tennant's horsehair mattress.

With one of those impulsive gestures of affection which occasionally betrayed Elizabeth's inner warmth, she went across to her sister and put her arms round Mary's shoulders.

'I'll find you another job, I promise I will. I lost you this one, so I'll have to get you another one, won't I? So you see, there's no need to cry any more.'

'I don't know what your father'll say, when he comes

home tomorrow,' Amy said, picking up the boiling kettle from the hob and making tea. 'A good job for you, Lizzie, my girl, that he's away. We'll all have calmed down a bit by the time he comes back.'

'Mr Evans has found some work, eh? That's good,' Jack put in, deflecting Amy's attention from Elizabeth to himself. 'Where is it? Not local by the sound of it.'

'A barn, down Bruton way,' Amy replied, putting the tea, in its brown-bellied pot, to stew on the hearth. 'Needs some plastering on the inside walls. Not a big job. Won't pay much, and it's not what he's used to. But beggars can't be choosers, as I told him. With Christmas so close, we need all the money we can get . . . Mary, take off your hat and coat for goodness' sake, and go up to bed. There's a hot brick in it, wrapped in your old flannel nightgown. I'll bring you a cup of tea as soon as it's brewed; and I'll rub your chest if I can find the camphorated oil. I don't like the sound of that cough.'

'It's not as bad as it was.' Mary heaved herself to her feet. She was extremely tired and still, now and then, light-headed. The realization that she need never go back to Mrs Tennant's, never climb, weary in every limb, to that miserable attic, never get up at the crack of dawn to black-lead the kitchen range or holystone the front door steps, suddenly hit her, leaving her weak with relief, although, oddly enough, not gratitude. She still resented her sister's actions. Given time, she told herself, she would have summoned up the courage to hand in her notice.

She went upstairs to the tiny box-room at the back of the house, which had been hers for the past five years, and which she preferred to the other, slightly larger, back bedroom. Mary loved her view of the narrow garden with its plum tree and narrow, but carefully tended, strip of grass. Immediately below the window was the flat roof of the bathroom, which her father had added on to the house twelve months earlier, when he had decided that the girls were getting too big to use the old tin tub in front of the kitchen fire. To the right of the bathroom was a covered area where her mother kept the big cast-iron clothes-mangle, a luxury which very few other women in Springtime Grove could afford. It had been given to William by a lady for whom he had worked, and Mary recalled going with her father, in the hired horse and cart, to bring it home. She remembered, too, the way Eileen Hennessey had looked on enviously from her doorway, as William and two of his friends had manhandled the mangle into the house. Jack's mother, like most women in the street, paid a halfpenny a time to use the unwieldy box-mangle in the public wash-house at the far end of Inkerman Street.

Too tired to unpack her carpet-bag, Mary undressed with the lethargic movements which were habitual to her, even when she was well. She unwrapped the flannel nightdress from around the cooling brick, tumbled the brick itself on to the linoleum and climbed thankfully into bed. The feather mattress was like lying on a cloud. Her eyes closed almost before her head touched the pillow.

Downstairs, Amy poured tea and took a loaf of bread from the oven at the side of the kitchen fire. As usual, parts of it were burnt to a cinder while others were almost raw, but that was one of the hazards, accepted by everyone, of cooking by an open fire. Minna had given her an old gas-stove, which now held pride of place in the outside scullery, next to the chipped and brown-stained sink, but Amy rarely used it, preferring the old-fashioned methods of cooking, however uncertain they might be.

As Elizabeth ripped a blackened crust from the loaf and crammed it into her mouth, her mother asked accusingly: 'Well? What are you going to do then, Miss Clever-Dick? How are you going to find your sister another situation?'

Elizabeth chewed thoughtfully for a moment or two,

then said: 'I'll go over to Sebastopol Street, to the main factory, and see Uncle Joe. I'll demand that he gives Mary a job. After all — ' she sipped her scalding tea ' — he was responsible for getting her sold into slavery at Mrs Tennant's.'

' "Demand"! "Sold into slavery"! You do talk wild, Lizzie, sometimes. I don't know where you get it from. It isn't from me or your Dad. You'll put your uncle's back up, that's all you'll do, and then *your* job'll be whistled down the wind. Besides, your father said we weren't to ask Joseph for any more favours.'

'I shan't be asking for a favour,' Elizabeth smiled. Sometimes, Jack thought, she looked just like a cat. No, not a cat, a tigress. 'I shall simply tell him that if he doesn't give Mary a job in the factory, I'll make sure that everyone at chapel, including the minister, knows of the conditions at Mrs Tennant's, and who got Mary her place there. That'll frighten him. You know how the old hypocrite loves to present a good front to the world.'

'You speak more respectfully to your elders,' Amy retorted angrily. 'You're too hasty in your judgements of people, Lizzie Evans! All the same,' she added, putting a cup of tea and a slice of bread and butter on a tray for Mary, 'perhaps seeing your uncle isn't such a bad idea. Your father need never know that we approached him. If we keep mum, he'll think the offer came from Joseph. But mind, Lizzie, you're not to be rude. Tell your uncle the facts and let him decide what's to be done.'

'All right I'll try to be civil, but I don't promise. Uncle Joe must have had a pretty shrewd idea of what things were like at Mrs Tennant's. You've only got to look at Mary to see how thin she is. That woman kept her on starvation rations. The other girl, Sarah something, is just the same. She's just a bit tougher than Mary, that's the only difference. And that old witch of a housekeeper looked just as bad. Jack, will you come with me?'

A smile spread slowly across Jack Hennessey's good-natured features. His deep blue eyes, inherited from his Irish father, began to twinkle.

'Try and stop me,' he invited. He ran his fingers through his thick black hair, another legacy from Padraic Hennessey. 'The trouble is, when you're in this mood, your fights are so one-sided.'

Helen was kneeling on the window-seat of her bedroom when the Daimler turned in through the gates and her father got out. It was unusual for him to be home so early, but this evening he and Minna were dining with the Harrisons, and Helen had been on the watch for him ever since tea-time. She slid off the seat and went to peer at herself in the mirror, patting her curls into place and smoothing her blue velvet dress. She always liked to look her best for Papa.

The bedroom reflected Helen's personality, soft, warm and feminine. The walls were covered with rose-patterned paper, the deep-piled carpet was a pale hydrangea-pink, and the counterpane was Nottingham lace over a backing of carnation-coloured Chinese silk. On the bedside table stood a row of her favourite books: *Ivanhoe*, *Tales of the Round Table*, *Robin Hood and His Merry Men*, *Little Women* and *Good Wives*, *Little Men* and *Jo's Boys*. *The Wide, Wide World* and *Jane Eyre* completed the selection. When they were younger, Elizabeth had tried to interest her in *Treasure Island* and *The Last of the Mohicans*, but adventure stories held no appeal for Helen.

She ran downstairs, hoping to snatch at least a quarter of an hour with her father before he went to dress. In the hall, however, she paused, suddenly aware of Joseph's raised voice from behind the study door. She tiptoed nearer to listen.

'And then she had the audacity — the audacity, mark you! — to threaten me. *Me!* Said she'd spread it all round chapel that I'd sold my own niece into slavery.'

'Oh, come now, dear,' Minna's voice protested nervously, 'I'm sure you must have misunderstood what she said.'

'Good God, woman! D'you think I'm a half-wit?' Helen, her ear pressed to the crack of the study door, frowned to herself in consternation. She had never heard her father swear before. Papa must be extremely perturbed to have so far forgotten himself, especially in front of Mama. After a moment's silence, Joseph continued explosively: 'She stood there as bold as brass, having forced herself into my office with that idiot Irish boy from next door grinning at her elbow, and told me that she expected me to find Mary a job in the factory, because she'd taken her away from Kathleen Tennant's. *She'd taken Mary away!* Not Amy, not William, you notice, but *she'd* taken it upon herself to remove Mary! How old is Lizzie? Fourteen? Fifteen? Young enough to be put over William's knee and leathered unmercifully, as she would be if she were mine! But your sister and that precious brother-in-law of yours are too weak to stand up to her. They've let Lizzie intimidate them just because she has a bit of book-learning. Haven't I always said that educating women would lead to disaster?'

Helen realized that her father was talking about Elizabeth and straightened up, sighing. She did so admire her cousin, in spite of the fact that it was wrong to do so. Elizabeth was forward, headstrong, even sometimes rude; everything that Papa said a gentlewoman never should be; everything that Helen herself was not, nor had any desire to be. She leaned down again and reapplied her ear to the crack.

'Yes, dear,' her mother was murmuring soothingly. 'You're always right about everything.' There was a pause, then Minna asked hesitantly: 'What happened?'

The pause lengthened into a thunderous silence, before Joseph answered curtly: 'I agreed.'

'You . . . you agreed?'

44

Helen could hear her father pacing up and down. After a while, he said virtuously: 'Mary is your sister's child, after all, and naturally I feel responsibility for her. I can't let her suffer because of Lizzie's actions.'

'Of course not, dear,' Minna's response was automatic. 'And ... well ... Kathleen Tennant is rather frugal in her ways.'

'Now understand me, Minna! I did not submit to Lizzie's blackmail — because I can give it no other name but that. Accusing me of not caring for Mary's welfare so long as I could oblige a friend! Saying I was a procurer of cheap labour! Threatening to run to the minister with her tales! None of that cut any ice with me, I assure you. Mary is starting in the packing department at Arley Street next week simply and solely because of family ties, and for no other reason.'

'Yes, dear,' Minna replied obediently, as Helen opened the door and walked in.

Joseph turned angrily to see who had dared enter without knocking, but when he saw his daughter, his heavy face lightened. The scowl was replaced by a smile and he held out his arms. Helen ran into them, clasping her own about her father's neck and pressing her cheek against his waistcoat. He smelled, as always, of tobacco and chocolate and other male scents which comforted and reassured her.

She felt safe with Joseph and his presence gave her confidence. He was a bulwark between her and an outside world which she found vaguely menacing. He gave her life direction; told her what she could and could not do. She accepted without question all his dictates, including that she and Charlie Harrison would one day marry. Whatever Papa decided must be for her good. Mama felt the same, Helen thought, smiling at Minna, who was embroidering a cushion-cover with skeins of brightly coloured wool. Papa protected them both and relieved them of the onerous task of making, and taking, decisions.

45

'Will you play a game with me, Papa?' she wheedled. 'Before you go and dress?'

'All right, Puss. What shall it be? The War Game? That reminds me.' He looked over her head at his wife. 'Bucharest has been captured by the Germans.'

'Oh dear,' Minna said placidly, selecting a long, emerald-green strand of wool and threading it through her needle. 'Is that bad?'

Joseph suppressed an exclamation of impatience and turned to Helen, who was laying out the board and assembling the counters on a nearby table.

'You'll have to tell me again how to play it, Papa,' she said, as he drew up a chair. 'I keep forgetting.' She giggled. 'You know what a feather-brain you always say I am.'

For one brief moment, the treacherous thought surfaced in Joseph's mind that he wished Helen could be more like Lizzie Evans. The idea shocked and dismayed him, leaving him distraught with its heresy. How could he possibly want his beautiful, sweet, womanly little girl to be even remotely like her young shrew of a cousin?

'Of course I'll explain it all to you again, my poppet. No one expects your pretty little head to retain all these complicated rules.' And he drew his counters towards him.

To everyone's surprise, and somewhat to her own, Mary quite enjoyed working in the chocolate factory. This fact went a long way towards mitigating Amy's anger with Elizabeth for losing her sister her place. William had said nothing on his return from Bruton, when regaled with the story, merely giving Elizabeth a quick hug when he discovered her alone.

'Did I do right, Dada?' she had asked, and he had nodded.

'Only don't tell your mother I said so. Life is hard enough as it is.'

Life was certainly becoming more difficult, that third

winter of the war. In January, a four-pound loaf of bread went up to tenpence-halfpenny, and coal rationing was stricter. Unrestricted German U-boat warfare caused shortages of many things in the shops, and Amy spent half her waking hours standing in queues. Work for William was scarcer than ever, and what jobs came his way seemed invariably to take him away from home. There was no question of Elizabeth remaining at school, even for an extra year, and it was arranged that she should leave in the summer. Her earning capacity was needed to add to the precarious family fortunes, and the position of filing clerk with Gordon's Quality Chocolates was still on offer.

'You see what a good man your Uncle Joseph is,' Amy told her younger daughter. 'Like a proper Christian, he doesn't bear a grudge. You remember that, Lizzie, and show your appreciation by doing your very best. After the way you behaved, Joe could have been forgiven for breaking his promise.'

Elizabeth said nothing, a little uneasy about her own conduct, but knowing, given the circumstances, she would act the same way again. In the meantime, she made the most of her last few months at school, captaining the hockey eleven and playing in the netball team. She wore with pride — a pride she had not always felt until now, when it was almost too late — the dark, ankle-length blue serge skirt and white cotton blouse, with its broad pale blue sailor collar. All too soon it would no longer be her right to wear it. Ahead lay the adult world with its attendant difficulties and problems. Sometimes she looked forward to it, but at others she wished she could stay a child for ever.

CHAPTER FOUR

Two centuries earlier, Eastwood had been an independent township, lying between Winterbourne to the north and Bristol to the south; and although the tentacles of the city had long since reached out to embrace it, the district still retained much of its village atmosphere. Farmers' and artisans' cottages had disappeared beneath streets of terraced houses, tenements and shops; the dusty country lane which had once been the main thoroughfare was now a busy arterial road; horses and shanks's pony had given place to omnibuses and trams. Yet Eastwood continued to be very self-contained, with its own grammar schools, park, hospital and station; even its own theatre, the Tivoli Music-Hall in Guelph Street, attracting a weekly bill of, admittedly, second-rate acts.

One of the two main reasons for Eastwood's strong sense of identity was its religious nonconformity, a legacy from the days of the Wesleys, whose idefatigable work in the Bristol area had resulted in wholesale conversion to Methodism by the rural population. The incidence had been particularly high among the miners of Kingswood and the neighbouring villages. The second reason was Gordon's chocolate factory which, for the past seventy years, had provided sufficient jobs to make it unnecessary for the bulk of

Eastwood's inhabitants to leave the area in search of employment.

It was in the summer of 1846 that Joseph's grandfather, Fergus Gordon, had moved south from Scotland for the sake of his health, bringing with him his wife and two small children. His family had been making Gordon's High Quality Chocolates in Glasgow for over a hundred years, and only the most urgent of warnings from his doctor that his lungs would not stand another bleak northern winter had made Fergus sell the business to his keenest rival and move away from his native land.

North of Eastwood was then open country, where Fergus bought Ellesmere House and its surrounding estate, settling down to the life of a country squire. But as his health improved in the milder climate, he became progressively more bored by his idle existence. Bristol was too commercial a port not to raise his competitive instincts. He was well aware that the city already boasted a thriving chocolate factory, founded in 1728 by the Quaker, Joseph Fry. Fergus, however, saw no reason why it should not have two, and when, shortly afterwards, a tobacco warehouse became vacant in the near-by suburb of Eastwood, Gordon's High Quality Chocolates reopened its doors. Within ten years, the words Gordon's and Eastwood had become synonymous.

Fergus, in common with many of his contemporaries, was a patriarchal employer, holding himself as much responsible for the spiritual as the material welfare of his employees. Brought up a Presbyterian, he switched painlessly to Methodism when he discovered that the majority of his workers belonged to that church. He was the leading spirit behind the building of Arley Street chapel, a stone's throw from the factory, although an unexpected recession and the need to retrench left the structure unfinished. He died suddenly in 1874, shortly after the birth of his grandson, Joseph.

For the next quarter of a century, his son, Ezekiel, reigned in his stead, expanding the business, presiding over the erection of a second factory in Sebastopol Street and selling off most of the land attached to Ellesmere House as the city sprawled ever further northward. By the time of Ezekiel's death, early in 1900, just after Joseph had married Minna Gould, the four-storey mansion was surrounded by houses, nothing left of the original estate but the formal gardens. When Helen was six years old, Joseph followed his friends, the Harrisons, to the heights of Clifton, and Ellesmere House became the local hospital, adding yet further to Eastwood's sense of self-containment.

'Don' need to go inta town, us don'. We got everything yer,' was a common enough saying, and one which made Elizabeth mad.

'Bristol, let alone Eastwood, isn't the be-all and end-all of existence!' she would remark scornfully to Jack Hennessey during that last hot summer at school. Although listening to her mother and sister talking it often seemed as though Gordon's factory was the compass of their world.

She was sick and tired of their reminiscences; of interminable questions begining: 'Do they still . . . ?' or 'Did they used to . . . ?' For Amy and her elder daughter had suddenly found a common ground of conversation, comparing past and present practices at Gordon's.

She heard how the workers were still fined if they were seen listening to the street-corner agitators with their seditious talk of 'people's rights'; how the girls, as well as the men, still had to hump the heavy wooden trays of confectionery between one floor and another because Joseph was too mean to install lifts and pulleys; how the workers still assembled each day for early morning prayers, although the men no longer tied the strings of the girls' aprons to the backs of their chairs, so that when they got up to sing the hymn, their chairs rose with them. It all made Elizabeth dread the begining of August, when she, too, would be one of her uncle's employees, even though she would be in the office. One form of slavery, she said, was much like another.

'You don't know when you're well off, my girl,' Amy scolded, trying to conceal her growing sense of relief that Joseph had refused to put Elizabeth through teacher-training college. She needed the extra housekeeping money, and had even considered the drastic expedient of going out charring, but William had put his foot down. There was no tradition in the south, as there was in the north, of married women working. Only widows or those, like Eileen Hennessey, abandoned by their husbands, laboured outside the home.

'Why am I well off?' Elizabeth was in an argumentative mood. 'There are more jobs for women now than ever before, with all the young men away at the Front. I could be a ticket-collector on an omnibus or tramcar. One or two women are even driving the trams.'

'I'm not having that, so forget it,' Amy retorted sharply. 'You're not throwing away your education doing manual work that any fool could do. Besides, now America's in the war, it'll soon be over. All the men will be home wanting their jobs back. And where would you be then?'

'Where I am now, wasting my education in Gordon's factory, when I should have been a teacher, if only Uncle Joseph wasn't such a bigot where women are concerned.'

'I forbid you to talk about your uncle like that.'

They were all seated in the kitchen, at Sunday breakfast, a meal which invariably meant boiled eggs and toast. In spite of the heat, the fire had been lit and the warm embers glowed gently in the black-barred

51

grate. Amy took the saucepan from the hob and banged it down in the middle of the table, spooning two eggs into her own and William's egg-cups. Then she up-ended the other two egg-cups on top and, with a sharp knife, sliced deftly through the centre of each egg. Quickly, she righted the top halves before the yolks could escape, and Mary, who had been kneeling in front of the fire, toasting the bread, came to the table, her face flushed, beads of perspiration standing out along her forehead.

'I wish we could have a whole egg, for a change,' she grumbled.

'We can't afford it, as well you know,' her mother snapped. 'Even if we could buy them, that is. You try queueing for hours, madam, or find your father some work. If you've money, you can get pretty well anything. Now get a move on, or we shall be late for chapel.'

'As a matter of fact,' William said, raising his eyes from his plate, 'I shall be going over to Leigh Woods next week. Miss Turner wants some of the library moulding replaced. You remember. The Miss Turners at The Brass Mill. You said it was a funny name for a house when I did some work for them last year. I shall be there on the fourth and the fifth.'

'Dada! Can I come with you?' Elizabeth laid down her spoon, her eyes bright with anticipation of a treat.

'You'll be at school,' Amy reminded her tartly. 'No excuse to slack, just because you're leaving at the end of term.'

'Why not? I know all I need for a chocolate factory! Anyway, the Bristol schools have a half-day's holiday on the fourth of July for American Independence Day. As a gesture of welcome to our new allies, Miss Redditch said. Can I come, Dada? Can I?'

William glanced at his wife, then shrugged. 'I don't see why not. She's right, Amy; there's no point in her going on stuffing her head with Shakespeare and the

52

like, when all she'll need to know at Joseph's is how to make out invoices and add up columns of figures. She might as well come with me. The Miss Turners are putting me up for the night to save the journey home, but they won't mind finding another bed for Lizzie. There's plenty of room. The Brass Mill's a rambling old place. It'll give the girl a chance to see how the other half lives, and a break before she starts work.'

'Oh . . . Very well,' Amy conceded, defeated as much by her own good nature as by the logic of her husband's argument. 'I'll write a note for Miss Redditch. Now, for goodness' sake hurry up, all of you, or we'll miss the opening hymn. And make sure that each one of you has enough change for the collection!'

Mary pushed her way through the chattering crowds of girls in the cloakroom to reach the row of lavatory cubicles at the back. The heat was intense, and she thought jealously of Lizzie over at Leigh Woods with her father. It wasn't fair. Her sister always had all the luck.

Before she could enter a cubicle, one of the supervisors, in her regulation grey poplin dress, appeared in the cloakroom doorway, raising her voice to command attention.

'Everyone home!' she shouted. 'The temperature's over eighty and the chocolate's melting. There'll be no work this afternoon!'

A general groan went up from the girls, who were busy taking sandwiches from their coat pockets, ready for their lunch break.

'Damn!' swore the girl nearest Mary. 'That's the second time in a fortnight. My Ma'll go spare. We can't afford for me to keep losing a half-day's wages.'

'Wants bleedin' modernizin', this place does,' someone put in, and there was a mutter of agreement.

Ignoring the unrest, the supervisor raised her voice once more. 'Is Evans anywhere about? Mary Evans?'

Mary waved her arm. 'Here I am, Miss Bullock.'

'Ah! First thing tomorrow morning, report to number two factory. They want another girl for tipping the Christmas cigars.' And Miss Bullock disappeared into the gloom of the green-tiled corridor, leaving Mary to face twenty or more hostile pairs of eyes.

The most famous of Gordon's Christmas novelties, made and packed in high summer, was its chocolate cigars, filled with white fondant cream and tipped with cochineal-coloured sugar to simulate the glowing end. Painting the tips of these chocolate cigars was, for some reason, regarded as a prestige job among the female work-force, and anyone selected for it was the envy of all her friends. It had been known for some of the less popular girls to be missing when it came time for them to report to Sebastopol Street, so that someone else had to be sent in their place. These unfortunates were usually found trussed up in the lavatory cubicles, using their own belts, and their own handkerchiefs as gags.

The girl who had complained about her loss of wages was the first to speak as the sound of Miss Bullock's footsteps died away down the corridor.

'I see,' she said, putting her hands on her hips and tapping her foot. 'Painting the cigars now, are we? And how come you've been chosen, Mary Evans, when you've only been in the factory six months?'

'Because she's old Joe's niece, that's why,' another girl shouted from inside one of the lavatories, and there was a loud, angry jeer of agreement.

Mary felt her legs begin to tremble, and backed against the wall for support, a clothes-hook digging her between the shoulder-blades. This sudden enmity, blowing up like a storm out of a clear summer sky, of girls she had worked with amicably until now, unnerved her. It had always frightened her at school when other children had set on her in the playground; but for most of the time there had been Elizabeth to come to her defence, a small tornado, lashing out with her fists if necessary. Not that Mary had ever been grateful. She had resented Elizabeth's interference as much as she had needed it, protesting afterwards that she could have managed perfectly well on her own. But she knew that Elizabeth had never believed her; and her innate honesty had prevented her believing it herself.

Now there was no Elizabeth, only a sea of angry faces and a torrent of abusive language, which still shocked her as much as it had done at Mrs Tennant's.

'Go away,' she begged. 'Go away and leave me alone. I didn't ask to help on the cigars, honestly I didn't. One of you can take my place if you want to. I'll run after Miss Bullock and ask her now.'

She could not guess that this placatory attitude was the very one to enrage the girls still further. Although nothing had ever been said, they resented the fact that, coming from a background no better — or not much better — than their own, Mary 'spoke posh' as they disparagingly described it. No one who lived in Springtime Grove, even though the houses there did not open directly on to the street, but had minuscule paved front 'gardens', had a right to sound every aspirate as Mary did, or avoid the pitfalls of Bristol vernacular.

'Above 'erself,' had been the consensus of opinion; but it was not the fact that she was Joseph Gordon's niece which had previously spared her the girls' sarcasm and unpleasantness. It was simply that until the present moment she had done whatever job she had been given quietly and uncomplainingly, and not pushed herself forward. Now, however, it was assumed that she had obtained a special privilege after a very short time by trading on her relationship with 'old Joe', and all their latent resentment of her had surfaced.

'Snivelling bastard!' yelled a tall girl with freckles. 'Lock 'er in the bog an' leave 'er there till tomorrow.'

Mary dredged up a little courage from somewhere. 'You're not allowed to swear,' she spat at her tormentors. 'My uncle would dock your wages if he knew.'

'You going to tell 'im?' demanded the first girl, advancing threateningly, and sniggering as Mary shrank back once more against the wall. 'You're right, Sylvia! Lock the sod in the bog and jam the door.'

Several hands had already been laid on Mary, when a fair girl with glasses, who had not spoken before, observed quietly: 'That's askin' for trouble. She is old Joe's niece, even though she isn't any better than the rest of us. And old Joe might turn nasty if he got to 'ear of it. Send 'er to Coventry, that's the best way. Don't nobody speak to 'er from now on unless they 'ave to. That'll learn 'er to give herself airs and graces.'

'But I don't!' Mary exclaimed desperately, almost in tears. The girls ignored her. 'Kath's right,' said the one who had been addressed as Sylvia. 'Too risky to do anything else.' She lifted down her straw hat from one of the pegs. 'Well, I'm off, then. See you lot tomorrow.'

One by one, the other girls followed suit, a few eyeing Mary, obviously longing to offer her violence if only they dared. But caution prevailed, and eventually the cloakroom was empty of everyone except herself, huddled against the wall and dabbing at her face with her handkerchief. After a while, she went over to the wash-basins and ran some water, splashing it on her hot cheeks and swollen eyes.

Mary had been happy for the last six months, believing that she was accepted and liked. Now, all at once, it seemed worse than Mrs Tennant's. There, at least, no one had offered her physical violence. She forgot the bleak attic, freezing in the winter, scorching in summer; forgot the back-breaking climb a dozen times a day, up and down the steep flights of stairs in answer to the imperious summons of a bell; forgot the never-ending chore of blackleading the kitchen range; forgot the housekeeper's sarcasm and the inadequate meals.

It was all Elizabeth's fault as usual, poking her nose in and getting her dismissed. Why couldn't her sister have minded her own business for once, instead of fighting other people's battles?

Mary peered at herself in the cracked mirror hanging over the middle of the three wash-basins. Her face was puffy and her skin blotched with crying, but even on a good day she knew she could never be called pretty. She had inherited the worst features of both parents, whereas Elizabeth had inherited the best. Elizabeth had also inherited more than her fair share of their father's brains; for there was no doubt in his elder daughter's mind that William Evans, given an education, could have become anything he chose. He read avidly and with a fluency which concealed the fact that he was self-taught. He wrote well and found no difficulty with figures. But he had left school at the age of eleven to learn his father's trade, and employers looking for clerical staff refused even to grant him an interview. Who had ever heard of an artisan working in an office?

Then there was Amy. She and Minna had been the children of a lady's maid who had been killed, along with their father, in a train accident when the girls were young; but not before Florrie Gould had inculcated into her daughters the patterns of speech and behaviour which she herself had learned in the big houses where she had spent her youth. Amy and Minna had passed them, in turn, to their daughters; but whereas Elizabeth found them a positive advantage, they only separated Mary from the people with whom, by lack of education, she was forced to mix.

Mary took off her overall and hung it on her peg, putting on her straw boater and cheap white cotton gloves. The factory was almost deserted now, a vast, empty, glittering shell of heat, while the unworkable chocolate oozed and glistened into the salvage runnels, ready to be re-formed and re-worked the following day. Slowly she went down the stairs and out into the stifling street.

Elizabeth had never been inside a house like The Brass Mill before. Set within sight of the Avon Gorge, on the fringe of Leigh woods, the entrance hall alone, with its dark oak panelling and high rococo ceiling, was bigger than the two first floor drawing-rooms of which Joseph Gordon was so proud. Mouldings of fruit, flowers and birds decorated the marble fireplace, and a huge statue of naked women, hands strategically placed on breast and thighs, stood in an alcove from which the paint was peeling.

The whole house was indeed extremely shabby, but its faded splendours fascinated Elizabeth far more than the pristine gentility of Joseph's villa or Mrs Tennant's mansion at Stapleton. Structurally, William declared The Brass Mill very sound.

'That's because Miss Turner and her sister spend what money they've got on the fabric of the building itself, making sure it's in good repair. They don't have enough to replace the furnishings as well.'

The two elderly spinsters, both alike with their soft grey hair, myopic brown eyes and gentle voices, had welcomed Elizabeth with an old-fashioned courtesy, quashing William's apologies for bringing her almost before they were uttered.

'We are very pleased to have company, Mr Evans,' said the slightly younger of the two, whom, to Elizabeth's amusement, her father called 'Miss Josephine'. It was a form of address which was new to her.

'Why don't you call her "Miss Turner"?' she asked William, once they were alone.

'Because that's the way the gentry do it,' he

explained. 'Otherwise, Miss Josephine wouldn't know whether you were speaking to her sister or herself. You get to know things like that when you've been inside as many country houses as I have.'

The touch of pride in her father's voice struck Elizabeth as odd in one who was an ardent suporter of the new Labour Party, but she supposed that that was human nature.

She had been given a bedroom at the front of the house, and from her window she could see, far below, the Avon, now at low tide, a thin, silver-grey thread between banks of shining mud.

There was a knock on the door and the elder Miss Turner came in, carrying some much darned but beautifully laundered sheets, smelling of lavender.

'I've come to make up your bed, my dear.' She glanced about her, dubiously. 'I hope you'll be comfortable here. It's rather a small room, I'm afraid, but so much of the house is shut up these days.' Elizabeth, thinking of her bedroom in Springtime Grove, barely large enough to accommodate a bed, a single wardrobe and a washstand, made no reply. Miss Turner went on wistfully: 'Of course, when Josephine and I were gels, there were at least fourteen indoor servants, as well as the grooms and stable-lads and three men just to do the garden. Now we have to see to everything ourselves with one woman, who comes daily.'

There was nothing boastful in this speech — not a hint of the way Joseph Gordon would have made it sound — just an unadorned statement of fact. Elizabeth realized she was expected to offer neither admiration for past glories nor sympathy for present troubles, and suspected that the two Miss Turners were what her mother would call 'proper ladies'. They had that indefinable something Amy referred to as 'class'.

For their part, the occupants of The Brass Mill were surprised and delighted by their uninvited guest. In the past, when William had done work for them and stayed the night, they had found him intelligent enough, but conversation had necessarily been limited. They had so few interests in common. In Elizabeth, however, they discovered not only a bright, sharp mind, but also knowledge. She was a girl on whom education had not been thrown away, and who was able to talk to them on those subjects which interested them most, art and literature.

William, sitting with his daughter and the Miss Turners that evening in what was known as the small parlour, listening to Elizabeth quoting from Milton and Shakespeare as easily as he could quote from *Das Kapital* — more easily, in fact, as he had always found Marx impossibly heavy-going — he suddenly regretted her future in his brother-in-law's chocolate factory. Somehow, he and Amy should have scraped the money together to send her to college: she seemed to him cut out for the academic life. Yet even as the thought occurred to him, he admitted that it would have been impossible. Things were difficult enough as they were.

And Elizabeth, lying in bed later that evening, enjoying the strangeness of her first night away from home, thought that perhaps an academic life would not have suited her, after all. What she would really like would be to be the mistress of a house like The Brass Mill; to have enough money to furnish it as it deserved to be furnished; to be able to show Uncle Joseph and Aunt Minna what good taste really meant; to be able to patronize them as they had always patronized her. She got out of bed and padded over to the open window. In the moonlight, on the other side of the Gorge, high on its rocky perch, she could see the cleft of blue shadow which was Clifton. She stared at it for a long time until, suddenly chilled by a fresh night breeze, she turned and went back to her lavender-scented bed.

CHAPTER FIVE

For once the tide was in, and sunlight reflected on the water in a ceaseless, wavering pattern. Minna and Helen, walking along Marine Parade towards Knightstone Road — the former in a new blue coat and skirt and broad-brimmed hat, the latter in a cream broderie-anglaise dress threaded with dark green ribbons — felt pleased both with themselves and with the weather. So often August Bank Holiday Monday was spoiled by rain, but today everything had conspired to make Weston-super-Mare pleasant. Even Joseph was in a good mood, which was not usually the case at the prospect of the factories being closed for an entire seven days. He was never tired of reminding his employees that a week's holiday had been an unknown luxury when he was young. Today, however, he was mellow, having just won a new American contract for the distribution and sale of Gordon's Linlithgow Assortment in the States. As he strolled along behind his wife and daughter, he felt a surge of pride to be escorting two such attractive women.

For there was no doubt that Helen, at fourteen, was suddenly blossoming into womanhood, and was going to be what Joe privately termed 'a stunner'. In three or four years' time she would have the men flocking around her. Best, maybe, in that case to insist on an early engagement and marriage to Charlie Harrison. At the thought of Charlie, however, Joe felt a twinge of unease. He wished the boy was more manly, both in looks and ways; not so delicate nor so prone to hang around his mother. Albert should really have insisted on sending him away to school, like his younger brother, but May had objected that the life would be too rigorous for him at Marlborough, and had had him educated at home by private tutors. Still, the lad was only fifteen; there was plenty of time for improvement, and he and Helen seemed genuinely fond of one another.

'When Charlie and I are married . . . ' or 'When I'm Charlie's wife . . . ' prefaced many of Helen's remarks, although Joe did wonder uncomfortably at times how much his daughter knew about the realities of life. He was not sure what, if anything, Minna had told the girl, because, except in bed, his wife was inclined to be prudish, shrinking from any discussion about 'that kind of thing'.

'Papa!' Helen turned round, breaking in on his thoughts. 'We're trying to remember. What's the new surname that the royal family have chosen for themselves?'

'Windsor, my poppet. That should be easy enough to remember, surely.'

'But why, Papa? Why have they done it? Why aren't they called Guelph any more?'

'Because Guelph's a German name, sweetheart, and we're at war with Germany. Windsor sounds much more English.'

'I thought they were English,' Helen said vaguely.

Joe frowned to himself. There were occasions when he wondered if Minna and that governess woman had managed to instil anything into that pretty little head during the past nine years. But then, he had always insisted that girls did not need education. Had he, perhaps, been hoist with his own petard? Angrily he dismissed the thought. He was never wrong.

'Good day, sir! I hope you are having a very pleasant day.'

Joseph blinked, suddenly aware of a young man blocking his path, raising the straw boater which he wore with a certain rakishness on his thatch of dark hair. The hair, oiled to a brilliant shine, was indeed almost black, as seemed the eyes, in reality a deep and liquid brown. A smart pearl-grey suit, the waistcoat adorned with a gold watch-chain, gave a deceptively dandified appearance to a tall and muscular frame. The material strained slightly across strong, broad shoulders, and the starched white shirt collar encircled a sinewy neck.

'Ah . . . Good day . . . ah . . . ' Who in heaven's name was the young blighter? Joseph was certain that he did not know the face.

'Sawyer, sir. Benjamin Sawyer. I work in the filing office in Sebastopol Street.'

A filing clerk! Impudent young dog, daring to accost him like this! No wonder he had not recognized him. Joseph took in the grey silk tie and black patent leather shoes. How was one of his junior staff able to dress in such a way? What was he paying him?

Before he could quell pretension, however, Helen had came running back to join them, taking her father's arm and bestowing her most bewitching smile on this extraordinarily handsome young man.

'Who is it, Papa? Won't you introduce me?'

'Um . . . yes . . . ah . . . ' Joseph hated to appear churlish before his daughter. He had no wish to forfeit her good opinion. 'One of my junior clerks in the filing department, my dear. Mr . . . ah . . . Sawyer.'

Helen immediately held out her hand. 'As in Mark Twain's book? How lovely! How do you do, Mr Sawyer?'

'It's a great pleasure to make your acquaintance, Miss Gordon. Unhappily, my name is Ben. I wish it was Tom for your sake.'

'Have you read the book? My favourite Mark Twain is *The Prince and the Pauper*.'

'You're a romantic,' Ben Sawyer said, and smiled. He had, Joe noted grimly, excellent teeth.

Helen giggled and her father firmly took their leave.

'Who was that good-looking boy?' Minna wanted to know, as they caught up with her.

'He works for Papa, in the office. I wonder why he isn't in the army.'

'Probably not as old as he looks,' Joseph said, but made a mental note to instigate enquiries on Monday morning, as soon as the factory reopened. 'Now, how about an ice-cream, my poppet?'

'I hate Weston,' Mary grumbled. 'I hate all that mud. The tide goes out for miles.'

'Well, it's in now,' Elizabeth argued patiently; but Jack Hennessey, between them and holding an arm of each girl, realized that she was very close to losing her temper.

He could hardly blame her. Mary had done nothing but moan since their arrival by train, earlier that morning. If she kept it up, it was going to be a miserable day. He said quickly: 'Let's go along to the whelk stall and get three-pennyworth of whelks for our dinner.'

'Can't we have a proper sit-down meal?' Mary asked plaintively. 'I'm starving.'

'If you can afford it,' Jack answered, shrugging. 'Myself, I'm skint. Harrison's aren't exactly good payers.'

'If we didn't have to treat Lizzie,' Mary began, but her sister interrupted her.

'I don't know what's the matter with you, Mary Evans! You've been like a bear with a sore head these past few weeks. And don't worry about paying for my dinner! Jack will look after me. I'll pay you back, Jack, as soon as I start earning next week.'

'Don't be silly.' Jack squeezed her arm, thinking how

attractive she was now that the sun and sea air had brought some colour into her normally pale skin. He wished he could tell her what he felt about her, but he knew she would only laugh. Next year, he would be conscription age and have to go away, if the war had not ended by then. He wondered if she had thought of that; and if she had, did she care?

'I'm hot,' Mary complained. 'I must have a rest, Let's sit on the wall for a minute and look at the sea.'

'Just for a minute then,' Elizabeth agreed. 'I thought you wanted your dinner.'

They sat on the promenade wall, twisting their bodies round to look at the broad expanse of sand and, beyond it, the arm of the Bristol Channel, stretching away into the distance, to the faint, grey line which was Wales.

There was silence for a moment, while they watched the children building sand-castles, or their parents, trouser-legs and skirts held up, paddling self-consciously in the water. Elizabeth said irrelevantly: 'In the library at The Brass Mill there was a concealed door. It looked like part of one of the bookcases with rows of real shelves and books.'

'I'm sick to death of hearing about that place,' Mary snapped irritably, 'and I should think Jack is, as well. You go on and on about it all the time. It's not Buckingham Palace, for goodness' sake! Just some old house that's falling apart.'

'That just shows how much you know about it!' Elizabeth exclaimed furiously, jumping to her feet. 'And I'm sick to death, too, of the way you cavil at everything I say!' She swung round, preparing to leave, but bumped into a young man, treading on the toes of his smart black patent leather shoes. 'I'm sorry,' she apologized, still holding on to him in order to steady herself, aware of a swarthy, handsome face smiling down into hers. Her heart gave an odd lurch, and there was a peculiar sensation in the pit of her stomach which she had never experienced before. She had rarely seen a more good-looking boy.

'That's quite all right,' he assured her gallantly. 'You've dropped your bag.' He picked up the tapestry pochette and returned it to her.

'Th-thank you,' Elizabeth stammered.

He nodded and moved on, leaving her staring after him.

'Hm,' Mary grunted, also getting to her feet, her annoyance with her sister temporarily forgotten as she found a new object on which to vent her unhappiness. 'That's Ben Sawyer from the filing department. He doesn't half fancy himself, that one! He dresses like that all the time. Always turned out like a regular dog's dinner! You'll be working alongside him next week, Lizzie, I shouldn't wonder. The office staff are usually started off in files. Well, come on. Let's go and get those whelks before we die of hunger.'

'Right-oh!' Jack stood up and touched Elizabeth's arm. 'Lizzie? How about it?'

'What? Oh, yes. Of course. Who did you say that was, Mary? Ben Sawyer?'

Ben Sawyer was the first person Elizabeth saw the following Monday morning, when she reported for work in the filing department of the Sebastopol Street factory. Earlier, walking along the pavement as she approached the redbrick building, fronting one entire side of the street, Elizabeth had been daunted. She had, for the first time in her life, felt utterly insignificant, dwarfed by the row of columns which marched along the façade, and by the green-tiled dome which towered above it. Inside, it had proved to be a rabbit-warren of scurrying people, no one in the least interested in her or where she was going.

The uniformed man peering out from behind a grille in the entrance lobby had traced her name on one of his numerous lists.

'Evans, E . . . Filing department. Up them stairs, third left, second right, up another flight, fourth door on your left. Ask for Miss Ronson. She's in charge.'

But when Elizabeth entered, there was no one in the big, ill-lit room, with its rows of filing cabinets, except Ben Sawyer, and it was obvious from the brief nod he gave her that he had no recollection of meeting her before. Elizabeth was too proud to remind him. She sat down at the desk he indicated and waited for Miss Ronson to arrive.

He was just as handsome and dashing as she remembered: first impressions in this case had not been deceptive. But it was not merely his looks which attracted her. She had known good-looking boys before. There was something about his general attitude, a swashbuckling air, a devil-may-care look in his extrordinarily dark eyes that excited her. He would know what he wanted and where he was going, she thought, and would probably be ruthless in obtaining his ends. She liked that. It struck in her an answering chord. She decided, however, not to push herself, but to sit back quietly and wait for him to notice her.

But after Elizabeth had been at the factory a month and was still no more to him than a piece of the office furniture, she decided that it was time to make a bid for his attention. She invested a shilling of the florin a week which Amy returned to her out of her half-guinea wages in a pair of black silk stockings, and when she had to mount the ladder to reach the files on the top shelf, flashed a pair of well-turned ankles.

Miss Ronson, a tiny, flat-chested, bird-like woman, watched these manoeuvres with an amused toleration.

'You won't attract his lordship by showing him your legs,' she observed one day, when she and Elizabeth were alone in the office. 'Mr Hall, now, he's very interested every time you go up the ladder.'

Elizabeth flushed scarlet. 'I don't know what you're talking about!' she disclaimed.

'Oh yes, you do.' Miss Ronson laid down her pen. 'I'm talking about you and Beau Brummel there.' She nodded towards Ben's empty desk. 'That's what I call him. Although sometimes I wonder if Machiavelli might not be more appropriate.'

'Why?' Elizabeth was interested in spite of herself. She dropped the pretence of outraged innocence.

'Ben's an intriguer. My guess is that he likes to manipulate people. For his own ends, naturally. That young man is extremely ambitious.'

'He dresses well.'

'Yes.' Miss Ronson's tone was dry. 'I know the family. Ben lives with his widowed mother and a maiden aunt, both of whom dote on him. They spend all their money on him, even if it means going without themselves, and he lets them. He's selfish, like most very handsome men. He takes adoration for granted.'

'How does one impress him, then?' Elizabeth asked. She put up a hand and smoothed a strand of silky reddish-brown hair into place. 'I'm not bad-looking.'

'You're a very pretty girl,' Miss Ronson conceded, 'especially when you smile, which, by the way, isn't often. Sometimes you look as though you have the cares of the world on your shoulders. Don't let that family of yours lean on you too much. You're also extremely intelligent. But the only way you'll impress Ben Sawyer is by telling him that you're Joseph Gordon's niece.' She smiled at Elizabeth's look of surprise. 'You thought everyone knew? I expect most people do, but that's the point I've been trying to make about Ben. He's so self-centred that he can't be bothered to find out about anyone else. So if you want to capture his interest, tell him who you are. If you think he's worth it, that is.'

The idea was totally repugnant to Elizabeth. That she should be beholden to her uncle for anyone's interest enraged her beyond expression. She was sure, with all the arrogance of youth, that Miss Ronson misjudged

Ben Sawyer. But by Christmas she was as far from attracting Ben's notice as ever.

'Oh, Papa, do I have to come?' Helen turned from the drawing-room mirror, where she had been adjusting her new fur hat at an even saucier angle, and pouted prettily. 'Tanks are for boys.'

'This is Tank War Bond Week, sweetheart, and I'm going to be on College Green when the Lord Mayor and Lady Mayoress inspect that great lump of metal this morning. Bristol's aiming to raise over a million pounds. All the picture-houses are showing the *Tanks in Action* film this week.'

Helen grimaced. 'I hope I'm not expected to sit through that,' she said. 'Mama and I would much rather go shopping.'

Minna looked disconcerted. 'Oh dear! I've promised to meet May Harrison for lunch when the ceremony is over. You can come if you want to, darling, but you said last time how bored you got listening to our chatter. I thought Papa could bring you back home before Hawken drives him on to the office.'

'That will be taking him out of his way . . . I know!' Helen clapped her hands excitedly. 'I'll go to the factory with Papa today! Oh Papa, please say I may. I'll be good and not get under anyone's feet, I promise. I'm sure your secretary can find something for me to do to keep me amused.' Helen wound her arms around Joseph's neck and covered his cheeks with kisses. 'Dear Papa! Nice Papa! Do say you'll let me.'

'Very well, just this once,' Joseph agreed, unable to resist her. 'But I don't want you making a habit of it. I must say I don't really understand why you want to come.'

Helen was not sure herself why she was possessed of this sudden urge to visit the factory. When she said: 'I could look into the filing department and see Elizabeth,' she really was convinced that it was her

69

cousin she wanted to see. And yet, somewhere at the back of her mind was a teasing memory of the handsome young man who had spoken to her on the sea-front at Weston. 'One of my junior clerks in the filing department.' Surely that was how Papa had introduced him. Why should she recall that so vividly now? It had nothing to do with her wish to visit Sebastopol Street.

She kept telling herself so all the time she was standing, bored, in the bitter wind blowing across College Green from the Cathedral and the river beyond, while the Lord Mayor and Joseph and some of the other visiting dignitaries scrambled up a ladder to the roof of the tank and peered inside. It was a long time since she had seen where Papa worked, and the factories which would one day be hers. It had absolutely nothing to do with Ben Sawyer.

Nevertheless, she was forced to admit to herself when, later in the day, she walked into the filing department and saw him sitting at his desk with the others, that she would have been unaccountably disappointed had he not been there.

As soon as Ben noticed her, he got respectfully to his feet, along with Miss Ronson and the two others, Miss Mills and young Mr Hall, who made up the staff on 'files'. Only Elizabeth, glancing up casually from her work, made no attempt to rise.

'Good afternoon, Miss Gordon,' Miss Ronson said, going forward to shake hands. 'This is indeed a pleasure. We haven't seen you here since you were quite a little girl.'

'I'm surprised that you remember me,' Helen replied with a nervous laugh.

'Your father keeps a portrait of you in his office, painted, I think, about two years ago. You haven't changed very much since then.'

'Yes, of course. I'd forgotten.'

'You are, if I may say so,' Miss Ronson continued, 'as pretty as ever.'

'Th-thank you,' Helen stammered. 'I hope you won't object, but I've come to have a word with my cousin.'

She grinned at Elizabeth, and Elizabeth was compelled to smile back. There was something irritatingly endearing about Helen which undermined Elizabeth's determination not to like her. If only she weren't Uncle Joe's daughter, they could have been friends.

'Perhaps you'd like to use the boardroom opposite,' Miss Ronson suggested. 'There's no meeting of the board today. Elizabeth, you can have ten minutes.'

The cousins went across the passage to the empty room, with its long refectory table and leather-covered chairs. A large oil-painting of Fergus Gordon dominated the pine-panelled walls.

Once there, however, with the door shut behind them, Helen could think of nothing she wanted to say. She had not seen so much of her cousin lately, the once-monthly Sunday visits having fallen off since the day, last year, when her father had refused to lend Uncle William money. He, her aunt and cousins had only visited Clifton twice in the intervening months, offering a variety of excuses for their absence. Nor did Helen go to Arley Street Sunday School any more. Joseph gave as the reason the scarcity of petrol, and he and his family now worshipped at the Methodist chapel in Blackboy Hill. Helen sometimes suspected him of trying to distance himself from his embarrassing in-laws. He had provided jobs for both Mary and Elizabeth, and probably felt that he had more than discharged his duty towards them.

'Why did you want to see me?' Elizabeth enquired, and Helen wished, as she so often did, that her elder cousin were not quite so matter of fact.

She wanted to say: 'Because I admire you. Because I'm fond of you,' but she had an idea that Elizabeth

71

would laugh. Instead, almost without realizing what she was saying, she asked: 'That's Ben Sawyer, isn't it? The young man working with you? He's very handsome. We met last August Bank Holiday at Weston.'

Elizabeth felt something so akin to jealousy that it startled her. She did not like the wistful gleam in Helen's eyes, nor the proprietary note of interest in her voice. She answered coolly: 'Yes. How's Charlie Harrison?'

'Charlie? Oh ... He's very well.' Helen became more confidential. 'Papa's talking about us getting engaged on my sixteenth birthday. Charlie will be seventeen by then.'

'How nice. Congratulations.' There was another silence before Elizabeth added abruptly: 'I must be getting back. Some of us have a living to earn.'

As she re-entered the filing department, she was aware of Ben Sawyer's eyes upon her. Suddenly, she was the object of his undivided attention.

'Well, well,' he remarked softly as she resumed her seat. 'So you're old Joe's niece. I hadn't realized.'

'There's a lot you don't realize,' she answered pertly, then checked herself, aware that she sounded like the green fifteen-year-old she really was. 'You should keep your ear closer to the ground, Mr Sawyer,' she finished lightly.

'Your cousin,' he said, 'is a very beautiful girl. I thought so when I met her at Weston.'

For the second time in half an hour, Elizabeth felt a sharp stab of jealousy. Anger, too, that Helen had only to be seen once to make an impression, while she herself had been unable to make any impact after five months of trying.

'Yes, isn't she?' She smiled at Ben as though perfectly indifferent to his interest in her cousin. 'Quite the family beauty. And in eighteen months' time, she's getting engaged to Charlie Harrison, the elder son of

Albert Harrison of Harrison's Universal Clothing Company. It's been arranged since they were children.'

Ben Sawyer's strongly marked eyebrows flew up. 'How very Victorian.'

'Not really. They aren't being forced into it against their will. Helen and Charlie are devoted to one another. They seem to be as anxious for the match as their parents.'

'A couple of children! What can they know about marriage?'

'I don't know. Margaret Beaufort was only fourteen when she gave birth to Henry the Seventh.'

He stared blankly at her for a moment, then started to laugh. He was, she knew, taking note of her for the first time as a person.

Miss Ronson frowned in their direction. 'That's enough chattering, you two. May I remind you, Mr Sawyer, and you, Miss Evans, that you have work to do. Invoicing wants those files on the Linlithgow Assortment by half-past three.'

Rebuked, Elizabeth bent once more to her desk, but not before she had caught Ben's eye and seen him wink.

A week later, he asked her to go out with him, and, unknown to her parents, took her to the Tivoli Music Hall in Guelph Street, both of them lying about their age. It was the first time Elizabeth had ever been inside a theatre, and the first time she had been out with any boy other than Jack.

CHAPTER SIX

In February of the following year, Elizabeth said goodbye to Jack Hennessey, who had celebrated his eighteenth birthday in January and had been conscripted into the Royal Navy almost immediately afterwards.

As he stood on Eastwood station, waiting for the connection which would take him to Bristol and, eventually, Chatham, misery welled up inside him. Jack was aware of Elizabeth's growing friendship with Ben Sawyer, and was afraid that he was losing her for good. Not that, if he were honest, he had ever had her; not in any lover-like way, at least. She looked upon him as her friend; her best friend; someone on whom she could lean, to whom she could confide her troubles, hopes and fears. He supposed she regarded him as the brother who had never grown to manhood, but he had always fostered the hope that, given time, she would come to love him in the same way that he loved her. Now he was going away, leaving the field clear for his rival, who had been exempted from military service because of flat feet. It was Jack's one crumb of consolation that the reason for Ben's exemption was so undignified.

'You'll write, won't you?' he asked Elizabeth the night before.

'Of course. Every day,' she had promised brightly, kissing his cheek. 'I'll miss you. I shan't have a shoulder to cry on.'

'You can tell me everything in your letters. And stop worrying about Mary. I'm sure she's all right.'

'No she isn't.' Elizabeth had shaken her head. 'She's unhappy, just like she was in domestic service. I don't know what's behind it, but I mean to find out.'

'Mary's a woman now,' he had protested. 'She's nearly as old as I am. Let her fight her own battles.'

But he knew she wouldn't. Elizabeth was a born protagonist. She could never resist a challenge.

'You'll get on the wrong side of your uncle again,' he had warned her, 'and find yourself without a job.'

She had laughed at that. 'I'm not worried about Uncle Joseph. I shall just threaten to tell Helen and Aunt Minna about him and his secretary. They're having an affair. Everyone in Sebastopol Street knows about it. The only two people who don't realize that it's an open secret are my uncle and the lady herself. They fondly imagine that they're pulling the wool over everybody's eyes.'

Jack had been shocked. 'Who was low enough to tell you about it?' he had wanted to know.

'Ben, of course,' was the careless reply; too careless in Jack's estimation.

The local train shunted into the station and he climbed aboard. He did not like Ben Sawyer, the little he had seen of him, and not just because Elizabeth so obviously did. There was something, Jack felt, untrustworthy about Ben. He was the sort who used people and then threw them aside after they had served his purpose. He prayed to God nightly that Elizabeth would not be hurt.

There were other young men, conscripts like himself, leaning out of carriage windows, saying good-byes to mothers, sweethearts, wives, but there was nobody to see him off. Elizabeth was at work, his sisters at school, his mother too busy washing and charring for other people.

'The Lord knows what we're goin' t' do without your wages,' Eileen Hennessey had wailed, when his call-up papers had fallen through the letter-box. 'Harrison's isn't good payers, but the money's better'n what you'll get in the navy, and that's a fact.'

Jack sighed and settled back in his corner for the ten-minute journey into Bristol centre. As the train pulled out of Eastwood station, familiar landmarks seemed suddenly strange and alien. He already felt as if he had been away from home for years.

On the fourth of July, 1918, Mary accompanied Elizabeth and Ben Sawyer to Durdham Downs to watch the march past of United States troops. Joseph had reluctantly closed both factories for half a day in acknowledgement not only of America's contribution to the war, but also of the Linlithgow Assortment's bumper sales across the Atlantic. Mary had wanted to see the Doughboys, but had not wanted to go alone. She seemed to have no friends, not even among the Hennessey girls next door.

'Let her go with you and Ben,' Amy had ordered. 'It's not right, anyway, for you to be rattling around on your own with that young man. If your father were in better health, he wouldn't allow it.'

Her voice was shrill with worry, and Elizabeth, recognizing it, had bitten back the refusal which had sprung to her lips. William Evan's health had been failing for the past six months. Under-nourishment and pernicious anaemia had been the doctor's diagnosis.

'Drink lots of milk and eat plenty of red meat,' he had prescribed, knowing full well that his advice could not be taken. Even with the children working, money was still tight for every family in Springtime Grove. And then there was rationing. The supply of margarine had been limited since the last week in February.

So Elizabeth had agreed that Mary could go with her, although she had known that Ben would not be pleased. He stigmatized Mary as a 'frump'.

'And stupid,' he had added unkindly, on one occasion. 'She has no ambition except to get married and have babies. Married! Who'd want to marry a dowdy like her?'

Mary knew what Ben thought of her and normally avoided his company, going upstairs to her room whenever he called to take her sister out. But she could be stubborn, and once she had made up her mind to something, no amount of snubs and insults would deter her.

Standing now amongst the crowds in Upper Belgrave Road, she was impervious to Ben's pointedly turned back. She was glad she had come, and cheered as loudly as anyone as the soldiers paraded past. There was a mounted officer in front, followed by the flags and their bearers — the Stars and Stripes and a regimental flag with the number 823 — and then rank upon rank of men in their belted tunics and puttees and distinctive, 'boy-scout' hats. They were on their way to the city centre for an Independence Day celebration at the Drill Hall.

When the last rank of American servicemen had passed the crowd began to disperse and Mary found herself separated temporarily from her companions. She was aware, suddenly, of an altercation taking place behind her. Turning she saw a man and woman and a little boy, about six years old.

'Letting go of his hand like that!' the man was shouting. 'You might have lost him, you silly bitch!'

'Bloody kid! He's all you think about!' the woman retaliated. 'Never mind me! You don't care about me!'

They both spoke with the lilting cadences of South Wales, and had come across the Severn for the day, Mary guessed, to see the parade. The little boy started to cry and the woman slapped him, whereupon the man promptly boxed her ears. Mary's sympathy, which had at first been with the woman, veered towards the man. He obviously cared for the boy, while the mother was indifferent. Nothing was more certain to arouse Mary's antagonism than cruelty to children.

Other people were staring at the couple, their attention attracted by the row. As though suddenly conscious of the spectacle they were making of themselves, the man seized the woman's arm and urged her forward.

'And keep hold of the boy,' he commanded.

As he pushed past Mary, their eyes met. He had the small, dark face of the typical Welshman, whereas the child was fair and large-featured, like his mother. They vanished into the crowds.

'Mary!' Elizabeth was craning her neck, trying to find her sister in the crush. 'We're over here.' She made her way to Mary's side and linked arms firmly. 'We're going for a walk to the Sea Walls. Do you want to come?'

Mary realized that she was meant to refuse. Instead, she said: 'Yes. All right.'

Why shouldn't they take her with them? Why should Lizzie have all the fun? Life wasn't fair. Why was it that some people had everything, and others, like herself, nothing? Elizabeth was even popular at work, not only in the office, but among the factory girls, as well. Yet she was also Joseph Gordon's niece, spoke as correctly as Mary, and could equally be accused of obtaining privileges for herself, because of her rapid promotion from the filing to the invoice department. But no one ever did accuse her of these things. The girls of the factory floor particularly liked her, in spite of the fact that she often used words they did not understand.

'All right, your sister,' they would say to Mary, when they bothered to speak to her at all. 'No side to 'er, not like some o' them up in the office. Some o' them thinks, jus' because they don't get their 'ands dirty, they'm bloody gods, or summat.'

Ben Sawyer was one of those meant, Mary was sure, and she glanced sideways at him, as they walked across the Downs to the Sea Walls. He was not generally liked, not even among his fellow office workers, probably because he was so arrogant and tipped to 'get on'. He intimidated people, even Lizzie. Well, he didn't intimidate her. She could see that he was looking black as thunder at her continued presence, but that only made her more determined to stick to him like a leech.

'You have a cantankerous nature,' Elizabeth had said to her, more times than she could remember.

At the Sea Walls, where the rocks of the Avon Gorge fell sheer away to the road and the river far below, they paused to look at the seeming miracle of Brunel's bridge, spun between one towering cliff and another, and at the opposite side to the one on which they stood, where the trees of Leigh Woods, heavy with summer foliage, spilled and foamed along the crest. The Avon, now at high tide, wound silver-grey along its slimy bed, and, away to their left, Nightingale Valley sprawled in deep violet shadow. The ghosts of Goram and Vincent, those fabulous giants who were reputed to have carved out the gorge in the dawn of time, hovered about them in the upper air.

Or so Mary fancied; she who was not normally given to flights of imagination. But the day had taken on an unusual significance for her: she did not know why. She just felt as though something special had happened to her, as she trailed after her sister and Ben, back to the top of Blackboy Hill, to catch their tram home.

'Don't bring her with us again, ever!' Ben said. 'Or you'll have to do without my company. It's not that she's miserable. One can ignore that. But she looks a mess.'

Elizabeth was sitting with him on the settee in the

front parlour of his mother's house in Temple Road, behind Eastwood station. He had refused to take her there at first, almost as though he were ashamed of where he lived. It was only after Elizabeth had taken him on a visit to Springtime Grove that he suddenly relented. Perhaps he had expected Joseph Gordon's niece to live in the better part of Eastwood, in one of the new stucco-fronted villas near the park, or in one of the larger Victorian houses in Pitch-and-Pay Lane. Ben was, Elizabeth reflected uneasily, a terrible snob. She suspected that he was ashamed of his aunt and mother. Whenever she went to Temple Road, he always hustled them off to the kitchen.

There were a lot of things about Ben which made her uneasy, not the least of which was that he might affect her in the same way. Elizabeth knew that she was a bit of a snob herself, and fought against it, because she realized how much it upset her father.

'We are all equal in the sight of God,' he would say. 'No one, not King George nor Queen Mary, nor the President of the United States, is better than you or me.'

And yet, perhaps that philosophy of life was in itself a kind of snobbery. The more one thought about things, the more difficult they became, she reflected with a sigh. All the same, even with Ben, who filled her every horizon, she had to fight injustice.

'You may not like the way Mary dresses,' she said flatly, 'but she's neat and clean. Not everyone is interested in clothes.'

Ben experienced a familiar surge of irritation. Elizabeth was a good-looking enough girl, dressed as well as she was able on the little money at her disposal. She was sharp and intelligent, and, young as she was, never disgraced him by giggling or making silly remarks in public. But for all that, she was not really the type of female he liked. He thought of Helen Gordon, of her soft, red, vulnerable mouth; of the gentle childish curves of her body; of the warm violet-blue of her enormous eyes. Ben had seen eyes like hers in young girls before, radiating innocence, but with something lurking in their depths; a langour, a beckoning of which they were, as yet, quite unconscious. He felt himself aroused just by looking at Helen Gordon. And she had the added attractions of wealth, position and of being her father's daughter.

In the meantime, however, he must do with Joseph Gordon's niece in the hope that, one day, he might, through her, come to know her cousin. The connection between the two girls was not as close as he would have wished, but he had time on his side. He moved closer to Elizabeth and slipped his arm around her shoulders. He felt her tremble, and she put up a hand and stroked his cheek. At sixteen, she was older in some ways than Helen Gordon would ever be.

Nevertheless, Elizabeth was still a minor in legal terms. He must be careful. He kissed her, holding her, mentally if not physically, at arm's length. He could sense her frustration, but her chapel upbringing prevented her from taking the initiative, as a less inhibited girl might have done. He wondered how inhibited Helen Gordon would prove, once her emotions had been touched. One thing was certain; Charlie Harrison would not be the one to arouse her, to rescue her from her ivory tower. He was already inside it with her. They would be like two children playing at keeping house, if all Elizabeth had told him about Charlie were true. He had the impression of a boy just as virginal as his prospective bride.

'What are you thinking about?' Elizabeth demanded jealously.

Ben smiled into her eyes. 'I was thinking how nice you'd look with your hair bobbed. It's all the rage in London.'

'Is that truly what you were thinking?' She cuddled closer to him, guiding one of his hands to her breasts. 'I love you,' she whispered, but he pretended not to hear.

'Mother's coming. Probably to ask if we want coffee before I walk you home to Springtime Grove.' He got up, smoothing down his immaculate suit.

Did he never relax at all? Elizabeth wondered; take off his coat and shirt collar as her father invariably did indoors?

Mrs Sawyer knocked tentatively and entered. She had once been an extremely pretty woman, but her beauty had been eroded by years of drudgery and trying to make ends meet; trying to live to her adored son's exacting standards, the only legacy which her profiligate husband had bequeathed his son before dying of cirrhosis of the liver at the age of forty-two, still deploring the fact that he had married beneath him. Had it not been for her spinster sister, who had inherited a little money from a friend, Ada Sawyer did not know how she would have managed.

'I've made the coffee,' she said apologetically, setting down the tray on a table near the window. She glanced anxiously at her son. 'I hope that's all right.'

'Quite all right, mother, thank you.' Ben smiled dismissively. 'Don't wait. I'll pour.'

Elizabeth had never tasted coffee until she had come to Temple Road. It was far too expensive and exotic for the Evans household, and Joseph did not waste it on poor relations. But there were a lot of things Elizabeth had never done before she met Ben Sawyer. She had never eaten in a restaurant, visited a theatre or been taken to an art gallery. Ben had what her father termed 'high falutin'' ideas, but Elizabeth realized that he opened doors for her into a world she had only guessed at before.

The first time they had eaten out, she had chosen the cutlet, and he had asked: 'You know what a cutlet is?' She had thought she knew; a piece of fish, such as cod, but cross-wise so that one of the vertebrae remained in the middle.

'Makes a change from fillets,' Amy would say, as she dished them up on a Friday.

But a cutlet, it seemed, was a neck-chop of lamb or a small piece of veal for frying. There were other such lessons to be learned, and Elizabeth was an apt pupil, deftly concealing much of her ignorance.

She took the tiny, wafer-thin coffee-cup from Ben and sat sipping the sweet brown liquid. A picture suddenly presented itself of her and Ben married and living in The Brass Mill, surrounded by elegant friends; the sort of scene she had read about in books . . . .

With a twinge of conscience, she remembered that she had not written to Jack for over a month, and then only a very brief letter. She felt guilty, but surely Jack would understand that she was busy. And when they were apart, there seemed so little to write about. They had nothing in common any more. She certainly could not envisage Jack drinking coffee and entertaining friends at The Brass Mill.

Jack Hennessey was demobbed from the Royal Navy late in 1919. The Armistice, a year earlier, had come as a surprise, for only months before the German army had been on the offensive, moving towards Compiègne. Then suddenly it was all over and everyone was dancing in the streets.

There was no one who would not remember the eleventh of November, 1918, as long as he or she lived. There had been an air of hushed expectancy during the early part of the morning. Then, at eleven o'clock, bedlam had reigned. Factory hooters, church bells, whistles all started sounding together. Work was finished for the day as people poured into the streets, laughing, crying, shouting, singing. Joseph had opened a bottle of champagne in the board-room for the senior staff, and had even drunk a glass himself. Teetotal principles were all very well, but not on such a memorable occasion.

At the Eastwood Brewery in Portland Place, it was free beer for anyone who wanted it, and in order to cope with the demand, the women had borrowed watering-cans from a neighbouring hardware store to use in place of jugs. Everyone seemed a little crazy that day, although the war was not officially at an end.

That came in July 1919, with the signing of the Treaty of Versailles. Bristol, like the rest of the country, celebrated with parades and street-parties, ignoring the atrocious weather. All the houses in Springtime Grove were decorated with flags and bunting. Union Jacks and the Stars and Stripes hung from every window. Trestle tables were set up in the middle of the street and each household contributed something towards the celebration tea, in spite of rationing. They sat huddled under umbrellas, laughing at the rain. Even William insisted on joining in, although Amy and the girls tried to persuade him against it. He was still weak from a persistent cough which he had been unable to shake off since the previous winter.

The mood of optimism engendered first by the Armistice and then by the Peace did not last. By the time Admiral of the Fleet, Earl Beatty, arrived in Bristol on October the twenty-third, to receive the Freedom of the City and of the Society of Merchant Venturers a rail strike was looming and the United States Senate had refused to ratify the Treaty of Versailles.

Jack came home on Christmas Eve, having witnessed, in June, the scuttling of the German fleet at Scapa Flow. He seemed older than he had done during his few brief leaves. Then he had been almost carefree, always smiling. Now there were shadows in his eyes and his new suit hung baggily on him, so that his sisters laughed and called him Charlie Chaplin. The jaunty naval hat, with its crown and anchor and letters RNVR had been replaced with a check cap, pulled well down over his brows. He was silent as he and Elizabeth walked down to the chapel on Christmas morning.

'What's the matter?' she asked.

He shrugged, unwilling to admit that he was jealous of her friendship with Ben Sawyer. Did she realize how full her letters had been of Ben lately? When, that was, she had bothered to write at all.

'There must be something,' she persisted, watching a couple of boys, holes in the seat of their trousers, elbows poking through the sleeves of their jumpers, sailing paper boats on the canal.

'Nothing but the thought of going back to work for old man Harrison, I suppose. Harassing a lot of poor women for money, when they can hardly buy enough to eat.'

'Harrison's harassers,' Elizabeth smiled, as they turned in through the main chapel gates.

'Wait for us, you two,' called Amy, who was following with Mary and the rest of the Hennesseys. William had felt too poorly to accompany her.

'I'll stay home and keep an eye on the dinner,' he had said, trying to smile as though there was nothing the matter with him.

Amy knew better. She knew William must be feeling bad to miss the Christmas morning service. He loved singing carols and listening to a good, rousing sermon, before walking home with a sharpened appetite for chicken and roast potatoes, and Christmas pudding salted with the threepenny bits which everyone had to be careful not to swallow. It was a tradition which Amy had not dropped, even after the girls grew up, hoarding the tiny silver threepenny pieces in an empty jam jar from the middle of November onwards.

She scarcely heard a word that Eileen Hennessey was saying, grumbling as usual, this time about the Post Office.

'Wanting everyone to post early for Christmas, indeed! I don't know what the world's coming to! Asking you not to post after midday, Christmas Eve! No one'll want to do a proper day's work in a minute.'

Amy agreed automatically, as she took a hymn book

85

from one of the piles stacked on a back pew. She wished William could get rid of that graveyard cough. It worried her. She felt a premonition of disaster. She bent her head and prayed God not to let anything happen to her husband.

But William Evans lived for only another seven months, dying in July, 1920, just after the opening of the Olympic Games at Antwerp.

Part Two 1921 – 1925

That's the nature of women . . . not to love when we love them, and to love when we love them not.

Miguel de Cervantes 1547 – 1616

CHAPTER SEVEN

'Stand still,' Minna instructed, 'and let me see the dress properly.' She circled Helen, while the dressmaker watched anxiously from where she knelt on the floor, a large purple pin-cushion strapped to her wrist. 'A little too much ankle showing, do you think, Miss Bond? This is a wedding gown. We don't want any immodest display.'

'Oh, mama!' Helen did a pirouette, peering over her shoulder at the folds of white French silk. 'The train is divine, Miss Bond, and the length just right. Take no notice of Mama.' But she accompanied the reproof with a quick kiss of Minna's cheek.

'I don't think the dress could be any longer, Mrs Gordon,' the dressmaker protested nervously. 'It would look so old-fashioned.'

Minna bit back the retort that fashion was hardly a consideration since Joe had decided that Helen should be married in the Arley Street chapel, and kept her vexation to herself. It was the first time in twenty-one years of marriage that she had dared to criticize her husband; but she felt so strongly on the subject that she had questioned his decision.

'Why, Joe? We haven't been to Arley Street for ages. Surely Clifton would be so much nicer than Eastwood. What do May and Albert think?'

Joe had laughed. 'I don't know what May thinks, and I don't particularly care. I'm paying for this wedding and in those circumstances Albert is only too willing to go along with anything I say.'

'But why?' Minna had repeated.

'I've made up my mind and that's it,' was all the answer she could elicit.

The fact was that Helen had proved adamant about her choice of bridesmaids. She wanted Elizabeth and Mary, and nothing would move her or make her alter her mind. Joseph, however, was damned if he would introduce his business friends and acquaintances to his wife's poor relations: he would feel so ashamed. So he had told everyone that, at the young couple's request, it would be a very quiet wedding in the old family chapel where Helen and Charlie had both been christened. At the same time, he had issued invitations for a lavish 'welcome home' reception at one of Bristol's biggest hotels, when the newly-weds returned from their honeymoon.

Helen had raised no opposition to being married in Eastwood, sensing that she had already antagonized her father far enough over her stand on the matter of the bridesmaids. Besides, she did not care where she was married. There was not an ounce of snobbery in her nature.

Minna's wish to order the wedding dress from Harrods had also been thwarted by Joe, who had recommended their usual dressmaker.

'Miss Bond always turns you both out pretty well. I see no reason for making a fuss and going to London.'

But at least Minna had her way over the material for Helen's dress. Miss Bond had been instructed to purchase six yards of the finest white French silk. Joseph had reluctantly agreed.

'You can cut down on the bridesmaids' rig-outs,' he had told her. 'I've no intention of spending money on Elizabeth and Mary. It's bad enough having to foot the bill at all.'

He had tried hard to persuade Helen not to choose her cousins, and had only given in when she burst into tears.

'But why you can't ask two of your friends, I don't know,' he had grumbled.

It never occurred to him that Helen had no close girl friends; that he and Minna had protected their darling so carefully from the outside world that she had never had the chance to form any lasting relationship other than those with her cousins and Charlie and Stanley Harrison. Mary and Elizabeth were the only contemporary members of her own sex whom she knew at all well.

There was a knock and the maid, Smithson, put her head round the bedroom door.

'Please, mum, Mr Charlie's here to see Miss Helen.'

Minna nodded. 'Thank you, Smithson. Tell him Miss Helen will be down in just a few minutes. We'll have to fit the going-away dress tomorrow, Miss Bond. Can you come back then?'

Quarter of an hour later, Helen entered the first-floor drawing-room to find Charlie seated in an armchair, flipping over the pages of *The Tatler*. His interest was perfunctory, and Helen reflected that Charlie never read. She felt again one of those pin-pricks of dissatisfaction which had disturbed her tranquillity of late, and which had started on that day last month, June the tenth, when she and Charlie had made two of the crowds thronging the city to welcome the Prince of Wales. At one o'clock, they had been near the steps of the Merchants' Hall, where the royal visitor had delivered an address. There was hardly a woman present unaffected by the handsome, dashing looks and wide, engaging smile of the King's eldest son, as the Prince recalled his first sight of America, and compared it with that of Cabot and his crew of Bristol seamen nearly five centuries before. Glancing at Charlie's rather vacuous features and uninterested expression, Helen had experienced a sudden stab of irritation which had taken her completely by surprise. She had immediately slipped her arm through his and squeezed it affectionately.

Then, as the Prince went into the Merchants' Hall for lunch and the crowd broke up, they had, literally, bumped into Elizabeth and Ben Sawyer, Charlie clumsily treading on the former's foot. And while he was apologizing to Elizabeth and she was assuring him that it really did not matter, she was not hurt, Helen and Ben had exchanged a few words. They had been trite and impersonal, about the royal visit and where the Prince would be appearing next; but for the second time in fifteen minutes, Helen had felt miserable and uncertain. She had found herself envying her cousin her handsome escort; wishing that Charlie had the presence and confidence of Ben Sawyer; thinking how young and immature he seemed in comparison.

She felt the same way now, watching him turn over the magazine pages without a spark of interest or intelligence. Then he looked up and saw her, and grinned.

How silly she was! This was Charlie, her friend with whom she was cosy and safe, just as she was with Papa. Ben Sawyer frightened her a little, he was so aggressively masculine, for all his dandified appearance.

'Oh, Charlie!' she breathed on a note of relief, rushing towards him. 'Put your arms round me and hold me tight. Oh, I wish we could get married right away.'

'Steady on, old girl,' he said, patting her back and nuzzling his cheek against her hair. 'Only another three weeks!' He gave his high, whinnying laugh. 'Just think! You'll be Mrs Charles Harrison. Doesn't that sound funny?'

She began to giggle and raised her face to be kissed. His lips felt soft, almost like her mother's. Helen led him to the sofa, where they sat side by side, holding hands, discussing the house which their parents were giving them jointly as a wedding present.

'Won't it be a lark?' she murmured. 'Our very own house and our very own servants. Oh, Charlie, I hope I shall know how to go on. I'm glad we decided on Bournemouth for the honeymoon, aren't you? Remember what good holidays we had there when we were children?'

He nodded, his thin hand clutching hers. 'After we're married,' he said, 'Father's going to start me in the firm.' His narrow chest swelled importantly. 'I'll be a proper businessman.'

They smiled at one another. As long as they were together everything was comfortably predictable: 'safe', Helen repeated to herself again.

'If it stays as hot as this for the wedding,' Amy remarked, 'it'll be lovely.' She and Elizabeth were sitting down to Sunday breakfast. 'They're saying it's been one of the driest Julys anyone can remember. Was that the post? I'm expecting a letter.'

'Sunday deliveries have been abolished, Mama,' Elizabeth reminded her impatiently. 'They were ended last month. You know they were. Where's Mary? Isn't she up yet? She'll be late for chapel.'

'Of course they were! How silly of me. I keep forgetting. Eileen Hennessey said that asking people to post early for Christmas would be the thin end of the wedge. No Sunday deliveries! Whoever would have believed such a thing?' Amy put a smear of margarine on a half-piece of bread, then performed the usual ritual with one boiled egg. 'Mary's staying in bed. Her back's still bad.'

'That's humping those heavy wooden trays up and downstairs at the factory. What an old Scrooge Uncle Joe is. He ought to have installed lifts by now. Goodness knows what yarn he spins the factory inspectors! Uses the war as an excuse I shouldn't wonder. He'll have to modernize the place one day, though. Meantime, why don't the girls come out on strike?'

'Because,' her mother responded drily, 'one of the conditions of employment at Gordon's is that you don't belong to a union, so the girls lack organization. You should know that. You work there.'

Elizabeth paused in her eating, an arrested look in her eyes. After a moment, she said: 'I don't belong to a union, it's true, because no one's ever asked me. But I didn't realize it was forbidden.'

'No, I suppose you might not. As Joe's niece, you never had a proper interview for the job. He just told them you were coming.' Amy noted the martial light in her younger daughter's eyes and begged: 'Now, for pity's sake, don't stir up trouble just before the wedding. I want you and Joe on speaking terms for Helen's sake. She's a good girl and I'm fond of her.'

'Oh, everyone's fond of Helen,' Elizabeth replied caustically, then leaned across and patted her mother's hand. 'Don't worry. Even I'm fond of her. I don't want to be, but I can't help myself. When we were children, I used to think her niceness was all front, but now I know better.' She began gathering up the dirty dishes. 'Who were you expecting to hear from this morning?'

'Hear from? Ah . . . Well . . . I'm not sure that there will be a letter. Letters,' Amy amended. She glanced at the clock on the kitchen mantlepiece. 'Sit down again a minute, Lizzie. There's something I want to say to you. We've time before we need to get ready for chapel. I meant to talk to you and Mary together, but perhaps it would be as well to sound you out first.'

'Sound me out? What is all this, Mama?' Elizabeth sank back into her chair. 'You're making me feel quite nervous.'

'I don't mean to. Lizzie, things haven't been easy this last year, since your father died.' Amy gave a little laugh. 'Things weren't easy before he died, but they've got worse.'

'We manage,' Elizabeth interrupted fiercely. 'You're not going out scrubbing, Mama! Or taking in laundry. I won't let you. You know how Dada would have hated it.'

There was a moment's silence, while the hot July sunshine poured in through the kitchen window. Elizabeth could not speak of her father without a constriction of the throat.

'I know,' Amy replied softly. 'That's why I thought, well, taking a lodger wouldn't be so bad. It's no good looking like that, Lizzie. I have to do something.'

'But we haven't got room for a lodger,' Elizabeth protested, her mind reeling from this totally un-expected suggestion.

'Yes we have, if you move in with me. You and I can share the double bed and the lodger can have your room. I'm sorry it has to be you, Lizzie, but your room is bigger than Mary's.'

'You've thought this all out, haven't you?' Elizabeth asked slowly, and Amy nodded.

'I've already put an advertisement in the *Eastwood Recorder*. I thought, by this morning, there might have been an answer. I'd forgotten about Sunday deliveries being stopped.'

'You wanted to make quite sure that Mary and I wouldn't prevent you.'

'Lizzie, dear, I have to do something. You and Mary can't go on giving me nearly all your wages every week. It's not fair on either of you. Look at that blouse you're wearing. You've turned the cuffs and collar, and it's going thin on both elbows. That young man of yours won't want to be seen with you soon.'

At the mention of Ben, Elizabeth's lips compressed, and she glanced involuntarily at the still bare third finger of her left hand. Ben was as attentive, but as unlover-like as ever. He never spoke the words 'engagement' or 'marriage'. The pair of them might be, if not brother and sister, then affectionate cousins. She told herself that they were young yet; both of them only nineteen. But here was Helen, two years younger, and already getting married.

'Helen and Charlie have security,' she told herself sharply. 'Ben still has his way to make in the world. And so have I.'

She had not forgotten her adolescent vow to make more money than her uncle, but she had as little idea now how to do it as she had five years before. She had less incentive, too, convinced, for all her misgivings, that Ben would eventually ask her to marry him. But supposing he didn't.

Elizabeth got up quickly from the table and continued stacking the dishes.

'Well?' Amy enquired, trying to read her daughter's face, and daunted by what she interpreted as a look of disapproval.

'Well what?'

'My idea about a lodger. What do you think?'

Elizabeth moved towards the scullery. 'Not much good my thinking anything,' she answered with a brittle smile, 'seeing that you've already made up your mind.'

Mary's back had improved by the day of the wedding. The strained muscles, which had cost her three days in bed and two days' pay, were sufficiently healed to allow her to walk down the aisle in her cousin's wake without too much pain.

She was miserably conscious, however, that the blue foulard silk dresses and organdie hats suited her sister far better than herself. The paper-thin silk — or in this case, owing to Joseph's parsimony, silk and cotton mixture — showed up her ungainly, big-boned frame to disadvantage. To make matters worse, the softness of both colour and material became Elizabeth, bringing out the blue of her eyes and flattering her very pale skin. Elizabeth had had her hair bobbed, giving in at last to Ben's insistence, and it swung in two thick curtains, one on either side of her face, the sun tinting the brown with copper. There had been red hair in their father's family several generations back, and it had been Elizabeth's luck to inherit those interesting auburn highlights. Mary's hair, still worn in a bun at the nape of her neck, was what she described as 'mouse'. She was thankful that it was not the anticipated big, fashionable wedding.

But Elizabeth, standing behind Helen and clutching her bouquet of tiny pink rosebuds, wondered why not. This modest congregation and the reception afterwards at the Eastwood Park Hotel was not at all what anyone had expected. When it had first been certain that she and Mary would be bridesmaids, Elizabeth had tried to calm Mary's fears that it would be an important, Clifton affair; but it had not been an exercise she believed in. She had thought herself to be simply allaying her sister's initial alarm. She had been quite prepared for her uncle to renounce his Methodist origins and turn to the Church of England. The Cathedral or St Mary Redcliffe would surely be more his idea of a suitable venue for the wedding of his only child.

Instead, here they were in the Arley Street chapel with very few of Joseph's friends in evidence. Even the Harrisons, bigger and fatter than ever in their wedding finery, looked faintly nonplussed. Later, however, in the William Penn suite of the Eastwood Park Hotel, Elizabeth got an inkling of the truth. While they were waiting for the first of the guests to arrive, she overheard Helen remark to Charlie: 'Papa's ordered me the most wonderful evening dress from Harrods for the Grand Hotel reception.'

Her husband, absorbed in picking a piece of white thread from his coat sleeve, merely grunted, but Elizabeth moved nearer.

'Is that the reception,' she hazarded, 'when you . . . ?'

'When we get back from our honeymoon. That's right. All Papa's smart friends are coming. Look out, Charlie!' Helen nudged him to attention. 'People are beginning to arrive.'

Elizabeth returned to her place beside Mary, in the receiving line. 'So that's it,' she muttered darkly.

'What is? Lizzie, you're standing on my shoe.'

Elizabeth moved, but made no answer. Inwardly, she was seething.

'I'll never forgive him! Never!' she burst out to Ben, when he called at Springtime Grove that evening to hear how the day had gone. 'He didn't want us mixing with his Clifton cronies. Not us. Not the poor relations.'

Amy was sitting at the kitchen table, darning stockings, but she looked up at that and said: 'Tell her she's making a fuss about nothing, Ben. I don't suppose such a thought ever crossed Joseph's mind.'

'Oh, don't be so naïve, Mama!' Elizabeth crammed her straw hat, with it's trimming of flowers and fruit, on to her short, swinging hair. 'Ben knows better, don't you?'

'I should guess that Lizzie's right in her assumption, Mrs Evans, but don't let it worry you.'

'Well I intend to let it worry me,' Elizabeth rapped out. 'And I'll tell you another thing, Mama. Our present wasn't even on display.'

'Wasn't it? I didn't notice,' Amy lied, her flushed cheeks giving her away. 'It wasn't a very good tea-service, anyway,' she added.

'It was more than we could afford,' Elizabeth retorted angrily. She glanced at Ben. 'You're very quiet this evening.'

'A bit tired, that's all. Any luck with your lodger yet, Mrs Evans?'

Amy bit off her thread of mending yarn, 'I've had one or two replies, but no one I consider really suitable.'

'What Mama means,' Elizabeth said with a laugh, 'is no one she considers really interesting. There were two very suitable applications, one from a spinster lady, another from a widow. But Mama fancies a pale young man whom she can mother.'

'Nonsense!' But Amy's heighted colour showed that Elizabeth was not far from the truth.

Later, as she and Ben walked along Springtime Grove in the direction of Portland Place, Elizabeth said: 'She's never got over the death of my young brother. Mama always wanted a son, and then, when she had one, he died at the age of six. Poor Edward. He was such a loving little boy.' Again she directed a look of concern at Ben. 'You are quiet this evening, and it's not just tiredness. What's wrong?'

'Nothing . . . All right, something. Call it the end of a dream.'

'That's very enigmatic. What is it supposed to mean?'

'I don't know.' He sounded peevish. 'Not much, perhaps. It's just that sometimes something happens which you've persuaded yourself won't take place.'

Elizabeth slowed to a halt. 'Are you by any chance talking about my cousin's wedding?'

Ben, who had overshot her when she stopped, turned round to face her. Would he be a fool to admit the truth? Probably, unless he wanted to alienate Elizabeth. He knew how much she loved him, and also how proud and stubborn she was. But now that Helen was married, did he want to go on seeing her? Was there any point? He decided he would do as well not to be too hasty with his answer.

'Don't be silly,' he reassured her, drawing Elizabeth's arm through his. 'You pressed me for a reason and I didn't have one. It was just something to say. Now, come on, or we shall be late for the film.'

They caught a tramcar in Portland Place and went to a cinema near the city centre which was showing a

German film, *The Cabinet of Doctor Caligari*, but for once neither of them paid much attention to the insubstantial shadows on the screen. Elizabeth, sitting beside Ben in the smoky darkness, holding his hand, tried to persuade herself that everything was all right between them; to convince herself that she really believed what he had said.

It had not occurred to her until that moment when she asked her question, that he might have been using her to reach her cousin. Even now, she did not really believe it. After all, Ben had known from the beginning that Helen was going to marry Charlie Harrison. She herself had told him so, that day two and a half years ago, when Helen had visited the factory. And certainly, since then, Ben had implied by neither word nor look that he was interested in Helen. She was being stupid, seeing danger where none existed. Ben would not have seriously supposed that the engagement between her cousin and Charlie Harrison would be broken, or, if it had been, that he would stand a chance with Uncle Joe. Because Ben was no fool, and he must know that Joseph Gordon would never tolerate him for a son-in-law. It was one thing for Joe to have married a girl from the factory floor, but he would never stand for one of his employees marrying Helen. 'Don't do as I do, do as I tell you,' was one of his favourite maxims. Elizabeth decided that she was worrying unnecessarily. She took a firmer grip on Ben's hand.

Ben, feeling the sudden pressure and the slackening of her body, was quick to interpret the signs. Elizabeth had convinced herself that her suspicions were unfounded. He smiled grimly to himself. How easy it was to bamboozle women. Although he kept it well hidden, Ben had as much contempt for the opposite sex as Joseph Gordon, an attitude of mind to which his doting mother and aunt had contributed. But Ben was cynical about most people: they let themselves be used easily.

What, then, was he going to do about Elizabeth? He genuinely liked her. She was more intelligent than most girls he had met, but, in natural corollary, was less controllable. Her dislike of her uncle, aggravated still further by this latest bee in her bonnet over the wedding, would lead one day to open confrontation. He could see it coming, and realized that no amount of lecturing and persuasion on his part could prevent it. That, however, did not of necessity mean that she would be estranged from Helen. There was a bond between the cousins which seemed to strengthen as they grew older. But Helen was now married. What a waste, he reflected savagely, to throw away a girl like that on a feeble creature such as Charlie Harrison. Ben remembered Helen's eyes; 'bedroom eyes' was what he called them. Could the marriage last? Surely Helen must be aware of her true nature eventually, and if so, wouldn't it be wise of him to be in a position to help her make that discovery?

As the credits rolled up on the screen and the house-lights brightened, he turned to Elizabeth with his most disarming smile.

CHAPTER EIGHT

Mary left the factory at half-past six, thankful to be quit of work for another day. Overhead, the melancholy autumn sky gave no promise of a break in the dismal weather. Rain-scuds from the west followed the path of the canal and left the tow-path deserted. Mary thought of home, the warm kitchen, the smell of hot food, and quickened her steps. She could not be bothered to wait for Elizabeth. Her umbrella was seized and rattled by a sudden squall of wind, and she locked her fingers around the spokes to stop it being blown inside out.

She enjoyed the rain. She liked the small, enclosed world of her sou'wester and umbrella, the shelter both gave her from prying glances. Her extreme shyness, which caused her at times to be both rude and aggressive, made walking along the street an ordeal. She tried to avoid other people's eyes, convinced that strangers pitied her for being such a plain young woman. Or perhaps, worse still, they did not even notice her; did not think of her at all.

As she turned into Springtime Grove, the wind buffeted her almost off her feet, then screamed away around the corner in a frenzy of destruction. One of the Miss Cohens, who kept the corner shop, was just closing for the night.

'Autumn gales!' she called. 'Nasty weather!'

'Lovely!' Mary shouted back, and went on down the street, leaving Miss Cohen staring after her in astonishment. She experienced a sense of freedom, of exhilaration. She had not felt like this since that day, three years ago, when she had walked to the Sea Walls with Elizabeth and Ben.

The hedge of thin shrubs which, together with a few brick tiles, comprised the front garden of number eighteen, was dancing frenziedly in the wind. As always, the front door stood wide until darkness fell, when it was no longer safe to leave it open. Beyond it the inner door, with its panels of coloured glass, winked and gleamed jewel-bright, reflecting the light from the kitchen. Mary slammed it shut behind her, standing in the narrow passage and shaking the water from her, like a dog. She dropped her still unfurled umbrella into the hall-stand, and hung up her dripping sou'wester and mackintosh. It was then she noticed that the light was coming not only from the kitchen, at the end of the passageway, but also from the doorway on her left, which opened into what was variously known as 'the front room', the 'drawing-room' or the 'parlour'.

'Lizzie?' Amy's voice sounded from inside the room. Mary recognized the tone; defiant, yet at the same time, defensive. Mama was planning to do something of which she knew Elizabeth would not approve.

'No, it's me.' Mary pushed the door wider and went inside, noting the look of relief on her mother's face. A fire had been lit, and the small room was filled to the ceiling with flickering light.

Amy was not alone. Standing beside her chair, twisting his cap in his hands, was a shabbily dressed, fair-haired boy of perhaps eight or nine years old. A small, dark man in his thirties was seated in the other armchair, and rose awkwardly to his feet as Mary came in.

She recognized them both at once. How odd that she

should have been thinking of that day when they had gone to see the American soldiers. To her superstitious mind, it seemed that the coincidence must have a special significance.

'This is my elder daughter, Mary.' Amy introduced her with a nervous little laugh. 'Mary, dear, this is Mr Davies and his son, Richard. I've agreed to let them have our middle bedroom.'

'How do you do?' Mary said, holding out her hand. For the first time in her life she felt neither shy nor embarrassed in the presence of a man.

'Very well, thank you,' he answered in the soft Welsh accent she remembered so clearly. 'How are you?'

'Mr Davies and his son are from Cardiff,' her mother rushed on, as Mary turned to smile at the boy. 'He's a widower, isn't that right, Mr Davies?'

'That's right, Mrs Evans, and please call me Alan. My wife died when Richie, here, was born.'

In the ensuing flow of Amy's commiseration, neither she nor Alan Davies noticed the arrested look on Mary's face. Her first thought was that she had been wrong; that the woman with him that day on the Downs had not been Mrs Davies. But a second, longer scrutiny of the boy recalled the woman's face vividly to mind. Richard Davies might have his father's brown eyes and high cheek bones, but he resembled the woman too nearly for her not to have been his mother. Or could she have been, perhaps, an aunt or a cousin?

'You left your family behind in Wales, then, Mr Davies?' Mary asked, sitting down on the sofa.

Alan Davies resumed his own seat. 'I haven't any family, Miss Evans. I was brought up in an orphanage. A man on his lonesome, I'm afraid. There's just been Richie and me ever since he was born.'

Amy clicked sympathetically. Mary said nothing: Alan Davies's reply had settled it. For some reason of his own, he was keeping the existence of his wife a secret. She wasn't dead, or he would have had no reason to lie about the date. He must be divorced, and naturally would not care to admit it. It would bar him from many good homes in his search for lodgings. Well, she certainly would not reveal his secret. She did not blame him in the least for ridding himself of that bad-tempered woman.

She asked: 'Have you work in Bristol, Mr Davies?'

'Yes. With the Bristol Tramways and Carriage Company, as a conductor on the trams. I'm very lucky. Unemployment's getting terrible in South Wales.'

'It's bad here, too,' Amy said. 'All over the country, in fact.' Her voice was suddenly high and strained.

Mary had also heard the rattle and slam of the inner door and voices in the passageway. A moment later, Elizabeth looked into the room.

'What's going on?' she enquired. 'What on earth are you doing in here?' She stared in surprise at Alan and Richard Davies, then entered the room properly. Jack Hennessey followed her in.

'Mama, you're out of your mind! One lodger, you said, not two!'

'Richard Davies is only a child.' Amy's face was set in determined lines. Mary could see that she had made up her mind.

'Children have a habit of growing,' Elizabeth pointed out. 'Where's that great lump of a boy going to sleep, I'd like to know?'

'For the time being, I'm borrowing a camp-bed from Eileen Hennessey. Richard can sleep on that in his father's room.'

The Davieses had departed half an hour previously and the controversy had raged ever since. Amy and the girls, together with Jack Hennessey, were seated round the table in the kitchen. Jack looked on as the three women ate their tea.

'And are you going to charge rent for two people?' Elizabeth demanded, reaching for a slice of bread to mop up the gravy on her plate. 'That boy will eat you out of house and home.'

'Mr Davies and I have come to a satisfactory arrangement,' was the guarded answer.

Elizabeth raised her eyes to heaven. 'That means you're going to charge him exactly what you would have charged for one. Mama, for goodness' sake! Apart from the money, we don't want a growing boy in the house.'

But that, thought Mary, was precisely what their mother did want. She wanted a substitute for the son who had been snatched from her in his infancy. Young Richard Davies was an answer to prayer.

Elizabeth put her knife and fork together on her empty plate and turned imploringly to Jack.

'What do you think?' she asked him.

Jack looked uncomfortable, torn between his desire to side with Elizabeth and his instinct to stay out of other people's quarrels.

'Not really my business,' he muttered.

'No, it's not,' Amy fired up. 'It's mine! And I've decided. Mr Davies and his son are coming on Monday, as arranged. That gives you Saturday afternoon and Sunday to move your stuff into my room, Lizzie.'

'It's sheer lunacy,' Elizabeth confided to Jack when they were alone in the kitchen.

The washing-up done, Amy suggested that they spend the rest of the evening in the parlour.

'A pity to waste the fire now it's lit,' she said.

Elizabeth had declined on the score that someone ought to start cleaning the silver, and Amy, visibly relieved, had tucked her arm through Mary's and withdrawn for a comfortable gossip. She had realized from the beginning that her elder daughter was on her side over this business of the lodger.

Jack sat at the kitchen table and watched while Elizabeth tipped the drawerful of knives, forks and spoons on to the newspaper which she had spread. He took one of the dusters.

'You put the stuff on and I'll polish,' he offered.

'Well don't you think it's lunacy?' Elizabeth asked as she picked up one of the knives. 'And when did she ask your mother if she might borrow your old camp-bed?'

'Must have been yesterday.' Jack rubbed vigorously. 'Ma mentioned it at breakfast this morning.'

'She'd made up her mind then, even before she'd seen them ... There's something about that man I don't trust.'

'Why not?' Jack was always reluctant to condemn without good reason.

'I don't know. Maybe it's the way he doesn't exactly meet your eyes when he speaks to you.'

'Shyness perhaps.' Jack polished a spoon. 'Mary avoids looking at people directly, and you wouldn't say there was anything shifty about her.' Abruptly he changed the subject. 'Lizzie, there's a lot of gossip going round about you and Ben Sawyer. People are asking when you are going to get married.'

'People can mind their own business, then,' Elizabeth rapped back. 'We're not doing anything we're ashamed of, if that's what your friends are suggesting.'

'They're not my friends, and even if they were, they'd know better than to suggest anything of the kind to me. I'd knock their teeth in! No, it's just that people wonder why, after going out together for so long, he doesn't pop the question.'

'"Pop the question"!' Elizabeth repeated scornfully. 'What an excruciatingly vulgar expression! Ben isn't feckless enough to ask a woman to marry him before he can afford to support her. We don't want a houseful of children and a life courtesy of Harrison's Universal Clothing Company, thank you. There's plenty of time to talk about marriage.'

Her vehemence and the look on her face warned Jack

not to proceed with what was all too evidently an unwelcome subject. He said no more, and after a while they settled into a companionable silence. But he disliked Ben Sawyer in the same instinctive way she seemed to dislike Alan Davies. He promised himself: 'If he hurts her, I'll half-kill him.'

'A Happy New Year, my poppet. A very happy nineteen twenty-two. Minna, May, Albert, here's to our children, God bless 'em!'

Joseph raised his glass and the other three followed his example. Helen and Charlie, standing beside the now rather bedraggled splendours of the Christmas tree, raised their glasses in return. A bottle of sherry to welcome in the New Year was an innovation insisted upon by Albert Harrison, who had never been as abstemious as his Methodist upbringing required.

The sound of church bells echoed in from the streets. Further down the row of solid Victorian houses could be heard the sound of voices raised in laughter. Someone was carrying out the old Scottish tradition of first-footing.

Minna said: 'I suppose we ought to be going. These young people need their beauty sleep.' She blushed as she saw May and Albert exchange amused glances. That wasn't what she had meant at all.

Nevertheless, as she followed Helen upstairs to collect the coats from the first-floor bedroom, she could not resist asking: 'You're . . . all right, darling . . . are you?'

Helen switched on the electric light. Joseph and Albert had insisted on the conversion from gas to electricity as soon as they had purchased the house in Pembroke Road. It was certainly a nice house, Minna thought; warm brick with clustering chimneys, and plenty of tall windows to let in the light. Joe had not stinted on his present, whatever he had done about the wedding.

Helen looked at her mother, faintly puzzled. 'Of course I'm all right, Mama. I told you. I've quite recovered from that cold.'

Minna picked up her evening wrap and the coats of the others from the bed. The clashing of church bells was making her head ache.

'That wasn't quite . . . what I meant,' she replied hesitantly. 'Are you . . . ? What I want to know is . . . are you expecting a baby?'

Helen flushed and avoided her mother's eyes. 'Not yet,' she answered shortly.

'Oh . . . I didn't mean to pry, darling. But as you've been married nearly six months . . . naturally, I wondered.'

Helen moved to the dressing-table and began to fiddle with one of the silver-backed hairbrushes. 'This is nineteen twenty-one — nineteen twenty-two now, Mama. People don't marry just to have babies any more. People take their time.'

Minna agreed hurriedly. 'Yes. Yes, of course.' She wondered unhappily if Helen had been reading any of those awful books which had been circulating recently. It was in 1916 that Mrs Margaret Sanger had established the first contraception centre in the U S A. Everyone — anyone who dared mention the subject, that was — had said at the time that it could never happen in England; but the year just ended had seen the opening of London's first birth-control clinic. 'It's just that I'm looking forward to being a grandmother, that's all.'

'I know.' Helen came across and kissed Minna affectionately. 'Don't worry. Charlie and I are . . . well, we feel we're a bit young, that's the trouble. Sometimes I feel I'm still a little girl myself.' She giggled, a habit she had when nervous or embarrassed.

'Of course.' Minna was relieved. 'You're only just eighteen.'

They went downstairs with the coats. While they

were all getting ready to leave, May Harrison suddenly remarked: 'I hear your sister's taking in lodgers now, Minna.'

Minna made no reply. She had often thought that there was a spiteful streak in May. She seemed to enjoy reminding Minna of her working-class origins.

'We don't have much to do with them nowadays,' Joseph said coldly, placing her fur wrap around Minna's shoulders. 'What Amy does is her own business. We don't want to know.'

'Oh, Papa! What a horrid thing to say.' Helen was distressed. 'I care, even if you don't.'

Joseph tried to bluster away her disapproval, but he saw May Harrison grin. May, he decided viciously, could sometimes be a bitch. He had not heard that particular item of news himself, and wondered where she had obtained her information.

They were gone at last, the front door shut behind them, Joseph's new Daimler purring away down the street, followed by the Harrisons' older, but no less grand Austin. Helen gave a sigh of pleasure as she returned to the drawing-room and kicked off her shoes. Charlie was stretched out on the sofa, sipping another glass of sherry.

'Well, that's over,' she said, sinking into one of the deep armchairs and warming her stockinged feet by the dying fire. 'Our first New Year in our own home. Mrs Bagot did us proud, I thought, at dinner.'

Charlie smiled sleepily. 'Yes. Jolly good. She's a damn fine cook when she puts her mind to it. We have to thank Mother for finding her for us.'

'Mmm.' Helen shifted, tucking her feet underneath her and propping her chin in her hand. 'Charlie, Mama asked me something tonight.'

'Hazard of having parents, old girl. They're always poking their noses in.'

'She wanted to know if I was going to have a baby.'

'Why?' Charlie looked bemused. 'You didn't say

110

anything to make her think so, did you?'

'No, of course not. How could I when . . . ? It's just that she expects it, Charlie, after six months of marriage.'

'Don't see why. Lots of people never have children.' Her husband's voice was drowsy and his eyes were closing. Helen got off her chair and went to kneel beside him.

'Charlie! Wake up. I want to talk to you.'

'Can't talk now,' he protested. 'It's nearly one in the morning.'

'Charlie! Isn't it time we . . . well . . . slept together?'

'We do sleep together.' He grinned fatuously.

'You've had too much to drink,' Helen accused him. 'You're not used to it. I didn't mean sharing the same bed, darling. I meant sleeping together like . . . like man and wife.'

'Oh that.' He sat up, shaken into brief sobriety. He stared at his feet in their elegant black leather evening shoes. 'Plenty of time for that sort of thing, old girl. You know I'm not strong.'

'I know you say you're not strong.'

'I'm not.' Charlie's tone was plaintive. 'The doctor told Mama years ago that I must not exert myself. He said my chest's weak. Excitement is bad for me.'

'But, darling, when people get married they expect . . . certain things. It's disappointing . . . if they don't get them.'

'I know. I know.' He smothered her cheek. 'But I don't feel well enough, sweetheart. I'm sure it wouldn't be good for me, not just yet. Later on, I shall be stronger. Much stronger. You'll see. Everything will be all right soon.'

Helen sat back on her heels, watching the last, dying flames on the hearth. A picture of Ben Sawyer flashed into her mind; so tall, so dark, so good-looking.

'Tall, dark and handsome'; the familiar phrase

suddenly made her giggle. That was better. She must not think that way about Ben, and laughing at him helped her not to take him too seriously. She was happy with Charlie. It was fun having her own home, making her own decisions, even though she was not very good at that. But there were always Papa and Mama to consult when she was unable to make up her mind. Charlie would get stronger.

She lay back, resting her head against his shoulder. They must go to bed. The fire was almost out, only a faint glow remaining amongst the embers. She closed her eyes, drifting on the borderland of sleep. She wished Papa had not spoken so slightingly of her aunt and cousins. It made her ashamed. Just before she lost consciousness, she wondered what their new lodger was like.

Mary saw him waiting at the corner of Canal Street before he saw her. She quickened her pace.

'Hello,' she said breathlessly. 'I didn't realize you were on early shift this week.'

Alan Davies raised his hat. 'Six until two. I hope you don't object to my coming to meet you. Again.'

They both laughed. It was a lovely, clear spring evening, with a hint of frost to come. The pale sunset glimmered into twilight and the first stars crackled overhead. Mary recalled with delight the utter disbelief she felt the first time that Alan had come to meet her from work. January the eleventh, 1922, was a day she would always remember. The next morning one of the girls had said: 'Saw you with a man yesterday evening, Evans. You're a dark horse.' It was the first time anyone had addressed her voluntarily for years. The original cause of the dispute had long since been forgotten, but its consequences lingered on because the other girls considered her dull and stand-offish. And then, in an instant, she had become an object of interest. Evans had a 'fellow'.

It was Mary's secret nightmare that Alan Davies's attentions would cease as suddenly as they had started. Three months later, however, there still seemed no danger of that happening. Whenever his shift work on the trams permitted, he met her from work and escorted her home. And tonight, it seemed, he was preparing to take the relationship one stage further.

'I wondered if you'd like to come to the pictures with me, this evening,' he said, as they crossed Portland Place. He put an arm about her shoulders to draw her out of the path of one of the drays, parked outside the brewery. 'I've spoken to your mother and she's very kindly consented to look after Richard, if you'll come. There's a double bill, *Broken Blossoms* and *Way Down East*, at the Tivoli. Your sister said that used to be a music-hall.'

'Yes, it did.' Mary's heart was beating so fast she could hardly breathe. He did like her. He liked her enough to want to take her to the pictures. She did not care if he was divorced. It did not matter. 'And I'd love to come with you. Thank you.'

They walked on in silence for a while, but as they turned into Springtime Grove, Mary blurted out: 'Why do you like me? Other men don't.'

'Perhaps that's why. I suffer the same way, you see. Women have never found me very attractive.' They had stopped on the corner of the street, oblivious to everyone and everything around them. 'Your sister doesn't like me, for example.'

'Take no notice of Lizzie. Did . . . Did you not get on with your wife?'

There was the slightest hesitation before he answered smoothly: 'Not very well. But we were only married a year, see, when Richie was born and she died.'

'Oh.' She had been hoping against hope that he would tell her the truth; confide in her to show that she had his trust. Perhaps when they knew one another better he would. She was expecting too much too soon.

They continued down the street towards number eighteen. He said: 'Of course, that isn't the only reason that I like you. I like you because you're so kind, not just to me, but to Richie. He's very fond of you, you know.'

'Is he? I thought he preferred Elizabeth.'

'How could you think that? They're always having words. Look how she went on at him last night for leaving his dirty shoes in the passage.'

'But he respects her. He doesn't even notice me.'

'He's young. He has a lot to learn.'

'That doesn't explain why he prefers Elizabeth.'

'She just forces herself on his notice by constantly nagging him.' There was a note of exasperation in his voice which he seemed to hear, and swiftly suppressed. 'She's always resented us, I realize that, and would like to be rid of us if she could. I can't blame her. She was the one turned out of her room.'

Mary paused with her hand on the gate. 'She'll come round when she knows you better.' Her voice and face lacked conviction.

Alan Davies followed her the two paces along the brick-tiled path to the front door. 'That neighbour of yours, Jack Hennessey, has been making enquiries about me, at work. I'm sure your sister put him up to it.'

'*Jack* has?' Mary turned red with indignation. 'That's too bad! I'll have a word with Lizzie about it.'

'No. Don't do that.' Alan Davies smiled at her. 'I can't be responsible for you quarrelling with your sister. Leave the matter to me. I'll sort things out.'

CHAPTER NINE

No one could ever give any satisfactory explanation as to why Inkerman Street was so called, because it was, in reality, a square. In the long-gone days when Eastwood had been in transition between village and suburb, it had been called Hanover Place and its now derelict Georgian houses had been the homes of the well-to-do. By the time it had been renamed, however, in 1854, the public wash-house already occupied the northern side, and the rest of the buildings were falling into disrepair.

Since the turn of the century it had become a favourite haunt for the soap-box orators, who also frequented the Horsefair and Old Market Street in the city; and its unfortunate proximity to Sebastopol Street had meant the imposing of a strict ban on all of Gordon's employees. Anyone from either factory seen in the little crowds which gathered around the advocates of communism, trades unionism or a united Ireland was threatened with instant dismissal. And, frequently, the threat was carried out.

Elizabeth had never been tempted to listen to any of the political agitators, her mind usually being full of other things. She scarcely even glanced into the square, as she hurried by on her way to the factory, except as a safety precaution. And even that was hardly necessary, there being very little traffic other than pedestrians. But on that particular morning in late July, she could not fail to notice the young Irishman, standing on an old three-legged milking-stool in the entrance to Inkerman Street, holding forth on the recent ambush and assassination of Michael Collins.

'And so perish all traitors who make deals with the British Government!' He punched a fist almost under Elizabeth's nose as he spoke. She dodged and crossed to the opposite pavement.

She had been worrying about the growing friendship between her sister and Alan Davies, and the row she had had with her mother the previous night.

'Leave Mary alone,' Amy had warned her, 'or you'll have me to reckon with. This is my house, and I say that Alan and Richard are going to stay. I don't know what it is you have against them, but whatever it is, it's all in your mind. I'm thankful I haven't your suspicious nature.'

Was it true that her dislike of Alan Davies was unfounded? Elizabeth was still trying to analyse the reasons for her antagonism towards him when she became conscious of a fist in front of her face and an Irish voice shouting in her ear.

As her eyes and mind focused on the young Irishman, another man came up behind him and toppled him from his perch.

'This is my stand today,' the second man shouted. 'I put my mark here yesterday evening.' He pointed to a chalk cross on the cobbles, then swung round on Elizabeth, seizing her arm. 'Did you know, my girl, that this month is the eighty-eighth anniversary of the Tolpuddle Martyrs? Tried and transported in eighteen thirty-four for daring to form a trade union! Honest, respectable men, one of them a Methodist lay preacher, treated like criminals for demanding their rights — a living wage for themselves and their families. John Ball preached the communistic law, and he was hanged,

116

drawn and quartered after the Peasants' Revolt. Two centuries later, Robert Kett was hanged from his own Oak of Reformation. And we are still struggling, my sister! The working classes are the source of this country's wealth, and yet . . . '

At that moment, the Irishman, who had been dazedly picking himself up from the pavement, recovered sufficiently to seize the trade unionist by the collar and slam his left fist into the other man's jaw. Elizabeth fled up the street to the main factory entrance before a nasty situation deteriorated yet further.

Apart from telling Ben about the brawl during their half-hour dinner-break, munching sandwiches and sharing a flask of tea at their desks, she thought no more of it. Street fights were common enough, especially in the rougher districts. Nor did she imagine it had anything to do with her summons, late that same afternoon, to that holy of holies, Joseph's office. She was certainly astounded by the command to present herself immediately to the sanctum on the top floor, as her uncle had never before, during the five years of her employment, asked to see her. As she had done nothing wrong, however, she was not worried.

Miss Folmer, cool and efficient in a grey flannel suit which defied the summer weather, showed her into Joseph's office, then retired to the ante-room, where she resumed her vigorous rattling of typewriter keys. Joseph was writing and did not at once look up. Nor did he invite Elizabeth to sit down.

She occupied herself by looking casually around the room, noting the panelled walls, the huge walnut desk, the deep pile of the green carpet, the leather armchairs and a table against one wall, bearing a sherry and a whisky decanter for Joseph's business friends. She noted that both decanters were of poor quality, and remembered some of the beautiful crystal-cut glassware she had seen at The Brass Mill.

Her uncle's voice recalled her wandering attention,

and she realized from his first word that this was not a friendly interview.

'It has come to my attention, Evans, that you have been listening to that scum in Inkerman Street. You were seen this morning in conversation with one of them, his hand actually on your arm. Well? Do you have anything to say for yourself?'

Elizabeth stared at him as though he had taken leave of his senses. 'I don't know what you're talking about,' she said.

'You will speak to me with respect, or not at all,' Joseph replied with precarious calm. 'And you are either very stupid or being wilfully silly. I repeat, you were seen on the corner of Inkerman Street and Sebastopol Street this morning, on your way to work, in conversation with one of the political speakers. Are you going to deny the truth of that statement?'

'Yes,' Elizabeth retorted hotly. 'And I'd like to know who has been spreading lies about me!'

'Lies are they?' Joseph's eyes were bulging with anger. He thumped his chest. 'I saw you, my girl! I saw you! What do you say to that, eh? I was passing by on the other side of the street, in the car.'

'Then you were mistaken in what you saw. The man gripped my arm and I was unable to get away, until the Irishman, whom he had knocked off his stool, got to his feet and knocked him down.' She could see by the look of baffled rage on her uncle's face that most of this scenario was new to him. All he had obtained was a brief glimpse of her and the second man as his car drove past. 'And that is all that happened,' she added defiantly.

Joseph bit his lip, tapping his fingers on his desk. Plainly he did not want to believe her, but he rang the bell for Miss Folmer, who hurried in.

'Telephone the police station,' he snapped at her, 'and find out if there was a disturbance in Inkerman Street this morning, involving an Irishman. Report back as soon as you can.'

Two furious spots of red burned in Elizabeth's cheeks. 'I am telling you the truth,' she said. 'You have no need to verify my story.'

'Mr Gordon will be the judge of that,' Miss Folmer reproved her icily, and withdrew to the outer office again.

Elizabeth turned to her uncle.

'I should like to be told,' she said, 'why I and my fellow workers are not permitted to listen to anyone we wish. It shows a singular lack of confidence in your employees.'

'Lack of confidence!' spluttered Joseph. 'Do you seriously imagine that most of the poor, muddled intellects in this factory would be able to resist the sort of rubbish those Bolshies are handing out? They'd be regimented like so many sheep.'

'Aren't they already? By the employers?'

Her uncle's jaw worked soundlessly up and down. The veins stood out on his neck. At last: 'You,' he said thickly, 'are dismissed.'

'For what reason?' Elizabeth asked. She took a deep breath to steady her nerves. 'Telling the truth?'

'For listening to seditious talk.'

'I've explained what happened.'

'You're lying,' he accused her.

Miss Folmer returned to the office. 'There was a disturbance in Inkerman Street this morning,' she announced ungraciously. 'An Irishman was involved. Sergeant Banner had a word with both men, who are at present in custody, and they corroborate Evans's story.'

'Thank you, Folmer,' Elizabeth said sweetly, and saw the secretary's fist clench at this gratuitous piece of impudence.

Elizabeth was not proud of it and regretted it almost at once. She must learn not to give way to childish impulse.

Joseph was obviously shaken, and she realized with

a sense of outrage that he had expected her to be lying.

'Am I still dismissed?' she asked calmly, but inwardly seething. How she disliked him!

Her uncle hesitated, glancing at the secretary, who gave a little shake of her head. Elizabeth could hardly contain her fury at having her fate decided by Miss Folmer, but she restrained her anger. She was not ready at the moment to leave Gordon's.

'Very well. Your notice is withdrawn,' Joseph rasped. 'But you will have a day's wages docked from your pay this week.'

'Why? I've done nothing wrong. You can't punish me for no reason.'

'Impudence, my girl! Impudence! That's the reason.' Her uncle was apoplectic again. Miss Folmer hurried solicitously to his side, ready to loosen his collar. 'Now get out, before I change my mind and insist on sacking you, instead.'

Elizabeth went. But she knew, as she returned to the invoice department, that she should begin making plans for her future. After today, she wished to remain no longer than was absolutely necessary at the factory. But could her plans include Ben Sawyer?

The garden lay grey and misty under the full moon. It had rained during the day, and from her bedroom window Mary could see the two small flower-beds, which her father had tended with loving, but inexpert care, their wet earth glistening in the ghostly light. The sharp angle of the bathroom roof jutted out below her, and, beyond it again, the little outhouse where the mangle was kept.

It had been a close day for late September and the factory had been stuffy, the work tiring and monotonous. She had noticed it less than usual, however, just as the other girls' perpetually hostile attitude had failed to hurt as much as usual. Today she had been almost indifferent to their dislike, seized by the conviction that her relationship with Alan Davies was nearing some sort of crisis.

She supposed she was in love with him, although having no experience of love, she could not be certain. She was very fond of both Alan and his son, and was very jealous of Elizabeth's odd, ambivalent intimacy with Richard. The pair quarrelled and argued incessantly, Elizabeth bossing and scolding, Richard as cheeky as the ten years' disparity between their ages allowed. Yet, at other times, they laughed and joked, even sharing secrets with one another. But at least Alan showed no inclination to fall under Elizabeth's spell. Mary fancied that he actively disliked her, although he never said so. He was always very respectful towards Elizabeth, but never treated her with the friendliness he used with Mary and Amy.

'You're like the Mam I never had, Mrs Evans,' he would say, as he sat with them in the evening, telling stories of his boyhood in a Cardiff orphanage and, later in Penarth, where for a short time he had owned his own cockle and mussel stall on the front. But when Elizabeth appeared, he would be quiet, making himself as inconspicuous as possible.

He was still wary of Jack Hennessey.

'He's your sister's man,' he had once said to Mary. 'He's in love with her, poor devil. But she'll have that tailor's dummy, if she can.'

Mary had never thought of Jack as being in love with Elizabeth, but once Alan had drawn her attention to the fact, she could see it for herself. She had had no problem in identifying the 'tailor's dummy'.

Ben Sawyer had been there tonight, filling the little kitchen with his commanding presence, condescending to Amy, ignoring the rest. He and Elizabeth had been to some musical concert in Bristol, and Mozart's Clarinet Quintet and Haydn's Symphony number 44 — 'In E minor; "Mourning",' Ben had

121

dropped casually into the conversation — had been under discussion.

'Pair of show-offs,' Alan had hissed in Mary's ear, as he handed her a cup of tea; even though it must have been obvious to him, as it was to her, that Elizabeth was showing off Ben Sawyer, not her own small, painfully acquired knowledge of music.

There had been an extra warmth, an additional intimacy in Alan's manner towards her this evening and also for the past few days, which made Mary's heart beat faster. It was responsible for her conviction that their relationship had reached a turning-point, whatever it might prove to be.

It was late, gone eleven, by the time Ben went home and everyone was ready for bed; but once undressed, Mary found that she could not sleep. She was filled with a sense of excitement, of anticipation. She got into bed and read for a while then blew out her bedside candle and got up again. She stood at the window, staring out at the moonlit strip of garden.

She had no idea how long it was before she heard the scratch of finger-nails at her bedroom door. At first, the sound was so faint she thought she was mistaken. Then it came again, accompanied this time by a very slight knock. She tiptoed across the room to avoid any tell-tale creak of the floorboards.

Alan Davies was outside in his nightshirt. He said nothing, merely raising his eyebrows in unspoken question. Mary hesitated for a moment, then stood back to let him enter. She glanced anxiously at the closed door a few feet away, at the other end of the narrow landing, but there was no sound from her mother's room, which Amy shared now with Elizabeth.

'Richie's fast asleep,' Alan murmured, slipping his arms around her and kissing her ready lips. He began pulling up her nightdress and forcing her back towards the bed.

Mary knew that she ought to struggle, to protest, to

produce some token of outraged modesty, but she had no will to resist. If this was love, she was ready for it. Every instinct was at war with her upbringing and religious training, and her instincts won. She could not even wait to reach the bed, but pulled Alan down to the floor, the rag rug slipping and rucking beneath her, on to the cold linoleum. His wiry body, surprisingly strong for someone so small and light, was on top of hers, pinioning her arms, forcing himself inside her almost as if he hated her. Just for a split second, before the pain began, Mary thought that, for him, she had suddenly become someone else.

She had never imagined that pain could be at once agonizing and ecstatic. She wanted to scream, but dared not. She could hear the rasp of his breathing and her own heart hammering against her ribs. Her back arched, the world splintered into fragments of joy and anguish; and then she was sobbing foolishly, her face pressed to his chest in an effort to muffle the noise.

Later, they made love again, this time less traumatically and more comfortably in bed. She did not mind the soreness. Every other sense was submerged by a feeling of triumph. Now, at last, she knew what the other girls at the factory giggled and whispered about; understood their elliptical remarks. She, plain, dull, uninteresting Mary Evans had a man and was as good as any of them. She thought of Elizabeth and Ben Sawyer and nearly laughed out loud. What a dry-as-dust relationship they had, with their discussions of music and books and paintings. Mary snuggled into Alan's side and wondered if she might be pregnant. If so, she did not care. Alan would marry her and they would have a home of their own. They would have very little money, but it did not worry her. She was used to that.

Presently, she sat up, her long hair, which she stubbornly refused to have cut, falling untidily about her shoulders. The bright moonlight poured in through the uncurtained window, throwing everything in its path into sharp relief. The rest of the room was a pall of shadow, but she could see that Alan, lying beside her, was fast asleep. She nudged him.

'What is it? Gwyneth?' His exhausted voice was startled into life.

'Wake up,' Mary whispered, 'I want to talk to you.'

So his wife's name was Gwyneth, but it did not matter that he had named her. He no longer loved her. She was the one he loved now.

Alan struggled into a sitting position, momentarily unsure of his surroundings. Then, as the moonlight touched his face, Mary noticed the sudden, cat-like blink of wariness, as he realized what he had said.

'It's all right,' she murmured soothingly. 'I know about your wife. I know she isn't dead.'

'What do you mean?' She could feel the tension of his naked body.

'I know that you and she are divorced. You see, I saw you both, and Richard, four years ago, just before the end of the war. You were on Durdham Downs. You were having a row about the boy.'

He stared, trying to adjust to what she was saying. Suddenly he relaxed and gave a bark of laughter.

'Ssh!' she implored him. 'Someone'll hear you.'

'Divorced,' he repeated. 'Yes, of course. Gwyneth and I are divorced. She left me and went off with another man.'

'I knew it must be something like that, or she'd have taken Richard. It must have been terrible for you.'

'Yes. Yes, it was a bad time. Well, I never! Fancy you knowing all along and never saying a word to anyone.'

'I knew Mama wouldn't approve of divorce, and Lizzie would have seized on any reason to stop you living here. She wanted some horrible, old, dried-up spinster.'

'So you were on Durdham Downs that day. I remember it clearly. The fourth of July, nineteen

124

eighteen. The Doughboys were having an Independence Day parade, and we'd come over from Cardiff to see it. Gwyneth had lost Richie in the crowds because she let go of his hand. Gave me a nasty five minutes until we found him again, and I lost my temper. Well, well. What a coincidence you being there. It's a small world and no mistake.'

Mary smiled at him, running an index finger slowly down his body. 'I don't mind you being divorced,' she said. 'We won't let on to Mama or Lizzie. Or to the minister. It won't have to come out, will it, when we get married?'

'Married?' He sounded startled, even frightened, but Mary told herself that he had not expected her to take the initiative. She was beginning to feel sleepy herself, and the clock on her bedside table showed that it was half-past two.

'We are getting married, aren't we?' she insisted. 'After tonight . . . I thought it meant that you loved me.'

'I do. Of course I do.' If the answer was a little too glib, he made up for it a moment later by putting his arms around her and kissing her. 'We'll be married as soon as we can, but you must give me time to sort things out. I'll have to break it to Richie, and we'll have to find somewhere to live.'

'We can go on living here,' Mary said promptly, 'until we've saved a bit, that is. I can move into your room and Richie can sleep in here.'

'You've got it all arranged, haven't you?' If he had not been smiling, his words might have sounded like an accusation.

'It's only just come to me,' she answered. 'But it makes sense. That way, Mama won't have to find another lodger right away. And you know how fond she is of you and Richard.'

'Don't say anything to anyone yet, then,' he wheedled. 'Let our engagement be a secret. Like I said,

I need time to sort myself out.'

Mary's face assumed the mulish expression which he had seen so often when she argued with her mother or sister. What a bloody fool he was! He should have known better.

'I should like to tell Mama,' Mary persisted. 'I don't see it would hurt to tell Mama, and she has to know sooner or later. I shan't let on about tonight, of course. I don't mind having a secret from Lizzie. In fact, I should rather enjoy it.'

There was a pause. Then: 'Tell your mother if you must,' he agreed. 'But I'd as soon no one else knows at present.'

Having carried her point regarding Amy, Mary, although puzzled, was willing to submit to his other demand. Doubtless Alan had his reasons, and she was too happy to admit to the suspicions nagging away just below the surface of conscious thought.

'You'll come again tomorrow night?' she whispered.

He nodded, wondering uneasily how insatiable she might prove to be. These butter-in-the-mouth, prunes-and-prisms misses were very often the worst, once their passions had been aroused. But it could be all to the good. It gave him a hold over her, and meant that she was more likely to do as she was told. And he was genuinely fond of her. He had recognized her from the start as a misfit, like himself; someone ignored or laughed at.

Because he was small and thin, and without good looks to recommend him, Alan Davies had always been discounted. The bigger boys at the orphanage had picked on and bullied him. In later years, when he was trying to make a go of his cockle stall on the front at Penarth, he had been an easy mark for other, unfriendly traders. When the wooden booth and its contents had been wrecked for the fourth time, he had given up and moved back to Cardiff as an odd-job man. His one talent had been in bed, which was how he had come to marry his wife, who was pregnant with Richie at the time.

For the boy's sake, he had tried to make a go of things, getting a steady job with the Cardiff City Council. It hadn't worked out, however. Gwyneth had never really cared for him, nor for the child, although she, too, had done her best for a while. But when that hulking ex-sergeant-major had come along, there had never been any question of her staying. She had been out of his life for two and a half years now, and he saw no reason why she should ever return.

He slid out of bed, shivering as his bare feet touched the linoleum. He dragged on his nightshirt and, bending down, kissed Mary goodnight. His natural optimism surfaced. He was very comfortable here. Perhaps everything had turned out for the best, after all.

CHAPTER TEN

Helen stopped the Buick at the end of Sebastopol Street and addressed the chauffeur.

'You can return to Clifton, George. My father will bring me home. Don't bother getting out of the car. I can manage on my own.'

'Very good, madam.' The chauffeur touched his uniform cap respectfully and waited until Helen, with a flash of pale silk stockings, had stepped on to the pavement, then pulled away from the kerb. He reckoned that Mrs Harrison junior had the best turned ankles in Bristol; probably in the whole of England.

Helen, oblivious of the admiration she aroused in her chauffeur's breast, stopped to buy a *Daily Mirror* from the newspaper seller on the corner. He had only one left, so great had been today's demand. 'Today's Great Abbey Wedding' ran the banner headline, and beneath was nearly a whole page photograph of the young Duke of York and his bride, Lady Elizabeth Bowes-Lyon. Above the name of the paper was printed in bold black type: 'First Royal Wedding Number: Pages of Special Pictures and New Serial.' Immediately under it was the day and date: Thursday, April 26, 1923.

Joseph had offered his daughter and son-in-law a week in London to see the decorations, and had even managed to buy them seats on a balcony overlooking

128

the bridal route to Westminster Abbey, but, at the last moment, Charlie had felt too ill to go. Charlie was alway too ill to go anywhere, Helen thought impatiently.

She reproached herself at once. What a mean thing to think about Charlie. He could not help his feeble health, poor lamb, but it did take some of the fun out of life. She went down the street to the main factory entrance. The doorkeeper, in his little cubby-hole, glanced up, resentful at being disturbed, then stared when he saw the elegant young woman in the navy-blue suit, with six inches of daringly flesh-coloured silk stockings revealed below the hem of the skirt. It was a moment or two before he recognized the face under the wide straw hat as belonging to his employer's daughter.

'Mrs Harrison, ma'am. I hardly knew you,' he said, coming out from behind his grille.

'I shouldn't expect you to,' Helen answered with a smile, 'considering how very infrequently I come here. I think the last time was five years ago. Is my father in his office?'

'Ah . . . I'm not too sure, ma'am. There's been some trouble today. Some of the factory girls have been protesting about there being no lifts between floors. Somebody said there'd been a walk out over at Arley Street.'

'Oh dear. Perhaps I ought not to worry Papa, then. But I've dismissed my car and I'm not sure how I'll get home. Maybe you could find me a taxi.'

The door-keeper seemed dubious. Taxis were not easy to come by in Eastwood.

'Not much call for them round here, you see.'

Helen stood irresolute. She did not want to bother her father if he were busy, with what was a purely social visit. She had only come on impulse and because she was bored.

'Can I be of assistance, Mrs Harrison?' asked a voice

behind her, and Helen turned round to see Ben Sawyer. 'You seem to be having some difficulty,' he added. 'I heard you asking for a taxi.'

Helen explained, finishing: 'I'll go up and sit with Miss Folmer.'

'I imagine she's as busy as Mr Gordon.' Ben was amused, but also impressed, that the idea of catching a 'bus or tramcar never so much as crossed Helen's mind. 'However, if you have no objection to driving with me, I'll take you home. I'm going to Redland. Clifton won't be so very far out of my way.' He saw her look of surprise. 'I'm out on the road now,' he explained.

'Oh. Do you like that?'

'Very much. I find selling easy. People seem to take to me, you see.'

Helen could understand that. He looked so handsome, so smart. She could see that retailers would be impressed. She was impressed herself.

'I'd be extremely grateful if you could give me a lift,' she replied a little breathlessly. 'You're sure it's no trouble?'

'None whatsoever.'

She preceded him out of the building and he guided her to a side-street, where one of the new Austin 7s was parked.

'Not what you're used to,' he apologized, opening the passenger door and handing her in. 'I know the 7s are regarded as rather vulgar by the owners of bigger Austins. Do you think you'll be warm enough if I leave the hood down?'

'Oh, yes. It's quite a mild day.' Helen glanced about her delightedly. 'What a darling little car.'

Ben laughed. 'I'm flattered you think so. The motor trade refused to have anything to do with it when it first came out, last year. It was only when Sir Herbert Austin threatened to sell it through the cycle trade that the dealers capitulated. The cycle shops could have sold it much cheaper.'

'And is it selling well?'

'Like hot cakes. This is a joint birthday present from my mother and aunt.'

'Lucky you,' she laughed, removing her hat and letting her short fair hair stream in the wind.

They travelled in silence for a while, then she asked: 'This trouble at Arley Street, is it serious?'

'One of the factory hands ricked her back carrying a load of trays upstairs. It's always happening, and there's invariably trouble when it does. It sounds a little bit more serious this time.'

'The place needs modernizing, doesn't it?' Helen remarked after another pause. 'And Papa won't spend the money.'

Ben negotiated a corner. 'To be honest, both factories need more lifts, more mechanization. Not a great deal has been done since well before the war. It's not really for me to say, however. I don't know Mr Gordon's financial position.'

'Healthy, I should guess. But there's a strong Scottish streak in Papa, which makes him chary of spending money. I'm the last person who should say so, because he's been generosity itself to me all my life. But he's canny when it comes to business.' There was a longer silence, which she did not know how to break. Eventually she enquired shyly: 'How's Elizabeth? I haven't seen her for an age.'

'Very well,' he answered coolly. 'She's been allowed the day off for Mary's wedding.'

Helen jumped. 'Mary's wedding!' she repeated incredulously. 'Surely, you must be joking.' He shook his head. 'But ... But who's she marrying? Why haven't Charlie and I been told about it? Why haven't we been asked?'

The car threaded its way across the Tramway Centre and began the steep ascent of Park Street before Ben answered.

'It's a quiet affair, I gather. No one but immediate

131

family, Jack Hennessey, who's giving Mary away, and a friend of Mr Davies as best man.'

'Who's Mr Davies?' Helen wanted to know.

'The lodger. He has a son nearly eleven years old, so your cousin will have a ready-made family.'

'But why didn't someone let me know?' Helen was distressed. 'Why didn't Papa? The least Charlie and I would wish to do is to send them a present. Where are they living?'

'They're remaining for the present in Springtime Grove.'

Conversation lapsed once more until Helen was called on for directions, and after that no more was said until the car drew up before the big house in Pembroke Road. Three Clifton College boys straggled past, out on a run.

Helen roused herself from her thoughts and turned to Ben.

'Won't you come in and have tea with me?' she asked. 'Charlie's ill in bed. You can give me more details about the marriage.'

He smiled regretfully. 'I'd love to, Mrs Harrison, but I daren't. I've three shops to visit this afternoon, and you don't keep potential customers waiting. Your father would be quite justified in sacking me for wasting the firm's valuable time.'

'I'd make things all right with Papa.'

'Thank you, but no. I prefer to stand on my own two feet.'

Helen, whose thoughts for the past ten minutes had been centred entirely on Mary and the peculiar circumstances of her cousin's wedding, became suddenly aware of Ben Sawyer's proximity in the little car; of the fact that their knees were almost touching; and that, in turning to speak to her, he had laid his left arm along the back of her seat. For some unaccountable reason she found herself blushing, and experienced again that mixture of arousal and panic which she felt whenever he was near. Did he guess that she was still a virgin? The mere thought filled her with shame. At that moment, she hated Charlie and his perpetual illness.

She was immediately contrite. She loved Charlie. They had grown up together. He represented a world of stability and continuity; he was her protection against that other world which often seemed dangerous and always on the change.

'You're afraid of life,' Elizabeth had once told her, and perhaps that was true. She needed to be looked after.

She met Ben's eyes — such bold, disturbing eyes — and looked quickly the other way.

'Thank you for bringing me home,' she murmured and got out of the car, not waiting for him to assist her.

She watched him drive away, then walked up the path to the door. A uniformed maid was on the look-out for her return, and appeared on the doorstep.

'Mrs Harrison senior is here, mum. We thought we'd better call her. The master has taken a turn for the worse.'

'Lizzie what is this all about?' Jack sat down on the arm of the sofa in Amy's front room, and ran his fingers through his spiky dark hair.

After the simple wedding ceremony at Arley Street chapel, he had returned with the bridal party to number eighteen Springtime Grove for high tea. The workmate who had been Alan Davies's best man had excused himself early and gone home; and by the time the meal was over, Jack, too, was feeling the strain of Elizabeth's silent disapproval. He had taken his leave, but to his surprise Elizabeth followed him into the passage, pulling him into the parlour and shutting the door behind them.

'I want you to go to Cardiff on Sunday,' she said in answer to his question. 'I've asked Ben to go, but he says he'll have nothing to do with it. You're the only other person I can trust.'

133

'Cardiff? What for? What am I supposed to do when I get there?'

'Make some enquiries about Alan Davies.' Elizabeth put her hand in her skirt pocket and drew out a folded sheet of paper. 'This is an old envelope I found in his room one day, when he was out. It has a Cardiff address on it. I want you to go there and see what you can discover. I'd go myself, but if I was absent for a whole day Mama would want to know where I was and what I was doing. I don't want to tell a pack of lies. It could make things unnecessarily complicated.' She held out the envelope, which Jack accepted reluctantly.

'But what do you think I'm going to find out, for goodness' sake? He and Mary are married. Surely, after what you told me, that's all that matters?'

'You mean he's made an honest woman of her? I wish I could be sure of that.'

'I don't know what you're on about, Lizzie. You see Alan Davies coming out of Mary's bedroom at three o'clock one morning, and when you tax him with it, he says they're engaged to be married. And two months later, they are. What more do you want? No one knew anything to his discredit at the Tramways Company.'

'No. He's spun them the same story as he's given us. I want to know why this wedding had to be so quiet. I want to know why he'd been promising my sister marriage for over six months, but did nothing about it until he had me to reckon with. What a poky little affair it's been today! Not even your mother and sisters invited.'

'If Mary and Mr Davies wanted a quiet wedding, I don't see what it's got to do with you. He was brought up in an orphanage. He has no relatives, and your sister has no friends. And it was hardly the sort of wedding your uncle and aunt would have wished to attend.'

'Helen would have come,' Elizabeth insisted stubbornly. 'But Alan wanted no unnecessary person either informed or invited. It smells fishy to me. That's why I want you to make some more enquiries. Will you do it? For me?'

'For heaven's sake, Lizzie, you don't have to twist my arm. Just tell me what it is you suspect. Although I think your boyfriend is wise, having nothing to do with it.'

'We'll leave Ben Sawyer out of this discussion,' Elizabeth answered shortly. 'As for what I suspect, I'm not quite sure. But instinct tells me that there's something wrong.'

But was there? Or was it wishful thinking on her part? It had been a shock to her that night, when, plagued by thirst, she had got quietly out of bed, so as not to disturb her mother, and started downstairs to the kitchen. When Mary's bedroom door had opened, she had assumed that her sister, too, was wakeful. To find herself face to face with Alan Davies had temporarily bereft her of speech and movement. She had clung to the banister rail, staring at him, her lower jaw dropping ludicrously. For a moment, he had been as horrified as she; then he had laughed and shrugged, like someone resigning himself to the inevitable. The next day, when Elizabeth had demanded an explanation from him in front of Amy, he had calmly announced that he and Mary were getting married. No one, he said, could blame two people in love for jumping the gun.

Further silenced by Amy's admission to having known of the secret engagement, Elizabeth had been given no opportunity to probe deeper. It was from a chance remark of Richard's that she deduced how long Mary had been Alan Davies's mistress, and her suspicions flared again. If he had promised marriage from the beginning, why had he waited so long?

Elizabeth's head ached from too much thinking. Was her new brother-in-law the shady character she believed him to be, or was she simply jealous? Jealous that Mary, her plain elder sister, whom men never looked at twice, had managed, after all, to get herself a lover while Elizabeth was still a virgin? Her own relationship with Ben seemed arid by comparison. She had always collected compliments on her intelligence as avidly as other women did on their appearance; but suddenly she knew that she would give a dozen concerts, theatre trips, art gallery visits for one night in bed with Ben.

Furiously she pushed the knowledge aside. There would be time enough for that when they were married, she told herself. Ben was just cautious. He would make no move until he could afford it. He knew the value of money in marriage.

She was conscious of Jack watching her intently. She asked: 'You will do it for me then? Go to Cardiff and make some enquiries? Just to put my mind at rest.'

'Yes, I'll do it. As you knew I would from the start.' Jack got to his feet and smiled self-mockingly. 'I'm a fool to myself and to you.'

'You're a dear.' She kissed his cheek.

Jack silently cursed himself for his weakness. How long would he let himself go on being used while she chased Ben Sawyer? But, in his heart of hearts, he knew the answer.

Mary pushed her way through the crowd of people chatting after evening service, receiving congratulations on her marriage from all sides. She and Alan had returned home yesterday after a week at Weston-super-mare.

'You'll find yourself the centre of attention at chapel,' Amy had warned them the previous night, during supper. 'And it's no good looking like that, Alan, my dear! People had to find out sometime. Getting married's not the sort of thing you can keep secret for ever.'

'We didn't expect to.' Mary had laid a hand proprietorially on her husband's. 'Especially now I've left the factory.'

She had offered no reason when she had handed in her notice two weeks ago, but she had had no intention of leaving her ex-workmates in ignorance for long. At the first opportunity, she would be outside the factory entrance when the girls came out; Mrs Alan Davies, sporting her new wedding ring.

And Amy, abetted by Eileen Hennessey, had done her work equally well the preceding Sunday at chapel. There was hardly anyone who did not accuse Mary of being either secretive or sly. She was in her element, the focus of an attention she had never experienced in her life before. Alan tried to smile, but she could sense that he was angry.

Walking home beside the canal, her hand tucked into the crook of his arm, she said timidly: 'Mama's right, you know. People were bound to find out. It would look so odd if we tried to keep it a secret any longer. And with Jack giving me away, his mother was bound to know, and that was as good as telling the whole of Eastwood.'

Alan made no answer for a moment. Then he nodded at Jack and Elizabeth, walking some yards ahead of them. He lowered his voice.

'Do you know where he was last Sunday, while we were down at Weston?' Mary shook her head. 'I was talking to one of the Hennessey girls on the way to chapel this evening, and she let the cat out of the bag. Jack went to Cardiff last Sunday. All day. Now why do you suppose he did that?'

'You mean . . . he was enquiring about you? Did he find out anything?'

'I don't imagine so, or we should have heard by now. Your sister could never have kept her tongue still.'

'Are divorces registered?'

'Divorces . . . ? Oh . . . Sure to be. Not locally, though, I shouldn't think. Probably in London. They don't seem to have thought of that.'

'Lizzie's not as clever as she thinks she is.' Mary

137

smiled complacently. 'Anyway, we're married now. Even if they find out about the divorce, everything's legal.'

Alan said nothing, but his expression, as he watched the pair in front, was tight-lipped. Elizabeth was not the woman to give up that easily. Failure on the first occasion would not deter her from persuading Jack to go again. And he was besotted enough to do as he was told. Alan chewed his lower lip thoughtfully.

There was a pub in one of the narrow streets leading off the Tramways Centre, where he and a few of his cronies went at lunchtime, when they were on the nine to six shift. It was a haunt of increasing numbers of the unemployed, looking for a hand-out or a free drink. Alan had noted one man, a big, loud-mouthed, aggressive lout, who looked as though he would murder his own grandmother for sixpence. For half-a-crown, Alan was sure that the man would have no objection to beating someone up. He would sound him out tomorrow.

He felt better at the thought of positive action, and returned the pressure of Mary's hand.

'Don't worry,' he reassured her. 'Everything will be all right. You'll see.'

It was dark by the time Jack finished work on Tuesday. It had been a particularly difficult day. As unemployment increased, it became harder for people to find the weekly instalment of sixpence or a shilling, which was their repayment on goods purchased in Alma Road, at Harrison's Universal Clothing Store. Jack, who, apart from his time in the navy, had been a collector for Harrison's ever since he left school, hated his job at the best of times. The articles sold were shoddy; poorly made so that they would wear out faster. And when anyone failed to make a payment, it was his and the other collectors' duty to report it at once, so that Albert Harrison's strong-arm boys could

138

repossess the goods. These men were highly trained in all forms of intimidation and very well paid; the only members of the company who were. Very few people argued with Harrison's repossessors. Those who did invariably ended up in hospital.

On more than one occasion, Jack had lent money to his clients, with no expectation of having it repaid. But he was unable to do it very often. He needed every penny he earned to support his mother and younger sisters. Only the eldest Hennessey girl was as yet out at work, having recently gone into domestic service. But whatever he did, it was only a drop in the ocean. Money was becoming scarcer as unemployment rose.

His last call that evening was in Guelph Street, in one of the block of tenement flats, soon due for demolition. The Tivoli Music Hall, renamed the Tivoli Picture Palace, was showing Charlie Chaplin and Jackie Coogan in *The Kid*. It was too small and unimportant a cinema to get any of the new releases. Just as its live shows had been second-rate, so now it struggled to keep its doors open with films which most people had already seen in town.

Jack paused for a moment to look at the still pictures outside, then turned towards home. The money he had collected was in a belt strapped round his waist, under his coat, but in all his years as a collector, no one had ever tried to rob him. He plunged into the maze of narrow streets and alleys which linked Guelph Street and Springtime Grove.

Suddenly, two men stepped out of a doorway in front of him. At first, he thought nothing of it, and was about to push his way past, when the bigger of the two seized him and threw him back against the wall.

'This the bloke?' he asked his companion.

The second man nodded, and immediately a fist like a sledge-hammer drove into Jack's stomach, winding him. As he doubled up in agony, he fell, hitting his head on the rough brickwork behind him. Blood trickled, warm and sticky, from his nose. A boot kicked him in the ribs.

Jack had instinctively clutched his arms about his waist to protect his money-belt, but neither man made a move to take it. Either they did not know it was there, or robbery was not their motive. But if not, what was? Then, just before he lost consciousness, Jack heard the small man speak.

'Let that be a lesson to you, Hennessey. Keep your nose out of my business in future. And if you tell that bitch of a sister-in-law of mine what's happened, I'll have you done over again tomorrow.'

The voice belonged to Alan Davies.

CHAPTER ELEVEN

'Charlie has been very ill indeed,' May Harrison said coldly. 'Had I not been there to nurse him properly, I shudder to think what might have happened. If his delicate consitution had been taken more seriously, if his wife had been present at his bedside, instead of gallivanting around the town with strange young men, the symptoms of relapse might have been noted in time and the doctor called earlier. A great deal of the poor boy's suffering might have been prevented.' She could feel Albert's foot nudging hers under the table, and Stanley was looking embarrassed, but neither husband nor son was going to stop her speaking her mind. 'Of course, it's the way Helen has been brought up. It's not really her fault that she's selfish.'

Joseph choked over his tea and lowered his cup. This, in his own house, at his own table, was the outside of enough! He had been growing bored with the Harrisons' Sunday visits for some time now, but he had put up with them for old times' sake, and because the families were linked by their children's marriage. He was aware that May thought Helen a less than perfect daughter-in-law, but to criticize his darling to his face was more than he was prepared to tolerate.

'If you hadn't made such a fool of Charlie when he was young,' he retaliated, 'encouraging him to think he was sick when he wasn't, molly-coddling him at home, instead of sending him away to school, he wouldn't have a delicate constitution, as you call it. If he thought a bit less of himself and more of his wife, he wouldn't have time to play at being ill.'

'Joe,' Minna adjured him anxiously, 'remember May and Albert are our guests.'

'Play at being ill!' May exclaimed furiously. 'Charlie is incapable of pretence, I'll have you know. Albert, don't just sit there! Back me up. Didn't the doctor tell me, when Charlie was only a few months old, that his chest would always be weak. He needs looking after. If I'd known that Helen was going to turn out such a flibbertigibbet, so callous and unconcerned — '

'Pardon me, May, but I take exception to that remark,' Minna interrupted, bridling. 'Helen would just have up and gone to London, to see the royal wedding, if what you say is true. But she never once complained because the trip had to be cancelled on account of Charlie's indisposition. Whatever that was.'

'All in the mind, if you ask me,' Joseph barked. 'Furthermore, having a lift home in my employee's car is not what I should call "gallivanting around the town with strange young men."'

'She shouldn't have left the house in the first place, that's all that May is saying,' Albert put in, trying to pour oil on troubled waters. But his words were more like a red rag to a bull.

'She came to see me!' Joseph roared angrily, thumping the table so that the cups jumped in their saucers. 'Her own father! Is that a crime?'

'She didn't see you, though, did she?' Albert retorted, stung by his friend's attitude and unable to resist a jibe. 'Having that spot of bother, weren't you, at the Arley Street factory? And I'll tell you something, Joe, for free. You'll have more trouble there if you don't do something soon about modernizing that place.

142

You're not fit to be a businessman. You're still living in Queen Victoria's reign.'

Joseph rose ponderously to his feet, his face contorted with rage.

'When I want advice on how to run my business, you're the last man I shall consult, Albert. At least mine's a decent Christian concern. I'm not a bloodsucker, living off the backs of the poor.'

Albert went as white as Joseph was red.

'That does it,' he said. 'I shall not stay a moment longer to be insulted. We should like our hats and coats, please, Minna. May! Stanley! We are going.'

'Oh, now, please, let's all calm down,' Minna implored, flustered by the unexpected turn which the afternoon had taken. 'I'm sure Joe didn't mean what he said just now.'

'Well, it sounded like it to me,' May pronounced majestically. 'And I certainly meant everything I said about Helen.'

Minna tugged violently at the bell-rope. 'In that case, perhaps it would be better if you went. Smithson!' She addressed the maid who came in answer to her summons. 'Mr and Mrs Harrison are leaving. Please fetch their outdoor clothes. Mr Stanley's also.'

The hats and coats were brought and donned in silence. A sullen, cold rage had replaced the earlier fire; something more permanent than a quarrel between friends. It had been brewing for a long time, Minna reflected later; probably ever since Helen's and Charlie's wedding, when the Harrisons had resented the fact that Joe had not done things in style. Perhaps, after all, the marriage which the four of them had planned for so long, ever since the children were in their cradles, had not been such a good idea.

In retrospect, Elizabeth decided that 1923 seemed to have been a year of innovation.

The Duke of York was the first of the King's children

to marry; and, in the same month, the first Cup Final was played between the football clubs of Bolton Wanderers and West Ham. King George and Queen Mary paid a state visit to Rome, to the King and Queen of Italy, and pictures of the royal occasion were rushed to the London newspapers by aeroplane. Bonar Law resigned and Stanley Baldwin became Prime Minister. Female breasts and waists almost disappeared. The Savoy Hill studios were opened for anyone who had a wireless receiver, and the first *Radio Times* was published on the twenty-eighth of September. At midnight on the thirty-first of December, the first broadcast of Big Ben's chimes welcomed in the New Year; and the impetus of change was carried on into 1924, when in January the first Labour Government took office under Ramsay MacDonald.

'And if that doesn't make Uncle Joe realize that the twentieth century really has arrived, nothing will!' Elizabeth declared, banging a pile of hot plates down on the kitchen table. She was followed by Amy, carrying the carving dish with its small joint of beef.

It was Sunday dinner-time, but for once, with the exception of young Richard Davies, no one wanted to eat. The brisk walk home from chapel in the raw winter air usually produced ravenous appetites, but today all the adults were too preoccupied to be hungry.

Mary was feeling unwell, as she had been ever since the beginning of her pregnancy two months earlier. She spent hours of each day being sick, and the rest of the time feeling sleepy. Her mother said the sickness was normal, but it seemed to Mary too violent to be natural. She was worried that she might miscarry, and she desperately wanted this child. She had always wished for children, and now she longed for one more than ever. Alan was less attentive, less loving than he had been before their marriage, and she hoped that the baby would forge a stronger bond between them. Sometimes she wondered if Alan had ever been in love with her; and, in rarer moments, if she had ever been in love with him. He had been lonely and needed a woman; her ambition had always been marriage and a family. But her incurably romantic nature would not let her entertain the notion for long. She needed to believe in love.

On the opposite side of the kitchen table, Elizabeth was experiencing disquiet over a number of different things. Foremost, as ever, was the state of her relationship with Ben; the way it never, on his side, progressed beyond friendship, and the way he continued to shy away from any talk of marriage. Whenever she raised the subject, occasions which were becoming ever more frequent, he repeated that he still had his way to make; that they were both young; and that he had no intention of saddling himself with the responsibilities of married life before he could afford them. He made it all sound so eminently reasonable that she was unable to quarrel with him, and ignored the warning voice inside her head which denied that reason and passion had anything in common.

A secondary source of irritation was Jack's refusal to do any more snooping — that was his word; hers was 'investigation' — into Alan Davies's past. Jack had been resolute, and it had come as a shock to Elizabeth to find that she could not always twist him around her little finger. Her sense of indignation equalled her feeling of betrayal. She had never connected the 'attempted robbery' on Jack last April, when he had been badly beaten up by a couple of thugs, with either her brother-in-law or Jack's present attitude towards him.

A third, less immediate cause of annoyance was the tame acceptance of their lot by the girls on the factory floor at Gordon's. After their brief, abortive action of the previous year, they had returned to work, continuing to hump the heavy trays of chocolates up and down stairs between the different processing departments. Membership of a trade union was still banned, as was listening to the speakers on Inkerman Street corner.

'Conditions at Gordon's are positively prehistoric!' she burst out now, pouring gravy over her meat and looking around the table for the bread. She knew no one else was interested, but it was the only one of her worries she could openly discuss. 'Someone ought to do something about it.'

'Why don't you then?' Amy snapped. 'Another slice of beef, Alan, dear?'

Why couldn't Elizabeth be pleasant any more? She had always been an odd, difficult girl, ever since she was born, but never as constantly bad-tempered as she was at present. Why could she not get on with Alan? It was so nice having a man and a young boy in the house once again. They could be such a happy family if only Elizabeth would let them. Soon there would be a grandchild, perhaps another boy. Mary would be so pleased to be a mother; and all Amy had ever wanted was a quiet life and a little extra money. The money had not been forthcoming, as Alan continued to pay exactly the same rent as he had done before his marriage, and Mary was no longer working. But hardship Amy could endure — she had put up with it all her life — just as long as the domestic atmosphere was happy.

Alan held out his plate. 'Thank you, Ma. Just a small slice, or you won't have any to cut up cold, tomorrow.'

He did not need to look at his sister-in-law to see her angry expression. He could picture it well enough, knowing how she resented him and what she called his sponging ways. He was well aware that she had expected him to pay more towards the housekeeping when Mary finished work, but he had no intention of doing so unless, most improbably, Amy insisted. But he knew just how to flatter and cajole his mother-in-law into backing him. He told Amy that he was saving so that he and Mary could one day buy their own house. It was true that he was saving, salting money away in an old tin box in the bottom of the wardrobe, but that was his insurance against a day when he might at last have to cut and run.

Young Richard Davies, cramming his mouth with hot food, thought that adults were a rum lot; moody, silent, for no apparent reason. Even his favourite, Elizabeth, had been more than usually short with him of late. One of the things he most enjoyed was their verbal sparring, and he had early learned not to take her abrasiveness too seriously. Besides, he always gave as good as he got. He liked her because she did not fuss over, or want to mother, him. Mary's and Amy's attempts he found especially cloying: they suffocated him with their over-anxiety. Perhaps things would get better when his little half-brother or – sister was born. They would have someone else to think about. Sometimes he speculated about what would happen if his real mother ever came back.

He did not miss her. He had disliked her, if the truth were told. He remembered her as someone constantly shouting and hitting him. He had been glad when she ran away and left him and his father on their own. Not that Richard had any particular affection for his father. He had realized from a precociously early age that Alan had one great talent; persuading people to accept him at his own valuation. Richard had always known that his father told lies — 'Just smoothing the path, boy-oh! Just smoothing the path!' — so he had not questioned the instruction that he was to pretend never to have known his mother. He had no wish to talk about her, anyway; not even to Elizabeth, who occasionally tried to pump him. The move to Bristol from Cardiff had not upset him. One school was much like another, and he had no close friends.

'Can I have some more Yorkshire pudding, Mrs

Evans?' he asked thickly, through a mouthful of meat and vegetables.

'Empty your mouth before you speak and say please!' Elizabeth cuffed his ear, but not hard enough to hurt. He grinned at her impudently.

'Leave him alone, Lizzie!' Mary was standing up, swaying slightly on her feet, her face chalk-white, her eyes wild. 'He's not your stepson! He's mine! Just for once, mind your own business.' She crouched forward suddenly, clutching her stomach. 'Oh God!' The cry was wrenched from her, without her realizing what she was saying. 'Alan! Oh God, the pain!' Her voice rose to a screech. 'Alan! Get the doctor! I'm losing the baby.'

Elizabeth glanced at her watch. Ten minutes yet before she was due to clock in. She had plenty of time to get from Arley Street to Sebastopol Street. As she passed the closed chapel gates, someone ran up behind her and caught hold of her arm.

''Ullo, Liz. 'Ow's Mary? We 'eard she'd lost the baby. We never liked 'er much. She was always such a miserable cow, but we was sorry about the miscarriage. She was fond of children.'

Elizabeth recognized the speaker as a girl called Sylvia Crocker, whom Mary always mentioned with particular venom. Elizabeth had never managed to find out why.

'Hullo Sylvie,' she said. 'I'll tell Mary you were asking about her. She's still in bed. The doctor says she's not to get up for another week at least. She's in a bad way. She won't be able to have any more children.'

'God! That's rotten. You'd better go on, Lizzie, or you'll be late. I've bin off with me back again. I'm dead slow this morning.'

But instead of hurrying on, Elizabeth slowed her steps. 'Not those boxes again?' she queried.

Sylvia nodded. 'What else? Occupational 'azard at Gordon's.'

'It wouldn't be if you had a union to fight for you.'

The other girl shrugged. 'We're not allowed to join a bleedin' union, are we?'

'Then go on strike. Withdraw your labour until you get the terms of employment you want.'

'It's all right you talkin'!' Sylvia exclaimed pettishly. 'Who's goin' to lead a strike, I'd like to know?'

'You could.'

Sylvia blinked. 'Think I could?' she asked after a moment.

'Of course, or I shouldn't suggest it.'

There was a pause, then Sylvia shook her head. They had reached the gates of the Arley Street factory, and the girls were streaming inside. Elizabeth noted that they far outnumbered the men. They were cheaper labour.

'I couldn't get it started,' Sylvia argued. 'I could keep 'em at it, once it got goin', but I 'aven't got the words to steam 'em up in the first place. Needs someone with education.'

Elizabeth recalled her mother's taunt, the Sunday that Mary had been taken ill. She had said that someone really ought to do something about conditions at Gordon's, and Amy had challenged: 'Why don't you, then?'

And here was her chance. But what on earth should she say? She hesitated, tempted to laugh the whole idea away and go on to Sebastopol Street as though nothing had happened. After all, it was neither her business nor her problem.

But it was. She too, worked for Gordon's, accepting the restrictions on her liberty. Moreover, the dislike of her uncle, which had been steadily building up over the years, now amounted almost to hatred. She and her family had been on the receiving end of many slights and rebuffs over the years. She swung on her heel, and entered the factory gates, dragging Sylvia Crocker with her.

'Hide me in one of the cloakrooms,' she ordered, 'until you assemble for morning prayers.'

The assembly in Arley Street was led by one of Joseph's under-managers, Norman Pound, whom Elizabeth remembered as Superintendent from her Sunday School days. A cadaverous man, with thinning grey hair and a straggling moustache, he was an ardent supporter of morning prayer-meetings, resisting all those who said they were an anachronism in 1924. His admiration for his employer rested largely on Joseph's perpetuation of these religious gatherings. It did not worry him that in all other respects, especially in those which really mattered, Joseph was a bad employer. Norman Pound saw him only as a kind of modern Saint George fighting the dragons of agnosticism, atheism and Catholicism.

The assembly hall was cold, the cheerless February sunshine filtering through the high windows to lose itself among the gas jets illuminating the room. Elizabeth, who had come from the cloakroom and entered the hall concealed by a group of Sylvia's friends, thought that the installation of electricity was a priority. Without it, there could be no proper automation. She must remember to prime Sylvia later.

She was wearing the white overall and cap of the factory operatives, spares found for her by one of the girls. By dint of pushing, she managed to get a seat on the gangway, near the front. Everyone stood as Mr Pound, followed by all the supervisors, entered through a door at the back of the hall and mounted the stage. He walked to the lectern and bent his head.

'We shall pray,' he announced.

Now was her moment. Elizabeth had expected to feel terrified, but instead experienced only a sensation of icy calm. She moved forward, taking off her cap and apron as she went. She ran up the three steps on to the platform. Mr Pound, having composed himself for prayer, did not immediately observe what was happening. He was too busy marshalling his thoughts.

Elizabeth clapped her hands. 'Listen to me, all of you!' she shouted.

Eyes opened, heads were raised, and a sea of faces blinked at her in astonishment. The first words, she had realized, were going to be the most difficult. She had to grab their attention. Waiting in the cloakroom, she had recalled the man in Inkerman Street telling her about the Tolpuddle Martyrs. She had barely listened to him at the time, but his words must have sunk in, for she remembered them now, just when she needed them.

'This coming July,' she said, and was amazed how well her tones carried in the silent hall, 'will be the ninetieth anniversary of the Tolpuddle Martyrs. Honest farm labourers, working-class folk like ourselves, who were tried and transported for the so-called crime of forming a union.' She raised her voice. 'Nearly a century later, nothing has changed! Are you allowed to join a union? No! Why not? Because Joseph Gordon makes it a condition of your employment that you don't. How can he do that? He can do it because individually you all accept it. Individually, you're afraid of losing your jobs! But if you band together, fight shoulder to shoulder, all for one, one for all — ' she realized with sudden gratitude that years of listening to Methodist sermons every Sunday morning and evening had taught her the necessary cadence and rhetoric ' — then you can become a force to be reckoned with! Unemployment is bad, but even Joseph Gordon would find it hard to replace you all. Sisters! Brothers! Strike now — ' she drove her fist into her palm ' — for the right to join a union! Strike now — ' again the gesture — 'for better conditions!'

'Listen to what she's saying! She's talking sense!' Sylvia Crocker was scrambling up the platform steps to range herself alongside Elizabeth. 'Sisters! We shouldn't 'ave to put up with carrying them 'eavy boxes. Other factories are goin' modern. Why don't Gordon's?'

A lot of people were on their feet now, shouting and yelling. Prayers were forgotten. Mr Pound and the supervisors, overtaken by the speed and turn of events, could think of nothing to do. One or two of the supervisors were not even sure that they wanted to do anything.

'Strike!' bawled Sylvia, now in her element. 'Everyone out!' She turned to Elizabeth, her freckled face beaming. 'Thanks, Liz. I'll take over from 'ere. I 'ope you office lot are goin' to come out on strike with us.'

Elizabeth felt deflated. This had been her show and it was being taken out of her hands.

'I don't suppose I'll be working at Gordon's much longer,' she said with a nervous little laugh.

Anger burned and flickered beneath the surface; she could see it in the set of his mouth and behind his eyes. But for once, Joseph Gordon preserved a calm exterior. It was as though what she had done was too great an enormity for rage.

'You will take a week's wages in lieu of notice,' her uncle said. 'You will collect your belongings and be out of the factory in half an hour.'

'I shall certainly be gone as soon as possible,' Elizabeth agreed, 'but I shall resign, and you will provide me with a reference. A good one.'

For a second, she thought that his anger would overflow, to wash away even the lines of worry fretting his brow. The Arley Street factory was reported at a standstill, and the action had already spread to Sebastopol Street.

Joseph gripped the arms of his chair, but his voice remained quiet. He had learned, too late, not to underestimate his niece.

'Tell me why I should,' he invited.

'Miss Folmer.' She saw his startled look and smiled. 'Everyone knows about you and Miss Folmer, Uncle Joe. You can't keep that sort of secret in a factory full of women. I'm sure you wouldn't want me to tell Aunt Minna about your little peccadillo.'

He was shocked, but he fought back.

'Your aunt wouldn't believe you. I'd say you were making it up.'

'And maybe Aunt Minna would believe you. But Helen wouldn't. She's a different generation. Modern novels, the cinema, have made people realize that such affairs are not uncommon. Helen might not want to believe me, but in the end, she would.'

Joseph slumped in his chair, defeat and also, Elizabeth noted uneasily, contempt in his eyes.

'By God,' he said, 'you're a hard-faced bitch. I don't know who you take after. It's not your Ma or Pa.'

'No,' she agreed. 'You always found them very easy to crush with your patronizing airs, your hand-me-down clothes, your lectures and second-rate presents. My family has always been an embarrassment to you, and you've shown it. Oh, how you've shown it! You wouldn't even lend them the money to put me through college. I swore then I'd get even with you one day. Now, about this reference. Will you call in Miss Folmer or shall I? She can type to your dictation.'

CHAPTER TWELVE

Helen sat on the edge of the bed, holding Charlie's hand. He really did look ill, she thought. She should never have dragged him up to London, all round the Wembley Exhibition. Her mother-in-law would be furious when she found out. She would say Helen was selfish and inconsiderate. And she was, Helen scolded herself; she was both those things. They had arrived home yesterday, and Charlie had gone straight to bed. He had remained there this morning.

'Have you been to see your parents?' he asked, in between bouts of coughing.

'Papa was at the factory, but I saw Mama. She wanted me to stay to lunch, but I said I had to get back. I've asked Cook to send us both up something on a tray.'

Charlie shook his head. 'I don't want anything. I'm not hungry. What's happening about the strike?'

'It's all over. Papa's had to give in. It's been three months. It started in February and now it's April. No one thought that the factory workers could have stayed out so long. Mama says some of the married men went back to work. They couldn't afford to go on with the strike, with no money coming in. But the single girls and men held on. Their families supported them, and some people at the chapel set up a fund. Papa will never forgive them for that. Mama told me he's thinking of joining the Church of England. And then the factory inspectors backed the strikers in their report. They said both factories badly needed modernizing. It's going to cost Papa an awful lot of money, just when profits are down. And it's meant a lot of bad publicity for the firm. He's had to lift his ban about unions, too. Mama reckons it will mean more trouble in the future.'

Charlie coughed again and wiped his lips with his handkerchief. 'What about your cousin? Did your Mama tell you anything more?'

'No. Papa still maintains that Lizzie had nothing to do with the strike, in spite of all the rumours to the contrary.' Helen transferred her gaze to the bedroom window. It was a cold, gusty day and she could see some starlings, trying to gain the shelter of a tree, tossed like bits of paper in the wind. 'There's something odd about it all, Charlie, but I don't know what it is.'

'Don't think about it,' he advised fretfully. 'There's nothing you can do. It won't do any good to worry. It won't bankrupt your Papa, whatever he has to pay. My father always says yours is a very downy bird. It'll mean less for us, of course, when he dies.'

There would have been a time when Helen would have been both shocked and hurt by this callous attitude, but three years of marriage had taught her that Charlie was very self-centred. She attributed it to his chronic bad health, something she was beginning to believe in as fervently as May. She blamed herself for the visit to London, although Charlie had looked forward to going as eagerly as she. He had long ago abandoned all pretence of working in his father's firm, and was quite content to live on the more than generous allowance made to him by his parents. But when he felt well, he got bored with doing nothing and insisted that he was perfectly capable of leading a normal life. He nagged Helen into expeditions which each knew would tire him almost at once, and which May roundly condemned. Helen, however, was as bored by their empty existence as her husband, and, against her better judgement, acquiesced in his schemes. This trip to Wembley, she now admitted, had been absolute folly. She would not blame May for being angry.

Helen was not very attached to either May or Albert Harrison, but she wished, nevertheless, that they would make up this stupid disagreement with her parents. Her warm, loving nature hated dissension of any kind, and to have it in the family distressed her. She guessed that the fight had been about herself and Charlie, and had done her best on both sides to soothe ruffled feelings. Her efforts had failed, and she had begun to suspect that perhaps her parents and parents-in-law had never really liked each other, and were glad to have quarrelled.

'What about your cousin?' Charlie asked for a second time. 'Has she found another job?'

He was not truly interested in Elizabeth, but it was a sure way of attracting Helen's attention. Sometimes he felt that he lost her; that her interest in him waned, and it frightened him. She was the only friend he had ever had in his life. He did not care for his younger brother Stanley, who, in spite of his equally fragile appearance, was as strong and healthy as a horse. Charlie had always been in awe of his parents; of their commanding size and domineering ways. Helen was his rock; his playmate and sister rolled into one. It never even dawned on him that the most vital role for a wife was missing from his list. He had never made love to her in three years of marriage, always pleading his failing health. The truth, which he would never permit himself to face, was that the idea was repugnant to him. He simply was not interested in sexual love.

At his question, Helen withdrew her gaze from the window and smiled sadly.

'I don't know what Lizzie's doing. I haven't seen her for ages. Or Aunt Amy and Mary. I wrote to Mary when

I heard she'd lost her baby, but she never replied. Now, I feel it would be disloyal to Papa to get in touch with either her or Lizzie. Whatever Papa says about Lizzie having nothing to do with the strike, I'm sure he's lying. It's too much of a coincidence her leaving just then. And he grows so silent whenever anyone mentions her name.'

'Isn't it time you found a proper job?' Amy demanded angrily, as Elizabeth came into the kitchen. 'The pittance those women are paying you is nearly all swallowed up in bus and tram fares.'

For answer, Elizabeth put her hand in her coat pocket and pulled out two pound notes and a handful of small change, which she deposited on the table.

'There you are, Mama. I only ride as far as the top of Blackboy Hill, then I walk the rest of the way. For what I'm doing, the Miss Turners pay me extremely well. More than they can afford, I daresay. Cataloguing the contents of The Brass Mill's various rooms isn't my idea of an arduous job — more like a labour of love — and anyway, it's nearly finished. Next week will see the end of it, then I must start looking for something more permanent.'

It had been pure chance that, two days after leaving the factory, Elizabeth should have met the younger Miss Turner on one of the latter's rare forays into town. Elizabeth had been walking up Park Street and Miss Josephine had been walking down. Miss Josephine had insisted on retracing her steps and treating Elizabeth to tea at a café near the brow of the hill. She had been saddened to hear of William's death.

'Your father was such a clever man with his hands,' she had said, stirring her tea. 'He made a splendid job of replacing the moulding in the library.'

She had then enquired about Elizabeth's own doings, which Elizabeth had told her with certain reservations. She said merely that she had left her uncle's factory and was looking for another line of work.

Miss Josephine had sighed. 'Unemployment is very bad at present. Forgive me, but do you think you were quite wise, my dear, to leave a steady job, however unsatisfying and unsatisfactory it might be?' This was her own assumption. Elizabeth had offered no explanation for her departure. 'However, my sister and I could give you temporary employment, if you care to take it. We're getting old, and so many of The Brass Mill's rooms have been shut up and under covers for so long that we're not sure what we have any more. We want to get our affairs in order; it will make things so much easier when we die. We want to throw out the rubbish and store the rest, and that means having an inventory of every room. We can't pay much, and I'm afraid we're a long way from Eastwood, but you could live in during the week and go home at weekends.'

Elizabeth had jumped at the chance. She remembered The Brass Mill and its occupants with the greatest affection, and an opportunity to renew acquaintances was too good to be missed. She had declined the offer to live in during the week, even though it meant that some of what she earned would be lost in travelling. But she wanted to be sure of meeting Ben at least one or two evenings a week now that she no longer saw him during the day, at work. She salved her conscience by walking as much of the distance as she could, and had come to look forward to her early morning and late evening rambles across the Downs. Now that the job was coming to an end, she felt sad.

Only this morning, she had unearthed from the bottom of a cupboard an exquisite set of plates, wrapped in tissue paper, put away and forgotten. The Miss Turners had exclaimed excitedly over the find, recalling the plates' existence from childhood days.

'It's the *famille verte* plates!' Miss Josephine had cried. 'Look, Clarissa! I remember Father saying they

158

date from the K'ang Hsi period. How ever could we have overlooked those?'

They had carried off their treasures to croon over them in the library, where they were assembling the more valuable items.

Amy poked the kitchen fire vigorously. After several days of fine May sunshine, the weather had again turned cold.

'A good thing, too,' she said. 'Although where you're going to find another job is more than I can fathom. You hear of more people being out of work every day. Throwing up a good job like you had! I don't know what came over you. You must be mad.'

'Mama! We've been into all that, months ago,' Elizabeth answered wearily. 'Can we let it alone?'

Amy straightened her back and put down the poker. 'They're still saying round here that you were responsible for that strike. I've never asked if it's true, because I don't want to know. I can't see, though, why Joe would have given you that reference if it were so, and that's what I tell people. Besides, everyone knows Sylvia Crocker was the ringleader. It's costing your uncle a pretty penny to modernize that place.'

'I'm sure he'll see his money back, eventually,' Elizabeth retorted unfeelingly. 'He ought to have done it years ago. Conditions in those factories were primitive.'

She felt no guilt about Joseph, but she did feel some for her own lack of earning power. With only Alan Davies's rent between them and starvation, she could not afford to become a liability on the household. She needed to find a new job quickly. But where? Even her spuriously glowing reference from Gordon's would not necessarily ensure her work.

There was a rap on the glass door at the end of the passage, and without waiting to be invited, Eileen Hennessey walked in. She was clutching an empty cup.

'I've come to borrow a bit of sugar,' she smiled. 'You don't mind, Amy, do you, there's a dear? Our Jack doesn't get paid until this evening, and the Miss Cohens won't let me have any more on tick.'

None too pleased, Amy went to a cupboard and pulled out the sugar tin.

'Mind you let me have it back, then, as soon as possible,' she said. 'I'm short myself.'

'Jack not home yet, Mrs Hennessey?' Elizabeth asked. She glanced at the clock on the kitchen mantelpiece, which showed almost nine o'clock. 'He isn't usually as late as this.'

'He's doin' two rounds this week. One of the other collectors died, sudden like, a few days ago, and they haven't taken anyone on in 'is place. Not in any hurry, if you asks me. As long as our Jack'll work 'imself to death doin' two people's jobs for one wage packet, why should they bother? Our Jack's a fool to himself, and so I tells 'im. Thanks, Amy, I'm ever so grateful. Our Bridget kicks up something awful if she can't have sugar in her tea. I'll let you 'ave it back tomorrow, as soon as I've been to the shop.'

'She's always on the cadge lately,' Amy grumbled, as the glass door clicked shut behind Eileen Hennessey. 'She never was much good at making the money go round, but she gets worse as she gets older. She's forever in debt to the Cohens. I'm surprised they allow her as much credit as they do . . . Lizzie! I'm talking to you! Miles away, as usual.'

'Sorry, Mama.' Elizabeth picked up her hat and coat from the old leather-covered settee, where she had dropped them. 'I've an idea, that's all.'

'I don't normally see applicants for jobs myself,' Albert Harrison said, his thumbs stuck in the pockets of his waistcoat, swinging gently to and fro in his swivel chair. 'But this time I've made an exception. I don't mind admitting that I'm frankly curious on several counts. First of all, Miss Evans, what makes you think I'd employ a female collector? There's never been such a thing at Harrison's.'

Elizabeth, seated in a chair on the opposite side of Albert's desk, looked challengingly at him.

'Are you implying that I'm less intelligent than a man, Mr Harrison? If so, I assure you that you're very much mistaken.'

Albert laughed. 'Your very intelligence, young woman, must tell you that we don't employ women collectors because it wouldn't be suitable. You meet some very nasty customers on the doorstep in this game. You could encounter, if not physical violence, then very bad language.'

It was Elizabeth's turn to laugh. 'Mr Harrison, during my years at Gordon's, I often had to go down to the factory floor for one reason or another. There is little in the way of bad language that I haven't heard at some time. And women are doing all sorts of jobs nowadays that were once the monopoly of men. The war has changed so much.'

'I'm aware of that fact. But women still aren't traipsing around back alleys in the dark collecting money. It would be asking for trouble.'

'I can make sure that I do all my collecting during daylight hours. I shan't stop to eat.'

'Difficult in winter.'

'Nevertheless, I should like to try. You see that Gordon's have given me an excellent reference.'

Albert glanced down at the paper on his desk. 'Yes. Now, that does intrigue me.' He raised his eyes again and stared consideringly at Elizabeth. 'I'd like to know how you wangled that out of old Joe. I have it on good authority that you were the moving spirit behind the strike.' She returned his gaze limpidly, neither accepting nor refuting the allegation. 'Well?' he barked. 'What do you have to say?'

'I should say that the stike was inevitable sooner or

later, in a factory where the conditions were so poor.'

'Hmm.' He made no comment for a moment. Then he said slowly: 'And I should say that you are a very dangerous young woman.' There was another silence while he flipped the edge of the reference with his thumb-nail. 'What's Joe Gordon up to?' he shot at her suddenly. 'Carrying on with that secretary of his, eh? You must have got something on him.'

Elizabeth sat poker-faced. She asked: 'Do you think my uncle is the sort of man to submit to blackmail?'

'Not giving anything away, eh? You got your reference in return for holding your tongue. Well, I admire a woman who believes in fair play. If you make a bargin, stand by it, that's my motto.'

'Do I get the job, Mr Harrison?'

'Give me one good reason why I should employ you, when there are so many men out of work.'

Elizabeth hesitated. She could offer all sorts of reasons; that she was unmarried, a wage-earner and also unemployed; that she would work as hard, probably harder, than a man and receive less wages; that he would be regarded as a pioneer in the field of female labour. But she rejected them all in favour of one which she guessed would have a greater appeal.

'Because,' she said, 'it would annoy my uncle.'

Albert picked up his half-smoked cigar from a big, onyx ashtray and drew on it steadily. The tip winked evilly. He grinned.

'So you know about our little disagreement, do you?'

Again Elizabeth judged it best to say nothing. She had not known about the quarrel until Albert Harrison had spoken of her uncle, but had gathered all her information from the tone of his voice, the look on his face. He would not thank her, however, for being told that he was so transparent.

Albert lay back in his swivel chair, watching her narrowly through the spiralling smoke. Then he nodded abruptly.

'You can start Monday morning,' he said. 'Eight o'clock sharp. A trial period of three weeks. We'll see how you go on.'

Elizabeth had anticipated all sorts of objections to her new job, and was ready with her arguments. But it was only her mother and Jack Hennessey who put up any opposition.

'You can't do it!' Amy wailed, horrified. 'It's not a fit job for a woman.'

'It's a job,' Elizabeth retorted grimly. 'If I make a go of it, it means another regular wage-packet coming into the house.'

Before this irrefutable argument, Amy's resistance melted.

Jack, however, was not so easily persuaded.

'You're asking for trouble all round,' he warned her. 'The other collectors at Harrison's will resent you. They'll blame you for taking the bread out of another man's mouth. The customers'll either try to diddle you or abuse you because you're a woman. Give up the idea, Lizzie, before it's too late.'

But Elizabeth was adamant. 'Find me alternative employment before next Monday,' she challenged him, 'and I'll do as you ask.'

It was Ben whom she had really dreaded facing with her news, expecting fierce criticism. She had, in one way, looked forward to arousing his anger, his protective instincts, his passionate avowals that he would not tolerate her exposing herself to abuse or physical harm. She had even hoped to elicit from him an immediate proposal of marriage. He might feel that marriage on a shoestring was preferable to allowing her to take such a risk.

None of these things happened. He seemed rather amused than otherwise by her initiative, and wished her luck.

'You've always had plenty of courage, I'll say that

for you. More like a man.'

She was frightened. Their relationship had become stagnant. He still took her out; he still, skilfully, held her at arm's length; but, subconsciously, she was no longer deceived by his talk of making a decent living wage before settling down to family life. He was rising fast in Gordon's but not fast enough. She knew his insatiable ambition. Senior clerk or section supervisor, with a gold watch and an illuminated address when he eventually retired, would not satisfy Ben Sawyer. Yet what else could he hope for at Gordon's? And he was too careful to risk throwing up his job for the hazards of unemployment. On some level of her mind, not openly acknowledged, Elizabeth recognized that Ben was not the sort of man to forge his own destiny out of small beginnings. He was too sybaritic. He would have to take short cuts to wealth and power or go under.

She threw herself into her work, intent on proving that she could do it. She dressed unfussily; her grey flannel suit for spring and autumn, plain cream or white poplin dresses for warm summer days. And when winter came, she unstitched the fur collar from her brown velour coat and trimmed the lapels with two rows of braid. Whatever the weather, she always wore a hat, finding that it gave her an added authority.

From the start, she adopted a no-nonsense approach making no concessions to her femininity; discouraging equally attempts by the women to enlist her sympathy and playful jocularity on the part of the men. When payments could not be met, she reported the matter to the main office in Alma Road, stifling any qualms she might feel as a woman. For as a woman, she had to be even more ruthless than her fellow collectors all of whom were waiting eagerly for her to show herself unfit for the job. She knew she was the source of much resentment, and was determined to overcome it. If the only way she could do it was to make everyone forget that she was a woman, then, as far as possible, that was what she would do.

In nineteen twenty-five, shingled and semi-shingled hair became fashionable and skirts rose above the knee. Elizabeth had her hair semi-shingled, but resisted the shorter length skirts for as long as she could without appearing positively dowdy. People, she found, were beginning to accept her without question; customers and Harrison's employees alike no longer found her a source of comment or surprise. She had grown accustomed to verbal abuse on the doorstep, and, so far, had never encountered physical violence. She was careful to visit less accessible tenements and houses during the hours of daylight, and to walk home on dark evenings through well-lighted streets. Whenever possible, Jack would accompany her.

He alone was unreconciled to her job. As far as he was concerned, it had only one recommendation; it had occupied Elizabeth's mind for the past year almost to the exclusion of everything else. She had had no time to worry about Mary and Alan: she had stopped trying to persuade him to take her to Cardiff so that they might make further enquiries.

'Mary's happy, your mother's content,' he had said the last time she had mentioned the subject. 'You've no grounds for your suspicions except a natural mistrust of people. You know the old adage about letting sleeping dogs lie. Forget it, Lizzie.'

And she had. He silently called himself a coward, knowing that the attack on him was proof that she was right. There was something in Alan Davies's past he did not want discovered.

Part Three 1926 – 1930

My care is like my shadow in the sun —
Follows me flying — flies when I pursue it.

Elizabeth I 1533 – 1603

CHAPTER THIRTEEN

The General Strike of 1926 passed for Helen like a dream.

It was on the first day of the strike, the fourth of May, that Charlie's cough grew worse. He went to bed early, and by the following morning he not only had a temperature of a hundred and four, but was spitting phlegm whose rusty colour warned Helen of the presence of blood. Panic-stricken, she sent for the doctor.

'Lobar-pneumonia, I'm afraid, Mrs Harrison,' Doctor Morgan said gravely. 'Your husband will need very careful nursing if we're to pull him through. I shall arrange straight away for a day- and night-nurse. Sleep and rest are essential. Plenty of fluids and as much light, nourishing foods as he can take. He won't want anything solid to begin with, but he may feel that he can manage an egg-custard, a coddled egg or a morsel of steamed fish in a day or two's time. Meanwhile, I shall suggest poultices to relieve the pain and difficult breathing, but he must be disturbed as little as possible. Don't worry too much. The nurses will see to everything. If all goes well, his temperature should drop in ten or twelve days' time, and we must concentrate on building up his strength to meet the crisis.'

Helen summoned May, who arrived full of recriminations, ready to dismiss the nurses and take charge of the sick-room herself. But when she saw her son's white face propped against his pillows, heard his laboured breathing and inspected the contents of the sputum cup, she said to Helen: 'I'll move into the spare room with you. We'll see this thing through together.'

They kept watch in turns, sitting in a corner of the bedroom, out of the way of the nurse on duty, running errands for cups of tea, boiling water, clean sheets, fresh poultices. Fear drew May and Helen closer, making them, for these few weeks at least, almost friends. Joe, Minna and Albert dropped in from time to time to enquire after the invalid and give news of the outside world. The expected revolution, the fighting in the streets, the bloodthirsty mobs after the pattern of France and Russia, had not materialized. Instead, the strike was fizzling out in typically British fashion, a welter of muddle, compromise and betrayal.

Helen and May were uninterested. They would not have cared, probably would not have known, if a guillotine had been set up outside their own front door. Every waking thought was concentrated on Charlie.

The General Strike came to an end on May the thirteenth, ten days after it had begun, and the same evening Doctor Morgan called to see his patient.

'We can expect the crisis soon,' he said to Helen. 'I shall go up and see Mr Harrison now, and report to you before I leave.'

Helen and May sat downstairs in the breakfast-room, May fiddling with a piece of embroidery. Helen pretended to read, but the book, Warwick Deeping's *Sorrell and Son*, had slipped unheeded to her lap, and she stared out of the window at the garden; at the small fruit trees splayed against the wall, at the formal, rectangular flower-beds and at the path, edged with miniature box-hedging. Some of the shrubs were already in flower.

'He'll be all right, won't he?' she asked suddenly. 'Charlie I mean. He will pull through?'

May raised her head and took off her glasses, which, nowadays, she used for close work.

'Yes, of course,' she said.

Helen heard the note of reservation in her mother-in-law's voice and thought: 'She doesn't really believe it. She thinks he's dying.'

But Charlie couldn't die! He mustn't! He was her friend and she needed him. All her feelings of exasperation and frustration seemed so petty to her now. She would be lost without him. She got up and began to walk up and down the room. When the door opened and the doctor reappeared, she jumped.

She knew at once by his face that something was wrong. May, too, got to her feet, her eyes wide with fear, her legs braced against the seat of her armchair.

'What is it?' Helen asked breathlessly.

Doctor Morgan shook his head. 'I'm afraid, Mrs Harrison, that there are complications. Your husband's temperature, instead of dropping has risen still further. I think . . . I'm almost sure it's empyema.'

'What does that mean?'

'It means that pus has formed in the pleural cavities. An operation may be necessary.'

'Could that be . . . serious?' Helen had intended to say 'fatal' but was unable to make herself use the word.

'Extremely. But we must hope, my dear. Hope and pray. I shall come again first thing tomorrow morning and if there is no change, I shall make immediate arrangements to have Mr Harrison removed to the Infirmary. I don't want to do so unless absolutely necessary. Moving him could be dangerous.'

Doctor Morgan went away, treading softly across the carpeted hall as though already, Helen thought resentfully, there was a death in the house. As soon as she had shut the front door behind him, she went upstairs to the bedroom next to the drawing-room, which she used to share with Charlie.

May had beaten her to it and was standing by the bed, her face rigid with fear. The day-nurse was in a huddled consultation with her replacement, who had arrived during the doctor's visit. Charlie, his body streaming with perspiration, tossed deliriously against his pillows. He did not know either his mother or his wife.

The day-nurse approached Helen.

'I'm going to stay on an hour or two, Mrs Harrison, until Mr Harrison is quieter. We're going to sponge him down and try and reduce the temperature.' She glanced at her watch. 'It's gone nine o'clock and there's nothing you can do at the moment. I suggest either you or your mother-in-law gets some rest. My colleague or myself will fetch you if there's any change.'

'What sort of change?' Helen could barely speak.

The nurse did not answer, but glanced significantly at May.

'You go, Helen,' May ordered. 'It's you Charlie will want to see and to be with when he comes to himself. We don't want you cracking up then, do we, nurse?'

'Certainly not. Your mother-in-law's right, Mrs Harrison. Go and lie down. Get your housekeeper to send you up a glass of hot milk. It might help you sleep. Take one of those pills the doctor gave you.'

Helen looked helplessly from the nurse to May. She wanted to stay with Charlie, but the habit of letting others make her decisions for her was too deeply ingrained.

She went upstairs to the second floor; to the spare bedroom she was sharing with May, and lay down on one of the two single beds. She did not want to send for anything from the kitchen: the thought of eating or drinking made her feel sick. She did not undress, either, merely kicking off her shoes. She lay on her back, her head turned to one side, staring at a branch of lilac in a vase on the dressing-table, and at its shadow on the wall behind. Charlie had bought her that vase, she remembered; a tall, slender trumpet of fluted pink glass, designed to hold a single flower. She went on staring at it as the light died and the shadowed pattern of the lilac branch faded, fainter and fainter, until it vanished altogether and the wall was blank.

Helen sat up abruptly and opened the drawer of her bedside-table. She could not sleep without one of the pills which Doctor Morgan had prescribed for her for over a year now, to alleviate what he called 'nervous indisposition'. If he guessed the truth about her marriage, he did not say so, nor did he invite her confidence. He was an elderly man, old-fashioned in his notions, and of the opinion that all this modern talk about sex in connection with health was vastly overrated.

'Plenty of exercise,' he had advised her. 'Take up tennis. Splendid for the system.' All the same, he had given her the pills.

Helen had used them sparingly at first, but as one sleepless night had followed another, had come to rely on them more and more, until now she found it difficult to sleep without them. She had recently increased the dose to two, and tonight she swallowed three with the glass of water which always stood by her bed. If she could only drop off, she told herself childishly, Charlie would have recovered by the time she woke up again.

Usually she slept dreamlessly, but this evening her mind was restless. She and Charlie were playing on the sands at Bournemouth, as they had done so often when they were children. She could see May and her mother sitting side by side on the rug, under the sunshade, watching them. Her father and Albert Harrison were paddling in the water, trouser-legs rolled up to reveal white, city-dwellers' ankles. She was throwing a cricket-ball to Charlie, who had set up his stumps on

173

the beach and was wielding his bat to the imminent danger of his brother, who was keeping wicket. But quite suddenly, Charlie was no longer there. He had disappeared, but no one else seemed to notice. Then she was running along the edge of the sea, where the waves curled and feathered across the sands, which now spread forbidding and lifeless to an empty horizon. She was alone and terrified.

'Charlie! Charlie!' she screamed.

She jerked awake to find herself sitting bolt upright, shivering uncontrollably. Someone was knocking on the bedroom door, and a voice she recognized as belonging to one of the nurses was calling to her urgently.

'Mrs Harrison! Mrs Harrison, are you awake? Come quickly please!'

'Will you go to Charlie Harrison's funeral?' Amy enquired, stirring the tea. She lifted the brown pot from the hob and set it on its stand, wiping her hands in her apron. 'Minna said that Helen particularly hopes you'll go.'

Elizabeth, eating her breakfast standing up because she and her mother had overslept that morning, shook her head.

'I can't get the time off,' she said. 'I daren't get behind with my collections.'

'Surely Mr Harrison would make allowances this once.' Amy looked shocked. 'It is his own son.'

'I haven't seen Albert Harrison since the day he engaged me,' Elizabeth retorted. 'He's the owner. I'm just an employee. Our paths don't cross.'

'But in the circumstances . . . '

'The circumstances, Mama, are just what he doesn't wish to be reminded of. I don't suppose he cares for his daughter-in-law's low connections any more than Uncle Joe.'

'I wish you wouldn't talk like that.' While Elizabeth

174

swallowed the last mouthful of bread and butter, Amy poured her a cup of tea. It came out dark brown and stewed, having been made by Alan two hours earlier. He was on the first shift this week. 'You were Helen's and Charlie's bridesmaid. Mary and I thought we'd go, especially since the funeral's at Arley Street.' She sighed and blinked away a tear. 'That was Helen's doing, you know. Minna said so in her letter. Helen wanted Charlie brought back to the place where he was born. He's to be buried in Eastwood cemetery.'

Trust Helen, Elizabeth thought impatiently, to make the charming, useless, sentimental gesture. As though it mattered to the dead where they were buried. And Charlie had lived most of his life in Clifton.

'I must be going,' she said, putting on her tight-fitting hat and kissing her mother. 'You can tell me all about the funeral this evening.'

Jack was waiting for her at the gate. The May day was warm, and as he took in her white poplin dress and cloche hat, he said: 'You're not going, then?'

'Don't you start.' Elizabeth shut the gate behind her. 'Mama's been on at me ever since we got up. We overslept. Neither of us heard the alarm. That's why I'm a few minutes late. What a rush! Young Richie will probably be late for school as well. Mama hasn't even called him yet.'

'"Young Richie",' Jack reminded her, 'is fourteen years old. I imagine he'll be leaving school pretty soon.'

'I'm afraid so. Richard is a bright boy, but even if he were as clever as Albert Einstein he wouldn't be allowed to remain at school or go on to university. My dear brother-in-law, like my uncle, has the idea that all education is suspect.'

They crossed Portland Place, past all the bustle of the brewery, and made their way towards Alma Road.

Jack said: 'You're fond of Richard.'

'In a way. Which is more than I can say for his father.

175

I still maintain that there's something very furtive about Alan.'

Jack hurriedly changed the subject. He and Alan Davies steered clear of one another as much as possible. Sometimes Jack wondered if he had not imagined Alan's involvement in that incident, two years ago.

'The strike has hit a lot of families round here hard,' he said. 'Ten days' loss of wages has made half my customers really short. The strong-arm boys are going to have a field-day. I do what I can, but it's not much.'

'What can you do?'

'Well, if it's only a matter of a penny or twopence, I lend them the money.' Jack grinned sheepishly.

'Lend them? *Give* them the money, you mean.' Elizabeth turned to look at him. 'Honestly, Jack, you're soft as butter.'

'Better than being hard as nails,' he threw at her. 'Besides, more often than not, I do get the money back. People are a lot more honest than you think.'

Elizabeth laughed. 'Oh, I know what your opinion of me is,' she said. 'But it's a good job some of us have our heads screwed on the right way. You and my cousin Helen would make a good pair. Or, on second thoughts, perhaps you wouldn't. You both need someone to take you in hand. Someone with backbone.'

They had, by this time, reached Alma Road and the chocolate-and-cream façade of Harrison's Universal Clothing Store. Today, the shop itself was closed, the blinds drawn in acknowledgement of the owner's bereavement, but the business of debt-collecting went on.

Jack and Elizabeth went in by the staff entrance and picked up their account books, and Jack, in addition, his money-belt. The sole concession to Elizabeth's sex had been permission to put what she collected into her handbag. It had been her own idea to carry over one wrist a canvas bag, partly filled with coppers and pebbles, to act as a decoy; but somewhat to her disappointment no one had ever tried to snatch it.

By midday, when she normally met Jack at a café near the station for a sandwich and a cup of tea, she had completed only half her usual number of calls. Jack had been right: the strike had left many families short of money and unable to meet their payments. Elizabeth had spent double her accustomed time on most doorsteps this morning, listening to excuses and prevarications and tearful demands for a few days' grace. So far, she had resolutely closed her ears to these pleadings, but she had not enjoyed it. Her sympathies during the General Strike had been with the strikers, and she refused to join any of the citizen-bands which had been formed in order to keep public services running. Now she found herself forced to penalize the very people whom she had so recently been supporting.

Elizabeth had tried very hard not to have favourites amongst her customers. Impartiality was an important factor in keeping her job. But she had to admit to a soft spot for the Fairchilds who lived in Inkerman Street. The husband had come home from the war in France badly shell-shocked and gassed, a mental and physical wreck. He had never worked since, and lay all day on the sofa, which was the one decent piece of furniture in the sparsely furnished, all-purpose room. His wife, a thin, prematurely old woman, went out charring to support him and their two younger children. The oldest boy had recently started on the railways.

As a general rule, Elizabeth called on the family late in the afternoon, when she knew Mrs Fairchild would be at home; but on the odd occasion when she had gone earlier, the money had always been laid out ready for her on the table. So, at twelve o'clock, finding herself close to Inkerman Street, Elizabeth decided to make her collection and save a return journey later.

For some reason, the square was free of speakers, only their abandoned placards and boxes testifying to their customary presence. Perhaps, thought Elizabeth, they had talked themselves to a standstill during the General Strike. There were one or two people either going into or coming out of the public wash-house, which, like the Georgian houses that flanked it, was falling into disrepair. The Fairchilds lived in one room, divided by a curtain to make living and sleeping areas, on the first floor of one of the houses, a tap on the landing being their only supply of running water. There was no bathroom, and they used the three communal lavatories built in what had once been the garden at the back.

Elizabeth had grown used to the smell of the place, but in the beginning it had made her retch. Dried urine, stale cabbage, stray cats and dogs all mingled their various odours to form one indescribably pungent scent. Two young children, filthy, one of them covered in sores, were playing on the landing, sitting in a cardboard box and pretending it was a ship. They paused in their chatter to give Elizabeth a baleful stare, then resumed their game.

She knocked on the door of the Fairchilds' room and, to her surpirse, it was Mrs Fairchild herself who opened it. She looked frightened when she saw who it was, and it was obvious that she had been crying.

'Ha . . . Hallo, Miss Evans. I wasn't expectin' you yet.' She hesitated, and for a moment, Elizabeth had the impression that the door was going to be slammed in her face. Then Mrs Fairchild opened it wide and motioned her in. 'I 'aven't got all yer money,' she said defensively.

Elizabeth entered the room, the bare boards creaking under her weight. Mr Fairchild lay, as always, on the couch. On the deal table were spread out ten pennies and four halfpennies. Beside them was an empty purse which had been turned almost inside out. Elizabeth could see at once that the payment was sixpence short.

Mrs Fairchild shrugged fatalistically, but she was twisting her hands together under her apron.

'I . . . I can't pay, Miss Evans. That's me last shillin' until the end o' the week, when me and our Tom gets paid. Our Tom's lost a week 'n' a 'alf's money as you well know, an' I've 'ad to stay 'ome today 'cos our Dad's real poorly.' She started to cry again, the tears running down her pale, tired cheeks. 'What with the rent 'n' food, it's bin a struggle, I c'n tell you.' She nodded towards her husband. 'Dad ain't 'ad 'is beer now for a fortnight, an' I 'ates deprivin' 'im. There ain't much else in un's life, now is there?'

Elizabeth stared at the coppers on the table with as much desperation as the Fairchilds themselves.

'Can't you find the money anywhere?' she asked. 'Isn't there anyone who would lend it to you?'

Mrs Fairchild shook her head. 'They'm all in the same boat roun' 'ere, Miss. Strike's 'it everyone. An' what good's it done, I'd like to know.' She sniffed and wiped her nose on the back of her hand. 'It's all right. I knows you've got to report it. But they'll come 'n' take the stuff away — our Johnnie's shoes what 'e needs fer school an' our Billie's coat. An' what's 'e going t' wear then when it rains? You tell me that. An' what about the money we've paid already? We lose all that, jus' like we'd thrown it in the dustbin. It ain't fair, Miss, on honest, 'ard-workin', decent folks.'

It wasn't fair, but they knew the rules when they bought the goods, and what would happen if they were unable to pay. Yet somehow, today, Elizabeth's glib, well-rehearsed responses stuck in her throat. The Farichilds were among her best customers, always had the money ready on time; were as honest as the day. The circumstances, too, were unusual, and had not arisen out of fecklessness or carelessness. At the same time, Elizabeth could imagine the reaction at Harrison's if she were to plead for the family, using the

General Strike as an excuse. She would be dismissed immediately. In the opinion of people like Albert Harrison and her uncle Joseph, anyone who had taken part in the strike should be clapped in irons.

She took a deep breath. 'I'll lend you the money until Friday, Mrs Fairchild,' she said. She saw the woman's look of disbelief and, delving into her handbag, produced a sixpence from her own purse which she placed on the table beside the coppers.

Mrs Fairchild began to stutter. 'Th-that is k-kind of you, Miss. Isn't it, Dad? Did you 'ear that? Miss Evans is goin' t' lend us the money. You'll get it back, Miss, I promise. Come roun' Friday night an' I'll 'ave it ready an' waitin'.'

'We don' want charity,' her husband whispered harshly. It was the first time Elizabeth had ever heard him speak, and she realized that his vocal chords must have been partially destroyed by the gas. 'I ain't acceptin' charity, an' that's that.'

His wife began a tearful protest, and Elizabeth cut in: 'It's not charity, Mr Fairchild. I shall get the money back.'

'Favour, then.' The voice rasped the words out with increasing difficulty. 'Not acceptin' favours, neither. Fought fer King an' Country with the best of 'em. Won't accept favours from the likes of you.'

'Fer goodness' sake, Dad, 'ave some sense!' Mrs Fairchild looked imploringly at her husband, but he turned his head away.

'No,' he grated.

'We'll lose Johnnie's shoes an' Billie's coat!'

'No, I said!' The man's voice was lost in a paroxysm of coughing.

When the fit had passed, Elizabeth said quietly: 'If that's how you feel, Mr Fairchild, we'll make it a business transaction. Your wife will give me a receipt for the sixpence and an I O U for — ' She broke off, at a loss. She had no idea of the going rates of interest, and suspected that neither did the Fairchilds. 'An I O U for sixpence farthing,' she finished lamely.

There was a moment's silence, interrupted only by Mr Fairchild's laboured breathing. Then he nodded. A farthing represented quarter of an ounce of tobacco, but he was prepared to sacrifice that for the sake of his pride.

Mrs Fairchild produced a grubby sheet of paper and a stub of old pencil, and, with Elizabeth's help, wrote: 'I O U 6¼d,' and signed her name. Elizabeth put it and the money into her bag, smiling at the relief on the other woman's face.

'I'll see you on Friday evening,' she promised.

CHAPTER FOURTEEN

'Ben Sawyer was at Charlie Harrison's funeral,' Mary said that same evening, 'representing the employees. Helen asked where you were.'

'She was very disappointed that you weren't there,' Amy added, straightening the folds of her black dress. 'She mentioned it to her father-in-law in my hearing, and Mr Harrison said you could've had the day off if you'd asked.'

'Without pay.' Elizabeth laughed shortly. 'What happened afterwards? Did they give you a meal?'

'Everyone was going back to Clifton.' Amy put a plate of ham and salad in front of Elizabeth. 'We said we wouldn't go. You're late home tonight. Good job it's still light. I don't like you walking around with all that money on you.'

'I don't like it much, myself,' Elizabeth conceded. 'But if I don't finish until after seven o'clock, the counting-house is shut.' She attacked her belated meal. 'The shop was closed today as a mark of respect to Charlie. The staff were furious at having to lose a whole day's pay. So Ben was at the funeral, was he? He didn't mention that he'd been invited.'

'He was asked back to Clifton, as well,' Mary said, watching her sister eat. 'Of course, we could have gone, too, couldn't we, Mama? It was just that we — '

'Weren't pressed?' Elizabeth was sarcastic.

'Helen wanted us to go back very much,' Amy replied, on the defensive, as always, with her younger daughter. 'It was just that we should've had to come all the way back again, and I thought you'd be in earlier than this.'

'It was a hard day.' Elizabeth chased the food around her plate, but she no longer had any appetite. She wondered why Ben had said nothing about going to Charlie's funeral. 'What will Helen do now? Go home to her parents?'

'I asked her that,' Amy replied, 'but she said "no". Not just yet, anyway. She's going to try living on her own.'

'Helen won't stand that for long. She never could bear being alone.' Elizabeth put her knife and fork together. 'I'm sorry, Mama. I'm not hungry this evening.'

'I'll eat it,' Richard offered. He had been lying supine on the horsehair sofa, reading a book, but at Elizabeth's words he sat up, then came to the table. 'Can't let all that lovely grub go to waste.' He wagged an admonitory finger and said, in a fair imitation of Mary: 'Think of all the starving children in Africa and India who'd be glad of it.'

Mary flushed angrily as Elizabeth laughed.

'Cheeky young devil,' Elizabeth said, but without rancour. 'I can tell your father isn't around. Where is Alan, by the way? I thought he was on early shift this week.'

'He's out,' Mary answered tersely.

'Gone to the pub,' Richard grinned, raising a forkful of ham and lettuce.

'One of his workmates who lives near here asked him to go, just for a quick one.' Mary glared at her step-son. 'Alan wouldn't have gone otherwise. You know he doesn't like drinking.'

'I know he says he doesn't.' Elizabeth ignored her

sister's indignant protestations and turned to her mother. 'Did Ben say anything about coming round tonight?'

Amy shook her head. 'Not to me. It's your evening for the pictures, isn't it?'

'He was too busy making himself agreeable to Aunt Minna and Uncle Joe,' Mary put in maliciously, 'to have time to speak to anyone else.'

'I'll be in anyway,' Elizabeth said. 'If he comes, he does. But he may not feel like going to town.'

She wished she felt as indifferent as she sounded. It was nine o'clock already; too late to go to the cinema, even to the Tivoli. She went out through the scullery to the bathroom and washed her hair; then, with it wrapped in a towel, wandered into the garden. The ghostly shape of a white May tree was silhouetted against the wall which divided the Evanses' plot from the Hennesseys'. A lighted window shone out above the bathroom roof: Richard had gone to bed in the room which used to be Mary's. Elizabeth smiled to herself. She could picture him sprawled across the counterpane, already half-asleep even before he had removed his clothes, his pale eyelashes like two half-moons against his cheeks. She had to admit to an ever growing affection for Richard, however much she disliked his father.

She returned to the kitchen to dry her hair, hoping that Ben might have arrived during her absence, but there was no sign of him. Mary looked smug because Alan was home. He had gone upstairs to change his boots for slippers.

Elizabeth sat with her back to the kitchen fire, releasing her hair from the towel.

'You'll be sick, with the heat on your back like that,' Amy said, as she had said, ritually, to both Elizabeth and Mary for years.

How we repeat ourselves, Elizabeth thought. She supposed that all families had patterns of conversation

184

which, with custom, had become almost meaningless; just words to be uttered like some ancient and secret charm.

'Mama,' she asked, 'do you know anything about money-lending? What the rate of interest is, for example.' She would hate to have cheated the Fairchilds.

Amy was immediately alarmed. Even Mary's attention was caught, and she looked up from the sock she was darning.

'You're in trouble,' Amy accused her younger daughter. 'You've been embezzling the firm's money, and now you can't pay it back. I knew no good would come of you taking this job. Money can be a terrible temptation.'

'I am not in any trouble,' Elizabeth told her, laughing. 'I just want to know, that's all.'

It took her a little while longer to allay her mother's fears, but once Amy was convinced, she gave her mind to the subject with all the concentration of which she was capable. She liked academic problems: real ones threw her into incoherency. But the upshot of all her deliberations was that she knew practically nothing about it.

'I remember my grandfather — your great-grandfather — talking about "sixty-per-cents",' she said finally. 'At least, I think that's what he called them. He was talking about money-lenders, I'm sure.'

'It doesn't sound right to me,' Elizabeth demurred. 'Wait a minute, though.' She sat up and turned sideways to dry the left side of her hair. 'I remember a play we did at school. One of the Elizabethan dramatists. Fletcher, I think. There was a bit in it that went something like, "There are a few gallants . . . something, something, something . . . who would receive favours from the devil, though he appeared like a broker and demand sixty in the hundred".'

'Well, there you are,' Amy said, vindicated.

'What a very unpleasant conversation!' Mary exclaimed, snipping off her darning wool and banging her scissors down on the table. 'It's not Christian! Can't we change the subject?'

Alan appeared, nodding briefly at Elizabeth.

'Not gone to the pictures, then?' he asked.

'Obviously not. I worked late.'

'No need to bite his head off.' Mary made room for her husband at the table beside her. 'Is Richie asleep?'

Alan nodded, turning his chair sideways and stretching his feet towards the fire, regardless of the fact that they were in Elizabeth's way. He seemed more relaxed and sure of himself these days, Elizabeth thought. If her suspicions had been correct, and he had been concealing some secret in his past, it had ceased to trouble him.

It was ten o'clock. Ben would not come now. Elizabeth's hair was dry and she got up from the floor, folding her towel.

'I'm for an early night,' she said. 'It's going to be another hard day tomorrow.'

Helen said aloud: 'The first Sunday of nineteen twenty-seven.' Silently she added: 'Nearly eight months since Charlie died.'

There was no one in the room with her; no one in the entire house. Mrs Bagot always had the first Sunday of the month off to visit her married son in Cheltenham, and the maid who lived in was a Sunday School teacher. She had disappeared for the afternoon as soon as she had served Helen with the hot soup and cold chicken left for her lunch by the housekeeper.

Normally, on these occasions, Helen spent the day with Joe and Minna, but both of them were suffering from 'flu, and Smithson had telephoned, advising her not to go.

'They're both pretty bad, Miss Helen. It wouldn't be sensible for you to come. The doctor says it's very

186

infectious. Cook's gone down with it as well.'

So Helen found herself totally alone in the house, and its emptiness frightened her. She wandered from room to room, looking out of the windows, but the road was almost as deserted as the leafless garden. A thin rain was falling into the Sunday quiet. A woman hurried past on the opposite pavement, her face partially concealed by an umbrella. Two motor cars went by in the space of half an hour, but for the last twenty minutes there had been no sign of life at all.

Helen sat down by the drawing-room fire and picked up *The Murder of Roger Ackroyd*, the detective novel which had caused such a sensation when it was published the previous year. But even the magical Mrs Christie could not hold her attention today. After a moment or two, she let it slip to the ground and bent forward to put some more coal on the fire. Then she leaned back and stared at the leaping flames through half-closed lids. Presently tears welled up and trickled slowly down her cheeks.

Minna and Joe had been urging her, ever since Charlie's death, to sell the house in Pembroke Road and return home to live, but Helen had resisted the pressure. She was not sure why. She wanted to go home, back to the petting and the spoiling which she had always known, and yet she could not bring herself to do it. She had, in her present state, a measure of independence which she might regret losing. Some days, when it was warm and sunny and the birds sang in the garden, she treasured the sense of being her own mistress; of being responsible to no one but herself. But on short winter days when the weather was bad, she hated being alone.

She felt lost. Charlie had been her future for as long as she could remember, and she had never envisaged it without him. They had been talked of, and thought of themselves, as a couple ever since they were children. Her sense of frustration with Charlie while he was alive only made his loss harder to bear. If only he had lived, she told herself, things would have worked out between them. As it was, she had been a wife and no wife. She still had no real idea what marriage was about, and she sometimes wondered if the chief difficulty between herself and Charlie hadn't been one of incest: they had been brought up so much like brother and sister that it had been inhibiting for both of them. For she had to admit, in her more honest moments, that she had not fancied him 'in that way', and had become reconciled to the platonic life which they had led together. She had even convinced herself that she preferred it.

The doorbell rang and jerked her out of the half-doze, half-reverie into which she had fallen. She glanced at the clock which showed a quarter to three. She was not expecting anyone, and did not know whether her excitement was caused by nervousness or anticipation. It was only when the bell was pressed for a second time that she remembered there was no one in the house but herself. Her nervousness increased. She got up and went slowly downstairs to the front door.

Ben Sawyer was standing outside when she opened it, holding a bunch of very expensive hot-house roses, his Austin 7 parked in the road. Helen stared at him mutely for a few seconds before managing to stammer: 'M-Mr Sawyer. How v-very unexpected.'

He raised his hat.

'I hope you'll forgive me for calling, Mrs Harrison,' he said, 'but I was in the vicinity, lunching with a friend, and I wondered if I might be a welcome caller.' He indicated the roses. 'I took the liberty of buying them yesterday. I hope you don't mind.'

Helen, recovering from her surprise, smiled at him. 'What woman would mind roses in January?' she asked. 'They must have cost the earth.'

'"Sweets to the sweet",' he said, but saw at once that

she did not recognize the quotation as Elizabeth would have done.

'Please . . . Come in.' She held open the door and he stepped into the hall, removing his hat. 'I'm on my own,' she explained. 'My housekeeper and the live-in maid are both out. Won't you stay and keep me company for a while? Here, let me take your hat and coat.'

'And the flowers,' he said.

'Yes, of course. Thank you.'

She led the way upstairs to the drawing-room, then excused herself while she went to put the roses in water. When she returned, he was sitting on the sofa in front of the fire, with no hint of embarrassment or awkwardness in his manner. She was the one who felt shy and ill at ease.

She resumed her seat in the armchair and smiled across at him, wondering what to say. It was the first time in her life she had been completely alone with a comparatively strange man.

'You've been lunching with a friend, you said. Does he live near here?'

Ben Sawyer looked directly into her eyes and returned the smile. He was handsomer than ever, Helen thought.

'That was a lie, I'm afraid, Mrs Harrison. I have no friend in Clifton. I came to see you.'

'I'm sorry . . . I thought you said . . . I'm being very silly, I know, but I don't understand.'

'I came to see you,' he repeated. 'I told you a lie about having a friend near here. I haven't. I had lunch at home. You're the most beautiful woman I've ever met and I wanted to be with you. I've never stopped thinking about you since I saw you that first time at Weston.'

His audacity took her breath away. She had never been the object of such direct and unabashed gallantry, and had no idea how to cope with it. She clasped her

189

hands tightly together around one upraised knee.

'But . . . But you're practically engaged to my cousin Elizabeth,' she protested. 'How can you possibly have been always thinking about me?'

'Elizabeth was always second-best,' he answered. 'Don't mistake me. I like her. I like her very much. And you were engaged and then married to Charlie Harrison. You were the unattainable, like the fair damsels in the medieval Courts of Love.'

'Oh.' The conversation, she decided, was moving at altogether too rapid a pace. She tried to slow it down.

'Would you like some tea?' she enquired. 'I could get some for you.'

'Could you?' He looked quizzical. 'Do you really know how to make tea? You, who would never dream of taking a tramcar or a 'bus? Have you ever made a pot of tea, Mrs Harrison?'

'No. No, I haven't.' She was suddenly struck by her uselessness and began to cry again, searching desperately in her pocket for her handkerchief.

'Here, have mine,' Ben said, passing her a clean white square of cambric, and reflecting that, with Helen, life would be a series of clichés. But it made a change from Elizabeth, so practical, so self-assured. The cousins were the opposite sides of the coin. Ideally, one needed both of them. Unfortunately, it was not an ideal world.

'Thank you,' she said, and wiped her eyes, whereas Elizabeth would have blown her nose. 'I'm sorry. I'm being stupid, but I've been very unhappy since Charlie died. I get so lonely, and I'm no use to anyone.' She gave a watery smile. 'I can't even make a cup of tea.'

'Why should you? There's no point when you can afford to pay someone to do it for you.'

'Money doesn't buy happiness,' she answered tritely and a little crossly.

'Try telling that to those who haven't any,' he advised her.

Handing her the handkerchief had been an excuse for moving along the sofa so that he was now seated in the corner next to her armchair. They were at right angles to one another, their knees almost touching. Once more, Helen experienced the familiar sensation of alarm and excitement. She shifted, and her silk stocking brushed against his trouser-leg. His hand shot out and gripped her knee.

'Mr Sawyer! You mustn't! Really!'

His other hand covered both of hers. Their eyes met and she could not look away.

'Don't you want me to make love to you?' he asked gently.

'No, of course not.' But the words were faint. She could barely find the voice to speak. She added, even more faintly: 'I'm a virgin. Charlie and I never . . . ' She was unable to finish the sentence, and closed her eyes.

Ben was startled. He had not imagined the marriage to have been a passionate one, but never for a moment had he considered the possibility of it not having been consummated at all. He disliked being thrown; not having foreseen all the possibilities. He had always prided himself on being the master of any situation. He had even been able to manage Elizabeth. Angry with himself and, more obscurely, with her, he made a move to rise — only to find that she was in his arms, clinging to him, begging him not to leave.

He pulled her down on the carpet between the sofa and the hearth, fumbling with the buttons of her dress. Impatiently, she pushed him aside and began tearing off her clothes; literally, for he heard the soft wool of the black dress rip. He removed his own clothes, catching fire from her urgency, so that what was to have been a practised seduction turned into a confused and passionate embrace. His fastidious nature revolted at the disorder and the haste, but he recognized, all the same, that he had not been deceived by those 'bedroom eyes'. Once aroused, Helen was a woman who would

191

always have to be in love, and he was going to make sure that, at least until they were married, he remained the object of that affection.

Presently, he sat up and drew her to rest against his shoulder. Her eyes were closed and she was breathing heavily. He watched the rise and fall of her breasts. Perspiration ran down her face and neck. He smoothed away the line of pain around her mouth with the tip of one of his fingers.

'It will be better next time,' he promised. 'The first time is always the worst. Or so I'm told.'

'Have you made love to many other women?' she demanded jealously.

His good humour had returned as he regained control of the situation.

'One or two,' he answered lightly, knowing exactly what she wanted to hear. 'But they didn't mean anything to me. They were just girls. Not like you. You're different.'

'Am I?' She opened her eyes and tilted her head back, looking up at him.

'You know you are.' How easy it all was! How boring! He could have had Elizabeth on exactly the same terms. She, too, would have let herself be deceived.

Helen tucked her head beneath his chin. 'Poor Lizzie,' she whispered. 'How are you going to tell her about us?' A thought struck her and she lifted her face. 'You do want to marry me, don't you?'

'You know I do.' That, at any rate, was the truth. All his life he had wanted money. And in Helen, he had beauty and wealth combined. His belief in his destiny had not been misplaced, although it had been shaken when she married Charlie Harrison.

He lowered his head and kissed her; lips, eyes, throat, breasts. She wanted him to make love to her a second time, but he knew he could not manage it twice in an hour; and it would wound his pride to disappoint

192

her. He said quickly: 'Won't someone be back soon?'

Helen glanced at her wristwatch, then scrambled to her feet.

'I didn't realize it was so late. My maid will be home in about quarter of an hour, and I must bath and change.' She dragged on her clothes, ruefully inspecting the ripped seam of her sleeve. 'I'll have to think up some story as to how that happened,' she said with a guilty laugh. She put her arms round Ben's neck. 'You'll visit me again soon?' she begged him.

He kissed her on the mouth. 'I'll come when it's suitable,' he promised her. 'We must be circumspect, my darling, just for a while. You haven't been widowed a year yet. We don't want to put up any backs, especially your father's.'

'Papa doesn't mind what I do, as long as I'm happy.'

'I think he'd mind about this. It's a question of your good name. People gossip. They like to believe the worst of others, and if we were too premature in announcing our engagement, they'd think we were having an affair before your husband died, and that would reflect on Charlie. You wouldn't want that, now would you?' Helen shook her head and he kissed her again. 'As soon as you're out of half-mourning, in November, we'll speak to your father. Meanwhile, we must take care.'

'But we'll be able to do . . . this again?' She indicated the floor, where they had so recently made love.

He soothed away her anxiety. 'Perhaps. We'll see. We mustn't attract attention to ourselves, whatever else we do. It's important that we both behave normally. I'll have to go on seeing Elizabeth, just for the time being.'

'Must you?' Her tone was sharp; and he realized with a little thrill of pleasure that she was not just the soft, sweet heart of the flower: there was a thorn lurking in there somewhere.

'Yes, and I've told you why.' His grip tightened

around her waist. 'Don't start being foolish, or I shall get cross.' He saw the sudden gleam in her eyes and added: 'You might think you'd enjoy it, but you wouldn't, you know. Besides, I might not come back.' The threat was enough to subdue her and he kissed her one last time. 'I'll let myself out,' he said.

She heard him run downstairs and the slam of the front door. Her mind was in a whirl. She wanted to sit down and think, but she had no time. Hurriedly, she straightened the cushions on the sofa, made up the fire and went next door to her bedroom, then to the bathroom, where she ran herself a bath. Only when she was immersed in the scented water did she let her thoughts range back over the events of the afternoon.

She could not really believe that it had happened, except for the tell-tale bruise on her left breast and another on one of her thighs. She was a complete woman at last. Making love, being made love to, was everything she had hoped and imagined it would be. The unfulfilled years with Charlie slid away, unregretted, into the past. They had been a mere extension of childhood: two adults who had never properly grown up, playing at keeping house. What she had experienced with Ben Sawyer was what she had been made for; love and its physical expression. She had always suspected it. Now she knew for sure.

CHAPTER FIFTEEN

The audience streamed out of the cinema into the cool of the autumn night. Mary, like almost every other woman in sight, was wiping her eyes and blowing her nose. She clung to Alan's arm, half-laughing, half-crying.

'It was lovely,' she enthused. 'To think you could actually hear him singing. When he sang that "Sonny Boy", I howled my eyes out.'

'I know. I could hear you,' Alan grumbled. 'It would have been embarrassing if everyone hadn't been doing the same. Even the bloke next to me was snivelling.'

'Well, didn't you think Al Jolson was lovely? How do they do it, Alan? Is there someone standing behind the screen, singing the song?'

'No!' he answered scathingly. 'Of course there isn't!' As ever, when he was annoyed or irritated, his Welsh accent thickened. 'It's recorded and played to the movement of Al Jolson's lips. It's only a film you're seeing. Moving photographs, that's all.'

Mary searched the crowds around her. 'Lizzie said Ben might be bringing her this evening. But I can't see them anywhere.'

Alan grunted as they made their way along the street to join the queue for the Eastwood tramcar.

'If he's brought her, it'll be the first time he's taken

her out in weeks. She's seen precious little of him for months.'

A man who had been coming towards them suddenly stopped and caught Alan by the shoulder.

'Hullo, Davies!' he exclaimed, in an accent that matched Alan's own. 'What are you doing in Bristol? How are you, Mrs Davies? Nice to see you both back together again. I always reckoned you'd make it up.'

Mary felt Alan's arm go rigid beneath her hand.

'I'm sorry. I don't think I know you,' he said in a strangled voice. 'You must have the wrong man.'

'Wrong man, my foot! I'd know you anywhere, even though you have put on a bit of weight. You remember me. Bill Jones, who used to live in the flat above you in Cardiff.' The man took another, longer look at Mary and his smile slid into a frown. He raised his hat. 'Oh dear. I'm sorry!' he apologized. 'I thought you were Mrs Davies.'

Mary answered coolly: 'I am the present Mrs Davies. Now, if you'll excuse us, we have a tram to catch. We'll have to walk home if we miss the last one. Come on, Alan.'

They moved away, leaving the man staring after them. As soon as they were out of earshot, Alan demanded furiously: 'Why did you have to say that?'

Mary was bewildered. 'Say what?'

'That you're the present Mrs Davies.'

'What's wrong with that? He obviously knew about your divorce or he wouldn't have said he was glad to see you and Gwyneth back together again. Why are you so angry? What have I done?'

'Keep your voice down,' Alan hissed, as they joined the queue for their tram. 'If you hadn't opened your mouth, Bill Jones might not have been certain afterwards that it was really me.'

'What does it matter?' Mary was beginning to cry and people near them were looking. 'It's not important.'

'Oh shut up!' Alan whispered violently.

The tram arrived and they followed the people ahead of them into the downstairs, because it was too cold to sit on the uncovered top deck. Neither of them noticed the man who ran to catch the tram just as it was moving off, and climbed the stairs. Neither were they aware of him slipping quietly through the streets behind them, after they reached their destination. Mary was still tearfully defending herself against Alan's displeasure, while he walked along, hands plunged deep into his overcoat pocket, head sunk into the upturned collar, staring morosely in front of him.

After they had disappeared indoors, the man who was tailing them strolled past, looking for the number of the house.

'Eighteen,' he muttered aloud to himself, then walked to the corner of the road and searched the wall above the Miss Cohens' shop. There was nothing there, so he crossed to the opposite pavement. A conveniently sited street-lamp illuminated the name Springtime Grove.

Mary entered the kitchen ahead of Alan to find Elizabeth and Ben already in possession. She was too absorbed in her own trouble to notice how worn and tired her sister looked. She went into the scullery, filled the kettle from the tap and came back, banging it down on the hob.

'The fire's nearly out,' she said accusingly.

Elizabeth raised her eyebrows. 'Your evening at the pictures doesn't seem to have done you much good. Didn't *The Jazz Singer* come up to expectations?'

'You didn't go then?' Alan enquired, sitting down at the table, while Mary busied herself making a pot of tea. 'Where's Mam? Gone to bed, I suppose.'

'Yes. She went up soon after Richard. She said she was tired.' Elizabeth got up to help Mary fetch the cups and saucers. 'No, we didn't go to see the picture after all. Ben didn't get here until nine.'

Ben said nothing. He was lounging on the horsehair sofa, gazing absently at his hands. Mary was suddenly aware of the atmosphere, and realized that she and Alan had walked into the middle of a row. It made her feel a little better to know that Elizabeth, too, was unhappy. She glared resentfully at Alan as she waited for the kettle to boil; then thought with sudden pleasure of making up the quarrel in bed. That was more than her sister and Ben Sawyer could do.

Alan and Ben discussed the film and the modern technology which made the new 'talkies' possible, but the conversation was desultory. Neither man's heart was really in it. Alan just wanted to be quiet and think.

After all these years, he had begun to feel safe. He had grown lax, failing to keep his eyes open, although it was doubtful if he could have avoided tonight's encounter. What damnable, abominable stroke of luck had brought Bill Jones across the Severn to Bristol? Even then, he might have got away with it in the semi-darkness and the confusion of the cinema crowds, if Mary hadn't opened her stupid mouth. The man was halfway to believing himself mistaken when he had realized she wasn't Gwyneth, and if nothing more had been said, would probably have convinced himself that it was so.

'I'm the present Mrs Davies.' Damn Mary! Why did she never have the sense to keep quiet?

But the damage was done, and he could hardly explain his anger without revealing the truth; that he and Gwyneth had never been divorced; that his marriage to Mary was bigamous. How had he let himself be trapped into this position? Elizabeth, of course! He could have coped with Mary; spun her some yarn which would have kept her his mistress, without taking that final, irrevocable step. Why, in heaven's name, had he not told the truth from the beginning? Said that his wife had left him with a child to look after while she ran off with another man. It would have earned him just as much sympathy from Amy: he had recognized her as a 'soft touch' as soon as he had answered her advertisement. But he had been too proud to admit that he could not hold a woman. He had always been sensitive about his appearance, and Gwyneth's desertion had left him vulnerable and raw. The story that she had died in childbirth had at least left him some tatters of pride.

Even so, no harm would have been done if he had not let his randier instincts get the better of him. He had considered prostitutes, but he had no experience of picking one up, and lacked the nerve when it came to the point. He was afraid of making a fool of himself, so he had turned to Mary. He had known from the first that she liked him, and recognized her as a social misfit like himself. She was unhappy at work: she wanted a man as desperately as he needed a woman, but for different reasons. He should have been warned by her often expressed feelings, her frequently touted desire for marriage and a family. Perhaps even if Elizabeth had not found out about them, he could not have fobbed her off for ever.

His mind was going round in circles and his head was spinning. He did not want to leave Springtime Grove. He was very comfortable with a 'wife' and 'mother-in-law' who thought him nearly perfect. Richard, too, was settled. He did not want to be forced on the run. But then, why should he be? Why should Bill Jones concern himself with Alan's affairs? They had barely known one another, even though they had lived in the same house for a couple of months. Alan's mood lightened. He was being foolish. Bill Jones had probably forgotten all about tonight's incident by now.

He swallowed the rest of his tea and winked across the table at Mary.

'Bed, I think,' he said, holding out his hand.

She rose with alacrity, the sullen expression wiped as if by magic from her face. It restored his vanity to have such power over the happiness of another human being.

He followed her upstairs, whistling under his breath. He had never known what Bill Jones did for a living, because he had never enquired. He had been too preoccupied with the final break-up of his marriage. And for one reason or another, during the two short months they had spent beneath the same roof Alan had never seen Bill Jones in his policeman's uniform.

Left alone in the kitchen, Elizabeth looked at Ben.

'It's late,' he said. 'I must be going.'

He got up from the sofa, but Elizabeth barred his way to the door.

'Before you do, I want to know where I stand,' she said. 'I don't see you for weeks on end, and then, when you do condescend to call, you arrive late and offer no explanation. You kiss me as though I were your mother. I think we've been going out together long enough for me to be told what's happening.'

He sighed and sat down again. 'Yes,' he agreed. 'I suppose you're right. And you'll have to know soon, in any case. I'm going to marry Helen.'

Even in that moment of paralysing shock, a corner of her mind registered his form of words. 'I'm going to marry Helen,' not 'Helen and I are going to be married.' It was so typically Ben.

'You and Helen?' she queried incredulously. 'But . . . you hardly know her.'

He raised his eyes to hers and gave a tight, cruel, little smile. 'She has been my mistress since January.'

'Your mistress? Helen?' Elizabeth realized that she was repeating everything he said and tried to shake herself free of the stupor which seemed to possess her. 'I'm sorry. You must think me very dull, but I just can't seem to take this in.'

He made no reply, but leaned back against the scuffed, black leather of the sofa, his arms spread wide along its low back. After a moment or two, Elizabeth spoke again.

'Does Uncle Joseph know of your intentions?'

'Not yet. We intend waiting until Helen is out of half-mourning, then no one, not even May and Albert Harrison, can accuse her of disrespect to Charlie's memory.'

Elizabeth gave a bark of laughter. 'I wouldn't bet on that,' she said, 'he's only been dead eighteen months. When . . . How did Helen become your mistress?'

'I called on her one Sunday afternoon at the beginning of the year. Quite fortuitously, she was alone in the house. Both the servants were out.'

Elizabeth sat down at the kitchen table. 'Sawyer's luck,' she said. 'Was it . . . Was it always Helen, from the beginning?'

'I'm afraid so. I like you, Elizabeth. But you're not really my sort of woman and you haven't the money.'

'That's honest, at any rate,' she said breathlessly. She was feeling sick and was having trouble controlling the muscles of her mouth.

'You deserved the truth. And you're a woman who can take it.'

'Am I?'

'I've always thought so. There's nothing soft or yielding about you, my dear. You meet life head-on.'

'Tough as old boots, in fact.'

Ben rose to his feet and dropped a kiss on the top of her head.

'Marry Jack Hennessey,' he advised her lightly. 'He's mad about you and just the sort of husband you need. He'd do anything you asked him, and not just within reason, either.'

She barely heard him, she was so wrapped up in her own thoughts.

'All these years we've been going out together, have you just used me? Have I been nothing more than your lifeline to Helen?'

'Not all the time, but mostly. Didn't you guess?'

She steadied her voice. 'I suppose I had an inkling now and then. Subconsciously, I suppose I must have known all along. I just didn't want to believe it, that's all.'

'What I've told you,' he said smoothly, 'is in confidence until Helen and I publicly announce our engagement.'

'Be careful Uncle Joe doesn't cut her off without a shilling.'

Ben laughed. 'That would serve me right, wouldn't it? But you know as well as I do that he won't do that.'

'No. Well!' She got up from the table and faced him. 'The correct sentiment on these occasions, I believe, is to wish you joy. I'm sure you and Helen's money will be very happy together.'

He grinned appreciatively. 'You've a sharp tongue, Lizzie, my dear. Watch you don't cut yourself one of these days. *Au revoir*, then. There's no point in saying goodbye, as we're bound to see one another from time to time. I'm sure you'll be at the wedding, if only to show the world how little you care.'

She smiled through stiff lips. 'You're probably right. Will you see yourself out?'

She heard the slam of the outer door as Ben left, and turned slowly to look at the dirty cups and saucers, the cold teapot, the milk-jug and sugar-bowl as though they were objects from an alien world. Nothing around her seemed to make sense; she could relate to none of it. She was moving and breathing in a vacuum. She felt she ought to cry; the situation demanded it, but no tears would come. She was turned to stone. She stacked the dirty crockery and carried it through to the scullery, where she piled it in the sink. Then she filled the kettle and set it on one of the gas-rings to boil.

'I'm going to marry him, Papa.' Joe had never seen his daughter so determined or less submissive to parental

202

advice. 'Ben and I will get married, with or without your permission. You can't stop us. We're both over twenty-one, and I'm a widow.'

'Now wait a minute, darling.' Ben laid a hand on Helen's wrist and smiled placatingly at Joe. 'We are very much in love, sir, but I wouldn't want to be the cause of a rift between you and Helen. I'm too fond of her, and I respect you too much, for that. We just hope very much that you and Mrs Gordon will give us your blessing.'

Joseph glowered. 'A nice Christmas present, I must say! When you asked us round here for Christmas Eve supper, I little thought what you were planning to surprise us with, my girl!'

But Joe was far from being as displeased as he tried to sound. Ben Sawyer was a bright, ambitious young man. He had proved to be one of the most successful representatives the firm had ever had, because the retailers liked him. He was good-looking, with a commanding presence; and if Joe were to take him into partnership, he would be an asset to the board-room. His background was the only objection: it was as lowly as — well, as Minna's, if Joe were honest. And he had not wanted Helen to commit the same social solecism as he had himself. Those sort of gaffes were easier for a man to live down than a woman. On the other hand, Ben Sawyer had received the benefit of a grammar school education, even if it were only in Eastwood, and the still greater benefit of a mother and aunt who had indulged him to the top of his bent. The result was a cultured, knowledgeable, personable young man who would certainly not disgrace any woman he married. Ben showed, too, a profound respect for Joe, in spite of the fact that he had been keeping company with Eizabeth for years.

And that, of course, was one of the strongest arguments in favour of this marriage. Joe smiled to himself. The strike which Elizabeth had started had forced him into enormous expenditure. The outlay had nearly bankrupted him and, financially, he was only just beginning to recover.

He hated his niece with a cordiality which, he suspected, was only equalled by her feelings for him. And to have blackmailed him about Dora Folmer was despicable! He had lost more nights' sleep over that than about the business, and it had inevitably meant the end of the affair. If Helen and Minna had ever found out . . . his blood ran cold at the thought. At least, he admitted grudgingly, Elizabeth had kept her word to keep silent. But he still felt vindictive enough towards her to relish the prospect of her being hurt. Yes; he would agree to this marriage.

He had no intention, however, of putting Helen's mind at rest too soon. He resented her sudden independence and the fact that she had kept a secret from him for the first time in her life. His little girl was showing alarming signs of maturity. Her defiance in the face of his displeasure was something quite new.

'You and Mama always come here on Christmas Eve, Papa, so don't pretend your visit is something out of the ordinary,' she reproved him now. 'I came out of half-mourning last month and Ben and I didn't want to go on deceiving you any longer than we had to.' She turned to her mother. 'Mama! You're on our side, aren't you?'

'Well . . . really . . . ' Minna began to dither. She found Ben's looks and his marked attentions towards herself quite irresistible. Any objections she might have could only be personal, and she found nothing about him to dislike. In all other respects, she was in a most invidious position.

'Now wait a minute,' Joe said, 'there's no question of taking sides, as you put it. I haven't said definitely yet that I won't give my consent.'

'Oh, Papa, you're an angel! I knew you wouldn't have the heart to refuse.' Helen was out of her chair, bending over her father, covering his face with kisses. 'You must realize how much Ben means to me.'

'Thank you, sir,' Ben was saying, 'we're most deeply grateful.'

'Hold on! Hold on!' Joe extricated himself from Helen's embrace. 'I haven't said "yes", either.'

But, as ever, he found himself outwitted by his daughter's assumption of his benevolence. She always took it for granted that he had the best of intentions, and he never had the courage to disillusion her. He liked the view of himself as seen through her eyes too much to risk spoiling it. No doubt he was just a sentimental old man!

Sentimental and foolish, was Ben's private opinion, as he smilingly produced the square-cut emerald ring, which had cost his aunt every penny of her last hundred pounds. If he had Joseph's money, he would want to know a future son-in-law's reasons for marrying into his family.

'Look, Papa!' Helen extended her hand for Joe to admire the ring. 'Isn't it beautiful?'

She moved to sit beside her father on the sofa, the only person in the room unsurprised by the speed of her victory. But her father had never denied her anything she wanted badly, and she wanted Ben Sawyer as she had never wanted anything before.

Contrary to his boast to Elizabeth, which had been intended merely to wound, Helen had not become Ben's mistress. After that first time, he had not made love to her again. His courtship, though secret, had been a model of propriety.

'We don't want to run any foolish risks,' he had told her. 'Besides, I respect you too much. I just got carried away that day.'

But when he kissed her, when he cuddled and petted her, Helen was left in no doubt that marriage with Ben Sawyer would be as unlike married life with Charlie as she could possibly imagine. The last eleven months had dragged so slowly for her that, on occasions, she had thought she was going out of her mind. She had wanted to tell everyone about herself and Ben, and only the threat of his gravest displeasure had prevented her. She had used more and more sleeping tablets. Now, at last, it was out in the open and they need waste no more time.

'Ben and I are going to be married as soon as possible,' she announced. 'We don't want any fuss. A registry office wedding will do.'

'Oh, no, you don't, Puss!' Here, at least, Joseph could recover some of his lost authority. 'You'll be married properly, in chapel. Are you a Methodist, young man?'

'C of E, sir. But naturally we shall be married wherever you wish.'

Joseph smiled triumphantly at his daughter. 'There you are, poppet! Two against one. You'll do as you're told.'

'Then I'll be married in my dear old Arley Street,' Helen said defiantly, and her father nodded.

Ben said nothing, although the last thing he had planned was to start his married life in Eastwod, the one place above all others he wanted to get away from.

'Where are you going to live?' asked Minna. 'You can't very well remain here. Half this house was paid for by May and Albert Harrison.'

'Heavens! So it was!' Helen sat up straight and looked at Joe. 'What do you suggest, Papa?'

'No reason at all why you shouldn't continue living here, if you want to,' he answered truculently. 'This house is yours. Charlie left everything to you in his will. This place was a gift. May and Albert don't have a leg to stand on if they're foolish enough to try raising objections.'

'They're not going to like it, Joe.' Minna was apprehensive.

'They're not going to like me marrying Ben,

206

anyway,' Helen retorted with spirit. 'They're bound to think it's too soon after Charlie's death. So I might as well be hung for a sheep as a lamb.'

Joseph was not too sure that he approved of this speech; it smacked too much of Elizabeth, instead of his own sweet, docile little girl. But the prospect of May's and Albert's discomfiture outweighed his misgivings, so he patted Helen's arm approvingly.

'That's right, poppet. Stick to your guns.' He looked across at Ben. 'I think it's time you and I had a serious talk, young man. Can we use the dining-room, Helen?'

'Of course. But don't keep Ben away from me too long, please, Papa.' Helen rose with the two men and put her arms around her fiancé's neck, kissing him hungrily, full on the mouth. Minna felt embarrassed and glanced at her husband, but Joe was already on his way to the door.

Helen turned to her mother with a radiant smile.

'Oh, I'm so happy, Mama! You can't imagine!'

CHAPTER SIXTEEN

'Couldn't you do it for us, Miss? Please. Christmas has left us terrible short, and we know you do it for other people. We'll let you 'ave your money back Friday, and we'll pay whatever they pays extra.'

Elizabeth looked at the earnest, pleading face of the woman who lived in one of the tenement flats just off Portland Place, and hesitated, knowing that in that moment of hesitation she was lost. But this whole business of lending money to her clients was getting out of hand, and sooner or later would be bound to reach Albert Harrison's ears. And he would have no compunction in giving her the sack. Since the public announcement of Helen's engagement to Ben, Elizabeth had been careful never to be anywhere near Albert's office when he was at Alma Road, correctly guessing what his feelings towards any member of her family must be. Rumour had it that May and Albert had taken the news very badly, and the fact that Elizabeth herself was an injured party could hardly be expected to temper their judgement. Charlie had been dead for less than two years, and Helen's remarriage must have been a bitter pill for them to swallow.

Elizabeth was desperately trying to preserve an air of calm detachment, and the overwhelming sympathy of her mother and Jack Hennessey, both of whom insisted on treating her as if she were some sort of invalid, was driving her mad. Much easier to cope with was Mary's and Alan's sly enjoyment of the situation; whilst Richard Davies's genuine indifference excited her deepest gratitude. She was glad to escape into her work, and in spite of the dark winter evenings was putting in longer and longer hours.

One of the reasons, however, for her extended working day was the steady increase in her financial activities. The Fairchilds, of course, had not kept quiet, and had advised other neighbours and friends, who found themselves temporarily financially embarrassed, to make the same arrangement with her. The additional repayment of a farthing, halfpenny or penny preserved a measure of self-respect, and Elizabeth discovered that she was able to add several shillings each week to her wages. Her fame was spreading and it was not only her own clients who now approached her. Some people, like the woman who was accosting her this moment in the open street, belonged to other collectors.

Elizabeth realized that her sex had something to do with it. Because she was a woman in what was essentially a man's world, people, particularly other women, felt that she was more approachable; that they could tell her their troubles and that she would be sympathetic. It was not the impression she had set out to create, but it had happened anyway because of people's preconceptions.

Misconceptions too, Elizabeth thought, giving only half her attention to the woman who was pouring out a long rigmarole of woes and difficulties. She was aware that she had hardened since that evening last autumn when Ben had told her that he was going to marry Helen. Common sense told her that she was well rid of him and that her cousin was to be pitied, but it was not easy to convince herself. What she had felt for Ben had not been a superficial emotion. She had loved him, even while recognizing all his faults; his selfishness, his self-centredness, his callous disregard for his mother's and aunt's affection. His treatment of her had altered nothing, and she could only wait for time to heal the wound he had inflicted. Meanwhile, she determined never again to let herself be taken in by any human being; never again to permit herself to fall in love. Most people were concerned only with themselves.

'How much are you asking to borrow, Mrs Brown?' she asked. 'Look, we can't talk here. Tell me where you live exactly. I mean the number of your flat, and I'll call round after work this evening.'

'Thank you, Miss. Thank you.'

The woman's gratitude was touching and caused Elizabeth a momentary pang of conscience, until she remembered that if she did not lend the sixpence or shilling or however much it was that Mrs Brown was short of, Albert Harrison's debt collectors would simply move in and repossess the goods.

She glanced at her wristwatch and realized that it was almost midday. As she was near Springtime Grove she might as well go home for a cup of tea and a sandwich. With luck, Mary and her mother would still be out shopping, and Alan this week was on the eight-to-six shift. That left Richard, who was now fifteen and had left school at the end of the summer term. So far, he had been unable to find employment in spite of trying hard, but the inevitable frustration and boredom in no way impaired his sunny nature. Elizabeth smiled at the prospect of seeing him.

But luck was not with her today. As she opened the glass door, there was no sign of Richard, but she could hear her mother's and sister's voices coming from the front room.

'Who's that?' Amy called. She sounded worried. A moment later Mary appeared in the doorway, her face extremely pale, her eyes dilated with fear. She gave a relieved gasp when she saw her sister.

'Oh, Lizzie! Whatever are you doing home at this time of day? I thought you were Alan.'

'Why? He's on the day shift. What would he be doing home now, I'd like to know? What's wrong? What's going on?' Elizabeth added suspiciously as her mother's face, equally drawn, appeared behind Mary's shoulder. She pushed past them into the cheerless room to find a policeman standing with his back to the empty grate. 'Who are you?' she demanded. 'What do you want?'

'This is Sergeant Banner from Eastwood police station,' Mary informed her sister in a constricted voice. 'He's come to see Alan.'

'What about?'

'My business is with Mr Davies, Miss,' Sergeant Banner answered. 'I understand he's at work at present.'

'Yes. He's a conductor on the trams and 'buses. He'll be out on one of the routes somewhere.' Elizabeth turned to Mary. 'Do you know which one?'

Mary shook her head, and Sergeant Banner continued: 'It doesn't matter. I'll come back this evening. There's a few questions I have to ask him. Half-past six he gets home. Have I got that correctly? Right, then. Meantime, I'd advise you ladies not to try to contact him, or you may find yourselves in trouble. Tamperin' with the course of the law. Is that understood?'

'Wh-what's my husband done?' Mary quavered.

'I didn't say he'd done anything, Mrs Davies. I just want to talk to him, that's all. I'll be off then. And remember what I told you.'

When the sergeant had gone Mary sat down, shaking violently. 'It has something to do with that man,' she said. 'I'm sure of it.'

'What man?' Elizabeth shivered. 'For goodness' sake come into the kitchen, the pair of you, where it's warm.

211

I'll put the kettle on and make some tea and you can tell me all about it.'

Between them, she and Amy supported Mary into the kitchen and settled her in the chair nearest the fire. Elizabeth filled the kettle and set it on the hob to boil.

'Now,' she said, 'what man are you talking about?'

'Someone Alan and I met a couple of months ago, the night we went to see *The Jazz Singer*. His name was Bill Jones and he'd lived in the same house as Alan for a while, in Cardiff. Alan was upset at seeing him.'

Elizabeth thought for a moment, all the old suspicions about her brother-in-law, which had recently lain dormant, suddenly surfacing again.

'Where's Richard?' she asked. 'Is he in the house?'

'He's upstairs,' Amy said, 'lying on his bed reading.'

Elizabeth went to the foot of the stairs and called: 'Richard! Come down please! We want you.'

Richard appeared a few minutes later, his hair tousled, blinking like an owl. 'What's the matter?' he asked. 'Is it dinner-time?'

'Never mind dinner,' Elizabeth said sharply. 'Do you remember someone in Cardiff called Bill Jones?'

He gave her his most engaging smile. 'Lizzie, *bach*, every other person in Wales is called Bill Jones.'

There was no answering smile from Elizabeth. 'Stop playing the Celtic charmer, Richard, I'm not in the mood. This might be serious, so think. Do you recall anyone of that name who lived in the same house as you and your father?'

He saw that she was worried and puckered his brow. 'I can hardly remember,' he protested, 'it's such a long time ago. Let me see now. Whereabouts in Cardiff? We didn't always live in the same place, you know.'

Elizabeth glanced enquiringly at Mary, who shook her head. 'Alan didn't mention the address. I got the impression he wasn't there very long. About two months, I think he said.'

'Oh there! I know where you mean.'

212

Richard tilted his head on one side as if considering his reply, a habit which, when younger, had seemed precociously endearing. As he grew older Elizabeth had continued to find it amusing, until this moment, when it suddenly dawned on her that he was indeed considering his words, and probably always had been. It occurred to her too, in a new light of clarity, that Richard never talked of his early years unless directly questioned, and then only with the greatest circumspection.

'Come on, Richard,' she said. 'You remember this Bill Jones. I can see it in your face. What can you tell us about him?'

'I think he was a policeman,' Richard answered casually. 'I seem to recall seeing him once in his uniform. He's probably been transferred to the Bristol force.'

'Alan didn't say anything about him being a policeman,' Mary objected. 'Are you sure you're right about that, Richie?'

'Almost positive. But it's quite possible that Dada and — that he never saw Mr Jones when he was going on duty. I did, because I played on the stairs.'

'Dada and who?' Elizabeth demanded swiftly. 'What were you going to say then, Richard, when you stopped yourself?'

'Nothing,' he blustered. 'You're mistaken.' It was the first slip he had made in all these years.

'It's all right, Richie.' Mary pushed her hair back from her forehead with a weary gesture. 'I've always known about your parents being divorced.' Suddenly there seemed no point in keeping it a secret any longer.

Amy and Elizabeth looked from her to Richard and back again. Elizabeth, who had been about to make the tea, slowly replaced the kettle on the hob.

'Divorced?' Amy breathed. 'Div . . . Mary, what on earth are you talking about?'

'Alan's first wife isn't dead. She and Alan are

213

divorced. She left him for another man.'

'Richie?' Amy turned, dazed, to the boy for confirmation.

'Mam ran away,' Richard said. 'While we were living in the flat near the docks. Mr Jones had rooms upstairs.'

Elizabeth sat down abruptly. 'Dear heaven!' she said. 'So that's it. What a blind fool I've been.'

'What do you mean?' Mary was indignant. 'There's nothing illegal about being divorced. I knew, though, that was how you and Mama would look at it. I knew how you'd disapprove. That's why I've never told you. But people are getting divorced every day.'

Elizabeth took no notice of her. 'How long was it, Richard, after your mother left that you and your father moved to Bristol?'

'Almost at once. Dada said he wanted a complete change. He was sick of Cardiff.'

'And how long were you here before you answered Mama's advertisement for a lodger?'

'I don't know. Three or four weeks perhaps. We rented a couple of rooms in St Paul's while Dada looked for work. When he was taken on by Bristol Tramways, he said we'd better look for somewhere decent to live. We had one horrible, poky little room near City Road. And he couldn't work and look after me as well, could he?'

Mary was frowning. Elizabeth saw the apprehension in her eyes.

'But Richie, are you sure you've remembered correctly?' Mary asked. 'I mean, if you came to Bristol almost at once, when ... when did Alan get his divorce?'

Richard looked blank. 'I don't know,' he said.

There was a long silence, then Mary gasped and clapped a hand to her mouth.

'I'm going to be sick,' she muttered and rushed into the scullery. Amy followed her, her own face white with consternation.

214

'What's the matter?' Richard asked Elizabeth. 'I don't understand.'

Elizabeth closed her eyes. What an idiot she had been! She, who prided herself on her cleverness, her astuteness, who had suspected Alan Davies of hiding something right from the start, had never thought of the obvious answer. She had thought of bad debts, of theft, even, in her wilder moments, of manslaughter and murder; but never of bigamy. And yet the clues had been there; Alan's initial reluctance to marry her sister, his insistence on the quietest possible wedding. She supposed he must have begun to feel safe after all this time, and then, quite by chance, he had walked into this man Jones. Even so, she imagined it could only have been a temporary alarm or he would have cleared out by now. Alan had not realized that the other man, a policeman, having scented something amiss, had set off, hot on the trail.

Mary returned to the kitchen and sat down again in her chair. She looked haggard.

'I'm not really married, am I?' she asked Elizabeth.

Elizabeth shook her head and Mary burst into tears.

'Will someone please tell me what's going on,' Richard demanded.

'Your parents were never divorced,' Elizabeth said shortly. 'Your father's marriage to Mary is bigamous. The police have found out and are after him.'

'What ... What will they do to him?' Amy whispered, appearing at the scullery door.

'Send him to prison if they catch him. Someone has to warn him. He might still be able to get away.'

'Lizzie.' Amy stretched out her hand anxiously. 'You know Sergeant Banner said we weren't to contact Alan. We'll be breaking the law if we try to help him.'

Mary groaned, rocking back and forth in her chair. 'I don't want him to go to prison.'

Richard was looking frightened and Elizabeth patted his shoulder. 'Don't worry, my dear,' she said. 'Your home's with us, whatever happens. Mama, do you want Mary's name in the papers and her peace of mind destroyed even more than it is at present? No? Then someone has to risk something to make sure that Alan gets safely away. Mary, for goodness' sake pull yourself together. Now, do you and Alan have any savings? You do? Good. Go and fetch them. Richard, as soon as you've had something to eat, see if you can locate Jack Hennessey. He should be in the vicinity of Guelph Street early this afternoon. Tell him what's happened and get him to cover for me if anyone should happen to ask where I am.' Mary came downstairs, carrying the tin box which Alan kept in the bottom of the wardrobe. Elizabeth opened it and looked inside. After a few minutes she said: 'There's over a hundred pounds here.' Her lips compressed before she added: 'I always told you he was no good, Mama. He's kept you short while he's been feathering his own little nest.' She extracted half the money and handed it back to Mary. 'I think he owes you that,' she said grimly. 'For heaven's sake, take it! We're relieving him of the support of his son.'

Hesitantly, Mary pocketed the wad of pound notes. Her eyes were red-rimmed; her face swollen with crying.

'You will be able to find him, Lizzie? See that he gets away? Oh, God! Perhaps we're wrong. Perhaps we're jumping to conclusions. Perhaps we should wait until Alan comes homes and ask him.'

Elizabeth put on her hat and coat and picked up her handbag. 'If we wait until he comes home, it'll be too late. The police will be here ahead of him. I'll ask him, all right, but don't entertain any false hopes. You both know as well as I do that we're right. Now, don't forget, if Sergeant Banner or any other policeman should return unexpectedly, I'm out on my rounds and you don't know when I'll be back.'

*   *   *

'You're crazy!' Jack fumed. 'You took a damnably stupid risk! You're an accessory after the fact. You could go to prison.'

Elizabeth stretched her hands towards the fire. 'Don't start on me, Jack,' she warned him quietly. 'I'm tired. I've had an exhausting day.'

It was ten minutes since Sergeant Banner had left, angry and thwarted. Schooled rigidly in their parts by Elizabeth, Amy and Mary had managed, if not to be convincing, at least to stick to their story knowing that Elizabeth's continued freedom depended on their performance. They had maintained ignorance of anything Alan might have done wrong, and exhibited surprise at his non-appearance. Eventually, at nine o'clock, after a wait of three hours, the sergeant had showed his hand, admitted that Alan was wanted for bigamy and openly accused them of helping him to evade the law. He had added, portentously, that he would be making further enquiries, and had gone, heavy-footed, away. Jack, who had seen the policeman's arrival and been watching ever since for his departure, had at once come in from next door. Amy and Mary had already gone up to bed, but were apparently not asleep, because Jack could still hear them talking in Mary's room overhead.

'What did you tell the sergeant you were doing this afternoon?' he demanded.

Elizabeth blinked. 'I told him I was working, of course. What else should I have told him?'

'He could ask around, Lizzie. Make enquiries of your customers. You do realize that? Did he ask who you'd visited?'

'No. I don't think he's entirely convinced yet that Alan has really skedaddled. He could be in some pub, drinking with his mates. That, I think, is at the back of Sergeant Banner's mind. He'll be here again tomorrow.' She got up and walked through to the parlour. When she came back, she said as she resumed

217

her seat: 'I thought as much. There's a constable over the road watching the house. Anyway, Jack, I'm relying on you to give me an alibi, if the sergeant should get suspicious.'

Jack groaned resignedly. 'I thought you might be. Tell me what it is I'm to say.'

'If you're asked — and only if you're asked — you met me this afternoon about three o'clock, near Arley Street.'

'Three o'clock, near Arley Street. All right. What time did you really get back?'

'Half-past four. I rushed around then and called on as many customers as possible. With luck, they won't remember exactly when. Half of them don't have clocks or watches anyway.'

'You did see Alan, I presume. How long did you have to wait?'

'About an hour, I think. I got to St Augustine's Parade at two. I had to wait ages for a tram. Then, when I arrived, Alan was out on a run. He returned to check in his money at three. I caught him then.'

'What did he say? Did he deny it?'

'There wasn't any point, once I'd told him the police were after him. All he could think of was saving his skin. Richard was right. Alan hadn't realized that the man Jones was a policeman. I suppose Jones must have been pursuing his enquiries — the right phrase, I believe — ever since that night he met Alan and Mary in Old Market Street. No; Alan just cursed all policemen and their nasty, suspicious minds, took the fifty pounds and left without a word to anyone. I imagine the Tramways Company is still wondering where he's gone.'

'And where has he gone? Do you have any idea?'

'None at all. He didn't say and I didn't ask. I told him we'd look after Richard. I just want him out of Mary's life for good.'

'Is it for "good", Lizzie?'

'What do you mean? Alan won't dare show his face round here again in a hurry. If he has any sense at all, he'll buy himself a new suit and get rid of that 'busman's uniform as soon as possible. Then he'll get the first train out of Temple Meads for Scotland or Cornwall.'

'I mean are you sure you know what's good for Mary's happiness? It seems to me that she'd be happier with Alan, whatever his circumstances, even living as his — ' Jack blushed slightly ' — as his mistress, than left on her own again, as she's always been.'

Elizabeth stared at him, not knowing whether to laugh or be blazingly angry.

'Well, really!' she exclaimed at length. 'I've underestimated you, Jack. I never realized that you were such a free-thinking person. Talk about still waters — ! Anyway, how can you suggest such a thing? You saw what the news has done to Mary. How ill she looks.'

'What Mary's going through now is the natural reaction of anyone who finds out something unpleasant about someone they love. But that doesn't mean to say that the discovery makes them stop loving that person.'

'Oh, for heaven's sake, Jack!' Elizabeth leaned forward again to poke the dying fire. 'Alan has duped Mary; made a fool of her, and would have gone off leaving her without a single penny if he'd managed to get wind of the police enquiries before the rest of us. That was the only thing he showed any emotion about this afternoon; not about leaving Mary; not about leaving Richard; but about the fact that I'd confiscated half his precious savings. I think he'd have hit me if other people hadn't been around.'

Jack sighed. 'You may be right. But Mary's going to be very lonely.'

'She has Richard. He's the one good thing to come out of this unsavoury episode.'

'Does she have him? Once he manages to get a job he'll be more or less independent. Besides, I've always had the impression that he prefers your company.'

'Nonsense!' But Elizabeth, Jack noticed, could not help looking pleased as she said it.

'Lizzie.' Jack knelt by her chair and took her hands in his. 'When are you going to stop shouldering your family's burdens? You can't go on protecting them, and running their lives for them, for ever. And now you've taken on Richard Davies as well. You'll soon be arranging *his* life for him, if he'll let you.'

She laughed uncertainly, her eyes searching his face. 'Is that what you think of me? A dragon? A horrid, bossy female? And I always thought you were fond of me, Jack.'

He tightened his grip on her hands. 'I am fond of you. You know that, but I don't know if you realize how much.' He felt her try to pull away from him, but held her fast. 'No you don't, Lizzie. For once you're going to listen to me. I love you. I always have. I want you to be my wife.'

Her smile grew even more uncertain, and she tried feebly to make his words into a joke.

'Jack, dear, this is so sudden.'

'I'm serious, Lizzie. Do me the courtesy of being serious too. Will you marry me?'

'Jack . . . I'm sorry . . . I honestly don't know what else to say.'

'The answer's no, then?'

'I'm afraid so . . . Oh, Jack, can't you see — ? I've never thought of you that way. You're more like . . . well, like my brother. Oh, God! I really am terribly sorry.' Tears welled up in her eyes. She released her hands and brushed the tears away with a little laugh. 'Now look what you've made me do. I never cry.' She put her arms round him, laying her damp cheek against his. 'What a ghastly day this has been. A ghastly year, if it comes to that. I just hope nineteen twenty-eight will be better.'

220

CHAPTER SEVENTEEN

Helen and Ben were married in Arley Street chapel one Saturday afternoon at the beginning of January. Of the Springtime Grove family, only Elizabeth attended. Amy and Mary refused, point-blank, to go.

'People are talking about us,' Amy said. 'I can't bear it.'

'People will only talk about you if you give them cause,' Elizabeth retorted. 'All right, you can't prevent people knowing that Alan has gone, and there are enough gossips in this part of Eastwood for some of them to know the truth. But most people don't know; and if they do, they don't care. It's happened to other women. Mary isn't the first or the last to be taken in by a plausible rogue.'

'It's all very well for you to talk,' Mary complained huddled over the kitchen fire. 'It didn't happen to you. You aren't the one who's been made a fool of.'

'Oh?' Elizabeth swung round on her sister, her face sharp with anger. 'And what do you think this wedding is making of me? I've been made to look a fool by a man just as much as you have. But I'm not going to sit down and whine and refuse to go out. I'm going to hold my head up and show everyone that I don't care a fig for Ben Sawyer.'

Amy glanced apologetically at her younger daughter before turning to Mary.

'Lizzie's right, you know. We can't stay indoors for ever. Perhaps we ought to go. Show people we've got our pride.'

But Mary proved obstinate. 'No, I can't,' she whispered. 'Not yet. Don't make me.'

'I'm sorry, Lizzie.' Amy suddenly felt guilty about Elizabeth. It was so easy to forget that she too had troubles, so little did she thrust them on other people's notice.

So Elizabeth went alone and sat defiantly in one of the front pews, delighted to notice how disconcerted Ben was when he first caught sight of her. She looked around her at the congregation.

There were a lot of people from the factory, who had been given time off to attend the wedding, but very few of Joseph's friends. And apart from Joseph himself, who gave Helen away, she and Minna seemed to be the only relations of the bride. The groom's side of the chapel fared little better, Ben's mother and aunt being all his family; and again the majority of guests were from the offices of Gordon's factory. Albert and May Harrison were nowhere to be seen.

The reception, Elizabeth was amused to discover, was again held in the William Penn suite of the Eastwood Park Hotel. This time, however, she was not in the receiving line.

The harried-looking receptionist at the door announced: 'Miss Elizabeth Evans,' in his nasal, rather complaining voice, and a moment later, Elizabeth was kissing her cousin and shaking hands with Ben.

'Lizzie, darling, I'm so pleased you could come.' Helen hung on to her hand, desperately seeking for reassurance that she had not hurt her cousin in any lasting way; that Ben was right when he told her that he and Elizabeth had long been no more than friends.

Elizabeth wanted to say something wounding; something that would spoil Helen's day; mar her happiness by making her realize how she had ruined

Elizabeth's own. But she could not bring herself to do it. It was not Helen's fault that she believed everything she was told by Ben. And that, of course, was the chief weapon in her cousin's defensive armoury: Helen was never really to blame.

Towards Ben, Elizabeth felt no such compunction. She held out her hand and said loudly: 'Not a partner in the firm yet, I hear. You should have made that a condition of the marriage.'

He crushed her hand in his as though he would like to break every bone in her fingers.

Elizabeth moved along the line, dutifully kissing Minna's cheek and smiling at Joseph.

'Uncle Joe,' she murmured, 'how thoughtful of you and Aunt Minna to invite me. Let me congratulate you on your new son-in-law. And let me add that you and he really deserve one another.'

Out of the corner of her eye, she saw Ben, who was greeting the guest behind her, flush scarlet. She kissed his mother and aunt, and for the first time felt a surge of emotion. Mrs Sawyer hugged her and whispered: 'We hoped it was going to be you.'

Elizabeth's smile became more brittle. 'Oh, no,' she said gently. 'Ben was never in love with me. And you'll be devoted to Helen, once you get to know her.'

If Ben ever lets them know her, she thought, as she entered the dining-room and was ushered to her seat at one of the lower tables. Now that Ben had Helen's money, he would have no further use for his mother and aunt. The expression on Mrs Sawyer's face convinced Elizabeth that the older woman had already worked that out for herself.

The places around her gradually filled up, but she knew no one intimately enough to start a conversation. She recognized Miss Ronson, wearing a most unsuitable butter-cup-yellow hat, but they were separated by several tables and could only wave. Elizabeth wondered if Miss Ronson were still looking after that old mother of hers, and reflected that society — male society — expected too much of women; mother, nurse, concubine. How could any one person have so diffuse a personality? She would like to find something to do which would shock all these smug men. She would like to take them on at their own game of making money and show them what a woman could do.

'Are you happy?' Helen asked shyly. 'Are you really, truly happy?' She put her hands on Ben's shoulders, drew down his head and kissed him.

Ben smiled. Through the closed hotel windows came the muffled sounds of traffic from The Strand. London had seemed to him the obvious choice for a winter honeymoon, although Helen had wanted to go to Paris. Ben, however, who had never yet been abroad, had no wish to find himself, this early in his marriage, at a disadvantage. He had been to London on various occasions and knew his way around. But tonight he had ordered dinner in their sitting-room. Tonight they would not be going out.

'Very happy,' he answered truthfully.

He unclasped her hands and wandered from the bedroom into the sitting-room. He had never had a suite before, nor stayed in so luxurious a hotel. He had always afforded the best he could, but that had been, of necessity, limited. These high-ceilinged, spacious rooms were what he had always dreamed about. He would not find it difficult to get used to the power and prestige of money.

Helen followed him and sat down on the cretonne-covered sofa. Her heavy velvet coat with its fox-fur trimming was flung over the arm of a chair, and her pale blue hat, with its winking diamond buckle, lay discarded on the seat of another. She was still wearing the powder-blue, fine wool dress in which she had been married. For some reason, this irritated Ben.

'I do think you might have changed to come away, darling,' he chided, sitting down beside her. 'It looked so penny-pinching not to have a different dress.'

Helen was surprised. 'But I thought you'd be pleased, sweetheart. Charlie always was when I saved him money. After all, it isn't as though I was married in white.'

Ben's smile vanished and he said angrily: 'I don't want to hear about you and Charlie Harrison. Don't ever mention him again. I'm your husband now. You're Mrs Ben Sawyer.'

'Darling, darling, I'm sorry.' Helen threw herself into his arms. She had never realized before how jealous Ben was of her, how possessive; but the knowledge gave her a nervous thrill. 'I'll try, honestly, not to mention Ch — him again.' Common sense told her how difficult that would be, but for the moment she did not care.

Ben was as astonished at his reaction as Helen. Had he been given to much self-analysis, he would have said that he had married Helen for her money, and for no other reason. She was an extremely pretty woman; soft, malleable and seductively feminine. But had she possessed only those attributes he would not have chosen her in preference to her cousin. It was her wealth, her even richer prospects when she finally inherited Gordon's, that had formed the major part of her attraction for him. Now, out of the blue, he found himself playing the jealous husband; found himself actually resenting poor, ineffectual Charlie Harrison, to whom Helen had never been a proper wife. She had been a virgin when he had first made love to her a year ago, and he had been the only man in her life ever since.

Or had he? He was well aware that Helen had a passionate and sensual nature, which, once aroused, would not be easily satisfied. Perhaps he had been foolish not to let her become his mistress during the past twelve months, but he had been afraid of discovery

225

by Joseph. It had been absolutely necessary to his plan that his future father-in-law should not be antagonized in any way. Charlie had left Helen comfortably off, but Joseph was the real source of her wealth. So Ben had held her at arm's length. But had she found comfort elsewhere?

Ben got up and went into the bathroom, closing the door behind him. He clung to the edge of the wash-basin, staring at his reflection in the mirror. What in God's name had come over him? This jealousy was totally unreasonable. It was like a sudden sickness which had mown him down. Even its symptons were physical. His heart was beating at a furious rate, his knees were shaking and his skin was clammy to the touch.

He took off his coat, ran the tap and washed his hands and face. The shock of the cold water seemed to bring him to his senses. He dried himself slowly on one of the hotel's thick white towels, and once again took stock of himself in the mirror.

He must be in love with Helen, there was no other satisfactory explanation. Over this past year he had been growing steadily more attracted to her without realizing what was happening, and now he could not bear to think of her with any other man. And there was no need to: he knew that perfectly well, now that the mad sickness of jealousy had left him and his judgement was no longer clouded.

Ben returned to the sitting-room, where he found that dinner had arrived. Two trolleys laden with food, shining napery and glass, gleaming silverware and plates, stood in front of the fire. The waiter was uncorking the wine. Ben tasted it, pronounced it drinkable and waited impatiently while the young Italian assured himself that all was in order. Finally, having poured two glasses of wine, he withdrew. Ben flung himself down beside Helen.

'Darling, I'm sorry. I was being stupid. Of course you

must mention Charlie whenever you like. Am I forgiven?'

'There's nothing to forgive,' she protested breathlessly, returning his kisses. 'Couldn't we leave dinner until later? Let's go straight to bed.'

On the third of September, 1930, Elizabeth was twenty-eight years old.

As she dressed that morning a sense of desperation crept over her. Amy Johnson had flown to Australia; Greta Garbo had talked in *Anna Christie*; Prunella Stack had formed the Women's League of Health and Beauty. But she, Elizabeth Anne Evans, had done nothing with her life, and seemed condemned to the same old dreary treadmill. Nothing ever happened, except Jack asking her to marry him at regular intervals. She still worked for Harrison's, but she was not the only woman collector any more. In spite of the fact that skirts, after the 'flapper' year, were getting longer and longer, women had gained a little emancipation. Everyone over twenty-one now had the vote, women doctors were becoming more prevalent and there was even talk of women lawyers, although the legal profession was resisting the notion with all its might.

Elizabeth went downstairs to breakfast, where the expected cards and presents were stacked by her plate; a scarf from Amy, a pair of silk stockings from Mary and a Woolworth's 'diamond' brooch from Richard. Jack would bring flowers, as always, later in the day.

'Happy birthday,' Richard said, looking up from his bacon sandwich and grinning.

Although unemployment was still rising, higher even than it had been in the twenties, he had managed to get a job as a porter on the railway. He was eighteen now, tall, fair-haired, blue-eyed, with the sort of looks that turned women's heads both literally and metaphorically. Elizabeth accused him of being conceited, but he only laughed and flitted from one girl to another as often, seemingly, as he changed his shirts.

'I can't help it if women find me attractive,' he protested, 'and with so many after me, it's difficult to choose.'

Mary was also up, having returned, a year ago, to work in her uncle's factory. She seemed to have got over Alan; she rarely mentiond him nowadays, although she still called herself Mrs Davies. She looked older than her thirty years, largely because her hair was turning prematurely white, but her skin had lost its unhealthy pallor and had the bloom imparted by fresh air and regular exercise.

She nodded as Elizabeth sat down and said: 'Many happy returns of the day.'

Amy came through from the scullery with the teapot in her hand. She had a new gas-stove, which Mary and Elizabeth had insisted on buying for her, and no longer used the hob over the fire for boiling water.

'Happy birthday, Lizzie dear.' She kissed her younger daughter, adding: 'Hurry up and open your cards.'

'I'm just going to, but I had to look at my presents first. It's a lovely scarf, Mama, thank you. Just the shade of red I wanted to go with my winter coat.' Elizabeth draped the scarf around her neck as she spoke, and began opening the envelopes.

The cards were fairly predictable; roses from her mother, bluebirds from Mary, a garden scene from Jack and an old Christmas card, with robins and snow, from Richard, who had as usual forgotten to buy a proper one. At the bottom of the little pile was a long, white envelope with the typed inscription: Miss E. Evans, 18 Springtime Grove, Eastwood, Bristol.

Elizabeth stared at it. 'Whatever's this?' she asked, turning the letter over in her hands.

Amy shook her head. 'Isn't it another card? Open it and see.'

228

In some trepidation, Elizabeth slit the top of the envelope with her knife and drew out the contents. The letter-heading on the sheet of white notepaper was the name and address of a firm of city solicitors.

'Well?' Amy demanded impatiently, after Elizabeth had sat in a dazed silence for several minutes.

'It's the Miss Turners,' Elizabeth said at last. 'Miss Josephine, the younger, died last month, two years after her sister. She's left me The Brass Mill.'

There was silence. Then Richard said in an awed voice: 'You mean you own a house?'

Elizabeth nodded. 'Apparently all the contents are to be auctioned and the proceeds given to Muller's Orphanage. The house itself is left to me.'

'But . . . What on earth will you do with it, Lizzie?' Amy managed to ask.

'I don't know. For heaven's sake, Mama, give me time to think. I haven't really taken it in.'

But she had. Underneath the shock and confusion, Elizabeth's mind was racing, making plans. She would have to get rid of the house, of course, much as she craved to live there. She must be practical. She could neither afford to furnish nor to maintain The Brass Mill, and its sale would provide her with capital. She wondered how much it would fetch. Her father had always said that it was structurally sound. How long, she wondered, would it take to sell? Whom should she approach? She glanced once more at the letter. She would have to see the solicitors. Perhaps they would act for her as well.

'Shall we all go and live there?' Richard wanted to know. 'Incidentally, if you're too excited to eat that bacon sandwich, don't let it go to waste.' His appetite was as voracious as ever, although he never seemed to gain an ounce in weight.

'Of course we shan't,' Mary answered pettishly. 'It's Lizzie's house, not ours. It's nothing to do with us.'

'You'd all be more than welcome to live there if I

229

intended keeping it,' Elizabeth assured her sister. She began gathering up her presents and cards. 'But I'm going to sell it. All the same, I'd like to see it once again before I get rid of it. I'll make arrangements with the solicitors to go one Sunday. And if you're not on duty that day, Richard, my lad, and if you're very good in the meantime, I might even let you come with me.'

She blew him a kiss as she vanished through the kitchen door.

'So this is the famous Brass Mill,' Jack said, looking around at the stained and faded wallpapers and the bare floorboards. He sounded disappointed. 'I always thought it was more palatial.'

Elizabeth laughed. 'I suppose it always seemed so to me. I never said it was Buckingham Palace.'

'You used to go on about it quite a bit when you were young. Good heavens! What's that?'

They had entered through a side door, but had now reached the entrance hall with its oak panelling, marble fireplace and the alcove with its naked statue.

'They haven't sold that, then,' Elizabeth said, intrigued. She walked round it. 'I see. It looks as if the plinth is bolted to the floor. It must be part of the integral furnishings.'

Richard, who had managed to change his Sunday shift with a friend at Temple Meads station, at that moment wandered in to join them.

'Couldn't you keep it, Lizzie?' he enquired wistfully. 'It's such a lovely old house.'

Elizabeth shook her head. 'I only wish I could, but I need the money. But one day, if I make my fortune, I promise we'll all come here to live. Whoever the owner is then, I'll make him an offer he can't refuse.'

'You're mad,' Jack said. He was beginning to realize that the house was bigger than he had first thought. 'Who'd want a rambling old barn of a place like this? It would cost the earth to keep warm.' He wandered over to a window and pulled back the half-closed shutters. Outside, the sun tipped the beech and birch trees with gold and shimmered in a soft haze across the surface of a little pond. Further off he could see the blue-shadowed gorge, and above it the wide sweep of the Downs. 'You'd be better off with a nice semi-detached at Southmead or Henbury.'

Richard stared at Elizabeth in horror. 'That's not what you're going to do with the money, is it, Lizzie?'

'No, of course not,' she answered irritably, and Richard, satisfied, went off to explore further on his own.

Jack asked: 'What *do* you intend doing with the money you get for this place? And how much do you think you'll get, anyway?'

'I'm not sure,' Elizabeth said, answering his second question first. 'The solicitors are putting me in touch with an estate agent. But the senior partner did say he thought I ought to get two thousand pounds. Perhaps more.'

Jack pursed his lips in a soundless whistle. Two thousand pounds was a great deal of money. He had a sudden vision of Elizabeth moving away from Eastwood, beyond his reach. It frightened him.

'What are you going to do with it?' he repeated.

Elizabeth crossed to the window and sat on the dusty window-seat. Gently she pulled Jack down beside her.

'I'm going into business, Jack, and I want you to come in with me; because I don't want to go on working for someone else for ever.'

'You don't have to,' he replied eagerly. 'If only you'd marry me . . . '

'Not another proposal, Jack, please!' She sounded angrier than she meant to, and saw the hurt expression on his face. She said swiftly: 'I'm sorry. I didn't mean to be so abrupt, but I've said "no" so many times. I mean it, Jack. Believe me. But I do want you as my business partner, because what I have in mind won't be regarded as respectable for a woman.' He looked resigned and she laughed. 'I want to go into the money-lending business.'

He gasped. Whatever he had expected, it had not been this. When he found his voice, he said: 'You're out of your mind! Not respectable for a woman? It's just plain not respectable, full stop.'

'Oh, don't start getting pious, Jack, for goodness' sake. There are perfectly respectable financial loan companies in the country, but there aren't many in Bristol. For one thing, there aren't many Jews.'

This Jack knew to be true enough. For the eighth largest city in the kingdom, Bristol had a surprisingly small Jewish community. It had Jewish families, certainly, and there was a synagogue in Park Row, but for various historical reasons Jews had never settled in any numbers in the city. All the same, money-lending was considered unchristian.

'Why?' Elizabeth demanded when Jack pointed this out to her. 'Because some Pope once issued a decree to that effect? And he probably only did it because he wanted to corner the market himself. Great heavens, we haven't been a Catholic country for centuries. It's not illegal to be a Christian money-lender, Jack. It's just unusual. Anyway, I prefer to call it a financial consultant.'

'That proves my point,' Jack said triumphantly, 'if you have to start calling it by fancy names.'

Elizabeth removed her hat as though its constriction was suddenly more than she could bear.

'There's a real need for some kind of money-lending business in Eastwood,' she argued. 'At the moment, people like Albert Harrison have it all their own way. There are good and bad in all types of business, Jack. Not everyone who lends money demands a pound of flesh.' She stood up. 'Are you coming in with me or not?'

He looked at her pleadingly. 'Tell me you're pulling my leg.'

She almost stamped her foot. 'I'm quite serious. I'm going to start the business whether you come in with me or not. Only I'd rather have you with me than against me. There will be plenty of the latter. So what do you say?'

Jack closed his eyes and leaned the back of his head against the window-frame.

'I say Ben Sawyer has a lot to answer for. You've turned into a hard woman, Lizzie Evans.'

Part Four 1931-1935

Keep thy shop and thy shop will keep thee.
Light gains make heavy purses.

George Chapman 1559 – 1634

CHAPTER EIGHTEEN

Helen came out of the Regent Cinema in Castle Street, blinking in the August sunshine. She had not really enjoyed the film, *Tons of Money*, starring Tom Walls and Ralph Lynn, partly because British films seemed amateurish when compared with their American counterparts, and partly because she was not in the mood for farce. She had spent the morning shopping, had lunched at Lyon's in Wine Street, and then wondering what to do with herself for the afternoon, had decided, almost on impulse, to go to the pictures.

Sitting in the cosy darkness, watching the silly antics on the flickering screen, she had twice fallen asleep, recalled uncomfortably to her surroundings by the sudden forward jerk of her head. She had taken an extra sleeping pill last night and it must still be affecting her. She felt stupid, bored and desperately unhappy.

Standing on the pavement outside the cinema, Helen glanced at her watch. There was another hour before she need think of going home. She had not driven herself today, and had arranged with the chauffeur to pick her up on the corner of Clare Street at half-past four. She wondered vaguely what she should do until then.

A man's voice said: 'It's Mrs Sawyer, isn't it? I recognize you from the wedding photograph Mrs

237

Evans keeps on her mantelpiece. Are you all right? You're looking rather pale.'

Helen turned, but she did not recognize the tall young man regarding her so solicitously. He was, she judged, about nineteen or twenty, cheaply, but smartly, dressed and very good-looking. Except that he was fair, he reminded her of Ben as she had first seen him, that long-ago day at Weston. This young man had the identical, almost flashy appearance; the jaunty, debonair manner which today owed more to Hollywood film-stars than to the stage-door Johnnies of Ben's extreme youth, but whose influence was much the same.

Helen tried to smile, conscious, woman-like, that she must look a mess in her crumpled summer frock and, also, that she was twenty-eight years old.

'I'm sorry,' she said, 'but I don't remember your name.'

'Not surprising, as we've never met.' He held out his hand. 'I'm Richard Davies, Mary's step-son.'

'Oh. Oh, yes, of course.' Helen took his hand, her gentle, compassionate nature intent on maintaining the polite fiction. 'You're her husband's son by his first marriage.'

'That's right. Although Mary and I don't live together any more since she left Springtime Grove.' He smiled. 'Excuse me for saying so, but you really don't look well. I expect it's the heat. Look, let's go to the café over the road and have a cup of tea.'

'Yes. Thank you, that would be nice.'

In a kind of trance, she let him pilot her across the street and into the café, where he took charge with a confidence and maturity which reminded her even more of Ben. Richard ordered tea and toast and fancy cakes from the becapped and aproned waitress, and relieved Helen of her hat and gloves, which he stowed on the shelf provided, beneath the table-top.

'There,' he said, 'that's better.'

'You're a very competent young man,' Helen remarked, taking a gold cigarette-case and monogrammed lighter from her expensive leather handbag. 'But I really don't want any food.'

'Maybe not,' he answered, and the smile became a grin, 'but I do. Lizzie says I'm greedy, and she's probably right.' He was aware, as soon as he mentioned Elizabeth's name, of the embarrassment on Helen's face. 'Don't you approve of her either?' he demanded. 'Mary's moved out altogether and taken furnished rooms near Eastwood Park. She said she wouldn't stay under the same roof as Lizzie. None of the neighbours speak to her, nor to Jack Hennessey any more.'

Helen tapped the end of her unlit cigarette on the tablecloth.

'How could she?' she asked in a low voice. 'How could Lizzie have gone in for . . . for . . . you know what?'

'Money-lending, do you mean? Why not?' He regarded her cheerfully. 'The Evans and Hennessey Financial Loan Company. What's wrong with that?'

Helen flushed. 'I should think it's obvious what's wrong with it. Living off other people's misfortunes. It's a terrible way to earn a living.'

'Is it?' The waitress arrived with the tea-things, and for a few moments, Richard could say no more. When the woman had gone, however, he went on: 'I'd say it was poverty and low wages which ought to be condemned, not Lizzie and Jack. There are a lot of people in Eastwood thankful to avail themselves of their services . . . Would you like to pour?'

Helen dropped the unsmoked cigarette and lighter back into her bag and picked up the teapot.

'Milk? Sugar?' she enquired with automatic politeness, but her thoughts were still running on her cousin. 'Apart from anything else, it's a most unsuitable job for a woman.'

Richard helped himself to three of the genteel fingers

of hot buttered toast, piled them one on top of the other and bit, the melting fat oozing down over his chin. He was still smiling, but there was a hostile glint in his eyes which Helen was not slow to observe.

'Well, I daresay,' he said, as soon as he could speak, 'that if her boyfriend hadn't been pinched by another woman, she'd have been married and settled down by now. Then you, and all the rest of her family, wouldn't be in a position to be ashamed.'

Helen's hand shook and she almost dropped her cup. A tide of red suffused her face and she blinked back the tears.

'How dare you?' she murmured angrily. She replaced her cup on its saucer and began hunting in her handbag. 'Ben didn't love Elizabeth. He loved me. You can't force people into marriage. That would be stupid. You can't blame me because Lizzie's done something everyone disapproves of. That's like saying you can't help being a thief or a murderer.' She found her handkerchief and defiantly blew her nose.

Richard nodded contritely. 'That's fair,' he conceded. 'I'm sorry. It's just that I get so angry over everyone's self-righteousness. All right, I admit I don't much like the business your cousin's chosen, but she's good at it. And what's the difference between making money out of lending other people money, and selling them over-priced chocolates made by underpaid workers? Or taking their money for shoddily-made goods which you're going to repossess as soon as they can't meet the payments?'

Helen stirred her tea resentfully, blocking all his attempts to ply her with food. 'Now you're getting at my father and Albert Harrison, I suppose.'

'Not them particularly.' Richard finished the toast and started on the plate of fancy cakes. 'What I'm saying is that most businesses have a disreputable side if you insist on looking for it. It just depends on your point of view. But we've created a society in which we

240

can't do without it, so we have to accept its faults as well as its virtues; its disadvantages as well as its advantages. You could, of course, put that the other way around. I'm just saying that one business is as good, or as bad, as another.'

'You seem to be "just saying" a good deal,' Helen retorted crossly. 'You're the greediest, most self-opinionated boy I've ever met.'

'I'm not a boy,' he answered, no longer smiling. 'I'm nineteen. Old enough to have fought and died for my country during the war. So don't patronize me, Mrs Sawyer.'

Helen felt under the table for her hat and gloves. 'I'm going,' she said. 'I don't have to sit here and be lectured by you.'

Richard carefully chose a third cake from the rapidly diminishing selection. 'That would be cowardly,' he accused her. 'It would be cowardly to run away. You know, you'd feel better tempered if you ate something. Food's a wonderful panacea. Let me order some more tea and toast. My treat, of course. You needn't be afraid that I shall expect you to pay the bill.'

In spite of her annoyance, Helen was betrayed into a smile. 'You really are the most insufferable person I've ever met! All right. I'll have some toast while you finish off the cakes, as that seems to be your intention. If you eat like this all the time, I can't imagine why you're not as fat as Billy Bunter.' She raised a hand and signalled to the waitress. 'Why aren't you at work?'

'I'm on the railways. Shift work.' His natural flow of conversation was impeded for the moment by sponge and fondant icing. By the time Helen had ordered the toast, he had managed to empty his mouth. 'Why are you on your own? Don't you have any friends to go with you to the pictures?'

'My husband doesn't care for me having friends,' she answered with some constraint.

'I meant women friends.'

241

'Of either sex. He's . . . he's a very jealous man.'

'He never used to be when he was going out with Lizzie.' Richard regarded her speculatively. 'You're not going to tell Ben about having tea with me, then?'

Helen glanced down at her plate. 'No. No, I don't expect so.'

'You'd like to meet me again for all that, wouldn't you?' He grinned at her impudently, but made no move to touch her, which he might well have done, considering the smallness of the table and their inevitable proximity.

'Why should you think that?' Helen tried to sound indignant, but spoilt her effect by adding: 'I'm much too old for you anyway.' When he made no reply, neither confirming nor denying her statement by so much as the lift of an eyebrow, she changed the subject by asking abruptly: 'Do you like working on the railways?'

'No, I hate it. I'd like to be an actor. I'd like to go to Hollywood and make my name.' She laughed and he frowned. 'You think I'm being childish, don't you? You think it's a silly dream. But it's neither so silly nor so impossible as you imagine. All sorts of people are being taken on by the film companies and turned into stars. Not in this country, I agree, where we're still obsessed by trained stage actors; but in Hollywood, discoveries don't necessarily have to be able to act, as long as they're photogenic. And I'm photogenic.'

He was, too: she had to admit it. 'How do you know all this?' she enquired.

'I read the film magazines. But you haven't answered my question. Would you like to meet me again? I'm on early shift for the next fortnight. There's a French film coming to the Empire next week; *Le Million*, directed by René Clair. How about it? Shall we go?'

Helen was on the verge of refusal when she hesitated. The idea of deceiving Ben frightened her, but the sexual attraction of the young man sitting opposite was

242

stronger than anything she had experienced since the early days of her marriage. And it would serve her husband right if she were to go out with another man. Since her father had made him a full partner in the firm two years previously, work had absorbed ninety per cent of all Ben's time. He was too tired to make love to her when he came home from the factory, but was still jealous and possessive enough to expect absolute fidelity as his right.

Life was beginning to seem just like being married to Charlie, except that it was lonelier, because Ben was away all day, and more frustrating, because now she knew what she was missing. Ben had taught her that she was a loving, passionate woman, only to leave her to her own devices on account of his driving ambition. Her father was fifty-seven and might be persuaded to retire in a few years' time, or at least become a sleeping partner, and Ben was going to prove himself capable of running Gordon's.

The new machinery, which Joseph had installed so reluctantly and at such cost after the stike, had paid for itself many times over in expanding production. Gordon's was now posing a serious threat to its major rivals, the Yorkshire-based Rowntree's and the Midlands' firm of Cadbury, who had taken over the Bristol company of J S Fry. And much of this expansion had occurred during the past two years, since Ben had thrust Gordon's forward into the twentieth century with updated management and marketing ideas. Joe might complain that his son-in-law's notions were too American, too commercialized, but he enjoyed the increased profits too well to make more than a token display of opposition. He worked Ben hard, whilst making sure that he retained the power invested in him by his majority shareholding.

When Helen expostulated that she hardly ever saw Ben nowadays, Joseph would kiss her and wag an admonitory finger, for all the world, Helen thought resentfully, as if she were a naughty child.

'Now, now then, Puss! Men must work and women must play, eh? What? You don't say no to all those fripperies and gew-gaws that your mother and I give you, do you? That Ben gives you? That new car, that nice fur coat, those diamond ear-rings. But they can't be got without money, Puss, just you remember that, when you're wishing that Ben was at home more often. You just go and buy yourself a new hat, poppet. A day in London, that's what you need.'

A shopping spree was her father's permanent remedy for her own and her mother's complaints. Spending money was his placebo for all mental ills; but the trouble was that in Helen's case, the placebo failed to provide even a temporary illusion of well-being.

She returned Richard's smile, feeling both terrified and defiant.

'That would be very nice,' she said. 'I've never seen a French film. Shall we say a week today? I'll meet you outside the Empire next Thursday at half-past one. A Dutch treat, so there won't be any hurt pride or any fighting about who's going to pay.'

Elizabeth closed her ledger and tipped her chair back on to its rear legs.

'I'm dying of thirst,' she said. 'Put the kettle on, Jack, there's a dear.'

Jack raised his head from the column of figures he was attempting to add, memorized the halfway total and kept his place with a stubby forefinger. 'I'm not the office boy,' he answered briefly and resumed his addition.

Elizabeth grinned. 'But we could do with one, couldn't we? And what's more, we shall soon be in a position to afford one. We're beginning to make a go of it, Jack. Aren't you pleased?'

He put down his pen with a sigh, abandoning for the moment his effort to reach a final total. The opportunity was too good to miss.

'I'd be better pleased,' he said, 'if we weren't doing it by undercutting the interest rates. Sooner or later it's bound to cause trouble.'

'Who from?' Elizabeth asked ungrammatically. 'There aren't any other financial loan companies in this part of the city.'

Jack had to smile in spite of himself; in spite of his constant, nagging worries about making ends meet, his misery at being ostracized by family and friends, the perpetual doubt of the wisdom, or folly, of what he had done in giving up his job at Harrison's for this. The Evans and Hennessey Financial Loan Company was such a grand name for such a dubiously thriving enterprise. He glanced round the dirty, shabby room which, with a smaller adjoining one, comprised the company's offices. All the furniture — two desks, a filing cabinet, an old-fashioned safe and a couple of chairs for clients — was second-hand, bought as cheaply as possible in the local flea-market. The rooms themselves, again the cheapest they could rent, were over an empty, near-derelict shop in Canal Street, and in Jack's mind, epitomized the seediness of the whole mad venture.

'Who from?' Elizabeth repeated, when he did not answer her question immediately.

Jack rubbed his chin, which was beginning to feel rough and unshaven.

'People are coming here, now, from outside Eastwood, Lizzie. The news of low interest rates is bound to spread, and you've cut the rate twice in the past three months. Word gets around. The man who was here this morning, the one with red hair, had come from the other side of Bristol. One of the women yesterday was from Bath. I have an appointment tomorrow with a couple of blokes who want to borrow money to start their own business in Gloucester.'

'Well? Surely that's all to the good. Our fame's spreading, as you say. For heaven's sake, Jack! After only a year, we're beginning to make a profit.'

'And we're taking money away from other companies in other parts of the west country. I don't like it, Lizzie! And our competitors won't like it, either, you can bet your bottom dollar on that!'

'So what can they do about it, except bring down their own rates of interest? What we're doing isn't illegal.' Elizabeth stretched her arms and yawned. 'I'd make that tea myself, except that I'm too tired. I think I'll go home early for once. Mama won't be expecting me, but I can have a rest while she gets the supper.' She grimaced. 'Not that she'll be pleased to see me. She never is these days.'

'At least she didn't throw you out, like my mother did me. Those lodgings of mine in Station Road are damnably uncomfortable. I'm sure the mattress is stuffed with straw.'

'Serve you right,' Elizabeth remarked unfeelingly. 'You should have refused to leave home, as I did. Your mother couldn't have forced you out.'

Jack made no reply, which, on reflection, Elizabeth thought was charitable, considering what he might have said. He might have pointed out that her refusal to leave Springtime Grove had driven her sister away from home. She would, of course, have argued that it had been entirely Mary's own choice, even though that was perhaps not altogether true. Mary was still sensitive to public opinion, as she had been since the revelation that her marriage to Alan was bigamous. She was aware that Elizabeth's venture would cause hostility even from those people who would avail themselves of the facility she provided. Mary could not face it, and had pressed Amy to make Elizabeth leave.

'Show people that we want nothing to do with her, Mama.'

But Amy, while violently disapproving and angry that Elizabeth should involve them in any more gossip, had a stubborn streak in her make-up. Her children

246

meant more to her than the goodwill of friends and acquaintances; so she had refused to turn Elizabeth out and had begged Mary to show the street a united family front.

'If we condemn her, others almost certainly will. After all, she's doing nothing wrong.'

'Legally no, morally yes,' Mary had replied, and set about finding herself lodgings.

She had assumed that Richard would accompany her.

'But you're my son!' she had exclaimed indignantly when he had announced his intention of remaining where he was.

'Oh no I'm not,' he had answered, adding, in her eyes unforgivably: 'I'm not even your step-son. Let's face it. You and Dada were never properly married.'

If he had been younger, Mary might have insisted, but Richard was too old now to be under anyone's jurisdiction.

Mary had been upset, and Elizabeth had accused Richard of callousness.

'I'm being kind,' he said, 'to her as well as to myself. Do you think tongues wouldn't wag about us before very long? There is absolutely no sort of relationship between us, Lizzie. People would soon remember that.'

Mary had therefore left alone for the rooms near Eastwood Park; and neighbours refused to speak to Elizabeth, or even to acknowledge her presence when they met. The chapel-goers were the worst. After a few weeks, she gave up going to Arley Street on Sundays. Most members of the congregation ignored her, and the Minister preached a very pointed sermon on Christ's overthrow of the money-changers in the Temple. The fact that Elizabeth appeared amused rather than ashamed by this homily only exacerbated the situation.

Whether or not she was really amused, Jack had never been sure. Elizabeth kept her emotions on a very tight rein these days. She had grown hard and cynical, and sometimes he found it difficult to recognize the woman he loved. The warm-heartedness which underlay so many apparently arrogant and high-handed actions of the past had given way to a more calculated approach to life. And yet, just when he despaired of ever finding the old Elizabeth again, he glimpsed a look, heard a word which indicated that she was still there, buried under layers of hurt and feelings of betrayal.

She said to him now, suddenly, impulsively: 'Why did you do it, Jack? Why did you agree to come into partnership with me? You hate the job. I sometimes think you hate me. Certainly, you despise me. Why, then? I've often wondered.'

He entered his final total at the foot of the column and closed the ledger.

'I don't hate you,' he answered quietly. 'I don't even despise you. How could I, when I love you? And I suppose that's the answer. I couldn't possibly have allowed you to get into this on your own. For the first time in your life, you needed me, and I suppose that was something I couldn't resist.'

She leaned forward, her elbows on the desk, propping her chin in her hands.

'You won't regret it, Jack. I'll make sure you don't.' She smiled at him, willing him to smile in return.

'If it makes you feel any easier,' he said, 'I don't regret it quite as much as I did. I can see that the need to borrow money is there, especially in a poor community like Eastwood. It's no more than bankers do for the rich. All the time. The real trouble is my nonconformist upbringing; the belief that it's wrong to buy anything that you know you can't afford. You save the money first. Self-denial.'

Elizabeth laughed. 'I know what you mean. Our puritan ancestors cast long shadows. But things are changing. People are getting impatient to have what they want today instead of tomorrow, when they might be dead.'

'Is that a good thing, do you think?'

'Why not?' She got up and slipped a lightweight summer jacket on over her pale cotton frock. 'As you've just pointed out, the rich have always done it. You don't find the Joseph Gordons and Albert Harrisons of this world — and you'll appreciate that I don't even mention the Rothschilds and the Rockefellers — saving up pennies in an old tea-caddy or a stocking until they can afford the extra Rolls Royce or fur coat or diamond necklace. And how much less do the people of Eastwood require, who only want the bare necessities to live.'

She stowed away the ledgers in the safe and dropped a friendly kiss on the top of Jack's head.

'Goodnight, Jack dear. Don't think I'm ungrateful. Mind you lock up before you leave.'

CHAPTER NINETEEN

Ben was still not ready when Helen entered the dressing-room. He was standing in his shirt sleeves in front of the pier glass, staring absently at his reflection in the mirror. She picked up his jacket from the chair and touched him on the shoulder.

'You'd better hurry up, darling, or we'll be late. And you know how you hate arriving after everyone else is seated.'

They were going to the Prince's Theatre in Park Row, to see Sybil Thorndike in *Saint Joan*. Helen knew she would be bored, but tonight it did not matter. She hugged to herself the secret of her lovely day.

It had rained heavily ever since last night, a thick, murky November downpour, and the traffic had been a slowmoving procession of headlights all afternoon. Mrs Bagot had thought Helen mad to insist on going out, driving around the town in such weather.

'The shop's will still be there tomorrow,' she had scolded.

'I want a new dress for this evening,' Helen had said; and hoped that the housekeeper would not notice that she was wearing the flame-coloured silk chiffon which she had bought for her parents' thirtieth wedding anniversary celebrations. Instinctively, although the dressing-room was hot, she wrapped her mink coat

250

more firmly around her and held it together at the neck.

She put down Ben's jacket and went to the window, drawing back the edge of one of the curtains. It had stopped raining at last, and the street lamps swam, each in its nimbus of light, through a delicate autumnal mist, like sleeping swans floating on the surface of a lake.

'Did you go out today?' Ben's voice startled her, and she turned to see him regarding her in the mirror. When she did not answer, he swung round to face her, picking up his tie from the top of the chest-of-drawers. He made no move, however, to put it on, but just stood there, running it backwards and forwards through his fingers. 'I said, did you go out today?' he repeated.

Helen's heart began to thump uncomfortably. Could she get away with a lie? Probably not. It was possible that Mrs Bagot had already mentioned her absence in casual conversation.

'Yes,' she said, trying to sound normal. 'I went into town. I wanted a dress for this evening, but I couldn't find anything I liked, so I'm wearing the red one again.' She let her fur coat fall open. 'Are you driving tonight, or have you asked George to take us?'

'It's George's evening off,' he reminded her. 'I'm driving us to the theatre myself.'

'We ought to hurry then,' she said once more. 'Time's going on. You were late getting home tonight.'

He turned back to the mirror and put on his tie, apparently satisfied by her explanation. Helen felt her heart-rate begin to slow, and took a deep breath to steady her nerves.

They were in the car, a big Morris Isis 6 saloon, with cream bodywork and a black top — Ben's pride and joy — before he reverted to the subject again. The headlamps speared through the mist ahead, cleaving two golden paths of light.

'Where were you this afternoon?' he asked, as they drove along Pembroke Road.

251

Helen jumped. 'What? I told you, shopping. I was looking for a dress.'

He replied quietly: 'Rather an odd place to look for a dress, I should have thought. On Temple Meads station.'

She felt frozen to her seat. Obviously someone had seen her. But who? She dared not ask. Her one hope now was to bluff it out. She gave a nervous, high-pitched laugh.

'Temple Meads station? What on earth should I be doing there?'

'I don't know. That's what I was wondering.'

'I wasn't there. I don't know why you should think I was.'

'One of the girls from the invoice department saw you. She'd been sent in with some urgent post which had to catch the mail train to Crewe. She mentioned the fact of seeing you to my secretary, Miss Beaumont.'

Helen told herself to keep calm; just to keep denying it. She said: 'She must have seen someone who looked like me.'

Why, in heaven's name, had she gone? It was not as though she and Richard had been able to do more than exchange a few words and snatch a quick kiss behind one of the luggage trolleys. Nor was she absolutely sure now that he had really been pleased to see her. Her secret pleasure began to evaporate.

She recalled that his initial greeting had been: 'What are you doing here?' and his eyes had been hostile beneath the peak of his porter's uniform hat.

'I've come to see you,' she said. 'I have to see you. I can't stand the thought of not being with you again until Friday.'

'I'm working,' he protested. No; hardly lover-like, now that she gave it her full consideration. 'Do you know the current rate of unemployment? GWR could replace me from about three dozen applicants any time they chose.' Then he had relented. 'Wait for me,' he had ordered; and she had sat on a seat outside the ladies' cloakroom, deafened by the hiss of smoke and steam and the drumming of rain on the platform roof.

He had joined her presently, drawing her behind one of the luggage trolleys, and gently kissed her lips. After that she had forgotten everything else, including his less than ecstatic greeting.

Ben made no further comment, and Helen tried to convince herself that he was satisfied that a mistake had been made. Seated in the theatre stalls, watching as the lights dimmed over the painted proscenium arch with its legend: *Our true intent is all for your delight*, Helen thought about Richard. She had to admit to herself that he had never said that he loved her; that, in fact, during the three months she had known him, he had been brutally frank with regard to his feelings. He liked her very much, he thought her beautiful; but made it plain that the affair was no more to him than a pleasant diversion.

The audience were applauding Sybil Thorndike's first entrance, and Helen mechanically joined in. Her eyes flicked sideways at Ben, sitting beside her in the darkness. Had she fooled him? The girl from Gordon's invoicing department might not be too familiar with her face, she visited the factory so seldom. Ben might accept that the girl had been mistaken. All the same, Helen thought, she had been stupid. Those people who accused her of being scatterbrained and impulsive, of never stopping to think, were right.

When had she fallen out of love with Ben? she wondered. Perhaps the process of disillusionment had begun on that first night of their honeymoon, when his furious outburst at the mention of Charlie's name had frightened her. Nowadays, his neglect fuelled her uneasiness with resentment. And there was always the underlying, unspoken threat of physical violence. He had never used any towards her, yet she felt the danger was there. It hung over her, a kind of unspoken blackmail.

Richard Davies had come into her life at a particularly vulnerable moment, when she was feeling more than ever lonely and unfulfilled. It was natural, therefore, that she should have endowed him with all the virtues. The age difference — she was nine years older than he — had inhibited her a little at first, but she had soon forgotten it in the rapid progress of the affair.

She had met him the following week as arranged, outside the Empire in Old Market Street, and they had seen René Clair's *Le Million*. The film had bored her, but she had not cared. Richard had held her hand and, later on, kissed her. By the end of the afternoon, they were sitting with their arms entwined. After the film, over tea at a café, he had proposed that they meet again the following week, not this time at the cinema. She could, he suggested, take him for a drive in her car. He supposed that she did have a car of her own.

So she had picked him up on the Tramways Centre in the new Austin 7, which had been Joseph's last birthday present to her, and driven him into the country, where they had made love very uncomfortably on the seats of the car, in a secluded lane.

After that they had gone to small country hotels and taken a private sitting-room for the afternoon. Because Richard was on shift work, however, it was not always possible for them to meet, and sometimes it would be a fortnight before they saw one another again. Helen found these enforced separations increasingly unendurable until, this afternoon, she could put up with it no longer. The need to see Richard had overcome the need for caution, and she had gone to the station to find him.

The first act had come to an end without either the actors or the words having made any impression on her whatsoever. The house-lights went up for the interval. Her head was aching.

Ben turned to her. 'Let's get some coffee,' he invited smoothly.

*   *   *

'Aren't you staying?' Elizabeth asked, as Jack began to pack away his ledgers and lock the safe for the night. 'I thought we'd agreed to go over those accounts this evening.'

'Do you mind if we postpone it until tomorrow? I feel all in.'

Elizabeth had to admit that he did look tired. There were shadows beneath his eyes and his skin had a waxy sheen.

'You're not coming down with 'flu, are you?' She was suddenly solicitous. 'There's an awful lot of it about. The Miss Cohens have had to shut up shop.'

'I don't think so. I just don't sleep well, that's all. It's the fault of that terrible bed at my digs. You look as though you could do with a good night's rest yourself.'

'Oh, I'm all right,' she reassured him. 'I'll stay on a bit and make a start on the accounts. I must go to the bank as usual in the morning. And we have three new customers to interview tomorrow afternoon, besides having to chase a couple of defaulters. If that man in Arley Street doesn't pay up soon, we'll have to threaten him with a solicitor's letter. Thank heaven the Miss Cohens recommended Henley and Junkin. They're proving worth their weight in gold.'

Jack snorted. 'And so they should. They're getting enough money out of us.'

'Now, don't get crochety,' Elizabeth begged. 'You admitted only yesterday that things are going much more smoothly than you expected. We'll soon be able to move to better premises at this rate.'

Jack tried to smile, although his head was throbbing. Perhaps he was gettin 'flu, although he hoped to God he wasn't. The thought of being ill, of having to spend any length of time in that lumpy bed with only the grudging attentions of his landlady to rely on, appalled him. He wanted to go home, back to Springtime Grove, but his mother refused to have him inside the house. She did not, however, refuse any financial help he could give her.

Jack got up and put on his coat, stooping to warm his hands at the small gas fire which was their only source of heat. He wished, more for Elizabeth's sake than his own, that he could stop feeling guilty, especially now, when they were beginning to make a go of the business. But that made him feel guiltier than ever. He wasn't cut out for such things. He should have stayed with Harrison's. Yet oddly enough, he could be far more ruthless than Elizabeth when it came to collecting bad debts. There were a couple which Elizabeth would have written off, when not even a solicitor's letter did the trick. It was Jack who had insisted that they take one defaulter to court, and had been quite unmoved when the man was sentenced to six months' imprisonment.

'If we're in business, we're in business,' he had snapped, when Elizabeth had expressed regrets and reservations. 'If we're to run it properly, we can't afford softer emotions.'

And that was how he felt, although it did not assuage his sense of self-recrimination. Nevertheless, there were moments when fleetingly, he recognized in himself sensations of actual enjoyment. But one thing did worry him; the fact that they had drummed up business by undercutting the rate of interest, thereby taking custom away from other, longer established firms. It astonished him that they continued to flourish.

'I must go,' he said, straightening his back. 'I feel rotten. But I trust a good night's sleep will put me right. I'll see you in the morning.'

'Don't come in if you're not fit. I can cope perfectly well on my own.'

'I don't doubt it.' Jack grinned and shivered. 'It's probably just the onset of a cold.'

'I expect so. I'd send you round to Mama, but with Richard still living with us we haven't a spare bed. If you hurry, you might get home before it's really dark. These November evenings are so damp and treacherous.'

256

He nodded. 'Don't work too long. I don't like the idea of you walking the streets at night on your own. I'll see you tomorrow.'

Jack clattered downstairs to the empty shop below. It had once been a gentleman's outfitters, but now, where hats and collars, socks and gloves, ties and scarves had been so lovingly displayed, there was nothing but dust and cobwebs. The counter was as bare as the floorboards, the shelves devoid of their tiers of neatly labelled boxes. The bell over the door jangled loudly in the quiet as Jack let himself out into Canal Street. The air smelled cold, reminding him of bonfires and burning leaves. It would be a busy time for them over the next few months, with people needing money for Christmas.

Again he stifled a pang of guilt before suddenly being swept with a wave of faintness and nausea. His vision was clouded by a thick yellow mist, and although he felt icy cold, his hands and face were sweating. He clung to one of the window frames, resting his forehead against the filthy, mud-spattered glass. After a moment or two, the feeling of sickness passed, leaving him weak and trembling. He must get home to his lodgings before it happened a second time and he disgraced himself by throwing up on the pavement. He crossed the cobbled roadway to the rusty iron railings which separated pedestrians from the slippery bank and murky waters of the canal, and clung to them for support. He felt so ill he did not recall leaving the shop door unlocked.

Left alone, Elizabeth collected together the various ledgers and account books that she needed, then went into the adjoining room where there was a gas-ring, and made herself a pot of tea. While she waited for it to brew, she went back through the office and down the stairs and out to the lavatory in a shed in the tiny back yard.

She was halfway up the stairs again when she heard the shop bell jangle. The staircase twisted in the middle, so she was unable to see directly into the shop and paused, one hand resting on the banister rail, beside her. Her heart was beating uncomfortably fast. Then she recollected that it was not yet five o'clock, and that the light from the upstairs room was visible from the street. It must be a customer. Nevertheless, she was surprised that Jack had not locked the door on his way out.

She descended the stairs for a second time. The shop had never been wired for electricity and she had no matches with her to light the gas. She could not help feeling a little uneasy. She stood on the bottom step, staring into the gloom.

'Who's there?' she called. There was no reply and her uneasiness increased. 'Is anyone there?' she asked loudly.

The street lamps had already been lit and a dull, yellow glow suffused the shop's bay windows, but was not strong enough to penetrate further. The main body of the shop was in darkness.

'Is anyone there?' Elizabeth called again, and again there was silence.

Steeling herself to meet the onslaught of a possible attacker, she left the comparative safety of the stairs and walked forward a few paces. Nothing happened. Emboldened, she advanced another couple of steps. She could see by now that the shop door was ajar and could feel the draught around her ankles. Obviously someone had come in, but, discouraged by the silence and darkness of the interior, had changed his mind and retreated. Elizabeth closed the door, bolting it top and bottom. Then she went back upstairs.

The office looked unexpectedly warm and inviting after the echoing emptiness and darkness of the shop. Elizabeth poured herself a cup of hot, sweet tea and took it back to her desk. She realized she was shivering and turned up the jets of the little gas fire.

She felt annoyed with herself for having given way to

258

nervousness. If she was unable to remain alone, especially so early in the evening, without giving in to ridiculous fancies, she was unfit to be running a business. She was even angrier to discover that she was still unhappy, still straining to hear footsteps on the stairs, although there was a rational explanation for what had happened. At one point she was even ready to go down and lock the door as well as bolting it; but she dropped the key back into her handbag with a grimace of disquiet. Really, she was behaving like a child! Jack would be highly amused if she ever decided to tell him about it.

Not that she would. Jack was far too solicitous already. His care of her was oppressive. One of the things she had liked most about Ben was his willingness not to interfere in her life. On the other hand, knowing what she did now, that could have been a symptom of indifference. It was best not to think about Ben.

She finished her tea and returned the dirty cup and saucer to the kitchen. She would wash them up before she went home, or in the morning. Meanwhile, she was here to do the accounts, to find out exactly where she and Jack stood financially. As she settled down to her work, she heard the Arley Street chapel clock strike six. She had already wasted far too much time.

She had been working for perhaps ten minutes when she became conscious of a curious smell. It was almost, she thought, as if someone had lit a fire in a nearby garden. But Guy Fawkes night was long over, and there were no trees in Canal Street for anyone to be burning dead leaves. She sniffed the air and decided that, in any case, the scent was too acrid for a bonfire. It was more like old, rotting timber which had been set alight.

The smell was getting stronger. She glanced round to see if the gas fire was safe, that she had not left anything too close, where it could scorch, and saw the smoke curling beneath the door which led to the stairs. For a moment she sat glued to her chair, unable to move, then she leapt for the door, wrenching it open. Smoke poured in, smoke shot through with flame, and she reeled back, coughing.

Within seconds, she had recovered enough to slam the door shut. She ran into the little kitchen, where she soaked the tea-towel under the tap. With this pressed to her nose and mouth, she cautiously reopened the door, this time no more than a crack. It was sufficient, however, to convince her that the staircase and ground floor of the shop were well alight. There was no escape for her that way. She was trapped.

Panic took over and she screamed. The sound of her own voice, and with it recognition of her own hysteria, steadied Elizabeth. She could see the landing door begin to scorch as the flames took hold. She opened the window which gave on to Canal Street and yelled: 'Help!' as loudly as she could. But there was no one about. Nobody had yet spotted the fire.

The door fell in with a crash and the flames started to lick the walls. Elizabeth rushed to turn off the gas fire, cursing herself for not making it her first priority. Then she remembered that the main gas tap was in a cupboard under the stairs, where she could not possibly reach it. At any second, the fire would burn through the floor boards and melt the pipes. The gas would explode.

Elizabeth ran to the other end of the room and tried to open the window which overlooked the yard. It had not been touched since the summer and was stuck in its warped, wooden frame. Conscious of the heat at her back, Elizabeth hammered with her fists, tears of rage, frustration and blind panic rolling down her face. Suddenly, the window gave, bursting outwards with such force that she almost went, head-first, with it. Unsteadily she climbed on to the window-sill, before recollecting the precious ledgers and files. Desperately she glanced over her shoulder, but could see that it was already too late. The desk where she had been sitting such a short time ago was blazing merrily, the papers nothing but charred heaps of ash. The paintwork on the ancient safe was beginning to blister.

Below her, brightly illuminated by the fire, Elizabeth was able to see the roof of the lavatory shed. She stood up, closed her eyes and jumped. Her body hit the shed roof with agonizing force, bounced once, then rolled sideways, and she saw the cobbled yard rush up to meet her. She lay still for a moment, all the breath knocked out of her, feeling as though she were one gigantic bruise from head to foot; then, somehow, she crawled on all fours towards the door in the yard wall, opened it and dragged herself through just as the first gas pipe exploded.

CHAPTER TWENTY

'I'm afraid it looks like arson, Miss Evans.'

Sergeant Banner, sitting squarely beside Elizabeth's hospital bed, hands planted on knees, helmet stowed neatly beneath his chair, could not prevent a note of satisfaction creeping into his voice. He had always been convinced that it was Elizabeth who had warned Alan Davies and connived at his escape, although he had never been able to gather sufficient reliable evidence to prove his suspicions correct. Furthermore, he was a good Christian, a good Methodist, and it outraged his sense of propriety, set his moral values at nought, to know that a fellow Methodist, and a woman at that, was engaged in such a heathenish practice as money-lending. He wished she was his daughter. He would soon knock some sense into her with his fists.

'Why do you think it's arson?' Elizabeth croaked. Her throat was still raw from contact with the smoke. She had two cracked ribs, a broken left wrist and a twisted ankle; but, as everyone told her she was lucky to be alive, she felt she could not complain. Her face, like her body, was a mass of bruises. She ached from head to toe and her temper suffered accordingly. She found Eastwood Hospital dull and depressing, painted everywhere a rather grubby cream and a dark, institutional green.

Sergeant Banner cleared his throat. 'The remains of an empty petrol tin was found under the stairs. Mr Hennessey assures me that no petrol was kept on the premises.'

'No, it wasn't,' Elizabeth agreed.

Sergeant Banner continued triumphantly: 'Moreover, in your statement to us, Miss Evans, you said that you had bolted the front door after Mr Hennessey left. The experts in these matters assure me that, from what is left of that door, it can be ascertained that the bolts had definitely been withdrawn, suggesting that some person or persons unknown started the fire before making their escape.'

It made sense, of course. Elizabeth remembered the jangling doorbell. Whoever had entered had not gone away, as she had supposed, but hidden, either beneath the counter or under the stairs, until she returned to her office. She gave an involuntary shudder. Whoever had started the fire had not been squeamish about the possibility of burning her alive.

'What we want to know,' Sergeant Banner continued, 'is who has a grudge against either you or Mr Hennessey? Or both? Do you have any ideas?'

'Everyone!' she wanted to yell at him. 'And you know it! People like you, you fat, smug, smiling little bastard!' But she was suddenly very tired and could no longer be bothered with the Sergeant and his questions. Her lids drooped. Her eyes closed. When she opened them again, the Sergeant had gone and Jack Hennessey was sitting in his place, clutching a large bunch of chrysanthemums.

'Jack!' She smiled a sleepy welcome. 'Are you all right? Should you be out of bed yet? Mama said she'd been to visit you and that you had a terrible cold.'

'I'm OK. Don't worry about me. Just concentrate on getting yourself better.' He placed the flowers carefully on the locker by Elizabeth's bed.

'Sergeant Banner's been here this afternoon,'

Elizabeth said. 'He told me the fire was started deliberately. I thought he seemed rather pleased about it.'

'I wasn't going to say anything until you were well again.' Jack pulled his chair a little closer to the bed. 'But since you know . . . Lizzie, that fire was a warning to us. I don't suppose the police will ever find the bloke who lit it. Just someone making the odd quid or two on the side, doing somebody else's dirty work for him. Or them. I'm convinced that it was a caution from one, or maybe a few, of our competitors not to undercut their rates. If we persist, next time it will be one of us lying dead in some back alley.'

'It was nearly me this time,' Elizabeth retorted with some asperity. She saw the look on Jack's face and smiled. 'All right, love, we'll conform.' She regarded him silently for a moment or two, then added: 'I assume from what you said just now that you do intend to carry on?'

His jaw hardened. 'I'm not going to let anyone frighten me out of business, Lizzie. Don't misunderstand me. I'm no keener on it than I ever was, but I won't run scared.' He had done that once before, with Alan Davies, and still despised himself for it.

Elizabeth moved one of her bandaged hands towards him across the white cotton counterpane.

'Jack, dear, if it wasn't so painful I'd kiss you, but, as you see, my lips are all blistered. Did we lose much?'

'Financially, no. Thanks to your habit of going to the bank every morning. But we've lost all our records; files, ledgers, that sort of thing. We've no proof of who's borrowed what and who owes what. We'll have to start again, from the beginning.'

It was no more than she expected to hear. What was unexpected was Jack's determination not to be beaten and his support in starting again. Elizabeth had been lying in her hospital bed concocting various specious arguments to persuade him into staying in the business,

264

only to find that she had been wasting her time. She experienced a rush of gratitude and affection whose intensity surprised her. But all she said was: 'We'll have to find new premises.'

He nodded. 'I've thought about that. I think we should move out of Eastwood. Move nearer the city centre. I've been making some enquiries and there are a couple of decent, first-floor rooms to let in Old Market Street. It's a reasonable location and the rent's not exorbitant. Kitchen and lavatory shared with other people on the same floor. If you're agreeable, I'll contact the landlord tomorrow.'

'We might lose some of our Eastwood customers, but the move would be worth it. You're right, Jack. Absolutely right.'

'That's settled then.' He got up and bent down to brush his lips against her scarred and peeling forehead. 'Take care of yourself,' he whispered. 'I can't do without you, you know.'

Helen stood petrified, flattened against the wall, while the fury raged all about her. Unemployed demonstrators and baton-charging police had met in head-on collision.

Old Market Street resembled a battlefield. Men, both demonstrators and police, lay on the ground, blood pouring from wounds, or sat in the roadway, nursing broken limbs. The rest were locked in hand to hand fighting, while an enterprising few, all unemployed, tried to overturn a stationary car. All traffic had been brought to a standstill the entire length of the broad thoroughfare, and some rioters had climbed on top of a tram and were threatening to throw passengers over the side. Anyone who looked well dressed enough to have a job or a little money was regarded as being a legitimate target. Helen, in her fur coat, model hat and expensive shoes had already attracted a number of vicious comments. The men, however, were reluctant to touch her.

But some of the wives had accompanied their menfolk on what had originally been planned as a peaceful demonstration. These women were now lined up on the edge of the pavement, screaming abuse at the constables, who were laying about them with their truncheons. One or two near Helen, becoming aware of her presence, were eyeing her with overt hostility. She glanced desperately around, trying to spot Richard.

He had agreed to meet her outside the Empire cinema after she had telephoned him at the station. She had not seen him since the week before Christmas, and it was now the twenty-third of February. She knew it was degrading to be chasing a man who had intimated so plainly that he was bored with the affair, but she could not help herself. The more afraid she grew of Ben and his possessive love, the greater was her need of a friend to whom she could turn. She did not want to confide in her parents, to confess that her marraige had been a terrible mistake. Besides, Minna and Joseph admired Ben. Joseph, particularly; her father and husband had developed into a two-man mutual admiration society, and Helen realized that nowadays it was useless to appeal to one against the other. She needed Richard. She had no one else.

Mrs Bagot had warned her before she had left the house that there was to be a march somewhere in the city. Helen had given it little thought, nor would it have alarmed her if she had. Demonstrations by the unemployed were becoming commonplace. As resentment mounted over the Means Test, introduced the previous autumn, hunger marchers were converging on London from all over the country. There had been clashes with police, but so far only in areas remote from Bristol.

But today it was happening in Old Market Street. The constables had tried to stop the marchers, and the result was a riot. Helen, having left her car near Castle

Ditch, suddenly found herself in the middle of it. A man was hit over the head by a policeman's truncheon only yards from where she cowered against the shop wall. He fell, screaming, into the gutter. A trader's barrow was overturned. One of the women launched herself at the policeman, shrieking imprecations, clawing for his eyes. The rest of the group made a concerted move towards Helen.

'Get the bitch!' one of them yelled. 'Get that bloody coat off 'er back. She i'n't goin' t' 'ave to put up with no Means Test!'

Helen stood where she was, shaking. She could not have moved to save her life. Suddenly a body interposed itself between her and her attackers. A young man seized her arm cursing the women in fluent, four-letter Anglo-Saxon, and pushed her inside the shop, slamming the door behind him.

'Get this lady a chair,' he ordered the shopkeeper, who was nervously sheltering behind the counter, 'and bolt that door before those harpies get in.'

The shopkeeper hurriedly obeyed the second command first, worried for the safety of his merchandise. Even as he did so, half a brick crashed through one of his plate-glass windows, scattering the carefully arranged display of ladies' coats and dresses.

'Let's go into the back,' the young man said, supporting Helen with an arm about her waist. 'Things are getting too dangerous out here. I've read about the Bristol Riots of last century, but I never expected to see one first-hand.'

The shopkeeper ushered them into the store-room behind the shop and produced a hard, cane-backed chair, which he dusted with his handkerchief. The young man gently lowered Helen on to it, saying: 'Sit there, ma'am. You've had a nasty experience.'

'You're a Yank,' the shopkeeper said, regarding this uninvited guest as though he were an interesting specimen. 'Aren't you?'

'Not exactly.' The young man held out his hand. 'My name's Christopher Morgan and I'm from Texas. That's the southern states of America.'

'That's what I said, a Yank. What you doing over here?'

'Just bumming around Europe before I settle down at home. I'm on my way to Wales to see where my Daddy's people originally came from.' He glanced down at Helen, who had recovered a little of her colour. 'How do you feel, ma'am?'

'Better, thank you, but very ashamed. I'm afraid I panicked.'

'Anyone would in those conditions,' he assured her.

Helen managed a laugh. 'It's very kind of you to say so, but I know one woman who wouldn't have done so. My name's Helen Sawyer, by the way.' It was her turn to hold out her hand.

The American took it in a firm grasp. Now that she looked at him properly, Helen decided that he was not as young as she had at first imagined. He was tall, very broad-shouldered, with fair, wavy hair and hazel eyes. He had a wide, mobile mouth which turned up at the corners, giving him a happy-go-lucky expression. But in spite of this, and in spite of the fact that he talked of 'bumming around Europe' as though he were not long out of college, she judged him to be all of twenty-five or twenty-six years of age.

The shopkeeper went to see what was happening, and came back two minutes later to report that the police at last seemed to have the situation under control. Ambulances were arriving to take away the injured, and he thought that in a quarter of an hour or so it would be perfectly safe for the lady to leave.

'Nevertheless, ma'am, I wouldn't 'ang about,' he advised. 'I'd go straight 'ome as soon as the trams get moving.'

'I have a car,' Helen said. 'I've left it in Castle Ditch.'

'I'll walk you there,' Chris Morgan offered. He

stretched himself to his full height and flexed his muscles. 'You'll be all right with me.'

'I can see I shall. But ... I was supposed to be meeting somebody.' Helen turned to the shopkeeper. 'Outside the Empire.'

The man pursed his lips and shook his head. 'You let this gentleman see you to your car, mum, and go back 'ome. Whoever you're meeting will understand. If 'e's any sense 'e won't 've 'ung about, 'imself.'

Helen wondered why the shopkeeper automatically assumed that she was meeting a man. She got up, fastening her fur coat to the neck.

'Yes. I'm sure you're right. Thank you very much for letting me take cover in your shop. You've been most kind.' She smiled at her rescuer. 'Right, Mr Morgan, shall we go? I don't think there's any need to wait any longer. With you beside me, I feel quite brave.'

Elizabeth said: 'What on earth are you doing in Old Market Street, anyway? I thought you're supposed to be at work. And for goodness' sake, Richard, come away from that window! In the mood those men down there are in, someone's quite likely to sling a brick.'

Richard laughed, but moved back into the centre of the room looking around him.

'So these are the new premises of the Evans and Hennessey Financial Loan Company,' he remarked.

Jack grinned. 'Not bad, are they?' he asked complacently.

'Better than the last lot.' Richard hitched one leg over the corner of Elizabeth's desk, moving aside her tray of pens and paper-clips so that he could settle himself more comfortably. He cocked an ear. 'Just listen to it out there! A good job I knew where to find you. It all happened so quickly. I was literally overtaken by events.'

'You still haven't said what you're doing here when you're supposed to be at work,' Elizabeth reminded him. 'I suppose we might as well have a cup of tea. No clients are likely to turn up with this going on. I wonder if it will spread. A hundred years ago, during the Corn Law riots, half the city was burned down.'

'Well, pray it doesn't happen this time,' Jack said, 'or they'll probably begin with the buildings in Old Market Street, and I couldn't go through that all over again.' He glanced at Elizabeth. 'And neither could you.'

All her injuries had healed, her bones mended, and she was left without even a single scar in memory of her three-month-old lucky escape. But Jack was aware that Elizabeth was edgier than she had been; more prone to lose her temper for no apparent reason. And sometimes, when she thought no one was watching her, she shed meaningless tears. She would recover completely in time, he had no doubt of it. She was too strong-willed for it to be otherwise; but for now she needed protecting, especially from herself.

'I'll make the tea,' he volunteered, getting to his feet. 'You sit here and talk to Richard.'

'You dirty rat,' Richard flung at Jack, in his best imitation of James Cagney. In his normal voice he added: 'You know darn well she's determined to find out what I'm doing here. She'll give me the third degree.'

Jack grinned, making for the door and the shared kitchen, a few rooms further along the landing.

'You see too many American gangster films,' he said.

When he had gone, Elizabeth returned to the attack.

'So?' she demanded. 'What's the explanation? I take it this is French leave? That's how it looks to me, at any rate. Is someone covering for you at Temple Meads?'

'I came to meet someone,' Richard replied airily. 'I shouldn't have, of course, if I'd realized for one moment that I'd be endangering my precious little life. Think of the loss to humanity if I'd been killed.'

Elizabeth snorted. 'A few broken heads, some cuts

270

and bruises, that's all this'll amount to when it's over. So why did you come? I get the impression that you were, in any case, reluctant.'

'Oh . . . pressures.' He went to sit in Jack's chair, stretching his long legs in their porter's uniform trousers towards the fire, burning merrily in the tiny grate.

'What sort of pressures? Female ones? It wouldn't be you if they weren't.'

'Female ones, as you say.' He moved the chair closer to the fire.

'Problems?'

'You might say that.'

'And what else might I say? That she's very keen and you're not?' He nodded and Elizabeth asked: 'Has it always been like that, from the beginning?'

'No, I was keen too, to start with. But it wasn't meant to last. I mean, she's married. I assumed I was just a passing distraction.'

'As she was to you?'

'Yes.'

'But it hasn't worked out like that?'

'No. She thinks she's in love with me. I wouldn't have come today, but she 'phoned me at the station, threatening to commit suicide if I didn't see her.'

Elizabeth frowned. The affair sounded more serious than she had at first imagined.

'And is she the sort who'd do it?'

There was silence for a moment. The coal in the grate sent up spurts of flame, and the noise from the street, penetrating the ill-fitting windows, began to die down. Elizabeth got up from her desk and went to look outside. Ambulances were arriving. The police were making arrests.

'Well?' she asked, turning back to look at Richard.

He shrugged and gave a rueful grin. 'You could probably answer that question as well as I could. The woman we're talking about is Helen.'

'Helen?' Elizabeth stared. 'Helen?' she queried again, unable to take it in. 'Where in the world . . . ? Where and when did you meet her?'

'Last year, in Castle Street. Outside the Regent cinema.' He sketched in the details for her as briefly as possible, ending: 'I honestly didn't believe that the affair would progress this far. That's the truth, Lizzie. I swear it. I thought it was just a bit of fun. For both of us.'

'Which goes to show,' Elizabeth pointed out grimly, 'how little you know about women.' She resumed her seat. 'Good heavens, Richie, aren't there enough single girls of your own age queuing up to go out with you, without you having to embark on an affair with a married woman?'

He had stopped smiling and was looking sulky. 'She's glamorous,' he explained defensively. 'She has a car. She wears expensive clothes and she smells nice. The girls I get to meet aren't like that.'

Elizabeth could see his point of view. Eastwood girls, with little money to spend on themselves in increasingly hard times, the majority handing over most of their wages for housekeeping, were unable to compete with someone like Helen. The surprising thing was that Richard had tired of her company so quickly. She asked him why.

Elizabeth supposed that he would be evasive, so he surprised her by answering without hesitation: 'She's too clinging. I like someone with more spunk; more self-reliance. Someone like you.'

She tried to look severe. 'It won't do you any good to flatter me, Richard. You've behaved very badly and I suspect you know it. And you're making matters worse by not being truthful with Helen; by not telling her that everything's over between you. Next time she contacts you, be resolute. Tell her gently but firmly that the affair is finished.'

'And if she threatens to kill herself again?'

'People who make those sort of threats don't usually

carry them out. The ones who commit suicide are, more often than not, those who have never so much as mentioned it.'

But even as she spoke, Elizabeth wondered if she was being unfair to her cousin. Yet she did not see what else Richard could do. He could not let himself be the victim of blackmail.

Jack came back with three cups of tea on an old tin tray.

'I went downstairs while I was waiting for the kettle to boil,' he said, 'and things are a lot quieter. It just remains now to clear up the mess and assess the damage.'

'I must go then,' Richard said, rising. 'I won't stop for the tea, Jack, thanks all the same. I've been out much longer than I foresaw, as it is. My mate'll have his work cut out to cover my absence.'

He went, and Jack raised his eyebrows at Elizabeth. 'Problems?' he asked, as she had asked Richard earlier.

'Yes.' She offered no further disclosures.

Recognizing that she was going to be uncommunicative, Jack sat down at his desk with his cup of tea. He glanced covertly at her and thought that she was looking tired. He hoped that whatever trouble Richard was in, Elizabeth would not take it upon herself to interfere.

CHAPTER TWENTY-ONE

In spite of Elizabeth's advice and his own inclinations, it was not until over a year later, during the long, hot summer of 1933, that Richard finally ended his affair with Helen.

He had by this time left the railways and was working in the offices of the Evans and Hennessey Financial Loan Company, one of three staff now employed by Elizabeth and Jack. The company had moved again, taking over the entire ground floor of what had once been a small fruit and vegetable warehouse at the back of Philadelphia Street in Broadmead. Elizabeth's exacting standards, her scrupulous fairness in all her dealings, were beginning to pay rich dividends as the firm's reputation grew. There were far fewer single borrowers on their books these days: they were financing a number of small businesses.

They took on staff; an elderly spinster, Miss Pringle, who, in spite of a Roman Catholic upbringing, seemed to have no qualms about the sort of work she was being offered, and a young boy called Norman Pargetter, who ran the errands and made the tea. It was when Elizabeth mentioned the possibility of employing a third person that Richard had suggested himself. He was bored with being a porter and saw no future in it. Elizabeth wondered why she had not thought of the idea herself, and with Jack's approval gave him the job.

Mary was furious and broke a three-year silence to tell Elizabeth exactly what she thought of her. She arrived in Springtime Grove one evening, a fortnight after Richard had started work and just as he and Amy and Elizabeth were finishing an early supper.

Elizabeth, who had not seen her sister for some time, was shocked by Mary's appearance. Mary looked slatternly. Although only thirty-three, her hair was liberally streaked with grey. She had never bothered to have it cut, and it straggled untidily from the old-fashioned bun at the nape of the neck. Her shoes were down-at-heel, and the print frock she was wearing looked as though it could do with a wash. Her pink woollen cardigan, on the other hand, seemed to have been washed all too often, being matted and faded. She was, Elizabeth suspected, a deeply unhappy woman.

Mary brushed aside her mother's welcome and brusquely rejected the inevitable offer of a cup of tea.

'I've come to see Lizzie,' she said. 'Is it true that Richard has left the GWR and is working for you in your office?'

'Why don't you ask Richard?' Elizabeth demanded impatiently. 'He's twenty-one. Old enough, I should have thought, to answer for himself.'

'I'm asking you.'

'Oh, for goodness' sake!' Richard jumped up from the table. 'Stop talking about me as if I wasn't here! Yes, it's true I'm working for Lizzie and Jack. What of it? I'm not a child. I make my own decisions.'

Mary ignored him, keeping her eyes fixed on her sister. 'You've taken everything away from me,' she said in a trembling voice. 'You're always the winner and I'm always the loser. Always.'

The sheer injustice and falsity of the accusation left Elizabeth temporarily bereft of speech. She looked round helplessly for support, but her mother said nothing, because although Amy knew that her elder daughter's claim was untrue, she could understand how it might seem that way to Mary. For Mary had been prejudiced against Elizabeth ever since she was born; the natural jealousy of the elder for the younger child.

Elizabeth said shortly: 'Don't be stupid! Don't tell lies!'

'You hounded Alan! You hounded him!' Mary was growing hysterical. 'And now you've taken away my son.'

'Richard is not your son.' Only brutal frankness would do, Elizabeth decided. 'Alan was not your husband. And Richie is old enough to decide for himself what he wants to do.'

Mary was beyond reasoning. 'You're a bad influence on him!' she shouted. 'You've always been a bad influence on him. Not only have you encouraged him into that heathenish business of yours, but you've let him run around with a married woman!' She turned on Richard. 'Oh yes, I've seen you with Helen. I saw you a couple of months ago on the Tramways' Centre. You were coming out of the Hippodrome together. You'd been to see that Marlene Dietrich thing, *Blonde Venus*.'

It was Elizabeth's turn to stare at Richard, her sister momentarily forgotten. Amy, too, was regarding him, horrified.

'Richard?' Elizabeth queried. 'I thought that was over. I thought you said that day . . .'

'I didn't make any promises.' He stared back sullenly at the three accusing faces. 'I couldn't, Lizzie. You know why.'

So Helen was still threatening to kill herself, was she? Elizabeth sighed. She would have to see her cousin; there was nothing else for it. She wouldn't mention it to Jack: he would only say she was interfering again. But she must extricate Richard and Helen from a situation which was making them both unhappy. She would have to try talking sense to the pair of them.

The slam of the inner glass door recalled Elizabeth to her surroundings. She looked round for her sister, but Mary had gone; home to the three dingy rooms she inhabited near Eastwood Park.

'I'm sorry if I'm forcing myself on you,' Elizabeth said, removing her navy-blue straw hat and shaking out her hair. 'I'm aware that I'm *persona non grata* with most people these days, but I had to see you. It's about Richard.'

The upstairs drawing-room in the Pembroke Road house was cool and inviting after the burning heat of the streets outside. The country was in the grip of a drought. People were beginning to wonder if they would ever see rain again.

If Elizabeth had been shocked by Mary's appearance, she was equally so by Helen's. Not that her cousin was slatternly, far from it. Helen's beige silk dress, with its fluted organdie collar, was beautifully cut and obviously very expensive. The fair hair was fashionably cut and permanently-waved. But her eyes were devoid of animation, and her complexion, which Elizabeth remembered as clear and vivid, was thick and muddy. A cold sore had blistered at one corner of Helen's mouth.

'Do you mind if I sit down?' Elizabeth asked, when her cousin failed to offer her a seat. She tossed her hat and handbag on to the sofa and settled herself comfortably in its velvet depths. Helen, who still had not spoken, sat on the edge of one of the armchairs, as if poised for flight. 'It's about Richard,' Elizabeth said again, more gently.

Helen focused her eyes on Elizabeth's face, as if suddenly aware of her presence.

'It's all right,' she said dully. 'I know what you've come to say. He doesn't want to see me any more. I'd be a fool if I hadn't worked that out for myself.'

'Helen . . . Helen, dear.' Elizabeth stretched out her

hand. She had come prepared to do battle. Instead, she found herself unexpectedly moved by her cousin's obvious desperation. 'Helen, dear, what's gone wrong between you and Ben?'

Helen shivered. She made no move to take Elizabeth's hand, but clutched her own together tightly on her lap.

'Nothing's gone wrong,' she answered sharply.

'If nothing is wrong, why are you searching for happiness elsewhere? Don't — forgive me — but don't you and Ben want children?'

'Ben doesn't like children. He says they'd be an encumbrance. He says we shouldn't be able to do as we pleased.'

'And do you do as you please? You, I'm talking about, not Ben.'

'He has the factory. It keeps him busy.'

'So I imagine. But where does that leave you? Does Ben know that you and Richard are friends?'

A look of such fear came into Helen's eyes that Elizabeth was startled.

'You won't tell him, Lizzie! You won't, will you?' her cousin implored. She got off her chair and knelt beside Elizabeth. 'Promise me! Please!'

'For heaven's sake!' Elizabeth put an arm around Helen's slender shoulders to find that they were shaking. 'What do you take me for? Of course I won't tell. But Helen, darling, you must see that Richard isn't the answer.'

'He wants to break free,' Helen said in a low voice. 'I've known it for a long time. It's only because I've said I'll kill myself if he does that he sees me any more.'

'You can't hold on to someone you love that way.' Elizabeth smoothed her cousin's hair. 'Doesn't Ben love you any more?'

Again there was the convulsive shiver. 'He loves me too much. Too much.' Helen buried her face in her hands.

Elizabeth continued petting and coaxing her cousin back to a steadier frame of mind, while trying to sort out the confusion in her own. She did not believe for a moment that Ben had married Helen because he was in love with her: he had used his marriage simply as a means to an end, just as he had used his friendship with herself. But if, by some trick of fate, he had genuinely fallen in love with Helen afterwards, what sort of lover would he make?

Jealous, came the answer; because love was an emotion so alien to Ben's character that he would not know how to handle it. His own overwhelming self-regard would make it a crime if his affection were not returned a hundredfold. The esteem in which he held himself would demand the sort of constant adoration, constant admiration, which would rapidly kill the very love that he sought to inspire. For the first time since Ben jilted her in favour of her cousin, Elizabeth experienced a sense of relief.

Gently she drew her cousin's hands away from her face. 'If you're so frightened, Helen dear, why don't you leave him? Get a divorce. Go home to your parents. Uncle Joe and Aunt Minna wouldn't want you to be unhappy.'

'Divorce?' Helen's tear-stained face was shocked into immobility. 'Oh, I couldn't. I couldn't possibly.'

'Why not? It's not so uncommon these days, you know, as it used to be. There isn't the same social stigma attached to it as there was, say, ten years ago. Not unless you want to storm the Royal Enclosure at Ascot or have ambitions to be presented at court,' she added, trying to induce a smile.

But Helen was not amused. Divorce, to her, was a terrible disgrace; an outward sign of failure. It was frowned on by all sections of the Church, not least by the Methodists.

Elizabeth's sympathy changed to impatience. 'And I suppose adultery isn't frowned on by the Church,' she snapped, when Helen, haltingly, made her sentiments known. 'It's all right for you to deceive Ben, to cuckold him —' she took pleasure from such a good, Shakespearean-sounding phrase ' — but not to be honest and tell him that you no longer love him. Oh Helen, love!' Compassion once more overcame annoyance. 'I'm sorry. I didn't mean to be harsh but you must try to sort this thing out. Richard isn't the answer, as I told you before. Truly he isn't. You must let him go before you destroy him and yourself. And you know, if you were only half as much in love with him as you think you are, you wouldn't hesitate to leave Ben, ask for a divorce or flout any of the other shibboleths and restrictions which society imposes upon women. Wait until you're really in love. You'll find out.'

'I am in love with Richard! I am!'

'No, you're not. You're in love with being in love, which is something quite different. Think about it honestly, and you'll have to admit that what I'm saying is true.' Elizabeth got up and reached for her hat and handbag. 'Grow up, Helen. Start behaving like an adult woman.'

Helen stared resentfully at Elizabeth as she, too, rose to her feet. Elizabeth did not understand; her cousin had never loved anyone in her life. But she was right about Richard. He did not want her. She was becoming an embarrassment to him. From the drawing-room window, she watched Elizabeth walk down the path and through the gate. Then she went next door to the bedroom she shared with Ben.

The sleeping pills prescribed for her by the doctor were in their usual place. She emptied the bottle on the bedspread and the tablets spilled like white confetti across the soft pink silk. Then she went to the bathroom and filled a glass with water, carrying it carefully back to the bedroom and feeling completely detached, as though she were observing someone else, someone whose actions no longer concerned her. She set the brimming glass down on the washstand and crossed to the little bureau in one corner of the room. Taking out a sheet of notepaper and her fountain-pen, she started to write.

Elizabeth glanced at the perspiring customer on the other side of her desk and said to Norman Pargetter, who had just entered with two cups of tea: 'Open another window, will you please, Mr Pargetter? The heat really is dreadful in here.' She smiled apologetically at the grey-suited man opposite. 'I'm awfully sorry.'

'Not your fault, dear.' He mopped his face with a large white handkerchief. 'Can't remember a summer like it, and that's a fact.'

'No,' she agreed. 'We're not used to it in this country. But we're never satisfied, are we? If it rains, we grumble just as much.' The preliminaries over with this almost ritual discussion of the weather, Elizabeth sipped her tea and said: 'Right. Let's get down to details, then, shall we? How much exactly, Mr Peters, did you and your partner want to borrow? Naturally you've brought proof of collateral.'

Before Mr Peters could reply, however, he was diverted by the sound of shouting from the outer office. His head jerked in comical surprise towards the closed door.

'Where is he? Where's that fucking little bastard? I'll break every bone in his body! Davies! Where the bloody hell are you?'

Elizabeth hastily got up and opened the door of her room just as Jack emerged from his. In the main office, where Richard, Norman Pargetter and Miss Pringle worked, Richard's desk was empty. Elizabeth turned to face Ben.

He looked ill. He was unshaven and his skin was grey. His clothes, judging by their crumpled state,

281

seemed to have been slept in. A terrible premonition seized Elizabeth, but she managed to say calmly: 'Please lower your voice and moderate your language, Mr Sawyer. There are customers present.'

'Sod your customers!' Ben advanced on her, his eyes wild and staring. Jack would have moved between them, but she signalled impatiently for him to remain where he was.

'What's the matter, Ben?' she asked quietly. 'Has something happened?'

'As if you didn't know, or couldn't guess!' He pushed his face close to hers. Was this the same suave, cultured, unflappable man she had been in love with for all those years? She felt, suddenly, she had never really known Ben at all. He went on thickly: 'You went to see her yesterday afternoon. Mrs Bagot told me. Doing that young turd's dirty work for him, weren't you? First he seduces her, then he gives her the brush-off.' He looked round furiously. 'Where is he, eh? Where's Richard Davies? I'm going to kill the little bastard!'

'Is it Helen?' Elizabeth asked urgently. 'For God's sake, Ben, tell me what's happened!'

'Of course it's Helen! She's swallowed a bottle of bloody sleeping pills, that's what's happened! She left a note saying she couldn't go on. Giving the whole story!'

'Is she dead?'

'She would have been if I hadn't happened to get home early yesterday evening. She's been in the bloody infirmary all night, having her stomach washed out.'

Elizabeth let out her pent-up breath on a long sigh of relief. 'Thank heaven,' she said devoutly.

Ben, who seemed to have grown calmer during the last few moments, turned on her, his anger rekindled.

'Where the hell is he? Where's that little whelp?'

'Mr Davies is out,' Miss Pringle volunteered primly.

'He's gone to the bank. He decided to go himself, Miss Evans, instead of sending Norman.'

Elizabeth was acutely conscious of Mr Peters behind her, a fascinated and slightly horrified spectator of the drama. She was also uncomfortably aware of Jack's silent condemnation. He was angry because of what she had done.

'Let people run their own lives, Lizzie. Let them fight their own battles.' He had no need to say the words aloud: she knew precisely what was running through his mind.

Damn Helen! Why had she felt it necessary to implicate Richard? If she wanted to commit suicide, why not take the responsibility on her own shoulders? It was what Elizabeth would have done.

Jack touched Ben's arm. 'Come and sit down,' he urged. 'Have a cup of tea. I'm afraid we've nothing stronger.'

Ben swung round, giving Jack a push which sent him reeling back against the wall. At the same moment, the street door opened and Richard came in.

'Sorry I've been so long,' he called out cheerfully. 'The bank was choc-a-bloc for some unknown reason. God, it's hot!'

He paused, suddenly aware that something was wrong. The next minute, a pair of hands fastened like a vice around his throat. He staggered back, falling across Miss Pringle's desk, struggling for breath, and Miss Pringle jumped up, screaming. Jack and Norman Pargetter, aided by Mr Peters, tried to drag Ben away, but in spite of their combined efforts, Ben still retained his hold on Richard's neck.

Elizabeth looked around frantically, then dashed into the kitchen behind the main office. The big, black kettle, still more than half-full of water, had been left simmering on the gas-ring, so that, if necessary, Norman could replenish the tea. Elizabeth picked it up, discarding the lid, and ran back to the heaving knot of men.

'Stand aside!' she commanded the others, and poured the scalding water over Ben's gripping hands.

Yelling with sudden pain, he released Richard, who rolled off the desk and knelt, gasping, on the floor.

'Someone telephone for an ambulance,' Elizabeth ordered, crouching down beside Richard and trying to assess the damage done to his bruised and swollen neck. 'Tell them one person's badly scalded and someone else has been nearly choked to death.'

'The story's in all the local papers,' Amy said.

Elizabeth shrugged. 'I suppose that was unavoidable. Hell and damnation! Richard's taking it hard enough, without this.'

'Don't you swear in this house, my girl!' Two angry spots burned in Amy's pale cheeks. 'I don't suppose you know how Helen is? I shan't be hearing from Minna.'

'No, I don't expect you will.' Elizabeth sat down and eased the shoes from her aching feet. The bad publicity over this affair was having an adverse effect on business. It gave plenty of ammunition to all those moralists opposed to her profession. She had arrived at the office that morning to find every window fronting the street either cracked or broken. She comforted herself with the thought that the public had short memories. By this time next week they would have found some other object for their censure.

Richard worried her, however. He blamed himself for Helen's attempted suicide. Even the fact that she was making a good recovery in no way consoled him. Elizabeth had tried telling him that if anyone was to blame, she was. Had she never gone to see Helen, it might never have happened.

'She would have tried it sooner or later,' was all he would say. 'It's my fault. I'll never go near another married woman as long as I live.'

But although she had to smile, Elizabeth could see

284

that he was making himself ill, which was why she had asked Jack round to supper this evening. She wanted his approval for a scheme she was hatching.

Amy went to the pictures, taking Richard with her, at Elizabeth's request. The Tivoli was still struggling on, keeping its doors open, but only just. This week, Frederick March was starring in *Dr Jekyll and Mr Hyde*, a film which had reached the main Bristol cinemas the preceding year. Jack arrived shortly after their departure.

'I'm afraid it's only macaroni cheese,' Elizabeth said, putting the hot dish on a mat in the middle of the kitchen table.

'After the food at my digs, your mother's macaroni cheese will taste like manna from heaven,' Jack grinned. 'All right. I know I should move. I know I can afford it. I ought to want to better myself. There. I've said it all for you. Now tell me why you invited me round here tonight.'

'Do I only ask you round when I want something?' Elizabeth asked guiltily. 'But you're right. I do want a favour.' She began dishing up, then paused to look earnestly at him. 'Jack, with your permission, I want some money from the firm. A substantial sum. About five hundred pounds. I want to pay Richard's fare to America and see that he has a reasonable start when he gets there. Enough money to support him for at least a year. I want to get him away from England for a while. Perhaps not for ever, but a sufficient time for him to get over what's happened. Sufficient time for Helen to get over him, without the temptation of trying to contact him again. Would you be agreeable? What do you say?'

CHAPTER TWENTY-TWO

Helen bought a copy of the *Daily Sketch* from the newspaper-stand at the corner of Apsley Road, then walked a little further down Blackboy Hill and went into one of the cafés. She found a secluded corner table and slid into the chair nearest the wall. She felt safer with some sort of protection at her back. The newspaper also acted as a barrier between her and the rest of the world.

She stared at the front page, a picture of the King and the Earl of Harewood with the two little princesses, Elizabeth and Margaret Rose, and the Earl's younger son, the Honourable Gerald Lascelles, standing on the balcony of Buckingham Palace. They were, the *Sketch* reported, acknowledging the cheers of the crowds who had gathered after the royal party's return from St Paul's Cathedral, where the Silver Jubilee Thanksgiving Service had been held. The date above the photograph was Tuesday, May 7, 1935. 'Pages of Jubilee pictures' the paper promised.

Helen then flicked through them without interest. There had been a time when any mention of the royal family, however trivial, would have commanded her whole attention. But for the past two years, ever since her abortive suicide attempt, she had found it difficult to take an interest in anything. She had come out today because she felt she must get out of the house, and not, like everyone else, to see the decorations — the flags, the bunting, the yards of red, white and blue ribbons, the loyal window displays which fronted every shop in Clifton.

Helen ordered coffee and a bun, the latter, when it arrived, being patriotically striped with red, white and blue icing. The lady at the next table had fancy cakes; 'butterfly' cakes, with pink, white and pale blue mock cream under the 'wings' of sponge. The white table-cloths had been decorated with strips of red and blue crêpe paper. Three Union Jacks hung from the ceiling.

Helen sipped her coffee and went on turning the pages of the *Sketch*. English people, normally so reticent, were inclined to unbend at times of national rejoicing and engage perfect strangers in conversation. She did not want that. She did not want to speak to anyone. Ben, with her parents' consent, had taken her to London to consult one of the new psychiatric doctors, but it had done no good. All the doctor's exhortations to her to relax, his attempts to probe the secrets of her childhood and first marriage, had elicited no response. How could she possibly say she was afraid of her husband, when Ben had done nothing to deserve it? She could not say why she was afraid of Ben. He had never laid a finger on her, and yet she felt perpetually menaced by him. She felt his presence permeating the house, even when he was not there. Her heart fluttered painfully every evening when he walked into the room where she was sitting; panic seized her when he kissed her; and when he made love to her, she shook with fear. A year ago, he had angrily moved into another bedroom, declaring he would get more response from a block of wood; but every now and then he insisted on sharing her bed.

'You're my wife and you'll sleep with me whenever I choose,' he had told her icily the last time it had happened.

Joseph and Minna could not understand her attitude towards her husband, nor reconcile themselves to the shame of her betrayal. Her father was still affectionate, but he treated her with reserve. Neither he nor her mother could forgive her for breaking the seventh commandment. She had betrayed them and her up-bringing, too. They pointed out how forbearing Ben was; how he loved her. And he did love her, but in a twisted way that wanted her for himself alone. He was jealous if she so much as spoke to another person.

The house had become a prison. And yet it was a prison she rarely voluntarily left; a prison she hated but clung to, because she was afraid of other people; afraid of Ben's jealousy; afraid of being hurt again. She relied heavily on her sleeping pills, and found that when she did not take them, she slept badly and had wild dreams. One of her most frequently recurring night-mares was that Ben was about to strangle her. She would wake, sitting up in bed, fighting for breath.

Someone sat down in the empty chair opposite her own. The café had filled up and Helen had feared that the table might have to be shared. She did not glance up, however, pretending an interest in what she was reading. And at that precise moment, her attention was genuinely caught by an item of news at the foot of the page. It was headed: British Discovery Signed by M-G-M. She began to tremble.

'Richard Davies,' she read, 'the latest British discovery to make his mark in Hollywood, has signed a three-year contract with the Metro-Goldwyn-Mayer studios. He is quoted as saying that he is absolutely thrilled. Mr Davies, who, like Cary Grant, hails from Bristol, has spent the last two years in America on what he describes as a working vacation. He has been touring the States doing a number of jobs, including garage attendant and waiter. It was while working as a waiter at a Hollywood party that an M-G-M talent scout spotted Richard's classical good looks. A successful screen test followed.'

'You look as though you'd seen a ghost, Mrs Sawyer,' said a pleasant American drawl in her ear. She looked up, still dazed, trying to place the man with the fair, wavy hair and hazel eyes, realizing that the face was somehow familiar. 'I'm Christopher Morgan,' he reminded her, holding out his hand. 'We met three years ago, in rather less pleasant circumstances than these.'

Helen frowned, then memories came flooding back. 'Oh! Oh yes. I remember now. Old Market Street, during the riot.'

'That's right. You didn't suffer any ill effects from that day, I trust?'

'No. I was quite all right, thank you.'

The American considered her. She seemed extraordinarily jumpy. When she lifted her coffee cup, her hand trembled and she spilled some of the liquid in the saucer. He thought, as he had thought before, what an extremely pretty woman she was; even when, as now, she looked so ill. But it was not her emaciated appearance which touched some chord deep within him: there was, even more now than three years ago, a lost expression, a vulnerability, which appealed to his innate chivalry, his desire to protect.

She seemed curiously incurious about him, like someone sleep-walking. He said: 'I'm still here, you see. I decided to stay on in Bristol for a while, and the months have just drifted into years. My Daddy's not exactly pleased with me, and he's stopped my allowance. But I get by.'

Helen smiled, and surprised herself by making an effort to keep the conversation going.

'You're not homesick, then?'

He grinned. 'What, in a city which boasts places like Philadelphia Street, Penn Street and the Cabot Tower? Yes, of course I'm homesick sometimes, but it hasn't been bad enough to shift me yet.'

'What do you do? For a living, I mean.'

'I've gotten myself a job managing a third-rate picture house on the other side of town. The Tivoli cinema in a place called Eastwood. You wouldn't know it.'

'I was born in Eastwood. My father's factory is there. Gordon's.'

'The chocolate people? Well, I'm darned! Seen your Daddy about, once or twice. Fine-looking man with grey hair. Saw him only last week, being driven to work in a big new Daimler.'

'Yes. My . . . my husband . . . is his partner.' Helen gathered together her handbag and gloves. She stood up, and for a moment, the American had the impression of panic. It was almost as though she were escaping from him. 'Goodbye, Mr Morgan,' she said breathlessly, half-extending her hand, then withdrawing it again before he could grasp it. 'I have to go. An . . . An appointment.'

He watched the café door swing closed behind her. He was frowning to himself when the waitress came to take his order.

Elizabeth glared at the American seated on the other side of her desk and demanded crossly: 'Didn't your father ever tell you not to get into the hands of moneylenders?'

Christopher Morgan shouted with laughter. 'He did, but I think he might have made an exception in your case. By the way, are you Hennessey or Evans?'

'I'm Elizabeth Evans. Why have you come to us, Mr Morgan?' She looked directly at him. 'We don't deal in small personal loans any more.'

'Oh.' He seemed disconcerted. 'Various people in Eastwood recommended you very highly. Said they used to deal with you in the old days, when you had a place in Canal Street. Local girl made good, they said. Though I gather that isn't the general consensus.'

'Far from it,' Elizabeth agreed drily. 'What are you doing in Eastwood, for heaven's sake?'

'At present, I'm managing the Tivoli cinema, but I've had other jobs before that. I rent an apartment — flat I guess you'd call it — round the back of the brewery.'

'You mean you've no collateral whatsoever?' Elizabeth asked despairingly. 'Why do you want two hundred pounds?'

'I want to buy myself a car.' He winked at her. 'I want to impress a lady.'

'You'd be far wiser to keep your money in your pocket,' she retorted with asperity, 'and go by 'bus or tramcar. But if it's desperate, won't your parents help? What about your father?'

Chris Morgan grimaced. 'Daddy won't do anything for me. He's angry because I haven't gone home. I only came to Europe for a year or two's travel, to broaden my mind, and I'm still here four years later. My Daddy wants me home to help run the family business.'

'What sort of business?'

'Oh, this and that. Mainly the grocery trade.'

A sudden suspicion made Elizabeth look even harder at him. 'Morgan's,' she said slowly. 'There's a big food chain in America called Morgan's. It's so well known we've even heard of it over here. There wouldn't be any connection, would there?'

'Hell! What's the point of denying it? You've guessed anyway. But the grocery business is so damn boring. If it was oil now, that would be different. My Daddy must be the only millionaire in Texas who hasn't made his fortune out of oil.'

'And roughing it in Eastwood and managing a flea-pit like the Tivoli isn't boring? Come on, Mr Morgan! Who do you think you're kidding? I suspect your trouble is that you had too much of everything too soon. Spoilt from the moment you were born. Just at present you're finding it fun to go slumming. It's a novelty that will wear off, believe me.'

'Look,' he said angrily, 'I'm nearly twenty-eight years old. Not so much younger than you are, I'll bet. So stop talking to me as if you were my mother. I came here to borrow money, not to get myself a lecture. OK?'

'Then you're old enough to have more sense. Grow up, Mr Morgan. You can't go on being irresponsible all you life.' Elizabeth drew in her breath. 'I'm sorry, but as I told you, we don't deal in small personal loans any more. Take my advice and save up for what you want. Or better still, go home and join the family business. There are plenty of people who would give their eye teeth for your chances in life. And what's more, they'd know what to do with them. It's not right that you should be frittering your life away in the way that you're doing.'

She expected the American to be angrier still, but instead, he just laughed.

'You're the darnedest woman I ever did meet! Don't you want to make money?'

'Not the kind a two hundred pound loan could bring me. Although I admit that's how we started. But those days are over.'

'Then why do you still live in Eastwood?' he wanted to know. 'I've seen you about, but I didn't know who you were or what you did.'

'Because I'm waiting for a particular house,' she answered. 'One which isn't on the market, and which the present owner won't part with, no matter how much I offer him. But I'll wear him down in time.'

'Poor guy. I'm sorry for him. You're a very determined lady.' Christopher Morgan got to his feet. 'You won't help me then? I'll just have to go to some other firm.'

He had reached the door when Elizabeth called him back. 'Sit down,' she ordered. 'If you go to somebody else, you could get fleeced. I'll tell you what I'll do. I'll make you a personal loan out of my own pocket. Don't ask me why. I must like you, I suppose. No terms, no contract. Just pretend I'm your aunt. You pay me back when and how you can. You know where I live. Springtime Grove. Number eighteen. Come round this evening and I'll give you my personal cheque.'

'Why should you take such a risk? You know nothing about me. And you don't look in the least like my maiden aunt.'

'A young friend of mine has been making his way round America for the past two years, in very similar circumstances to yours, and he has met with nothing but kindness from your compatriots.'

'And I suppose you're helping him out, too. You're a generous lady, Miss Evans.'

'I have been helping him out,' she agreed, ignoring the compliment, 'but I shan't need to any more. He's in Hollywood at the moment. He's just landed a film contract with M-G-M.'

'Hey! Now that's real enterprise,' Chris Morgan said admiringly, rising once more. 'Thanks for your offer, Miss Evans, but I can't accept.' He made his way to the door where he paused with his hand on the handle. 'You know, you remind me of someone, but I can't think who. Anyway, thanks again. See you around.'

He was gone, and Elizabeth was left staring after him. She heard the telephone ring in Jack's office next door, then pressed the buzzer on her desk for one of the two secretaries they now employed.

But when the door opened, it was neither Miss White nor Miss Gimple who entered, but Jack, looking rather pale. He crossed the room to Elizabeth and put his arm round her shoulders.

'Lizzie, dear,' he began, then stopped, as though he did not know how to continue.

'Well?' she demanded. '"Lizzie, dear" what? Do go on, Jack. I have another client to see at three.'

'Lizzie . . . Mary's just telephoned.' Elizabeth raised her head in astonishment and his grip on her shoulders tightened. 'She asked me to tell you . . . It's your mother. She was knocked down by a car outside the house. Lizzie, love . . . I'm afraid she's dead.'

Elizabeth sat in the kitchen, staring at the empty grate. She remembered the fires which used to burn there even during a heat-wave, before the new gas-stove made them unnecessary, except for winter warmth. But May this year was hot, and Amy had not bothered even to lay a fire.

Mary, dry-eyed, but haggard, had made tea. Eileen Hennessey, in floods of tears, was stretched out on the old black leather sofa.

'How did it happen?' Elizabeth asked. 'Did anyone see the accident?'

'I did,' Eileen Hennessey sobbed, and was unable to say more for several minutes.

Mary, with a patience which drove Elizabeth wild, persuaded their neighbour to sit up straight and handed her a cup and saucer.

'Drink the tea while it's hot. It'll steady your nerves.'

Elizabeth clenched both fists. 'Will one of you please tell me what happened!'

'Eileen was standing at her gate,' Mary said, 'talking to one of the women who lives further up the street — '

'The one who's just moved into number twenty-seven,' Eileen Hennessey put in, then burst once more into tears.

'Mama heard them chatting and went out to join them — '

'We were discussing that knitting pattern in last week's *Woman's Weekly*.' Jack's mother blew her nose in an extremely grubby handkerchief. 'And then Mrs Chubb, opposite, came out of her front door and shouted across to Amy. Something about some recipe Amy had wanted to borrow. Mrs Chubb was waving it in her hand . . . Oh dear God! Why didn't she look where she was going?'

'Mama, you mean?'

294

'Yes. She was standing by my gate, and she just turned and stepped straight into the road. The driver of the car didn't have time to do anything about it. He just knocked her flying. The doctor says her neck was broke.'

Eileen Hennessey's teeth began to chatter against the rim of her cup, and some of the hot tea spilled down the front of her blouse. Gently, Mary took the cup and saucer from her and helped the older woman to her feet.

'I'll take you home,' she offered. 'The doctor said you'd had a bad shock and were to rest. The girls are home from work. I can hear them moving about next door.' She added over her shoulder to Elizabeth: 'I'll be back in a minute.'

Elizabeth nodded bleakly. It had not even occurred to her as odd that Mary was speaking to her again after all these years. She felt nothing but a cold, unreasoning anger with God, with fate, with the whole world, ever since Jack had broken the news to her. Haphazard, indiscriminate accidents were something she read about in the newspapers or heard about over the radio. They were not something that happened to people she knew.

She had returned home in a kind of daze. Jack had insisted that she take a taxi. He would have come with her, but he had to stay behind to interview both her client and his own. He had wanted either Miss Gimple or Miss Pringle to accompany her, but Elizabeth had refused. She had needed to be alone. She had not even been surprised to find Mary at home, so right and proper had it seemed.

The shock of her mother's death had shaken Mary out of the lethargy into which she had fallen during the years of her self-imposed exile from Springtime Grove. With only herself to please and care for, she had grown apathetic about everything except her dislike of her sister, whom she regarded as the author of all her ills.

295

Deep down, she had recognized the injustice of this attitude, but she had to have someone to blame, because she was incapable of blaming herself. The tragedy of Amy's fatal accident, however, had brought her up short, facing the realization that there was no one close to her now, except Elizabeth.

Arriving home, she had found the police and the doctor in possession, with various neighbours drifting in and out, all anxious to give their version of events; and instead of going to pieces, as everyone, including herself, had expected her to do, Mary had taken charge with a calm and efficiency worthy of Elizabeth. And when Elizabeth herself arrived, she was, for once in their lives, less able to cope with the situation than Mary. She had clung to her elder sister, shaking and crying, until Mary had forced her to sit down and drink some tea.

Mary returned from next door, where she had left Eileen Hennessey to the ministrations of her two younger daughters, to find Elizabeth still gazing at the empty grate.

'Finish your tea,' she ordered. 'Here, let me pour you another cup. That one's cold.'

'Where is she?' Elizabeth asked. 'Is she ... upstairs?'

'Yes. In the front bedroom. The doctor's sending the nurse round presently to lay her out. I shouldn't go up till then.' Mary nodded towards the mantelpiece. 'There's a letter for you. Must have come after you left this morning.' She took an envelope down from the shelf as she spoke, and handed it to her sister.

Elizabeth turned the letter over in her hand. It bore a Bristol postmark. She did not recognize the handwriting.

'I wonder who it's from,' she said without interest.

'Read it and see.' Mary took back the envelope, slitting it open and handing the contents to Elizabeth. They looked at one another and, after a moment's hesitation, smiled, both suddenly struck by this strange reversal of roles.

Elizabeth spread out the single sheet of notepaper, covered by a few lines of writing in a large and sprawling hand. When she had finished reading, she leaned back in her chair, closing her eyes.

'It would come now, wouldn't it?' she asked. 'Now that Mama's dead and can't share it with me.'

'What's the matter? Has someone left you a fortune?'

'Better than that. The present owner of The Brass Mill has decided to accept my offer, after all. I suppose he's realized that he'll never get more for it than I'm prepared to give him.'

Mary was startled. 'You mean . . . You mean you can afford to buy a place like that?'

Elizabeth opened her eyes in surprise. 'Of course. Jack could, too, if he wanted to. Now, don't put on your prunes-and-prisms face, Mary, for heaven's sake! Jack and I have made a legitimate profit from a legitimate business. In fact, we're thinking of expanding and opening up a second branch of the firm in Gloucester.' She glanced around her. 'It's time I got out of here. I've been telling Mama so for a long time, but she didn't want to leave, and I didn't want to move until I could get The Brass Mill. So we just stayed on. In any case, this house and its contents will have to be sold now. Presumably Mama left everything between us.' She looked again at her sister. 'I suppose you wouldn't care to come and live with me?'

Mary shook her head decidedly. 'No. No, I couldn't.'

Elizabeth sighed. 'That's what I thought you'd say.' She got up. 'I'll just have to live on my own then. I can't ask Jack. It wouldn't be proper.'

'Since when has that worried you? Why don't you marry him, Lizzie? He loves you, you know.'

'But I don't love him, that's the problem. I'm extremely fond of Jack, but that isn't enough. I don't feel about him as I felt about Ben.'

'Are you still in love with Ben?' Mary asked. It seemed a moment for confidences.

Elizabeth shivered. 'No. No, I'm not. I think I had a lucky escape there. Helen's frightened to death of him; and, with hindsight, I think she has a right to be. There's a streak of violence in Ben, buried deep beneath that elegant exterior.'

'There is in a lot of men. There was in Alan.'

'You've never heard any more of Alan?' It was Elizabeth's turn to probe.

'No, I shan't, either. He was no more in love with me than Ben was with you.'

Elizabeth smiled sadly. 'We're a bright pair, aren't we? Unloved and alone. Lonely. So why don't we stick together, you and I? You could keep house for me at The Brass Mill. I'd pay you a very good wage.'

Mary hesitated. Accepting her sister's proposition would mean abandoning many of her most rigidly held principles. But all at once she was sick of principles. They were no compensation for loneliness and advancing age. It was true, too, that she and Elizabeth only had each other now. One of the chief bones of contention between them, Richard, had been removed. And if she earned her keep, it made her independent.

'All right, then,' she said. 'I will. Tell me when everything's settled and I'll hand in my notice at Gordon's.' She smiled at Elizabeth's astonished face. 'We'll work out something together. Somehow or other, we'll make it work.'

Part Five 1936-1940

Come live with me and be my love;
And we will all the pleasures prove.
                    Christopher Marlowe 1564 – 1593

CHAPTER TWENTY-THREE

Ben's secretary came into his office and said: 'Mr Gordon would like to see you, Mr Sawyer.'

Ben cursed under his breath and laid down his pen. 'You wouldn't happen to know what he wants, would you, Miss Beaumont?'

'I think it's something to do with the lid design for the coronation toffee-tin. Mr Gordon doesn't think the photographic reproduction is good enough.'

'Hell and damnation! Sorry, Miss Beaumont, but it's not my province and well he knows it. Why doesn't he get on to Chesney's? They're doing the art work.'

'I believe Mr Gordon wants to scrap the existing lid altogether. He wants some more suggestions.'

'That's up to the Chesney people, surely! They're the ones who should be coming up with ideas. Then it's for us to say "yes" or "no".'

Miss Beaumont made no reply, merely standing pointedly by the open door. Ben savagely screwed the top on his fountain pen and scraped back his chair.

'I'll have to go and see the old man, I suppose. I'm expecting a call from my wife. Let me know the minute she 'phones.'

The secretary nodded, moving aside to let Ben through. There was something unnatural, she thought, in the way he was always expecting his wife to contact him. Miss Beaumont knew — everyone in the office knew — why Helen Sawyer had tried to commit suicide three years ago. She had been involved with another man. But while Ben seemed ready to forgive, it was obvious that he was unwilling to forget. Miss Beaumont returned to her desk, took the cover off her typewriter and opened her pad of shorthand notes. She like being Ben's secretary, he was a good boss, but he was the first man she had ever worked for with whom she had not been just a little in love. For some reason or other, the idea of any physical contact with him made her shiver.

Ben entered his father-in-law's office without knocking, a small discourtesy which gave him disproportionate satisfaction.

Joseph scowled but said nothing. 'Sit down, lad,' he ordered, indicating the chair drawn up on the other side of his desk, 'and tell me what you think about this.' He pushed across the sample, circular toffee-tin lid. 'I think we shall have to scrap the photograph idea. It doesn't do His Majesty justice.'

Ben glanced at the still boyish face of his new sovereign and the gold lettering around the raised rim of the lid. 'To Commemorate the Coronation of His Majesty King Edward VIII, May 12th, 1937. God Save the King.'

'It looks all right to me,' Ben commented. He shrugged. 'Perhaps it's not the best of likenesses, but you'll see a lot worse before this year and next are out.'

'I don't want second-best for Gordon's,' Joe objected. 'Not for such an auspicious occasion. And the Bond Street Assortment has always been one of our classiest lines. I want a distinguished container. The colour's fine. I like this dark green with the gold lettering. Also the royal coat-of-arms repeated round the body of the tin. It's the lid that spoils it.'

Ben pursed his lips. 'There's over a twelvemonth yet to the coronation, and I don't know that I'd be in too much of a hurry to come to any firm decision. We may find that we have to change the lid again before we're through.'

'What do you mean?' Joe stared. 'If you're referring to this Mrs Simpson business, in my view it's just a lot of newspaper gossip. Besides, even if there were something in it, Edward would never marry her. He knows better than to make a twice-divorced woman Queen of England.'

'He could abdicate.'

'Rubbish! Queen Mary wouldn't let him. He wouldn't do it. He knows which side his bread is buttered.'

'Nevertheless, I suggest that until the situation is clarified, we hold fire on the special coronation lines. Put them into six months' abeyance.'

'And have our competitors beat us to it?

'It's a risk we'll have to take. We might well have the laugh on them.'

Joseph hesitated. He respected his son-in-law's judgement, but on this occasion it conflicted with his sense of loyalty. He would canvas the opinions of the firm's other senior members. He wanted to settle this matter of packaging the coronation assortments.

He changed the subject, slipping a hand into one of his pockets and producing an oblong of white pasteboard with gilt lettering.

'Have you and Helen received one of these things?' he demanded.

'An invitation to Elizabeth's house-warming at this place she's bought in Leigh Woods? Yes. Ours arrived this morning.'

'Are you going?'

'No. Are you?'

For answer, Joe ripped the invitation card several times across and dropped the pieces into his wastepaper basket.

'That's the proper place for that,' he snorted. 'A

godless, heathen way to make money! I wouldn't let Minna be contaminated by mixing in Lizzie's society. I always said no good would come of educating women, and Lizzie Evans is the living proof that I was right. A Judas! That's what that girl was to me. After all Minna and I did for her and her family.'

Ben had heard the complaint too often for it to excite his sympathy. Indeed, until the affair between Helen and Richard Davies, he had derived a certain amusement from his father-in-law's discomfiture, guessing that Joe was motivated more by jealousy of his niece's success than by any moral or religious scruples regarding the way in which she had made her money. Ben had once remarked to Helen that Elizabeth was probably more ethical in her business dealings than Joe was.

But Ben's attitude had changed. He had grown to hate Elizabeth since her championing of Richard Davies and her assistance in getting the boy away to the United States. Nor could he ever forgive her for making him look a fool that day in her office. The physical hurt he had not minded; it was the wound she had dealt his pride. If the thought ever occurred to him that her prompt action had saved him from the crime and consequences of murder, he suppressed it. He did not want to be grateful to her. Nor could he believe, at this distance of time, that he had intended any serious harm to Richard Davies. He had simply meant to give the young bastard a well deserved thrashing.

So when Elizabeth's invitation to her house-warming party at The Brass Mill had dropped through the letter-box that morning, he had anticipated Joe's action by tossing it into the dining-room fire. Helen had made no comment; but he remembered now, uneasily, how she had sat watching the thin slip of pasteboard curl and blacken in the flames.

Elizabeth paused, framed in the library doorway, a

cocktail glass half-full of an Old Fashioned held in one hand. The brilliant light from the room behind her made her nothing but a silhouette. Yet Jack, descending the stairs, recognized her at once. His heart thumped with pleasure, as it always did at the sight of her. How ridiculous that after all these years she could still have the power to affect him in such a way.

'Is she coming down?' Elizabeth asked hopefully, but Jack shook his head.

'She says she'd rather stay in her room. She says she doesn't know anyone and she'd only feel awkward.' Jack grimaced. 'I told her I didn't know many of the people, either. I said they were mostly business acquaintances, not really friends.'

'Well, upon my word.' Elizabeth advanced a few paces into the hall. 'You know them every bit as well as I do. Most of them. Bother Mary! Why will she insist on behaving like a servant? And before you make the retort I read in your eyes, Jack, it's simply not true. I've tried my best to convince my sister that this is as much her home now as mine.'

'I know you have. But it's too grand for her, Lizzie, as it is for me. A nice detached house somewhere in a Bristol suburb would suit her much better. Even then she'd miss Eastwood. Eastwood's a bit like a village.'

'Don't I know it!' Elizabeth retorted grimly. 'With a village mentality, all gossip and petty-mindedness. Why on earth you stay there I really can't fathom.'

'I've told you. I feel comfortable there.'

Jack had recently bought one of the solid Victorian mansions on the far side of Eastwood park, relics of the district's little spurt of renewed prosperity in the late eighteen-nineties, before it slid into its final decline. Elizabeth had not approved. She had wanted Jack to move right away from Eastwood; away from the animosity which, though fainter, continued to dog them and make them outcasts from the close-knit Methodist society they had always known. Number

305

eighteen Springtime Grove had passed into other hands. If Elizabeth regretted it, she gave no sign.

She moved into the centre of the hall and glanced around her. 'There's still a lot to do, but I don't intend rushing to fill the place up with a lot of second-rate stuff. I want it, eventually, to look as the Miss Turners would have remembered it when they were young. Only the very best, Jack. Only the very best.'

She was beautiful tonight, he thought. Her hair, with its auburn highlights, waved back from her broad, high forehead to nestle in a cluster of little curls at the nape of her neck. Her dress was made of floating black georgette, setting off her pale, smooth skin to perfection. Her wide-set blue eyes were sparkling with excitement. The total absence of jewellery, and its significance, were not lost upon Jack: all Elizabeth's share of the profits went into The Brass Mill. Personal adornment of that kind would have to wait.

'Mary's worth her weight in gold,' she mused. 'She looks after the place magnificently. Later on, when I've opened up some of the other rooms, she'll have to have assistance . . . For heaven's sake, Jack, we can't stand here nattering. It's being rude to our other guests.'

He followed her into the library, the only room as yet fully restored to its former glory, but with an absence of books which made its title a mockery. Elizabeth, however, had refused here, as everywhere else in the house, to do anything of which the Miss Turners would not have approved.

'I know I could buy a crate-load of books from George's,' she had said disparagingly. 'I know I could haunt the sales and purchase job lots by the yard. But that's not what making a library is all about. It has to be a personal choice, each volume meaning something to me, reflecting my tastes. It will be a long haul, but I have plenty of time. I hope to live the rest of my life here.'

The room was filled with just sufficient people to

dignify the event with the status of a party, but not enough to be uncomfortably crowded. Nearly all of those present were business acquaintances, as Jack had said, there being a notable absence of family. Miss Pringle and Norman Pargetter were there as the two senior members of an ever-increasing staff; for as well as retaining the premises behind Philadelphia Street, the Evans and Hennessey Financial Loan Company had recently acquired another building in Cotham, and it seemed likely that offices would be opened in both Gloucestershire and Somerset during the course of the next few years.

The only person present who seemed unconnected with the business was an American, whom Jack knew vaguely by sight as the manager of Eastwood's Tivoli cinema.

'I didn't realize that you and young — ah — what's-his-name were friendly,' he murmured, nodding his head in Chris Morgan's direction.

'"Young what's-his-name" — who, incidentally, is getting on for twenty-nine — and I have met twice. The first time was when he came to borrow some money, which I refused to lend him, the day Mama was killed. The second occasion was more recent, when he came to see me here one evening, to inform me that the present owner of the Tivoli is putting it up for sale. He wondered if you and I might like to expand our interests, Jack, and go into the cinema business. He thinks it would be a good time to buy. He says the movie industry is booming.'

Jack laughed, mixing himself a cocktail from the laden table set between two of the long windows.

'I trust you told him what he could do with his proposition.'

'No.' Something in Elizabeth's tone made Jack glance up sharply. 'I invited him here tonight to talk to you.'

Jack put down his glass with a snap. 'You're not serious,' he pleaded.

'Why not? It would be good for us to try something different. Something in addition to what we're doing. A second string to our bow. And I trust Mr Morgan's judgement. His father is one of the shrewdest business brains in the US. Even you, Jack, must have heard of Morgan's, the food-store chain.'

Jack looked astonished, as well he might, she reflected. But before he could ask any questions, she signalled to Chris, who was hovering near, and made the necessary introductions.

'You two have a little chat,' she murmured, preparing to leave them. 'Go in the garden, if you wish. It's a nice, warmish April night. I have to go and talk to some of these other people. I really am being a very poor hostess.'

'Elizabeth!' Jack exclaimed in minatory accents, but she took no notice and moved away.

By nine o'clock, some guests had already left and others were preparing to make their excuses, bored by the rather sedate nature of the house-warming. It was not that there was a lack of conviviality or even of drink — pink gins, Old Fashioneds, White Ladies and Manhattans had been consumed in quantity — but there was something about Elizabeth herself which they found slightly daunting. As one wife complained bitterly to her husband during the drive home: 'She asked me if I'd read *The Rock Pool* by somebody called Cyril Connolly, and then looked down her nose when I said I'd never heard of it. I almost expected her to dish me out a hundred lines.'

Her husband nodded. 'I know what you mean. I've always felt that if she wasn't so damn good at making money, Liz Evans would have made a very fine school-marm.'

At The Brass Mill itself, there was a feeling of relief as the guests departed. Jack had never liked social gatherings of any kind, because they made him feel inadequate. Elizabeth, while perfectly hospitable, nevertheless experienced a feeling of disappointment. The people she had played host to that evening were not the company she had once envisaged herself and Ben entertaining. But then, in those days, she had not foreseen the path her life would follow.

Finally, everyone had left except Chris Morgan, whom Elizabeth had encouraged to stay behind.

'Well?' she asked Jack. 'Has he convinced you?'

'About this scheme of yours to buy the Tivoli? Lizzie, do you know the difficulties facing independent cinemas? You need to be part of a chain, linked with one of the major distributors.'

'That's part of the fun, Jack. The challenge of making it work. Cinema audiences are increasing. People need to escape from reality, from the drabness of their lives, from unemployment and despair. There's a big potential audience in a district like Eastwood. We'll spend some money on the place. Do it up. Put in new seating. Make it the focal point for the whole community. Chris has agreed to stay on and run things for us. For a substantial rise in salary, of course.'

'Of course,' the American grinned.

Jack said nothing, still looking dubious. Mary cautiously poked her head round the library door, then relaxed and came in.

'I thought it was quiet,' she remarked. 'I guessed everyone must have gone.' She posed the inevitable question. 'How about a nice cup of tea?'

'Lovely,' Elizabeth breathed, kicking off her shoes and lying full length on the leather sofa. 'It's funny, but I've never really taken to alcohol. My Methodist upbringing engenders a terrible sense of guilt whenever I drink it.'

'Quite right, too,' was Mary's trenchant comment, before withdrawing to the kitchen regions.

Jack nodded approvingly at Elizabeth. 'She's looking well, Liz. You've done wonders there. I haven't seen Mary appear to such advantage for a long time.'

Elizabeth laughed. 'It wasn't easy. I practically had to kidnap her to get her to the hairdresser's. And the fuss she made about having it cut! But once the deed was done, even she admitted how much better she looked. After that, it wasn't so difficult getting her to throw out all those terrible, frumpish clothes and buy new ones. Under my aegis, of course.'

'Oh, I can see that yours has been the guiding hand.' Jack turned to Chris. 'You'll soon discover, Mr Morgan, that you have to guard your independence very jealously where Lizzie is concerned. She'll be running not only the picture-house, but your life as well, if you don't watch out.'

'Jack!' Elizabeth clapped her hands delightedly. 'Does that mean you agree? That we can go ahead and negotiate to buy the Tivoli?'

'I agree, but I'm not saying that I approve. As far as I'm concerned it's just self-preservation. I know you'll make my life a misery if I say "no".'

Elizabeth threw a cushion at his head. 'A fine reputation you're giving me, I must say!'

The front door bell jangled. Elizabeth had insisted on leaving the original, rather ancient bell in place, feeling that one of the modern push-button affairs would not only be out of keeping with the appearance of the house, but also be largely inaudible. She stared at Jack with lifted eyebrows, then glanced at the tall-case clock. The time was almost five to ten.

'I didn't hear a car, did you?' she asked the two men.

Mary's brisk footsteps sounded as she crossed the hall, followed by the murmur of voices. A moment later the library door opened and Helen stood in the doorway.

'I've come t' the party,' she said, slurring her words together as though she were drunk. 'Ben said . . . wasn't t' come . . . Said I w's goin' to.' As she advanced into the room, it became apparent that she was in a very dishevelled state; and as though suddenly conscious

310

that her appearance needed some explanation, she added, smiling beatifically: 'Locked me in my room. Tied sheets t'gether. Climbed down.'

Elizabeth had risen and gone over to her cousin. She put an arm around Helen's waist, supporting her.

'Helen, love, you haven't *driven* here, have you?'

Helen turned her head and blinked, as though not quite certain to whom she was speaking.

'Not drunk,' she said, solemnly shaking her head. 'Had a pill. Calm me down. Di'n't drive. Ben took keys . . . Car keys. Walked.'

'Ye gods!' Elizabeth led her cousin to the vacated sofa and made Helen sit down.

Mary, who had been watching from the doorway, remarked severely: 'I'll get the tea and bring an extra cup.' She vanished with a disapproving hunch of her shoulders.

Jack and Chris Morgan, who had risen when Helen entered, stood awkwardly, looking down at her. She returned their look, smiling vacantly into their faces.

'She's had more than one pill, I reckon,' Chris Morgan said, leaning forward and taking her wrist between his fingers. 'Her pulse is very low.'

'We'll have to get her to bed,' Elizabeth said decisively. 'She can't possibly go home like this. Mary will help me undress her.'

'I could run her home on my way back to Eastwood,' Jack offered. 'We could put her on the back seat of the car.'

Elizabeth shook her head. 'No, thanks all the same, Jack. I really think I should keep her here. I guess she and Ben have had a pretty bad fight. It must have been sheer will-power that got her this far. It's a miracle she didn't collapse on the Downs, or throw herself off the Suspension Bridge. I'd better telephone Ben, I suppose, and let him know that she's safe.'

Even as she spoke, they all heard the throb of an engine as a car bumped and bucketed its way down the narrow, tree-lined lane, which was The Brass Mill's only access from the main Portishead and Clevedon road. Through the long, uncurtained library windows, they could see headlights blossoming in the darkness, then heard the whoosh of tyres on gravel as the car pulled up before the main door of the house. The bell was jerked again, violently this time, and Mary, who had just reappeared carrying a tray, thumped it down bad-temperedly on the circular table and went to answer the summons.

There was no doubt about the identity of this caller. Elizabeth and Jack recognized Ben's upraised voice as soon as Mary opened the door.

'Where is she? Where's my wife? Don't tell me she isn't here, because I know damn well she must be.'

Elizabeth called out: 'Helen is in the library. You may come in, Ben, but kindly moderate your tone. This is my house, and I won't have shouting.'

He came in, looking murderous. Only acute anxiety on Helen's behalf, Elizabeth guessed, could have induced him to set foot in The Brass Mill.

'Where is she?' Ben's gaze flicked past Elizabeth, taking in Jack and Chris Morgan. Then he saw Helen slumped on the sofa and went forward.

'My God!' he breathed, staring down at her. 'Stupid bitch! She might have broken her neck, climbing out of that window.'

'Or lost herself on the Downs. Or been raped or murdered. Or thrown herself into the Gorge,' Elizabeth suggested. 'However, none of those things happened, for which we must be thankful. I was just going to 'phone you to tell you she was here.'

'Oh, I knew she'd be here,' Ben answered roughly. 'She was determined to come to your bloody party.' He reached down and hauled Helen ungently to her feet, but her body was too slack to remain upright, and she collapsed against him. He raised a hand and slapped her across the face. 'Stand up, you little whore!' he ordered her coldly. 'I'm taking you home.' He slapped her a second time, and, with a little sigh, Helen slipped from his grasp to the floor.

There was a sudden movement, and before Elizabeth could stop him Chris Morgan had swung his fist to Ben's jaw, knocking him flying.

'Leave her alone, you bastard!' Chris shouted.

CHAPTER TWENTY-FOUR

'What do you think?' Jack asked. 'Do you like it? There's a lot still to be done, but we're hoping to open it in time for the Coronation in May.'

Mary looked around at the Tivoli's newly enlarged and decorated foyer. The smell of paint was everywhere. The floor, as yet uncarpeted, had little drifts of wood shavings in all the corners. The plate glass of the ticket-office needed a clean, and half a dozen unwashed milk bottles stood on the bottom step of the balcony staircase, the cardboard discs which had stoppered them thrown negligently down beside a tumble of dirty overalls. Step-ladders, paint-pots and brushes cluttered the entrance. In spite of the chaos, however, Mary could see how imposing it would look when finished. The dark green and old-gold décor hinted at elegance and taste.

She pulled down the corners of her mouth. 'A bit grand for Eastwood, isn't it?' she asked.

Jack nodded. 'Just what I said to Lizzie. But she and Chris had it all planned out between them. The pair of them are as thick as thieves. Come and see the auditorium. Some of the seating should be in by now.'

Mary followed him through a swing door. The old, moth-eaten rows of red armchairs had vanished, and workmen were banging and hammering sections of the new dark green seats into place. Wall lights sported lampshades of coloured glass, Tiffany style, and the front of the balcony had been decorated with garlands of plaster roses, which would be picked out in gold.

'It'll look nice,' Mary conceded, 'but I still think Eastwood would have preferred the old colour scheme of red and yellow.'

Jack laughed. '"Very vulgar" Lizzie called it. She said it reminded her of court jesters in the Middle Ages.'

'But court jesters were the cinema entertainment of their day,' Mary pointed out. 'Perhaps, after all, it would have been more appropriate.'

It occurred to Jack that Mary had changed in the past year. It was not simply her appearance: she was less wary of her own intelligence; less wary of airing her opinions. Living at The Brass Mill with only one another for company, without Amy to act as referee and Court of Appeal between them, had done both the sisters good. They had come to appreciate each other's qualities and be more tolerant of one another's faults. What might have been a disastrous experiment had turned out to be beneficial for them both.

Nevertheless, Jack could sense that Mary was unhappy. She had made the greater sacrifice by abandoning her principles. She sincerely believed money-lending to be un-christian and therefore wrong. And she missed Eastwood, where she felt comfortable and knew her way around.

They emerged from the Tivoli's brightly lit interior into the grey drizzle of the December afternoon. The street lamps were already glowing; little phosphorescent buds of light flowering in the gloom. People scurried along the pavements, huddled beneath umbrellas; and the newspaper placards made sombre reading with their headlines on the King's abdication.

Jack had parked his car just around the corner from the cinema, and they got in quickly, glad to be out of the cold.

315

'Thank you for bringing me to see it,' Mary said. 'Lizzie never seems to have time.'

'You haven't seen my new house, have you?' Jack asked. 'Do you have to get back to The Brass Mill right away or could you come and have tea? My mother keeps house for me now, as I daresay you know from Lizzie, but she's out this afternoon, visiting a friend, so we'll have the place to ourselves.'

'I'd like that very much,' Mary said, as he switched on the engine. 'What made Mrs Hennessey change her mind?'

'About living with the black sheep of the family, you mean?' Jack smiled. 'Loneliness, I should suppose. After my sisters got married, and without your mother next door, Springtime Grove wasn't the same. Besides, money is a powerful persuader.'

'Yes, I know.' Mary's tone was subdued.

'I wasn't getting at you!' Jack exclaimed. 'I don't think for a minute that Lizzie's money influenced your decision.'

'Perhaps not. It's feeding and clothing me, nonetheless. But it doesn't seem important any more, compared with the need for human relationships.' Jack negotiated a corner and the car tyres hissed on the wet surface of the road. The trees and railings of the park came into view. 'I do miss Eastwood,' Mary sighed. And ten minutes later, as Jack ushered her into the spacious, high-ceilinged drawing-room of Avebury Villa, she gave another sigh, but this time of contentment. 'This is nice,' she said. 'Just the right size. Not cramped, like Springtime Grove, but not to big, either, like The Brass Mill.'

Jack helped her out of her mackintosh and glanced complacently about him. 'My sentiments exactly. That place of Lizzie's is far too large. You and she must be rattling around inside it like two peas in a pod. Sit down, while I go and make the tea.'

'I'll make it. Show me where the kitchen is.' A

thought struck her. 'It's not in the basement, is it?'

'Shades of Mrs Tennant's? No, not any more. It used to be, but when I bought the house I had the breakfast-room converted. I mean, what use was a breakfast-room to me? All my life I've eaten in the kitchen. We use the basement now only for storing coal.'

Mary was in her element. 'This is what I call a real kitchen,' she said happily as she entered. 'Comfortable. Compact. Nice and bright. The kitchen at the Mill is like a museum and although I persuaded Lizzie to put in a new gas stove, she won't hear of a refrigerator or a washing machine. She says they'd ruin the atmosphere.'

'Well, you won't find either of those things here,' Jack apologized. 'But they could be got.'

'Your mother would find them a real boon. I should love a really modern kitchen,' Mary observed wistfully, as they waited for the kettle to boil. 'At least we have a vacuum cleaner at the Mill. That's something, I suppose. That house is almost a religion with Lizzie.' She poured boiling water into the tea-pot. 'It's not natural.' She coloured slightly and kept her eyes averted. 'Why don't you make her marry you, Jack?'

'Oh, come on!' he protested. 'Who do you know who can make Lizzie do anything she doesn't want to, or prevent her from doing anything she's set her heart on? Besides, a person can only be rejected so many times, and I've reached my limit. I'm tired of being "good old Jack"; of being a shoulder to cry on, or someone who's handy to console her when things don't go exactly as she's planned. Here, let me carry the tray. We'll have tea in the drawing-room. It'll be warmer.'

The rain had increased and was lashing against the windows. Jack switched on the lights and drew the curtains, while Mary removed the guard which Eileen Hennessey had left in front of the banked-down fire. Mary had picked up the poker and prodded it into life. Meanwhile, Jack pulled up a table, whose glass top and chrome legs sorted ill with the chintz-covered three-piece suite, but whose clean, modern, functional lines delighted Mary's heart. She liked a jumble of objects, an assortment of styles. It made a room homelier and more interesting. She had no patience with Elizabeth's scrupulous regard for period.

'So,' she asked curiously when she had poured the tea, 'you honestly don't want to marry Lizzie any more?'

'I didn't say I didn't want to. I said I wasn't going to ask her any more.' Jack smiled wryly. 'And I have my mother to think of. Even if by some miracle I could persuade Lizzie to change her mind, can you imagine her and Mother under one roof?'

Mary shook her head. 'And that roof would have to be the Mill, Jack. Lizzie wouldn't live anywhere else. Mrs Hennessey wouldn't enjoy that at all.'

'No. So you see, what with one consideration and another, I've decided it's high time to put that particular dream behind me. And it never was anything more than a dream; I realized that a long time ago. What about you? Have you finally reconciled yourself to Alan's disappearance?'

'Yes. But more than that, I've also managed to reconcile myself to the idea that we were never really married; to the idea that I have never been married and am never likely to be so; to the idea that I shall never have children of my own; to the idea that Richard always preferred Lizzie.' She laughed bravely. 'There's a catalogue of woe for you. But I know now that Alan was no great loss.'

Jack leaned forward, the firelight touching his face, high-lighting the round, smooth cheeks, the snub nose. At thirty-six, his hair was as black as ever, his eyes the same deep, fierce, Celtic blue.

'He wasn't,' he said. 'And I'll tell you something about Alan Davies which I've never told to another soul.' Jack recounted the incident when he had been set upon by Alan and his hired attacker.

Mary was horrified. 'Why ever didn't you tell someone? Me, at least?'

'Would you have believed me, in the face of Alan's denial? Anyway, he would only have had me beaten up again.'

Mary made no reply, staring into the leaping flames. The rain continued beating at the windows as the storm lashed itself into a frenzy. She could hear the little crying noises borne on the wind and echoing down the chimney. Suddenly she buried her face in her hands.

'Are you all right? What's the matter?' Jack reached out and touched her hair. It was almost totally, prematurely grey.

'I don't know.' Mary's voice was muffled by her masking fingers. 'Yes, I do. I've made such a mess of my life.'

Gently Jack drew her hands down into her lap and held them there, imprisoned by his own.

'No, you haven't. Not more than anyone else. You mustn't feel sorry for yourself. It's so destructive.'

She began to weep silently. 'All I ever wanted was a home and family of my own. Was that such an awful lot to ask?'

He moved from his armchair to sit beside her on the sofa, putting an arm about her shoulders.

'Shush. Shush. You mustn't cry. I can't bear to see you so unhappy.'

She became more distressed, her whole body shaking. 'You knew I was miserable, didn't you?' she asked between stifled sobs. 'When you met me in Corn Street, at lunchtime, you could see how low I was feeling. You were sorry for me. That's why you took the afternoon off and brought me over to see the Tivoli. Poor old Mary, you thought. Give her a little treat. Buck her up. No clients to see this afternoon, so I can spare her an hour of my valuable time. Everyone pities me, and I hate it!'

319

Jack pulled her, stiff and resisting, into his arms. Presently, her body relaxed and she clung to him, crying as if her heart would break.

'I'm so lonely. So lonely!' she gasped. 'And I detest that place. I loathe The Brass Mill. What a silly, stupid ridiculous name for a house!'

Jack soothed her, rocking her to and fro until she was quieter. At last, Mary raised her tear-stained face and released herself from his embrace. She began searching on the floor for her handbag and the handkerchief inside it. When she had blown her nose and dried her eyes, she gave Jack a shamefaced grin.

'I'm sorry,' she whispered. 'A woman of thirty-six behaving like a girl of sixteen! You must find me pathetic.'

'No, I don't.' Jack shook his head. 'I find you very human. Very warm and loving. Mary . . . You get on well with my mother, don't you? You always did. Do you like this house? Would you . . . ? How would you feel about living here for good?'

Mary frowned, puzzled. 'But you don't need a housekeeper, Jack. You have Mrs Hennessey. I don't understand what you mean.'

'I'm asking you to marry me. Would you . . . ? Could you ever consider becoming my wife?'

'Honey, please!' Chris Morgan sat up in bed and took two cigarettes from the packet on the little fly-blown table beside him. He lit them both and handed one to Helen. 'Honey, you have to tell him.'

Helen, leaning back against the hard, under-filled pillows, pulled on the cigarette, watching the smoke curl in the air like pale blue ribbons. Outside, the same storm which had disturbed Mary and Jack an hour earlier took hold of the hotel windows and rattled them savagely. A draught of cold December air found its way beneath the ill-fitting frame and made Helen shiver. She drew the sheets and blankets closer about her naked body.

'I can't, darling,' she said. 'I daren't.'

Chris turned towards her, supporting his weight on one elbow.

'For Pete's sake, Helen! I'm sick and tired of seedy hotels! Of secrecy. Of telling lies. I ought to be over at the Tivoli now, supervising those workmen. Instead of which I'm out on "business" — again! Helen, I want to marry you, for Christ's sake! I want you to get a divorce and be my wife. I love you. And I think you love me.'

'You know I do.' Helen looked at him reproachfully. How could he doubt it, even for a second?

She had not expected to see him again after that night last April, when she had made such a spectacle of herself at The Brass Mill. High on drugs as she had been, she still, amazingly, retained some memory of events the following day. She could remember Ben shouting and hitting her, and Chris Morgan knocking him down. She also, even more miraculously, knew who Chris was, and could recall the two occasions on which she had met him before. She had been overwhelmed with shame.

Helen had told herself that she was unlikely to meet the American for a fourth time — and had been so appalled by the thought that she had telephoned Elizabeth to apologize for her behaviour and the ensuing scene.

Elizabeth had been busy and rather abrupt, but Helen had persevered until she had elicited everything her cousin could tell her about Chris. A week later, she had paid an unexpected visit to her father's factory, camouflage for the fact that, earlier, she had dropped in at the Tivoli, ostensibly as an interested party in her cousin Elizabeth's concerns.

'Lizzie tells me she's going to buy this place,' she had said shyly, when, having asked for the manager, Chris had been fetched from his office next to the projection room.

'Miss Evans and her partner are certainly very

interested,' he had answered formally. Then, his reserve breaking down a little, he added: 'I had no idea that you and she were related. It was quite a surprise to see you that evening.'

'Not a very pleasant surprise, I'm afraid . . . I came really to thank you, Mr Morgan. You seem to be forever rescuing me from difficult situations.'

She had turned to leave, but he caught her arm and asked when he could see her again. She knew what she ought to say, but was unable to frame the words.

She had said: 'Can you . . . I mean, are you free tomorrow afternoon? I could pick you up on the corner of Clare Street, at two o'clock.'

It was her affair with Richard all over again, but with a difference. This time, Chris was as much in love with her as she was with him. The emotion she had felt for Richard Davies paled into insignificance. Richard had been a precocious boy. Christopher Morgan was a man.

So why could she not bring herself to do as Chris wanted? Leave Ben and run away with him? But there was the rub: Chris refused to run away. He had no intention at present of quitting England, not even of leaving Bristol. He was making his own way independently of his powerful father, and enjoying it. He was committed to turning the Tivoli cinema into a showcase; an example of what could be achieved by the small local picture-house in opposition to the big central chains. He saw his immediate future linked to Elizabeth and Jack. Only the imminent threat of another war would send him back across the Atlantic, convinced that if that happened, America would have to get involved sooner or later. He wanted to be ready to fight for his own country, and nobody else's, when the time came.

Helen was not interested in the possibility of war. All that concerned her was the subsequent scandal if she left Ben to live with another man in the same city and in the same district in which she was born.

She said now: 'You know I love you. But I can't live with you; not as your mistress.'

'Helen, honey, you're my mistress anyway,' he pointed out gently.

'But not openly. Not so that everyone knows.'

'Isn't that worse? Living a lie?' He smoothed back the tendrils of hair which wisped about her face. 'I love you. I need you. I'm asking you please to tell Ben.'

'No. No, I can't. He'll kill me. I know he will. He frightens me so.'

'He can't frighten you that much, my darling, or you wouldn't be willing to risk his anger by meeting me like this. Don't you think, over the years, you've exaggerated your fear of him in your mind? Haven't you let it grow into an obsession, so that you can no longer separate fiction from fact? Have you stopped taking those pills, as you promised?'

'Yes . . . No . . . I don't take them as often as I used to.' Her eyes filled with tears. 'You think it's that, don't you? You think I'm high again. Well, I'm not. I haven't had a pill for days. You saw Ben hit me that night.'

'It was reaction. He was frantic because you'd disappeared; because he knew you weren't fit to be out alone. You know how terrified parents get when children go missing. How they larrup them when the kids turn up safe and sound.'

'No, I don't know!' Helen exclaimed petulantly. 'I've never had children. I've no idea what mothers feel.'

'Now, stop it,' he chided her patiently. 'You're just being silly.' He stubbed out his half-finished cigarette, and then hers, in an ashtray shaped like a fish, with the words 'A Present From Weston-Super-Mare' painted in bilious pink lettering around the edge. 'We won't talk about it any more just now. But honey, you'll have to come to a decision some day soon.'

'I will. I promise,' she murmured gratefully, snuggling down into his arms and sighing with pleasure as he began making love to her again. Her whole being flowed out to him, loving him; giving and being given in return.

Mary and Jack were married in Arley Street Chapel at the end of the following April. Elizabeth, noting Jack's air of quiet contentment and Mary's overflowing happiness, told herself that it was churlish to feel betrayed. She had no right to expect Jack to remain single. Nor was there any reason why Mary should devote the rest of her life to her sister's comfort. This desire to burst into tears was just delayed shock, because who had ever considered the possibility of Jack and Marry getting married?

'Well, whoever would have thought it?' Eileen Hennessey demanded, echoing Elizabeth's thoughts, as they drove together to the reception. 'Your Mary and our Jack! Your Ma'd 'ave bin pleased. She used to worry a lot about Mary . . . Ooh! Look! They're starting to put up the decorations for the Coronation!'

After the reception, Elizabeth drove home alone to The Brass Mill. It was early evening, and the April sunshine had turned to showers. As she neared the Suspension Bridge, the wind rose in sudden, fresh gusts, tossing the trees against a darkening sky. The dim grey spaces of the Downs looked suddenly forlorn, the woods of Nightingale Valley shrouded in a desolate mist. Elizabeth recalled the view as she had seen it that morning driving into town; sparkling skies trailing blue shadows and the long line of emerald grasses. But this change suited her own change of mood.

The house, too, for the first time since she had set foot in it all those years ago, seemed an alien place, full of ghosts which were not hers. She had not yet engaged anyone else to live with her. Listening to her own footfalls, the sound of her own voice as she greeted Trojan, the cat — the big, ginger tom had been the result of Mary's insistence that there were mice in the kitchen — Elizabeth felt more alone, and more lonely, than at any previous time in her life.

What was she doing in a place this size, half the rooms still shut up, the other half not yet properly furnished? She had always intended gathering all her family around her here; Amy, Mary, Richard and later on, perhaps Richard's wife and children. And, of course, Jack; because Jack had always seemed a part of her family. She had pictured them all living together in peace and plenty: a delusion, as she now admitted to herself with a mocking smile. For why should they have achieved the harmony here, which they never achieved in Springtime Grove?

Elizabeth glowered balefully at the statue in the entrance hall, before going upstairs to take off her hat and coat. Trojan followed at her heels, miaowing pitifully to remind her that he had not been fed for some hours.

'You fat, greedy brute,' she admonished him. 'It won't hurt you to wait five minutes.' Trojan rubbed against her legs, smirking.

Elizabeth tossed her fox furs on to the bed and unpinned her eye-catching little velvet hat. It was garnet coloured to match her suit, and had a froth of pale grey veiling. Her grey silk blouse was adorned at the neck with her first piece of jewellery; a winking diamond clip. Elizabeth constantly had to remind herself that they were indeed real diamonds, not glass or paste, courtesy of Woolworth's.

She could see her reflection in the long mirror which hung on one wall of her bedroom; belted, nipped-in waist, skirt ending just a few inches above a well-turned ankle. Not bad, she thought; still slim and graceful. Not bad for thirty-four. But what was the point of taking the trouble to look good. Who was she doing it for?

The sudden shrilling of the telephone bell interrupted her thoughts. She made a rush for the door, nearly falling over Trojan on the way. Then she took a grip of herself, forcing herself to walk downstairs slowly. What had she come to, when the prospect of a few minutes' disembodied contact with another human being could so excite her? Decorously, she lifted the receiver.

'I have a transatlantic call for you,' announced the operator. 'From Los Angeles. Please could you hold the line.' There were some muffled clicks before the operator's voice came again. 'Stand by caller. I am ready to connect you now.'

CHAPTER TWENTY-FIVE

'Well,' Jack said appreciatively, 'you've turned it into quite an occasion.'

Elizabeth, in a silver lamé dress and matching fox furs, smiled happily.

'No thanks to me. It's all Richard's doing. A real live film star at the opening of the New Tivoli cinema in Eastwood is quite an event. It's even brought a couple of reporters down from London.'

'You kept it pretty quiet until last week. How long have you known he was coming?'

'Only since the end of April. The evening of your wedding day. Where is Mary, by the way? I saw her earlier looking very elegant. That wine colour suits her. Are you both happy?'

Jack sipped his champagne and glanced round the crowded foyer, where a buffet and bar had been installed for tonight's gala opening. Visiting dignitaries milled all about them. The noise was deafening.

'Content, I think, is perhaps a better word. Very content. I assume Richard is staying at the Mill while he's in England?'

'Of course. Look at him. Doesn't he look wonderful? He's so fit and bronzed. It's all that Californian sunshine. I'd better go and rescue him. He's done nothing but sign autographs for the last half-hour. I must speak to the Lord Mayor, too, before we go in for the film. Wasn't it clever of me to get *Elephant Boy*?'

'Very. I don't know how you managed it. Did Richard pull a few strings?'

'No, it was Chris. It turns out our manager has a contact in Wardour Street. Some friend of his father's. Daddy, it would seem, has influential friends all over the world.'

At that moment, Chris Morgan pushed his way through the crowd to Elizabeth's side.

'Would you pose for a couple of photographs?' he asked her. 'One of the national dailies wants a picture of you and Jack with Richard Davies. That boy's been worth a small fortune in publicity. Did you invite him to come?'

Elizabeth shook her head and diamond earrings sparkled. She had bought them as a special indulgence for tonight.

'It was his own idea, after he'd received my letter telling him that we'd decided on a date for the opening.'

'Thank goodness you avoided Coronation Day itself,' Chris said, 'or we shouldn't have seen anyone from London.'

'That's what I figured, in the end. Now, let's get this photograph taken or it will be time for the film.' She turned to follow Chris, then paused, clutching Jack's arm. 'Look who's just come in,' she breathed. 'Helen and Ben.'

Both Jack and Chris Morgan looked towards the plate glass doors.

'You didn't invite them, did you?' Jack asked in consternation. 'You wouldn't have been so stupid, Lizzie, surely? Not with Richard here.'

'I didn't know when I sent them their invitation that Richard would be here. The invitations went out weeks and weeks ago. Besides, I didn't think for a moment that they'd come.'

'Ben problably decided he didn't want a repetition of what happened at your house-warming. He must have thought it safer to escort Helen himself.'

The press photographer, impatient at the delay, appeared at their elbow and bore Elizabeth and Jack away to stand by Richard. Chris pushed his way towards the foyer doors. There was shouting and laughter, flash bulbs exploded, champagne corks popped and someone was trying to make an impromptu speech.

Helen and Ben were standing on the very edge of the crowd. Helen, who was wearing a pale blue, clinging silk dress, looked tired and strained. Ben, on the other hand, appeared to great advantage in his evening clothes.

As he approached them, Chris could see that some kind of altercation was in progress. He caught the words, uttered low and furiously by Ben: ' . . . Richard Davies! So that's why you were so anxious to come tonight.'

Helen was confused. 'No. Honestly. I didn't know that he'd be here.'

'You expect me to believe that?'

'Yes. I don't care if Richard's here or not. He doesn't mean anything to me any more. I've told you.' She glanced round and saw Chris. Her eyes dilated and one hand went up to fiddle nervously with the clasp on her chinchilla cape. 'G-good evening, Mr Morgan. Ben . . . darling . . . You remember Christopher Morgan, the cinema manager?'

Chris extended his hand and exerted all his Southern charm. He wanted nothing to mar the evening, for Elizabeth's sake.

'Mr Sawyer, how do you do, sir? Let me get you and Mrs Sawyer some champagne.'

Ben eyed him narrowly, then recognition dawned. 'You're the bastard,' he said, 'who knocked me down.'

'Darling, please!' Helen slipped her arm through

her husband's. 'Not here. Not now.'

Ben shook himself free of her and glared at Chris. 'You're the American who was at The Brass Mill that night.' His voice was rising. People nearby were beginning to turn their heads. 'I have a score to settle with you. If Helen hadn't been in such a state, I'd have done it at the time.'

'I'm perfectly willing to accommodate you on some other occasion, Mr Sawyer, but not tonight. So please lower your voice and follow me.'

Ben rounded on Helen, who shrank away from him. 'I suppose this amuses you,' he accused her savagely, 'getting me under the same roof with two men, one of whom has assaulted me, while the other has been your lover. It's your idea of a joke!'

'Ben! Helen!' It was Elizabeth's voice, gay and impersonal, as she dodged through the crowd towards them. 'I'm absolutely delighted that you could come. Chris, darling, look after my cousin for me, would you? Now, Ben.' She took his arm as indifferently as if she had never once hoped to marry him, or poured scalding water all over his hands. 'Let me introduce you to the Lord Mayor and Lady Mayoress. The Sheriff and his lady are here, somewhere, as well. And there are lots of other people simply dying to meet you.' She urged him forwards, adding: 'Quite like the old days, isn't it? You first brought me here when it was still a music hall, remember?'

Left alone, Chris looked anxiously at Helen. She was trembling, and tears glittered on the ends of her lashes.

'You still haven't told Ben about us, have you?' he asked gently.

'No. Not yet.'

'Are you going to?'

'I . . . Oh, Chris, not here. Please.'

'How did you persuade him to come tonight?'

'I said I'd come on my own if he refused to bring me. He said he'd lock me in my room again, only this time

330

he'd be sure and take away the bed clothes, so I couldn't get out of the window, like I did before.' The breath caught in her throat and she choked slightly. 'So, I told him I'd jump. I said I didn't care if I broke my neck. In the end, he gave in. I didn't know Richard was going to be here.' She looked up at him, suddenly defiant. 'I suppose Lizzie's told you all about Richard and me?'

'I don't really know who told me. I wish it had been you, but it doesn't matter. I'm sure it's me that you love.'

'I do. Oh, I do,' she whispered passionately.

'Then why won't you leave your husband and come to me?'

'I can't!'

People were beginning to move towards the auditorium. Chris offered Helen his arm.

'Would you come with me,' he asked, 'if I decided to go home, to the States?'

He felt her jump. 'Go to America? Right away from England? Not come back?'

'Yes. Not immediately. I won't leave Miss Evans in the lurch. I must stay until this place has really got going. But in six months, or a year, say, would you be willing to come with me then?'

'You shouldn't have waited up, Miss Maple.' Elizabeth smiled at her housekeeper of three weeks, a tall, plump woman with grey hair and a no-nonsense manner, who ran The Brass Mill with a quiet efficiency and kept the two young daily maids firmly under her thumb.

'The trouble with society nowadays,' Miss Maple was fond of remarking, 'is that people no longer know their place.'

'And the awful thing is,' Elizabeth confided to Richard, as she preceded him into the dining-room, where the housekeeper had laid out drinks and sandwiches on the sideboard, 'that I find myself agreeing with her. Me! Lizzie Evans, who once organized a strike. Who once bearded the dreaded Mrs Tennant in her lair and told her that Mary and I were every bit as good as she was.' She sank into an armchair and kicked off her silver high-heeled shoes. 'Ah! That's better. Help yourself to whatever you want, Richie, love.' She nodded towards the sideboard. 'I don't think I could eat or drink another thing.'

'Nor me,' he said, leaning against the dining-table, watching her.

'Then come and sit down for five minutes before you go to bed. I haven't really told you how extraordinarily grateful I am to you for coming all this way, and turning what would have been a very modest occasion into an evening worthy of national attention.'

Richard smiled, but made no move to sit down. 'I came because I wanted to,' he replied. 'Because I was homesick. Because I wanted to see you.'

Elizabeth was about to return a flippant answer, when something in his tone, a serious note, stopped her. She raised her eyes uncertainly to his face.

'That . . . That's very sweet of you, Richard. Thank you.' When he made no answer, she added with forced brightness: 'Tell me some more about Hollywood. The parties sound perfectly crazy. In fact, the whole way of life sounds mad. Do you really, truly enjoy it?'

'Some of it. But I'm not a big star to be invited to the top-notch shindigs.'

'But you will be, one day,' she reassured him.

'I might, given time. But time is a commodity which is running out.'

'Whatever do you mean? You're not ill, are you?' Her heart almost stopped with fear.

'I'm talking about war. If there is going to be another war with Germany, I don't want to be stuck on the wrong side of the Atlantic. I want to be here, doing my bit.'

Elizabeth gasped with relief. 'You're as bad as Chris

Morgan,' she complained. 'He's convinced there's going to be another war. And he's so sure that America will have to join in, if there is, that he wants to do the same thing as you, but in reverse.'

'Don't you think there will be a war?'

'No, of course not. The Germans want peace as badly as we do. Good heavens! It's only nineteen years since the end of the last little lot! Hitler seems an eminently reasonable man. Why are men never satisfied unless they're at each other's throats? It makes me cross!'

Why was she getting so het up? Why did the prospect of war suddenly seem so much worse than it had done? Trojan jumped on her lap and started to clean himself. Normally, dressed as she was, she would have turned him off, but all at once silver lamé seemed unimportant. She glanced up at Richard, then looked away again, her eyes brimming with tears.

Next moment, he was kneeling beside her chair, holding her in his arms, covering her face with kisses.

'I love you,' he said fiercely. 'I've suspected it for a long time, but I knew it for certain the moment I saw you again.'

She returned his kisses hungrily, her fingers digging into his shoulders, her heart beating so fast she could scarcely breathe. Trojan, squashed, leapt to the floor with an indignant screech, and his action brought Elizabeth to her senses. She pushed Richard away and got hurriedly to her feet.

'This is ridiculous. Good God! Do you know how old I am? I'm nearly thirty-five. Ten years older than you.'

'What does that matter?' Richard also rose and took her in his arms again. 'Lizzie. My lovely, lovely Lizzie.' His lips found hers.

'No,' she managed to say at last. She laughed shakily, fending him off with both hands. 'This is madness. Do you honestly mean to tell me that after being in Hollywood with all those beautiful film stars, you fancy me?'

'They are the ones I fancied,' he answered quietly. 'You, I love. I think I knew it before I went away. I want to marry you.'

'Madness!' The word was torn from her with a virulence increased by the realization that she wanted him quite as badly as he seemed to want her; that she longed desperately to be his wife. 'No, Richard,' she went on more gently. 'I couldn't tie you to a woman so much older than yourself. It wouldn't be fair. Besides, I can't go to America with you. I have a business to run.'

'I know that. But my contract expires in twelve months, and after that, I shall come home, regardless of the political situation. The Rank orgaization has expressed an interest in me. They're keen to sign me up. And before you say anything, I realize you wouldn't live in London; that you won't live anywhere but here. That's all right. We'll work something out between us.'

She returned his gaze steadily. Why had she never understood how much she loved him; that he was the one she had been waiting for all her life? But she wouldn't marry him; not now, not in a year's time, not ever. For both their sakes he must always be free. He must never feel tied to an older wife. Even now, she could hardly believe they were having this conversation, everything had happened so fast and so unexpectedly.

She put her arms round him, holding him close. She was remembering the little boy who had arrived in Springtime Grove with his father, on an evening long ago.

'I'll make you a promise,' she whispered. 'I'll be your mistress for as long as you want me. This is your home whenever you're in England, to come and go as you choose. And when you're tired of me, you have only to say.'

Richard's arms tightened until she could scarcely breathe.

'No, Lizzie. Just for once in your life you'll take orders, instead of giving them. When I return from the States, next year, we're going to be married, and to hell with what people either think or say!'

She saw that he meant it, and decided not to argue. She would fight it out with him when the time came, and that was still a whole twelve months away. A lot of things could happen in that time, but for now he was here, and that was enough.

'I hope you fancy a thirty-four-year-old virgin,' she told him, half-serious, half-laughing, 'because you'll be the first man I've ever slept with.'

Mary sat at the dressing-table, brushing her hair. It was a girlhood habit which she had recently resumed, even though the hairdresser had warned her that it would ruin her permanent wave. It gave her a few moments quiet contemplation before she finally climbed into bed.

She could see Jack reflected in the mirror, and watched him undress. She liked his meticulous movements, the preciseness with which he folded his clothes.

'What did you think of it, then?' she asked. 'This evening I mean.'

Jack laughed. 'Typically Lizzie! Carrying all before her, as usual. She even sorted out Helen and Ben.'

'Yes. Their arrival was an uncomfortable moment. I often wonder what went wrong between those two. Guilt, probably, for the way they treated Lizzie.'

Jack threw her an affectionate, slightly derisory glance. Everything was black and white to Mary. In her world, there was no such thing as a complicated motive. He put on his pyjamas and got into bed. From the next room, he could hear his mother, snoring. He stretched his arms above his head, listening to the cracking of his bones.

'I'm tired,' he yawned. 'I shall sleep like a log.' He

frowned impatiently. 'Stop fiddling with your hair, love, and come to bed.'

Mary clambered in beside him and he found her hand, squeezing it. His marriage had brought him a great deal of quiet contentment, and he was grateful. He still loved Elizabeth: he always would. But with Mary, he had been able to find a happiness which he knew would have been impossible with her sister. At least now he could come home at night and shut the door on all the turmoil and bustle of the day. Under Elizabeth's direction, the business continued to expand, and they had branched out into the cinema world. Jack doubted if Elizabeth would be content for long with just the New Tivoli at Eastwood. Soon she would be looking for other picture-houses, and before long there would be an Evans and Hennessey chain. He had a lot to thank her for. Without her and her relentless ambition, he would be just another collector at Harrison's, living in Springtime Grove. Yet he could not escape the sneaking suspicion that that was all he had ever wanted to be. He was a man who had been made rich by force of circumstance, because of his devotion to just one woman. It was ironic, therefore, that he should have found happiness with somebody else.

'Lizzie was nagging me again tonight,' he said, 'telling me we ought to move out of Eastwood. She thinks we should find the same sort of place that she's done. I told her we're contented as we are. She's always been out to prove something ever since your Uncle Joe refused to send her to college.' Jack settled himself to sleep. 'Richard's looking fine,' he murmured. 'Every inch the film star. But no side to him. Not in the least conceited.' His voice tailed away, and soon he was snoring almost as loudly as his mother.

Mary lay on her back, without moving, staring into the darkness. The constant, nagging pain in her side, which she had first noticed over a year ago, had begun to worry her. If it persisted much longer, she supposed that she ought to consult a doctor.

Helen lay huddled on her side, crying quietly. The marks of Ben's fingers were on her wrists and forearms. A bruise was spreading at one corner of her mouth.

Ben rolled off the bed and stood looking down at her, filled with a mixture of love and hate.

'What is it about me,' he demanded with suppressed violence, 'that repels you so? Why don't I attract you like that little fart, Richard Davies? I bet you didn't try to fight him off when he made love to you.'

'I keep telling you,' Helen sobbed, 'that I didn't know he was going to be there tonight. I haven't seen him in years. He doesn't mean anything to me any more.'

'You've probably been corresponding secretly with him, while he's been in America. You have, haven't you? Answer me!'

'No!' The word was a shriek. Helen sat up, thumping impotently with her fists against the mattress. 'How could I? When you read all my letters first?'

She opened her mouth to scream again and Ben slapped her smartly across the face.

'Stop it! You're becoming hysterical. Do you want Mrs Bagot to hear?'

'I don't care who hears me! Mrs Bagot knows what goes on in this house. What you have just done to me is rape!'

Ben was so astounded by her words that for several moments he could do nothing but stare. Then he laughed in genuine amusement.

'You stupid woman!' he exclaimed contemptuously. 'How can a husand rape his own wife? Of all the foolish things to say!'

'I'll divorce you,' she wailed. 'I'll stand up in court and tell them what you just did.'

'What judge and jury do you imagine would convict

me? I believe you're losing your mind. Pull yourself together. Here.' Ben tugged open the drawer of her bedside table with such force that it fell out, spilling its contents on the floor. He stooped and retrieved the bottle of sleeping tablets. 'Take a couple of these. They'll calm you down.' He gathered up the rest of the things and bent down to replace the drawer. As he did so, he noticed an envelope, jammed at the back of the recess. With shaking hands, he managed to fish it out.

There was no name or address or stamp, but part of the letter was protruding from the envelope. The words 'My Darling Helen,' written in a strong, male hand, could clearly be seen.

'It's from him. It's from Richard Davies,' he accused her. 'You did know he was in England after all.'

'No! No, it's not from him. Give it to me!' Frantically Helen tried to snatch the letter from him.

Ben pushed her back on the bed, almost tearing the sheet of notepaper from its covering. He turned it over, searching for the telltale signature.

'Chris?' he queried. 'Who the hell is Chris?' Then: 'It's that bloody American,' he said slowly, answering his own question. 'The one who's managing the Tivoli for Liz . . . No wonder the bastard knocked me down that evening.' Ben turned to look at Helen, who had shrunk back guiltily amongst the pillows. 'You little slut! You cheap, bloody, little whore! When did this begin?' He came close to the bed, towering over her. Helen was too frightened to move. 'You don't want *me*, do you?' he went on thickly. 'You can't bear *me* near you. But anyone else, oh yes! The whole of bloody Bristol can screw my wife and she won't object. Anything in trousers, isn't that right?'

'I . . . I know how it must look,' Helen eventually managed to croak, 'but it isn't like that, Ben. It isn't, I promise. I love Chris Morgan, and he loves me. He wants me to get a divorce and marry him.'

'Love!' Ben spat out the word as if it were poison.

'You don't know the meaning of love! You imagined you were in love with Charlie! You were so much in love with Richard Davies that you tried to commit suicide when he left you. You even once thought you were in love with me!'

Helen began to cry. 'This is different,' she sobbed. 'I really do love Chris.'

Ben took a deep breath. Helen was the one person in his life who had refused to dance to his tune. All the rest, his mother, his aunt, Joseph Gordon, even Elizabeth, he had been able to manipulate to further his ends. Helen herself, at the start, had fallen a willing victim to his schemes. But then the tables had been turned: he had become the victim. From then on, things had gone wrong for him. He had lost control of the situation between himself and Helen. He had fallen in love with her, and instead of returning his love, she had grown away from him; elusive, fey, living her own secret life. He was unable to hold her, except by fear.

He leaned over the bed, supporting himself on one hand and placing the other on her throat. Slowly he tightened his grip, until the pressure on his fingers began to hurt.

'If you ever mention the word "divorce" again,' he said, 'this will be for real. Do you understand what I'm saying?' She nodded, her eyes dilated with terror. 'I won't let you leave me. Wherever you go, I'll find you and kill you. I won't let anyone else have you. You belong to me.'

CHAPTER TWENTY-SIX

'Why, for Christ's sake, didn't you tell me? A whole year — more than a year — you've been terrified half out of your wits, and you haven't said a word. Helen, you're crazy! So what's happened, that you're telling me now?'

Helen leaned against the railings of Bristol Bridge, lifting her face gratefully to the hot, July sunshine. All around her was bustle and life. A Tramways Company employee was cleaning the points in front of the Knowle tram, which bore gaily coloured advertisements for Harris's Wiltshire sausages and B & P Ginger Ale. Cars, bicycles and motor-bikes were jamming the turning into Baldwin Street outside St Nicholas's church. High Street and Bridge Street were packed with shoppers, bright with the women's summer clothes.

'Honey, are you all right?' Chris slipped an arm about Helen's waist. His face was full of concern. 'Let's walk to College Green,' he suggested. 'It'll be quieter there.'

It was lunchtime, but he was not hungry. In an hour, the New Tivoli would open its doors for the matinée performance of *Modern Times*, but he did not care. Ever since Helen had telephoned him at the cinema that morning, he had been ill with worry. She had sounded so strange, so detached, as she had told him that she had called to say goodbye.

Chris had been vaguely aware that something was wrong for the past few months. During their stolen encounters, Helen had been quieter, more withdrawn. She had been edgier, too, making what he had thought were unnecessary difficulties about the secrecy of their meetings; exasperating him sometimes beyond endurance by her stubborn refusal to leave her husband and go to him.

'No,' she had said, 'not until you go back to America. Ben would only come after me. Wherever we lived in this country, I'd be frightened to set foot outside, or answer the door.'

They had quarrelled, and he had taunted her with her Methodist conscience, saying that the hypocrisy of the British appalled him. This was not altogether true, and he was perfectly well aware that there were plenty of like-minded people in America, particularly in the Bible Belt of the middle-west. But certainly Elizabeth was the only person he had met in England who had the direct, honest approach to the pleasure of making money which was so taken for granted in the United States.

'I can see absolutely nothing wrong with wealth,' she had once said to him, 'providing you use it wisely and don't abuse the power that it gives you.'

Chris's admiration for, and loyalty to, Elizabeth, was the only reason he had delayed his departure. Since that night of the New Tivoli opening, when Helen had told him that she would go with him to America, he had made up his mind to return home. There were other reasons, also, why he wanted to go back to Texas. His mother had been unwell, and, after nearly eight years abroad, he was at last growing homesick. The war clouds over Europe, too, were getting darker. On the eleventh of March, the Germans had entered Austria, London had staged its first black-out trials and there

341

were plans to dig ARP trenches in Hyde Park. As long ago as the preceding November the Air Raids Precautions Bill had been introduced in the House of Commons. Nobody would admit to believing that there would be another war, but all the signs and portents were there.

Chris had already hinted at his intentions to Elizabeth, but until today he had felt no great urgency to hurry home. Then, this morning, had come Helen's telephone call.

'I'm ringing to say goodbye, darling,' she had said, adding listlessly: 'I can't go on any longer, Chris. It's too much of an effort.'

With mounting panic, he had recalled being told of her suicide attempt, and there was something in the way she spoke which made him fear that she would try it again. Under his breath, he had savagely cursed the doctor who kept her supplied with sleeping pills; a means of self-destruction always conveniently to hand. He had kept on talking, bullying and cajoling and scolding her until she had at last agreed to meet him on Bristol Bridge. He had rushed down from his office, informed his staff that he was going out on urgent business and dashed out of the cinema without even stopping to put on his hat. By the time the cashier had finished exchanging significant glances with the commissionaire, Chris was revving the engine of his car.

He had been half-afraid that, after all, Helen would not come, and had experienced an enormous surge of relief when he saw her slight, still girlish figure leaning against the railings of the bridge. He parked the Ford in Welsh Back and ran to meet her, taking her in his arms.

'No, Chris, you mustn't! Someone might see!' Just for a moment, Helen had been her normal self; then the depression and apathy had returned to her voice and manner. She had shrugged. 'What does it matter, though, if anyone does?'

But, finally, he had pried the story out of her; Ben's threat to kill her if she left him; his increasing tendency to violence when they were alone together; his recent insistence on returning permanently to her bed. Only Mrs Bagot's sympathy and connivance had made Chris and Helen's meetings possible during the last year.

'He interrogates Mrs Bagot every evening,' Helen said. 'Have I been out? How long was I out? Could I have slipped out at any time without her seeing me? Have I telephoned anyone during the day? She's been wonderful. She even tells Ben downright lies when she has to, and she always makes sure that the daily maids have gone home before Ben comes in at night. I never realized that she was so fond of me.'

Chris was horrified, yet, at the same time, he could not rid himself of the notion that she was just a hysterically inclined woman, exaggerating her problems and difficulties. He had been brought up as a Southern gentleman, to regard women as fragile and fallible objects.

They mounted the steps by Queen Victoria's statue and sat on a seat on College Green, facing the Cathedral.

'I shall go to see your cousin as soon as I leave you,' Chris said, 'and hand in my notice. Then I shall go straight to the shipping office and book two passages home. As soon as I have the details, I'll let you know. Of course, you're coming with me.'

'Am I?' There was no spark of animation in Helen's voice.

Chris turned round to face her. 'Of course you're coming with me! It's what we've always planned. If I'd realized what was going on, we'd have left before now.'

'I don't know, Chris. I think I'll still be frightened. Ben could follow me to America, you know.'

'Honey, not even a screwball like your husband is going to go thousands of miles across the Atlantic just

343

to wreak his revenge. He's just trying to scare you, that's all. Once he finds you've gone, he'll just accept it. He'll agree to a divorce, you'll see.'

She seemed unconvinced, but at last agreed to do what Chris wanted. The only decision she had ever taken for herself, marrying Ben, had led to disaster. She listened docilely while Chris told her what to do, agreeing with everything he said.

'As soon as I've made all the necessary arrangements, I'll telephone you, during the day, when Ben's not at home. In the meantime, behave normally. Don't do anything to arouse Ben's suspicions.'

'I'm very sorry indeed that you're leaving, Chris.' Elizabeth smiled at him across her desk in some consternation. 'I didn't realize that your mother was quite so unwell. But I told you years ago where I thought your duty lay, and I'm glad to see you've at last come to your senses. Of course we'll miss you. I was counting on your invaluable help when we open our new cinema in Gloucester next month, but I daresay we'll manage.'

He returned her smile, but with an effort. He hated deceiving her, and wondered if he might tell her the truth. On second thoughts, however, it was unfair to embroil her in his concerns. He wished she and Helen were closer, but he sensed constraint between the two women whenever they met.

'I'm sure you'll do very nicely without me,' he answered, glancing round the plushly carpeted office which, with Jack's next door, occupied the entire top floor of the new Evans and Hennessey building. The windows commanded a view of the Tramways Centre and that part of the river Frome which was soon to be covered. A staff of forty occupied the two lower floors, one reason why the offices behind Philadelphia Street had been abandoned, as they were now far too small.

Elizabeth rose and held out her hand. 'Jack will be sorry to have missed you, but he's in London today. I'll 'phone the cashier and make sure you get your full month's salary. No arguments. It isn't your fault that you have to leave in a hurry. I shall look forward to renewing our acquaintance in the future when you're head of the Morgan chain of stores.'

There was something different about Elizabeth lately, Chris thought, as he left her office and took the lift to the ground floor. She had always been a handsome woman, but now she positively glowed. She seemed filled with anticipation, as though she were in possession of some lovely secret.

Left alone, Elizabeth stared for a moment at the closed door, dwelling on the need to advertise at once for a new manager for the Tivoli, before recollecting with a smile that she now had a whole department which dealt with her growing cinema concerns. Her smile broadened and grew tender as she opened a drawer in her desk and extracted an airmail letter, posted from California. She withdrew the sheets of notepaper, covered in Richard's familiar handwriting, and read the letter again. Sentences which she already knew by heart leapt at her from the page.

'So provided this damn film finishes on schedule, I shall be with you by the middle of December, in time for Christmas. I love you, darling. Always, always. We're going to be married, whatever you say. You'll find that I can be every bit as stubborn as you.'

Briefly, she pressed the letter to her lips before returning it to its envelope. She mustn't sit here, mooning like a lovesick schoolgirl. There was work to be done. She touched the bell on her desk, and a moment later, her secretary entered, notebook and pencil at the ready.

The board meeting seemed endless. It was time his father-in-law retired, Ben thought resentfully. Joe was sixty-four. As soon as he took over the reins, Ben had a number of new ideas he wanted to put into operation: ideas for streamlining the factories, modernizing the canteen facilities and introducing one or two up to date confectionery lines. Gordon's needed another face-lift, similar to the one forced on it by Elizabeth, all those years ago. But Joe was still as reactionary now as he had been then. It would take either such another apocalyptic event or his removal to produce the necessary changes.

Ben was conscious of feeling unwell, and he remembered that the canteen pie had been somewhat suspect at lunchtime. He shouldn't have eaten it, but everyone else had appeared satisfied, and he had not liked to grumble. Now he was paying the price with a queasy stomach. To add to his discomfort, the August sun was beating through the long windows of the boardroom straight on to his back. He was thankful when at three o'clock, the meeting at last broke up.

'You don't look at all the thing, Mr Sawyer, if I may say so,' Miss Beaumont observed solicitously as he entered his office a few minutes later. 'Would you like some asprin?'

Ben shook his head. 'I don't think they'd do much good, thank you, Miss Beaumont. I'm feeling rather sick. I'll just dictate a couple of letters which must catch this afternoon's post, then I'm going home. Lying down in a darkened room will do most good, I fancy.'

The secretary, who had a date with a new man-friend that evening and wanted to get away early herself, agreed with enthusiasm.

'You work too hard, Mr Sawyer. You've been here until gone eight o'clock every night this week.'

'And I ought to be staying tonight,' he answered wearily, 'but I feel too unwell. The rest of the correspondence will have to wait.'

'Nothing that can't be left until tomorrow,' Miss Beaumont reassured him. 'It'll be a nice surprise for

Mrs Sawyer to have you home early for once.'

Ben glanced sharply at the secretary to see if she were being sarcastic, but her slightly coarse features were blandly innocent of any such intention. By half-past three, he was in his car, threading his way through the Eastwood traffic and out on to the main city road.

As he drove up Park Street, he became aware that his stomach was settling. His head ached less and he felt generally much improved. Perhaps Miss Beaumont was right. Perhaps he worked too long and too hard, and played too little. Maybe he and Helen should take a holiday more often. The odd week at Brighton or Torquay was not sufficient. And these last years, since things had been so difficult between them, they had not gone away at all. They ought to go abroad. Helen had never been out of the country, and he had only been on business trips to Switzerland and Holland.

The thought of Helen, as always, made him break into a sweat. Why did he still feel this way about her, when she had deceived him twice? Why did he still want her with this burning desire of complete possession? It was an ironic fact that had he married Elizabeth, he would be a happier and a richer man. Once, such a consolation would have driven him crazy with anger and frustration, but now it did not matter. All he wanted, all he had ever wanted since his honeymoon, was Helen, the woman he had married, like any brazen opportunist, to further his career.

He turned the car into Pembroke Road. He was within fifty yards of home when he saw Chris Morgan's Ford parked outside. He drew up behind it and sat perfectly still, trying to ward off a sudden sensation of panic. The American was here, in broad daylight, in his own home. And Helen was not expecting him back until late. Chris Morgan and his wife were in bed together . . .

The front door opened and the American came out of the house, carrying two of Helen's smart crocodile leather suitcases, part of a set which Joe and Minna had given her last Christmas. Chris Morgan opened the Ford's boot and carefully stowed them beside some luggage already there. He did not notice Ben and hurried back inside the house.

Ben got out of his car and went to inspect the contents of the Ford's boot. Apart from Helen's two cases there were, as Ben had anticipated, three other pieces of luggage, including a small steamer-trunk, all stamped with Chris Morgan's initials. They also bore labels directing them aboard the Queen Mary at Southampton docks, with a sailing date for two days' time. Helen's cases had similar labels, and as he stared at them, Ben began quietly and mirthlessly to laugh.

'When we reach Southampton, we go straight to the Dolphin Hotel,' Chris said. 'I've made reservations for tonight and tomorrow, in the names of Mr and Mrs Christopher Morgan. Tomorrow I'll sell the car, and first thing the following morning we go on board.'

Helen, almost as pale as the white silk frock she was wearing, hugged her handbag as if for support, like a child taking comfort from a teddy-bear.

'You don't think he'll find out where we've gone, and follow us?' she asked anxiously. 'Elizabeth knows you're going back to the States. If Ben should contact her . . . She doesn't know about you and me. She'd have no reason not to tell him.'

'It's a risk we must take. Look, darling!' Chris regarded Helen with a twinge of exasperation. 'All of us have to take a risk or two now and then. And what can Ben do in a public hotel, except kick up a row? And I don't think he'd do that, do you? Your husband's the last man to advertise the fact that he's been made a fool of.'

Helen tried to smile. 'Of course, you're right. Oh darling, I do love you so. I promise I'll be the perfect wife.'

Chris's momentary irritation evaporated. He put his arm around her and kissed her passionately. She had a lovely body, and she really was a miracle in bed.

'Is that all your luggage?' he asked.

'There's just the small case there and my vanity-box. And two hat-boxes,' she added defiantly.

Again, for some reason he could not clearly define, Chris felt irritated. 'You'd think we were going to the Australian outback,' he chided her, 'instead of to the greatest consumer society in the world. OK! OK! We'll make room for everything. The hat-boxes can go on the back seat. Now, come along. Have you said goodbye to Mrs Bagot?'

'I don't think that will be necessary,' Ben's voice said, just behind him.

Helen screamed and spun round to see her husband framed in the dining-room doorway.

'Ben! What are you doing home?' she demanded faintly. 'I thought you wouldn't be home until late tonight.'

'Obviously.' Ben strolled into the room and, drawing out a chair, sat down at the dining-table.

Chris tucked one of Helen's trembling hands into the crook of his arm and squeezed it.

'You can't stop her coming with me, Sawyer,' he said. 'She's thirty-five years old and her own mistress.'

'Your mistress, too,' Ben pointed out with an offensive grin. 'And Richard Davies's and possibly other men's, as well, if we did but know. But I don't wish to disillusion you.'

Chris controlled himself with an effort. 'You won't,' he answered shortly. 'I know all about Richard Davies, and I'm sure there hasn't been anyone else.'

'Really? What a very trusting fellow you are. But then, all Americans are such romantics.'

'Helen is coming with me to the States,' Chris said steadily. 'She's leaving you, Sawyer, and it's no use trying your tricks.'

'My dear chap, I shouldn't dream of it.' Ben spread deprecating hands.

Chris shot him a suspicious glance. What the devil was the bastard up to? He was being far too affable and urbane.

'That's OK then. Come along, honey.' Chris picked up Helen's light summer coat and draped it round her shoulders. 'If we're going to make Southampton in time for dinner, we have to get going.'

Helen looked nervously from Chris to her husband. 'G-goodbye, then, Ben. I . . . I'm sorry.'

'Don't be, my dear. I'll see you back here in — what shall we say? Three days' time?'

'Look, Sawyer, I've told you — ' Chris was beginning, but stopped. It dawned on him that Ben was holding some trump card or other, and had not yet revealed his hand. 'If you have something to say, damn well say it!' he went on explosively. 'I'm sick of this bloody cat-and-mouse.'

'Well, it's a small point, but, I think, a vital one.' Ben's smile deepened. 'I daresay you might not realize . . . What I mean is, I daresay it might never have cropped up in conversation between you — after all, you've had other things on your minds — '

'For God's sake, get on with it!' Chris shouted.

'I was merely going to comment on the fact that Helen has never before been abroad.' Ben saw the baffled look of incomprehension on the American's face and added with quiet relish: 'She has no passport.'

There was a moment's complete silence. Then Chris closed his eyes. He had checked all the arrangements, and double-checked, but had overlooked this one vital detail. It had never occurred to him to ask Helen such a simple, obvious question.

Helen herself stood as though turned to stone, her hands pressed to her burning cheeks. She had never thought about a passport, she was so accustomed to having all such details taken care of for her. Her father,

Charlie, Ben had always looked after such matters.

'Oh, no!' she murmured. 'Oh, no! Oh, no!'

Chris Morgan, for all his placid exterior, had a temper which could suddenly erupt, as on the night he had lashed out at Ben. Now, baffled and disappointed, Helen received the full brunt of his rage.

'You stupid bitch!' She could not, at first, believe that Chris was speaking to her, and stared at him in mounting horror. It occurred to her that he sounded exactly like Ben. 'Do I have to do all your thinking for you? In God's name, why didn't you tell me?'

'I never thought of it,' Helen whispered, her world collapsing around her. 'It never so much as entered my head.'

Chris groaned and sank his face in his hands. Ben sat watching the pair of them in open enjoyment.

'Does that mean we can't go?' Helen knew how foolish the question was, but felt compelled to ask it.

Chris made no answer, turning angrily away from her when she would have touched him.

She gave a choking cry and fled from the room.

CHAPTER TWENTY-SEVEN

'So you were the only person I could think of,' Helen explained miserably, sitting forward on the edge of her chair and twisting her white rayon gloves between her hands. 'I'm desperate, Lizzie. I can't stay with Ben any longer.'

'But . . . what about Aunt Minna and Uncle Joe?'

Helen shook her head. 'I couldn't go to them. They'd only try to force a reconciliation.'

Elizabeth bit her lip. It was late September and the country was in the midst of the Munich crisis. War was looming ominously close. Richard was still on the other side of the Atlantic and she was worried sick in case hostilities were declared before he could return to England. The last thing she wanted at this present time was to be burdened with anyone else's trouble.

'For pity's sake go home,' Jack had ordered her earlier in the day. 'You're no good to anyone like this.'

So she had left the office and driven back to the peace and quiet of The Brass Mill. She had spent the afternoon and early evening restlessly prowling around the house or glued to the radio, waiting anxiously for the next news bulletin. She found no comfort in the fact that the Royal Navy had been mobilized or that more trenches were being dug in Hyde Park. Miss Maple, too, had been nagging her about buying black-out material to line all The Brass Mill's curtains.

'We shall need a fair bit, Miss Evans, and if I don't get it soon, it'll all be gone. I understand the shops are running out fast.'

'Do what you think fit,' Elizabeth had told her indifferently. 'Go to Taylor's and buy what we need. Charge it to my account.'

After tea, which she had forced down in order to placate her housekeeper, Elizabeth went into the little back parlour and tried to read. But the tribulations of Scarlett and Melanie failed, for once, to hold her interest. She closed her eyes, willing Richard to telephone her from California to say that the film had been completed ahead of schedule; that he was catching the next boat home. And for one blissful moment, she believed her prayers had been answered, until she realized with a sinking heart that it was not the telephone she had heard but the front door bell. Before she could pull herself together sufficiently to instruct Miss Maple that she was not at home, the housekeeper opened the door and announced: 'Mrs Sawyer to see you, Madam.'

Elizabeth barely had time to recover from her astonishment before Helen had thrown herself into her arms, sobbing: 'I've left Ben.'

Now, half an hour later, having pieced together her cousin's incoherent and rambling story, Elizabeth was wondering desperately what she should do. With Richard due home in less than three months' time, any permanent visitor at The Brass Mill would be an embarrassment, but Helen's presence would be a positive disaster.

She regarded her cousin in mounting irritation. It had come as a surprise and something of a shock to her to learn of Helen's involvement with Chris Morgan. It shed a new and unwelcome light on his sudden departure, and, to use that most American of phrases,

Elizabeth felt that she had been 'taken for a ride'.

She got up and went to a side-table, where a decanter and glasses were set out, and poured two brandies. She handed one to Helen.

'Drink it,' she advised. 'I realize it's a bit early in the evening to be tippling, but it will do us both good. Steady our nerves.' Elizabeth sat down again. 'Haven't you heard at all from Chris since he went home?'

'No. He hasn't written or telephoned or anything. And he's right to wash his hands of me, Lizzie. I'm such a fool. I'm no good to anyone.'

'Stop talking like that. Helen, love, feeling sorry for yourself won't help.' There was an awkward pause before Elizabeth went on: 'It's not that I don't want you here, my dear, but there's something you ought to know. Richard and I are going to be married. He's coming home for good in December, when his Hollywood contract ends. So you see . . . in view of the past . . . well, having you here could be rather difficult, to say the least.'

The colour flooded up under Helen's fair skin. 'Oh, Lizzie, I'm sorry. If I'd known, of course I wouldn't have come.' Helen was on her feet, spilling brandy down her dress in agitation. 'I'll go at once.'

'Don't be foolish, love. Richard isn't going to walk in this minute. Sit down and we'll talk this thing over.' Elizabeth rose and gently pushed her cousin back into her chair. 'Darling, the proper people for you to go to are your parents, if Ben has thrown you out.'

'He hasn't.' Helen's voice became momentarily suspended, as the breath caught in her throat. She recovered and went on: 'I wish he had. It would make things so much easier.'

Elizabeth blinked. 'You mean that in spite of first Richard and now Chris, Ben still wants you? Darling, there are very few men, you know, who would be prepared to show such forbearance.' She knelt beside her cousin's chair and stroked the hair back from

Helen's forehead. 'He must love you very much. Don't you think, if you put your mind to it, you could love him? After all, you did so once.'

Helen said nothing, not knowing how to reply. She realized how Ben's attitude must look to outsiders; how her own conduct must make her seem a silly, loose woman. No doubt if she told Elizabeth that Ben persistently ill-treated her, her cousin would let her stay but pride forbade the confidence. She smiled tremulously.

'You're right, of course. Ben has been very forgiving and understanding. I owe him something. I ought to remain with him, and he still wants me. And when all's said and done, who else does?' She gave a little laugh which broke in the middle. 'I'm sorry to have bothered you, Lizzie. I was feeling a bit down. What I really wanted was someone to talk to. Thank you for letting me do that. And for the brandy. I'm feeling better. Honestly.'

Elizabeth asked uneasily: 'Helen, love, you are telling me the truth?'

'Yes. Ben's a saint. Everybody says so.'

'Oh, come . . . !'

'They do you know. Mama and Papa do, and other people who know about me and Richard, me and Chris. Even people who just guess at the truth.' Helen smiled brightly. 'So, you and Richard are going to be married! I'm glad. I hope you'll both be very happy.'

'You're not still in love with him, are you?' Another spectre had raised its ugly head. 'Truthfully?' Elizabeth pressed.

'Heaven's no!' Helen laughed, brighter than ever. 'I thought I was once, as you know, but that was just infatuation. I love Chris.'

'Then for goodness' sake apply for a passport and go out to Texas to join him. Before this bloody war starts and it's too late.'

'If he contacts me, I'll go. If not, I shan't.' Helen's

355

smile wavered for a moment; then she rallied. 'I'm not forcing myself on him. I'm not going to make that mistake a second time.' She got up and kissed Elizabeth's cheek. 'Thanks again, Lizzie. I'm sorry I was so hysterical when I arrived, but I'm fine now. Really.'

'Did you drive yourself here? Right. Telephone me as soon as you get home to let me know that you're still OK.'

'I will. Goodbye, Lizzie.' The door closed and Helen was gone.

'Damn! Damn! Damn!' Elizabeth swore out loud. Her conscience was troubled. She should have let her cousin stay. She had been mean and selfish, but she did not want to believe that, so she transferred her anger with herself to Chris Morgan. What a bastard he'd turned out to be! Going off in a huff and leaving Helen flat, just because her silliness had landed him in an embarrassing situation. Men! She could do without them! All but one.

Elizabeth and Richard were married at Bristol Registry Office early in January, 1939. They did their best to keep it quiet, to limit their secret to Mary and Jack. But, inevitably, word got around, and when they emerged after the ceremony into the dusk and chilling rain of a winter's afternoon, there were little knots of spectators waiting near the entrance. There were also photographers and reporters, not only from the local press, but from several national dailies as well. The wedding of a Hollywood film star, however minor provided some blessedly light relief from the constant threat and talk of war. The agreement at Munich the previous September, Neville Chamberlain and his bit of paper, had really fooled no one, in spite of the relief and jubilation at the time.

But however much the Prime Minister might have been reviled by fellow Members of Parliament, he had at least earned Elizabeth's undying gratitude for gaining sufficient breathing space to bring Richard safely home.

Standing on the pavement outside the registry office, sheltering beneath the umbrella which Jack was holding over her, Elizabeth heard a woman nearby remark to her friend: 'She looks a fair bit older than him.'

'They say she's thirty-six,' the other woman answered in equally carrying accents. 'Baby-snatching, that's what it is.'

How unfair, Elizabeth thought angrily. If their ages had been the other way around, no one would have considered Richard too old to marry her.

There was no official reception. Richard, between contracts, had no publicity manager breathing down his neck, urging him to capitalize on the occasion. With Mary and Jack, he and Elizabeth returned to a cold buffet at The Brass Mill, prepared by the capable hands of Miss Maple.

Nibbling chicken breast in aspic, Elizabeth asked her sister: 'Do you remember how Mama used to cut boiled eggs in half to make two do the work of four?'

Mary nodded, smiling. 'And at Christmas, we used to be given half an orange each, because at a farthing apiece, it was considered too expensive to give us a whole one.'

The rest of the evening, until it was time for Mary and Jack to go, was spent in happy reminiscence. But when Mary disappeared upstairs, prior to leaving, Elizabeth grew serious and asked: 'What's wrong with her, Jack? She looks ill to me.'

Jack blinked in surprise. 'Mary? She looks the same as she always does, to *me*.'

'Nonsense!' Elizabeth rapped out sharply. 'Anyone can see she's lost weight. Don't you think so, Richard?'

'She does seem thinner,' Richard admitted warily. 'But then, I haven't seen her for quite some time.'

'She's much thinner now than when you first came

357

home, just before Christmas,' Elizabeth reproached him. 'You must see that she is.' She turned her attention back to her brother-in-law. 'You really should persuade her to talk to a doctor, Jack.'

Jack sighed. 'It isn't easy to persuade her to do anything she doesn't want to do. You ought to know that, Lizzie. She's your sister. But if you think it necessary, I'll try.'

Elizabeth got up and kissed his cheek. 'Thank you. And if the doctor says there's nothing wrong with her, so much the better. It will have put my mind at ease.'

Mary came back into the room at that moment and Elizabeth adroitly turned the conversation. But a little later, when they were standing in the hall, saying good-night, she whispered in Jack's ear: 'You won't forget?'

He smiled and shook his head. 'I'll do what I can.' He glanced towards his wife, who was talking to Richard. 'She seems to have forgiven him at last for refusing to be the son she always wanted. Funny, isn't it, that he's ended up being her brother-in-law, instead? It's been a bit like musical chairs; Helen and Ben, Richard and you, Mary and me. Not the couplings that anyone would once have predicted.'

'No,' Elizabeth agreed with some constraint. 'Jack . . . I'm sorry.'

'Don't be,' he answered gently. 'You're happy. That's all that matters.'

'And you? Are you happy, Jack?'

'You asked me that once before, and I told you I'm content. Now, for heaven's sake, Lizzie, don't dream of coming to the office for at least a fortnight. A month, if you can possibly tear yourself away for that long. The Evans and Hennessey Financial Loan Company is too well established by now to fall apart if you're not there. It has a life and momentum all of its own.'

Elizabeth grimaced. 'I presume that's a tactful way of reminding me that I'm not indispensable. Quite right, too. Goodnight, Jack dear. God bless.' She kissed him again.

Then she and Richard waved goodbye, standing on the doorstep, huddled close for warmth in the bitter night air, until the noise of Jack's car engine had dwindled to a hum in the distance.

'That's that,' Elizabeth said, as she closed the front door. 'The dastardly deed is done.' She turned the plain gold wedding ring on her finger. 'Mrs Richard Davies. I can't believe it.'

'You're regretting it already!' Richard cried in mock alarm, dramatically clutching his heart. 'Divorce after only four hours of marriage. M'lud, I ask you, is this some kind of record?'

'Idiot!' Elizabeth wrapped her arms about his neck. 'Although I warn you, it's no more than many people expect.'

'Well, they're going to be disappointed then, aren't they?' He kissed her hard, his tongue probing her mouth. 'Let's go to bed,' he whispered, 'and to blazes with the rest of the world.'

But she held back, suddenly gripped by self-doubt. 'You do love me, darling, don't you? I mean . . . there won't ever be anyone else?'

'I swear it.'

'And . . . Helen? You were never really in love with her?'

'Lizzie! What's got into you?' Richard paused at the foot of the stairs and cupped her chin in one of his hands. 'I love you,' he repeated. 'You and only you. I guess I always have done, since I was a little boy.'

'And it makes no difference, my being ten years older?'

'No. No, no, no!' He hugged her. 'Does that satisfy you? Don't let stupid people get to you, sweetheart. Age isn't important when two people are in love. Now, Mrs Davies, would you like to come up to bed?'

*   *   *

War was declared against Germany on Sunday,

September the third, at eleven o'clock in the morning. Richard, who had completed a film at Denham studios the previous day, packed up and returned home the same night.

He had been telling Elizabeth for months that war was imminent. 'Don't let yourself hope for a single second,' he had said, 'that it can possibly be averted. It's just a question of waiting for the actual moment.'

In March Hitler had consolidated his position in Czechoslovakia, then turned his predatory gaze on Poland, to whom the British Government had pledged support. Throughout the summer, however, most people had tried to pretend that everything was normal. The French President, Monsieur Lebrun, had visited England, while the King and Queen had received a rapturous reception both in Canada and the United States. Turning on their radios to the comedy of *Band Waggon* and the even zanier humour of *ITMA*, people reassured themselves that in such a world nothing could be seriously wrong, carefully turning a blind eye to the fact that the Government, determined not to repeat the mistakes of the last war, had already introduced conscription.

By August, however, it was impossible to ignore black-out trials and their frightening implications; and on the last day of that month, the evacuation of women and children from London began. The following morning, Hitler invaded Poland and the British Government issued its ultimatum to the German Third Reich. Forty-eight hours later, the two countries were again at war.

Richard, Elizabeth and Miss Maple sat quietly by the wireless in the library, listening to the voice of Neville Chamberlain. The Prime Minister sounded suddenly an old, defeated and broken man. When he had finished speaking, Elizabeth got up and switched off the radio, before returning to her seat. Her eyes went to the windows, where she half-expected to see the sky full of German planes. Instead, the familiar trees and grass and flower-beds met her gaze. Sunlight flickered across the surface of the small stone fishpond, turning it into a mirror of gold. A lark soared, shrilling its song to the clouded blue vault of the sky. Nothing had changed during the past five minutes; no great, apocalyptic thunder-clap had marked the transition from peace to war. For one blessed, self-deluding moment, Elizabeth was able to persuade herself that it was all a bad dream; a nightmare from which she would soon be awakened.

Richard's voice dispelled this illusion. 'I've volunteered for the RAF,' he said. 'If I pass my medical, I shall be off next week.'

Miss Maple rose and tactfully withdrew. Elizabeth sat staring at her husband in a state of acute misery.

'I suppose you have to go.'

Richard went to her and took her hands in his. 'Darling, you know I do. I haven't any choice. And I'd much rather volunteer than be conscripted.'

'We'd better make the most of the time you have left, then, hadn't we?'

They went into town the next day, and already, Elizabeth noticed, there were signs of the altered times. The trams had white lines painted around the coachwork, top and bottom, so that they could be seen by pedestrians in the black-out, and their route indicator boxes were empty. Council workmen were busy removing signposts and, in some places, road signs. Street lamps were being painted black. She shivered and clutched Richard's arm.

'You should have gone to the office as usual,' he told her. 'It would have given you something to occupy your mind.'

Elizabeth shook her head. 'I want to be with you every minute that I'm able. Perhaps,' she added hopefully, 'you'll fail your medical.'

But he passed easily, as she had known he would. He

had always been strong, and the Californian food and sunshine had made him even fitter. Two days later he was gone. She walked blindly out of Temple Meads station, along with dozens of other women all trying to blink back their tears, and made her way to the Centre, and Evans and Hennessey House. She went up in the lift to her office, where her secretary wisely decided to give her a little time to herself before going in to take dictation.

Elizabeth pitched her hat and handbag on to the elegant Regency couch which stood near one of the windows, and sat down at her desk. She felt extraordinarily tired; drained of strength and energy. All she wanted to do was sleep, forgetting, in oblivion, the outrage of another war, only twenty-one years after the last one had ended; just long enough to breed another generation of young men. She thought of all those thousands upon thousands of her own generation who had been killed at Ypres and Mons and Gallipoli in the 'war to end wars', and who now appeared to have died in vain.

She heard the door between her room and Jack's open and close, and knew that he must have come into the office; but she did not look round. She had no wish to speak to anyone, not even Jack, just at present. If she ignored him, he might go away again.

'Lizzie.' He put a hand on her shoulder. 'Lizzie, I'm sorry to bother you at such a moment, but I have to talk to you. It's about Mary.'

Elizabeth's head turned sharply. 'What about Mary?' she demanded in a tight little voice, wholly unlike her own.

Jack drew up a chair and sat down next to her. He sucked in his breath.

'You remember your wedding night? You told me I should make her consult a doctor. Well, I tried for a long time to make her see reason, but she refused to do as I asked. I realize now that she had suspicions herself

362

about her illness and was scared that a doctor would only confirm them.'

'Her illness? She is sick then?' Elizabeth was suddenly frightened.

'Very sick, I'm afraid. It's cancer. She's dying.'

'No!' Elizabeth jumped up, putting her hands over her ears. 'I won't listen to you. You're lying!'

He made no answer, but sat watching her, his face sad and drawn and a look of hopelessness in his eyes. Ashamed, Elizabeth resumed her seat beside him, and held out her hands.

'Please forgive me, Jack. That was an awful thing to say. It's the shock . . . One thing on top of another.' She started to cry softly. 'When did you find out?'

'Three weeks ago. During the summer, I at last got her to see sense. The doctor sent her to the hospital for various check-ups and tests. And I took her to London to see a Harley Street specialist. Every verdict was the same.'

'But . . . But surely there must be something they can do!'

'Apparently not. The disease is too far advanced.'

'But we can't do nothing! We can't just stand idly by and watch her die!'

'I'm afraid we have no choice, my dear. All we can do is give her our love and support. She's going to need it. The pain is already very bad, and it's going to get worse.'

'Oh, God! How unfair and rotten life is!'

'Come on, Lizzie, that's not like you. You've always been a fighter. Fight now. Don't let things get you down. I'd like to get Mary away from Eastwood for her last few months. It's too noisy and grimy; and Mother will look after the house. If you agree, I'd like to bring her to The Brass Mill, where she can look out at the gorge and the woods.'

'If I agree?' Elizabeth tears flowed, unchecked. 'You foolish man, of course I agree. You're to bring her there at once, do you hear me? You must pack up and bring her tonight.'

Mary died quietly on January the seventh, nineteen-forty. During the final weeks of her life she seemed to rally, to be in less pain and more like her old self. She had followed with interest radio and newspaper reports on the chase, cornering and subsequent scuttling of the German pocket battleship *Graf Spee*. But by the beginning of the new year, it was obvious that the end was close at hand. She lost even more weight and her skin seemed to be falling away from her bones. For the last few days, neither Elizabeth nor Jack was ever far from her side.

She was buried, as she had requested, in Eastwood cemetery. As Elizabeth and Jack walked back to the waiting car, between the rows of graves, she asked him: 'What will you do now?'

'Go home. I can't stay at The Brass Mill now that Mary's gone, and besides, Mother is feeling neglected.' Jack braced his shoulders against the driving rain. 'And there's plenty to occupy me. This phoney war won't last forever. Sooner or later, Hitler's going to make a move, and this time civilians are going to be in the front line just as much as the troops. It's more than probable that men of my age group will eventually be called up. I'm only thirty-nine. There will be no time to brood, Lizzie, my girl. Until we've beaten Hitler, life will be too full for that.'

Part Six 1941 – 1945

Time takes all and gives all.
                    Giordano Bruno 1548 – 1600

CHAPTER TWENTY-EIGHT

Elizabeth peered from the office window at the barrage balloons, floating above the city skyline like stranded silver whales.

'They're high,' she remarked over her shoulder to Jack. 'I should say they're expecting a raid. It's my turn for firewatching, too.'

Jack came to her side and looked out. He was wearing his warden's navy-blue battledress uniform, in readiness for going on duty the moment he left work. Elizabeth knew how it had irked him to be turned down for active service because of his weak chest. Jack had always prided himself on his physical fitness, and the Army Medical Board's verdict had come not only as a shock, but also as something in the nature of a personal affront. In a huff, he had joined the Civil Defence as an Air Raid Warden, because, unlike many of his fellow citizens, he had never been sceptical of the Luftwaffe's ability to reach Bristol.

'They won't get this far,' people had declared, remembering the last war and the Zepplins' failure to foray much beyond London. To substantiate this contention, they had pointed out that the BBC and many of the Whitehall departments were moving into the city.

And for many months, throughout the 'phoney' war,

the worst inconveniences which Bristolians had had to suffer were either having strangers billeted on them, or being turned out of their homes altogether, the houses being commandeered by the military or one of the ministries. The Brass Mill had been taken over by the Ministry of Aircraft Production, and Elizabeth had moved to a flat in Clifton. At Jack's house in Eastwood Eileen Hennessey had cheerfully coped with a bunch of evacuees, all of whom had now been taken home again by their parents.

Then, the previous summer, there had been vicious daylight attacks on the aircraft works at Filton and on Avonmouth docks. The illusion of safety was shattered. In November, night raids had started; London, Coventry and, on the twenty-fourth, Bristol. The centre of the city, as generations had known it, disappeared overnight; the Old Dutch House, the medieval street of St Mary-le-Port, the historic St Peter's Hospital were all swept away.

And the raids had continued relentlessly until now, on this Good Friday of 1941, the prospect of another night of death and destruction raining down from the skies merely filled people with resignation. The initial fear and horror had receded, leaving in their wake a fierce determination to see the war through at all costs and to resist Nazi Germany to the bitter end.

Staring at the floating barrage balloons, Jack remarked pensively: 'The Huns may have got wind of the fact that Churchill will be here tomorrow. I suppose he might even be staying in the city overnight.'

Elizabeth turned away from the window. 'I'd forgotten that,' she said.

Winston Churchill, who had replaced the late Neville Chamberlain as Prime Minister in the first half of 1940, was visiting Bristol the following day in his capacity as Chancellor of the University, and was to confer Honorary Law Degrees on the United States Ambassador, John Winant, the Australian Prime

Minister and the President of Harvard University, Dr J B Conant. Elizabeth glanced back uneasily at the still empty skies beyond the window and consulted her wristwatch.

'I'll send the staff home early, except those of us who are fire-watching. Mind you, we may be worrying unnecessarily. We had a bad raid last Friday. They say lightning never strikes twice ... ' She broke off, shrugging. 'However, just in case, I'll issue instructions for everyone to leave at half-past four. Half of them will be on duty somewhere, anyway; at the Report Centres or with the Red Cross.' She touched the bell on her desk and her secretary appeared. Elizabeth gave her instructions, then put on her hat and coat and gathered up her handbag and gas-mask. 'I'm going to get something to eat,' she said. She crossed the room and squeezed Jack's arm. 'Take care tonight, won't you?'

For a second, his hand lightly covered hers. 'And you. How's Richard? Have you heard from him lately?'

'I had a letter last week. Heavily censored, of course, I've no idea where he's stationed, but I should think he's due for some leave pretty soon. Well, I'll be off. Don't forget what I said. Take care.'

She crossed the Centre and walked up Park Street to a little basement restaurant near the Victoria Rooms, run by a French woman. With the increasing shortages and rationing, Elizabeth maintained that only the culinary genius of the French could produce anything palatable in the way of food. She passed the now ubiquitous pig-bins, chained to lamp-posts, every few hundred yards, where people put their left-over scraps and peelings, and the one-legged wooden tables, whose green paint would change colour in the presence of gas. So far, thank God, there had been no gas attacks, although everyone had to carry at all times a Government issue mask. Once a week the staff of Evans and Hennessey House had to work for at least half an hour in their masks to get used to the discomfort and difficulty of breathing.

The staff now mainly comprised elderly or unfit men or married women, all the able-bodied being either in the Armed Forces or working in munitions factories or on the land. And nearly every one of those left was involved in some form of voluntary service. There was, Elizabeth reflected, as she took a seat at her favourite corner table in the restaurant, a public-spiritedness abroad these days normally lacking in the British character. Every man, woman and child was determined to beat Adolf Hitler.

After she had given her order to Madame, Elizabeth sat staring at a poster on the opposite wall. Beneath two crossed Tricolours, big, black letters shouted *A Tous Les Français*. Beneath this again, were the words *La France a perdu une bataille! Mais la France n'a pas perdu la guerre!* There followed a long exhortation, urging all free Frenchmen to fight for victory, ending with *Vive La France!* in even bigger, blacker letters than before. It was signed C. de Gaulle, General de Gaulle, Quartier-General, 4, Carlton Gardens, London SW1.

The fall of France and the evacuation of the British Expeditionary Force from Dunkirk, the previous summer, had been the most unexpected and most dramatic event of the war so far. Even the Battle of Britain had not been so traumatic, for no one had seriously considered the possibility of a German victory. In spite of the notices and the instructions and the booby-trapped beaches, the hastily improvised tank-traps and the miles of barbed wire, it had seemed incredible that Hitler should succeed in invading Britain, where everyone since William the Conqueror had failed. Similarly, it had been taken for granted that France would hold out as she had done from 1914 to 1918. But the French Government, remembering perhaps the carnage of the Great War and the vicious rape of their country, had surrendered, leaving Britain to fight on alone. The only hope now of defeating the Nazis was for the British to hold out for as long as it took to draw the United States into the war on their side.

Elizabeth ate and paid for her meal, then mounted to street level again. It was five o'clock, and there was an hour before she need return to the office for firewatching. She supposed she could go back to the flat to change and rest, but she was already wearing her slacks, and she did not feel tired. On a sudden, almost blind impulse, she found herself threading the Clifton streets until she arrived at the quiet cul-de-sac where four big houses formed the shape of a bow. The dark cupressus trees still sheltered the inmates from the road, but the railings and iron gates had been removed, taken away to be melted down to help the war effort. She passed between the stone pillars of Evelyn Villa, mounted the steps and rang the bell.

It was her Aunt Minna who answered the door. Domestic staff, for the time being, were a thing of the past. Minna stared for a moment, as if unable to believe her eyes, then she said faintly: 'Good heavens! Lizzie! Come in! Please do come in!'

Elizabeth stepped cautiously over the doorstep into the gloomy hall, which she had not seen since adolescence, wondering what on earth had prompted her to come. Then she saw Minna's face, old, drawn, tired, the tears coursing down the lined cheeks, and the next moment the two women were in one another's arms.

When she could steady her voice sufficiently, Elizabeth asked: 'Is Uncle Joe in?'

Minna shook her head and dried her eyes. 'No, but it's just as well. He hasn't forgiven you, Lizzie, and I'm afraid he never will. He hates it because you've been a success. He'd be very angry if he knew you were here. But he won't know. I shan't tell him. You're my sister's daughter, and I've wanted to make up our differences ever since Amy died. Come into the parlour and tell me all your news.'

The siren sounded its warning shortly after ten o'clock, and almost immediately the anti-aircraft guns hammered into the silence. Elizabeth, who had been trying to sleep on the camp bed in her office, swung her feet to the ground and switched on the heavily shaded lamp which stood on her desk. The low-powered bulb gleamed thinly, throwing a sad little puddle of light, while she groped under the bed for her shoes. Once they were on and laced up, she pulled a heavy jumper over her slacks and blouse and donned her tin helmet. Then she joined the other four women in the outer office.

They had found it too early to sleep and had been playing cards, betting by the look of it, with farthings and halfpennies. Elizabeth would have liked to join them, but she had discovered at the very beginning of the firewatching rota that her presence inhibited the others' fun. Even during a raid, the staff found it difficult to forget that she was one of the firm's co-owners.

Tonight, her companions were a couple of junior typists, too young as yet to be called up, an elderly woman from the accounts department and the large, rather mannish, extremely competent Miss Bird from publicity. Together they checked fire buckets, sandbags, stirrup-pumps and hoses, before making their way to the roof of the building.

'My God,' murmured Miss Bird, awe-stricken, stepping outside. And as they followed her into the open air, each woman realized that there really was nothing more anyone could say. The city was ablaze.

As well as the hail of incendiaries, high explosive bombs were also dropping. Their dull thud and crunch could plainly be heard in the distance. One of the typists started to cry, and the other one was shaking with fright.

372

'Pull yourselves together, both of you,' Elizabeth reprimanded them sharply. She hated doing it, but knew that sympathy would only make them worse. She was scared to death herself, but in this inferno they had to have their wits about them. They could receive a direct hit any minute, and if it were only an incendiary, it would, literally, be all hands to the pump. If it were a high explosive ... But Elizabeth refused to contemplate that possibility. For a fleeting second, however, it did occur to her to be glad that she had made her peace with Minna earlier in the evening.

'This is the worst yet,' Miss Bird whispered to Elizabeth. 'Worse even than last week.' She added grimly: 'Good Friday, too. In this case, definitely not the better the day, the better the deed. I should think ... '

Her final words were lost under the whistle of a falling bomb.

'Everyone down!' yelled Elizabeth, and threw herself flat behind the nearest chimney.

The flat expanse of roof seemed suddenly bathed in light. In fact, only one bomb had dropped on Evans and Hennessey House, but it was part of a stick which had also set neighbouring offices ablaze. As she sprang to her feet, Elizabeth glimpsed the scurrying activity on the next roof-top, where the building was already burning merrily.

There was a jet of flame, and she could no longer spare half an eye for what was happening elsewhere. Elizabeth and her four companions had to deal with their own fire. The real danger of incendiaries, as everyone well knew, was that they made a flare path for the bombers dropping the high explosives. It was imperative to extinguish the flames as soon as possible.

And by the time the 'All Clear' went, just before midnight, the five women had succeeded in doing just that. With smoke-grimed faces, hands raw from working the stirrup-pump and carrying buckets of water, clothes scorched from playing the hose too near the fire, dog-tired and bone-weary, they stood grinning triumphantly at one another. Only Miss Bird, wiping the dirt from the glass of her wristwatch, sounded a note of pessimism.

'Five minues to twelve,' she grunted. 'That's a bit early for Jerry to call off the dogs, don't you think? Especially when he's got the whole place lit up like Castle Street on a pre-war Saturday night.' She took a deep breath, and all she could smell was burning. Over the entire city hung a great pall of smoke.

Elizabeth, too, consulted her watch. 'Perhaps they're moving on elsewhere,' she suggested hopefully. But underneath her encouraging manner, she felt uneasy. She put an arm round the younger typist's shoulder. 'You did excellently,' she told her. 'Let's go and have that flask of tea we made earlier. We can assess what damage has been done when it's light.'

Helen heard the steady note of the 'All Clear' with relief, and rose to her feet. She put on the peaked navy-blue cap which was part of her Red Cross uniform, and smiled at the Detachment Commandant.

'Thank you for the coffee, Miss Griffiths. You and your mother have been most kind.'

'Don't be foolish,' the older woman retorted briskly. 'Do you think we would have turned you out to go to a public shelter? The very idea! And if it hadn't been for my suggestion that the detachment members met at my home tonight for an extra first-aid practice, you wouldn't have been here in the first place. It was a bit cramped, I'm afraid, but St John's have the use of our usual room this evening.'

'But if I'd left with the others, instead of remaining behind, I shouldn't have had to impose.' Helen picked up her navy-blue shoulder-bag and her gas-mask, said goodnight to old Mrs Griffiths and accompanied Miss Griffiths to the outer door.

'You'll be all right, I suppose, on your own?' the Commandant queried, a little doubtfully. Helen looked so youthful in the navy-blue suit, white shirt and black tie, that it was hard to realize she was a grown woman. The flat black shoes and grey rayon stockings only added to the illusion of the schoolgirl.

'Good heavens, yes! After all, it isn't very far. I shall be home in twenty minutes.'

'Mmm.' Miss Griffiths glanced at the hall clock. 'Midnight. The blighters have pushed off early for once. Well, at least your husband knew where you were. Good job I persuaded Mother to have the telephone installed two years ago. There wouldn't be a hope of getting it put in now.' She opened the door and gingerly peeped outside. 'I'm afraid it's been every bit as bad as it sounded. My dear, just look at that sky.'

The night sky was glowing with the reflection of a hundred fires. The Redland district seemed to have escaped the brunt of the attack, but from the direction of Whiteladies Road and Blackboy Hill they could hear the rattle of ambulances and fire-engines.

Miss Griffiths clapped Helen on the back. 'Don't loiter,' she advised, 'unless, of course, you're called on for assistance. Good job you're in uniform. People will know you can be of help.'

Helen's heart sank. 'Oh, please God, no!' she prayed silently.

The stupid thing was that she really enjoyed Red Cross work. She liked the weekly meetings, learning the theory of first-aid and home nursing, practising with splints and bandages on the other women. She even enjoyed the two nights a week she spent on the maternity ward of a Clifton nursing home, carrying round supper trays, emptying bed-pans and scrubbing bucket-loads of babies' dirty napkins. She liked gossiping in the sluice with the V A Ds, while they rolled bandages and sanitary towels to put in the sterilizer. And she had been allowed into the delivery room on a couple of occasions, and managed to see the babies born without disgracing herself by fainting.

Yes, she had done well since she joined the Red Cross, Helen reflected, as she hurried through the maze of Redland's streets and out on to the main road. She had gained her proficiency certificates in both first-aid and home nursing, and had recently added a life-saving badge to the tally. She sported on her sleeve the two stripes of a Section Leader. But, in spite of everything, she still had no confidence in herself; not the sort of confidence to cope calmly and efficiently in an emergency. She was fine in the practice or examination room, but was terrified of being called upon to translate theory into deeds. She saw a fire-engine and an ambulance ahead of her, outside a house which had obviously received a direct hit, and was now nothing but a smouldering ruin. Helen dodged down a side-street and began to run.

The ululating cry of the warning siren wailed out again at a quarter-past midnight, just twenty minutes after the 'All Clear' had blown. The second wave of German bombers hit the city with even more ferocity than before; and this raid was to last for nearly four hours.

Almost at once there was the crunch of high explosives as the enemy pilots dropped bombs on a city illuminated as clearly as if it were day. Helen had just crossed the wide thoroughfare of Whiteladies Road when she heard the familiar whistle, and instinctively flung herself down on the pavement. The noise of the explosion was deafening, and she realized that the bomb must have fallen very close at hand. For a moment she was unable to move. She could hear the crash of masonry and the tinkle of breaking glass, people shouting, a woman screaming, but still she continued to lie where she was. Someone bent over her.

'Are you OK?' a man's voice asked roughly.

Slowly, Helen got to her feet, brushing the dirt from her jacket and skirt, and searching around for her gas-mask, which she had lost in the panic. The man, an air-raid warden, retrieved it for her, at the same time noting her uniform and the red cross on her cap badge.

'Sure you're all right?' he asked again; and when she nodded, seized her elbow. 'Good. Because we need you in Apsley Road. You can help out until the ambulance arrives.'

Helen froze in her tracks. 'No! No, I can't,' she whispered.

The man stared at her, then jerked her forward. 'What do you mean, you can't? You're in the bloody Red Cross, aren't you? There are people badly injured round there. Dying, probably. So come on, woman! Get a move on!'

Helen went with him, in a trance, breathless from panic. 'Dear God, please no! What am I going to do?'

A house halfway along the street had been demolished, and the one next to it badly damaged. There was nothing to be done for the occupants of the former, and rescuers knew that they would find only dead bodies. But in front of the second house, a man was sitting on the wall, looking white and dazed, supporting his right elbow with his other hand. A woman was lying on the ground.

Helen freed herself from the warden's grip and took a deep breath. 'Think,' she told herself. 'Take it slowly and think!'

Neighbours had appeared with blankets and flasks. Helen dropped to her knees and examined the woman, who was moaning and clutching her chest. She was exceedingly pale and her pulse was soft and rapid. The eyes flickered open and she murmured: 'Thirsty.'

'Give her some of this tea,' an onlooker said, pouring the hot liquid into the cap of the vacuum flask.

'No!' Helen rapped out. 'There's probably a chest injury, caused by broken ribs. There may be internal bleeding. I'll have the blankets. All you've got.'

Competently, with hands which no longer trembled, she loosened the woman's clothing and ordered the rest of the people to stand well back, before covering her patient with the proffered blankets. She had seen, when she opened the nightdress, marks of bruising across the breast.

'Is there an ambulance available?' she asked the warden over her shoulder.

'I've telephoned in, and I've sent a man to the corner of the road with instructions to stop the first one he sees. Bad, is she?'

Helen considered. 'I think she'll live. No need, yet, to raise the legs or bandage the arms. Please, everyone, give her as much air as possible.' She turned her attention to the man sitting on the wall. 'You've broken your right collar bone, I think.'

He grunted. 'Slipped and fell as I was leaving the shelter. Put my arm out to save myself, and heard the damn thing snap.'

Helen opened his shirt and traced the line of the right clavicle with a gentle finger. She could feel the break and the lower level of the outer fragment. Otherwise, he seemed unharmed. She glanced up at the woman who had offered the tea.

'I want a big towel and a scarf, a big headsquare, if you have one. Also something to make a pad with. Something about the size of a Bath bun, to go underneath his arm. In the armpit.'

There was a concerted movement as most of the neighbours disappeared indoors, to return a few moments with a variety of scarves and towels of all shapes and sizes. Within minutes, Helen had improvised a St John's sling and was wrapping the patient in blankets. She could detect no sign of internal injury, and was certain enough by now of her own diagnosis to allow him to be given some sips of hot, sweet tea.

The warden patted her shoulder. 'Good girl,' he said approvingly, and Helen smiled to herself, realizing that the light must be dimmer than she had thought. 'Pretending to be scared, back there! Shock, most likely. Got you all of a doo-dah for a minute. If I was a bit rough, I'm sorry.'

'That's all right,' Helen said, aware, as she had not been for the past ten minutes, of the barrage of continuous noise going on all around them. It was certainly Bristol's worst raid since night bombing had begun last November.

An ambulance appeared round the corner of the road, and Helen saw her patients into it before wearily resuming her interrupted walk home. She was no longer afraid or felt the slightest urge to take cover, ignoring several people who shouted at her to do so. She felt as she did on those rare occasions when she had had too much to drink; or, alternatively, on those all too frequent occasions when she had taken a pill. She was drunk, she supposed, with success. For the first time in her life, she had been forced to rely on her own resources, and they had not failed her. Before she returned home, she would go not so very much out of her way and see that her parents were all right. Joe and Minna would be down in the cellar, but Helen had her own key and could let herself in.

She turned into the little cul-de-sac and stood transfixed. Evelyn Villa, the second house in the crescent, was nothing but a pile of smoking rubble.

CHAPTER TWENTY-NINE

'Your uncle left everything to Ben? I can't believe it.'

In the back of the taxi, Elizabeth snuggled close to Richard's side, trying to convince herself that he really was home on leave at last. It was such a long time since she had seen him. He looked thin and tired, and there were dark circles under his eyes. His Flight Lieutenant's uniform hung loosely on his spare frame. He was quieter, too; less exuberant than she remembered him. Now, however, he had ten days' leave. Ten whole days in which to make him forget, however temporarily, the war.

But that was impossible. He was already peering from the taxi windows at the scarred and battered landscape; at the empty spaces where once thriving shops and houses had been. Even the mention of Joe brought vividly to Elizabeth's mind the memory of that terrible Good Friday raid.

She said, as lightly as possible: 'Yes, shocking, isn't it? An awful thing to have done, but typical, of course, of Uncle Joe. He never had any faith in women's business ability. My success simply reinforced his prejudice that women were unfit to be loosed on the world.' She tugged off the fashionable 'Robin Hood' hat she was wearing and crushed the black felt in her lap. 'I suspect that there was another reason for him acting the way he did. Deep down, I'm sure he realized that Helen's and Ben's marriage was on the rocks, but he refused to admit it. Everything about Helen had to be perfection for him, always. She was his ideal; the perfect woman, and he couldn't bear to acknowledge that as a wife, she was a failure; that she had affairs and ran after other men. This will was a way of ensuring her dependency on Ben.'

Richard snorted disgustedly. 'In other words, pulling strings from beyond the grave. Doesn't she get anything at all?'

'Only if Ben dies before her. Then she gets the lot.'

'Ben hasn't been called up, I suppose?'

'Heavens no! Running Gordon's is a reserved occupation. All Sebastopol Street and most of Arley Street are producing cocoa and chocolate rations for the troops. It's damn near impossible for civilians to get sweets these days.'

Richard's eyes twinkled as he turned and kissed her. 'I've managed to get you a box of chocolate liqueurs. A little shop in the village near where we're stationed had a couple of boxes, strictly under the counter, last week. And the lady in charge succumbed to a handsome Flight Lieutenant's smile.'

'I trust that's all she succumbed to,' Elizabeth retorted with asperity.

He kissed her again, harder. 'I've told you, you need never have any fears on that score.' He held her away from him, but still within the circle of his arms. 'You're working too hard. You look tired. But at least things must be a bit easier now, now that the bombing has stopped.'

'A miracle, isn't it? Everyone presumed it would get worse in the summer, but instead, it just finished. And now that Adolf has invaded Russia, let's hope he'll have his hands full, and won't have time to bother with us.' She frowned. 'They said on the wireless this morning that the Russians are retreating.'

'They were taken by surprise. No one expected Hitler to break his pact with Stalin so soon.' Richard nestled his cheek against her hair. 'Do you mind if we don't talk about the war for the next ten days?'

'Of course not. I didn't intend mentioning it. It just slipped out.' She held him tightly. 'Let's spend the entire time in bed. I've told them at the office not to expect me in.'

He laughed. 'No eating?'

'Mmm ... Yes. I think we might allow ourselves time off for eating and sleeping. But otherwise ... '

'You're insatiable, do you know that? You may have been a virgin until the age of thirty-four, but you've made up for it ever since.'

The taxi drew to a halt in front of the slender Georgian house near Clifton's Mall, where Elizabeth had the ground floor flat. While Richard paid the driver and collected the luggage from the boot, Elizabeth eyed it with dislike.

'What's the matter?' Richard enquired, noting the expression on her face.

'I was just recalling my vow to live and die at the Mill. I promised you once it should always be your home. Now there are clerks and typists and other sundry M A P staff swarming all over it.'

'You'll get it back when this show is ended. Beating Hitler, that's all that matters now.'

'I know. I'm not complaining. I know I'm lucky — damn lucky — compared with most people. We're arranging loans for the Government now, did I tell you?'

'No, but I guessed you'd be up to something like that.' He followed her into the flat through a side door which led in from the garden, dumped his service gas-mask and case on the floor and took her in his arms.

'How I've missed you,' he murmured against her hair.

Elizabeth clung to him, her lips seeking his, one

hand fumbling with the buttons of his uniform jacket. He lifted her bodily and carried her into the bedroom.

Half an hour later, she lay back contentedly, her head pillowed on his shoulder, and lit a cigarette, watching the smoke spirals, faintly blue, curling away into the darkness. The July sunshine found a chink in the black-out curtains and dazzled her eyes with a bright star of gold. Elizabeth picked up her discarded petticoat from the counterpane and sighed.

'That was my last pre-war, silk slip. Did you have to tear it like that, you impatient man? You do realize that clothes are rationed now for us poor civilians?' She propped herself on one elbow and tickled the end of Richard's nose. 'They're going to introduce utility furniture and utility clothing in the autumn. Doesn't that sound absolutely foul?'

'I thought we weren't going to discuss the war,' he reminded her, then smiled. 'Stupid, really. You can't possibly forget it. What would you like to do this evening?'

Elizabeth climbed out of bed and put on her dressing-gown. 'First, I'm going to make a meal for us and feed Trojan, who, incidentally, is probably chewing his tail in jealousy and frustration. Food is his one comfort nowadays. He took the move from the Mill even worse than I did. Being reduced to a flat offends his aristocratic sensibilities, but I tell him it's his contribution to the war effort ... Sorry, there I go again. Well, as I said, I'll get us both something to eat. After that ... '

'What after that?'

Elizabeth blew her husband a provocative kiss. 'After that, I suggest we pick up where we've just left off. I can't think of anything nicer. Can you?'

'If we're going to do it, let's get on with it,' Eileen Hennessey advised. 'It's no good putting it off any longer, Jack. They're crying out for clothes for people

383

who have been bombed out and lost everything. And there's all Mary's stuff hanging in the wardrobe, doing nothing. We'll parcel it up this afternoon, and you can get the W V S or someone to collect it.'

Jack sighed. 'Mother, I have a pile of work I've brought home for the weekend, which I ought to be looking at. With Elizabeth away the entertainments side of the busines is being neglected. Oh, all right,' he agreed, noting the mulish expression on his mother's face. 'Let's get on with it then, and get it over.'

For some reason which he found difficult to explain, even to himself, Jack had been reluctant to get rid of Mary's things after her death. The sight of her clothes — the rack of shoes, the shelf of hats, the row of coats, suits and dresses neatly lined up in the wardrobe — somehow eased his loneliness. He could at least pretend that Mary was still around; that she had merely gone on holiday; that there was someone else who cared about his comfort and well-being other than his mother. Once those traces of their life together had been removed, he would be forced to accept the truth. He was on his own, as he had been all his life, emotionally isolated by his love for a woman who had never loved him. He had a sudden, sharp picture of Elizabeth and Richard in one another's arms, and had to suppress a cry of almost physical pain.

'Right,' he said tersely, putting aside his papers and getting up from the roll-top desk which he had bought for himself when Avebury Villa's original back parlour had been converted into his study. 'Let's get on with it.'

Eileen Hennessey, who had been standing in the doorway like some avenging angel, nodded in satisfaction. 'It won't take long. I've plenty of brown paper and string all ready. You haven't forgotten your sister and her family are coming to tea, I hope? It's Bridget's birthday.'

Jack made no answer. He might have retorted that he

had not been permitted to forget it; that he was expected to augment the incomes of all his sisters, their husbands and assorted children, with various gifts of money, as well as generous Christmas and birthday presents. But as his mother was perfectly well aware of these facts, it seemed pointless to mention them. Dutifully, he followed Eileen upstairs.

The big front bedroom he had shared with Mary was stuffy with summer heat, Eileen having drawn the heavily lined curtains against the bright July sunshine when she made the bed that morning. Jack impatiently threw them back, at the same time opening a window. The deathly, Nonconformist hush of an Eastwood Sunday pervaded the room. Even the war, Jack thought wryly, had not altered that.

'Well?' he asked. 'Where shall we begin?'

Eileen indicated the array of cardboard boxes and brown paper which she had laid ready on the bed. The brown paper she had grudgingly spared from her pre-war hoard. Like most other commodities, it was in short supply these days.

'I'll do the cupboards and drawers,' she said. 'Things like shoes, hats, underwear, bits and pieces can go in the boxes. You fold the clothes from the wardrobe and lay them on the paper. I'll parcel them up later. Check all the pockets to make sure there's nothing in them.'

Jack hesitated. He wanted to turn tail and run. There was something so final in tidying away the residue of a person's life. There ought to be people one could pay to do such things; people for whom the flotsam and jetsam of a human existence conjured up no regrets or pain . . . Savagely, he slipped the first coat from its hanger.

They had almost finished when a ring at the front doorbell announced the arrival of his sister Bridget and her family.

'You go down,' Jack urged his mother. 'I shan't be a

385

couple of minutes. There are only these last few dresses and that coat and suit to fold now.'

Eileen, whose enthusiasm for any project waned before the prospect of seeing her grandchildren, nodded briskly.

'Right,' she said. 'But don't be long. They'll be dying to see you.'

'Me and my money,' Jack thought grimly.

Left to himself, he made a final sweep of everything remaining on the hangers and laid the clothes on the bed, sorting them methodically into the various piles, winter dresses, summer dresses, coats, suits, jackets. The last but one item he picked up was a coat of white bouclé wool, which he had bought for Mary shortly after they were married. She had only worn it twice, complaining that it was too light a colour for autumn or winter use, but too warm and too heavy to wear in spring or summer. It was a beautiful garment which Elizabeth had helped him choose, and it seemed criminal to give it away. But his mother and sister were not Mary's size, and had been unable to utilize as many of her things as they would have liked.

He felt in the pockets. So far, all he had found was a couple of handkerchiefs and a receipted bill for a pair of gloves from Taylor's of the Green, one of the many shops gutted by fire in the Good Friday air raid. This time, however, his fingers closed on a more substantial piece of paper than an account-book flimsy. He drew out a ruled sheet, torn from a child's exercise book, and spread it open. It was some seconds before he realized it was a letter.

Helen left the nursing home just after ten o'clock, turning into the pleached alleyway which bisected the neighbouring churchyard. Tonight under her navy greatcoat, she was wearing the blue-grey cotton dress worn by all V A Ds when nursing. In her attaché case reposed the white apron and white, triangular headdress, each item bearing its red cross. Over her left shoulder was slung, as well as her handbag, her gas-mask in a black, leatherette case; for the making of gas-mask cases, in a variety of cheap materials, had proved to be one of the growth industries of the war.

She was feeling pleased with herself: this evening, Sister Morris had actually allowed her to assist at a birth. It had been a forceps delivery and she had acquitted herself well. Afterwards, Sister had praised her.

'You've improved out of all knowledge these past few months, Nurse Sawyer. You've twice the confidence that you used to have, when you first came here. Ever thought of taking up nursing full time?'

Helen had smiled, shaking her head. 'Not really, Sister. I'm thirty-eight. Too old to start as a probationer, don't you think? I enjoy my V A D work very much, though. If you want me a couple of extra nights each week, I have the time.'

She swung through the churchyard now with brisk, confident steps. The almost total darkness, the corpse-like gleam of the gravestones on either side of the pleached alleyway, did not disturb her as they once had, sending her round the long way, by the road. The pallid glimmer of light from her torch was directed carefully downwards, to the ground.

As she emerged from the graveyard, two soldiers lurched drunkenly across her path.

'Hallo, darlin',' said the taller one, in a broad Scots accent. 'What are yew doin' out this late, a' on yer own?' He lunged at her, trying to kiss her.

Helen laughed and side-stepped him neatly.

'The same as you, I expect. Beating Jerry. Isn't it time you went back to barracks, like a good lad, and let your C O tuck you up in bed?'

Both soldiers guffawed loudly, and stood aside good-naturedly to let her pass.

'Ye're nae bad fer a Sassenach!' the Scot yelled after her. 'Nae bad at a'.'

On the corner, Helen turned and waved. The two men waved back and blew kisses. She smiled to herself, recognizing how calmly and competently she had dealt with what could have been a tricky situation; the sort of situation which would once have seen her gibbering with fear. She walked on, humming to herself. She had almost reached home, when she stopped abruptly, paused for a second, then swung round and retraced her steps. Left turn, right turn, left again, and there was the little cul-de-sac where her parents had lived for so many years. Three of the houses still stood, tall and gaunt behind their cupressus trees, but the largest was nothing now but a shell, the ruined walls thrusting skyward, hollow and sightless. Already, nature was taking over, reclaiming her own, living proof that whatever men did, however extensively they built, they were impermanent, transitory creatures. In the long run, only the jungle survived.

Helen mounted the steps, tufted with moss, to the gaping hole where the front door had been. Broken masonry and charred wood littered the hall, and a piece of banister swayed drunkenly in the wind. The stairs ended abruptly, less than halfway up, and somewhere, a door creaked maddeningly on torn hinges. Helen shivered and turned away.

She had hoped, by coming, to exorcize the anger she felt for her father; to forgive him for leaving everything to Ben; for treating her as if she were a silly incompetent child. She ought to forgive him, she knew; for wasn't that the way she had always behaved? But, deep down, was the knowledge that Joe had made her that way, carefully moulding her character from birth so that she conformed to his ideal of the pretty, ineffectual little woman. The masculine ideal; for weren't all men conditioned by centuries of literature, example, and precepts to think of women as soft and compliant? Some men were able to accept that, in reality, this was not so. Her father and Ben were not among them.

When she arrived home, Ben was in his study, working — she could see the line of light beneath the door — but he came out as soon as he heard her step in the hall. He had lost weight, putting in long hours at the factory and bringing work home with him at night. He suffered, too, from the results of being comparatively young and in a reserved occupation. Handing out white feathers was not so prevalent in this war as it had been in the last, but it had happened to Ben on more than one occasion. More often, he had to endure snide, *sotto voce* remarks. They wounded that most vulnerable part of him, his pride, and left unhealed scars. Helen felt a sudden, unexpected rush of sympathy for him, which his opening words instantly dispelled.

'You're late. Where have you been? I've enough worries without wondering what's become of you, knowing you're out alone in the black-out. It's high time you gave up this Red Cross nonsense after dark. Surely there's plenty you can do during the day?'

'I've volunteered for two more evenings a week,' Helen informed him, moving towards the staircase, 'if the nursing home will have me. This is war, Ben. Everyone has to do their bit.'

'And what do you do?' His tone was truculent. 'Taking round supper trays and bed-pans to a lot of expensive women, who can afford to have their babies in a private nursing home! You call that war work?'

'It releases proper nurses for essential nursing.' Helen was surprised how detached she felt from Ben and his anger. His approval or disapproval was a matter of indifference to her: either way, she was no longer afraid. 'If it weren't for me and other V A Ds, there would be fewer nurses in the armed forces.' She smiled serenely at him. 'Well, I'm tired. I'm going to bed. And if you've any sense, you'll do the same.' Unhurriedly, she went upstairs.

Once inside her bedroom, she did pause for a moment, listening; but all she heard was the click of the study door as Ben returned to his work. She had scored another little triumph. She took off her overcoat and cap and tossed them on the bed, catching sight of herself in the mirror as she did so. Even the shapeless cotton dress looked good on her slender figure. She was still a very attractive woman, but her looks seemed suddenly unimportant. The Good Friday air raid had changed her life. The events of that night had shown her that she could rely on herself completely; that she was a grown-up woman, fully able to stand on her own two feet.

Helen stared at her reflection for a moment or two, then crossed the room to her bedside table. She opened the drawer and rummaged at the back until she found a small glass bottle; her sleeping pills, symbols of inadequacy and dependence. She carried the bottle into the bathroom and emptied its contents into the wash-basin, watching the tablets disappear one by one down the plug-hole, as she swilled them away with water.

Elizabeth sat on the edge of the bed, watching Richard dress. His uniform, carefully cleaned and pressed, lay over the back of a chair; his train left Temple Meads station in just over one hour's time. The ten days had passed like a dream. Now, he had to be gone.

She got up, and went to put her arms around him, holding him tight.

'Take care of yourself,' she whispered. 'Don't take any unnecessary risks.'

'Of course not. You won't lose me very easily, you know.'

She held him closer. 'I don't intend losing you at all.' She found that she was crying; silly, weak tears that scalded her cheeks. She was furious with herself, after all her good resolutions not to give way. 'I love you. I love you,' she kept saying, over and over again like a broken gramophone record.

'I know.' He raised her wet face and kissed her. 'And I love you.'

'Please let me come with you to the station.'

He shook his head. 'No. We promised one another at the start of this war that we wouldn't have any protracted goodbyes.'

'But if it gives us more time together . . . '

'No.' He kissed her again, then gently released himself and finished dressing. Elizabeth put on her dressing gown, feeling cold.

'At least let me make you a flask of tea,' she urged him. 'There won't be anything on the train. It'll be hot and crowded.'

'You know I don't like eating and drinking on trains. I should only spill it and ruin my uniform.' He smiled at her. 'I honestly don't want anything, darling. I shan't notice the journey, anyway. In spirit, I shall be here, with you.' He held out his hands. 'Come here. It's been a wonderful leave and you're a marvellous woman; you know that, don't you?' Half-laughing, half-crying, she shook her head, then laid her cheek against his shoulder, while he stroked her hair. 'Well, you are. Thank you for ten happy days. Especially for this afternoon.' He added: 'Strange, isn't it, how two people are just right for one another? I wonder sometimes what you see in me to love so much.'

Elizabeth quoted softly: '"If you press me to say why I love him, I can say no more than it was because he was he and I was I." Michel de Montaigne wrote that, four hundred years ago. Nothing changes.' She lifted her face and tried to smile bravely. 'I shall be living for your next leave,' she said.

The doorbell of the flat shrilled loudly, making the pair of them jump.

'The taxi.' Richard looked down at her, his own face drawn with unhappiness. They embraced passionately, before he thrust her away. 'I must go.' He put on his cap, slung his greatcoat over one arm and picked up his case and respirator. 'Goodbye, darling. Don't come to the door.' He gave a half-laugh. 'For one thing, you're not decent.'

The bedroom door closed behind him. Elizabeth could hear him speaking to the taxi driver; then the outer door of the flat slammed and there was a deathly silence.

Elizabeth turned back to the bed, with its crumpled sheets, the stubs of Richard's Craven A littering the big onyx ashtray on the bedside table. She could see the dent in one pillow, where his head had so recently lain. The dark blue silk dressing-gown which he used at home was where he had dropped it, on the floor beside a ghastly pair of gold-embroidered, oriental slippers, relics of his Hollywood days. His presence was everywhere in the room.

Elizabeth gave a despairing sob and put her hand to her throat. Then she flung herself down on the bed, hugging his pillow, crying as if her heart would break.

CHAPTER THIRTY

Elizabeth was never to forget Sunday, the seventh of December, 1941. Whatever else faded from her mind, however much the events of those war years ran together into a confused and ill-delineated whole, that day remained etched on her memory so vividly that she had only to shut her eyes to re-live it all over again.

She woke early, before it was light and switched on her bedside lamp. Her alarm clock showed half-past six, and she swore softly knowing that she would not be able to sleep again. So she got up, shivering in the cold room, but refusing to put a match to the gas fire. The Government had recently renewed its pleas for care to be taken with essential services. Elizabeth padded into the kitchen and made herself a cup of tea, which she took back to bed with her, hoping it would warm her.

The Sunday papers, when they came, were full of gloom. The British army in North Africa had been overrun, Leningrad was under siege, the German troops had reached the outskirts of Moscow. The only good news was Bomber Command's nightly attacks on German cities; but even that brought no consolation to Elizabeth. Her thoughts immediately centred on Richard, who was flying Lancasters from an airfield 'somewhere in England'. His tour of operational duty was due to end soon. He would be coming home on leave.

At nine o'clock she got up and ran her bath, no more than a few inches of water. She had always loved wallowing, and had to be strict with herself not to exceed the official limit. Afterwards she cooked some scrambled eggs, made with egg powder, and washed the unappetizing meal down with another cup of tea. Just as she was clearing away the doorbell rang. When she opened the door, she was astonished to find Jack outside.

'What on earth brings you here on a Sunday morning?' she asked, ushering him into the sitting-room, with its view of the pocket-sized back garden.

Jack grinned faintly. 'Always so pleased to see me. That's my girl!'

Elizabeth had the grace to look ashamed. 'I'm too old a friend to stand on ceremony with you, my dear,' she excused herself. 'And it must be something urgent to bring you all the way from Eastwood by half-past ten on a Sunday morning. Something that obviously won't keep until tomorrow. So sit down and tell me what it is.' From the flat above came the pounding rhythm of *We'll Hang Out the Washing on the Siegfried Line*, and Elizabeth sighed. 'I wish those two girls would give that damn record a miss. It was a stupid enough song when we all believed it to be true, but now — ! Jerry seems unstoppable.' She indicated the newspapers, lying in an untidy heap on the sofa. 'Wouldn't it be lovely to hear a church bell again?'

'Not if it meant invasion,' Jack answered shortly. 'But I know what you mean.'

Elizabeth sat down in the chair opposite him and crossed her legs. She was wearing navy-blue slacks and a scarlet twin-set, whose strong colour emphasized her pallor and general air of fatigue.

'Go on, then,' she said. 'Tell me why you've come.'

There was a silence for a moment or two before Jack

394

replied. Elizabeth regarded him curiously.

'We-ell,' he began at last, 'it's not exactly urgent. In fact, it's something I've known for months. I haven't said anything to you because I thought you had enough on your plate, worrying about Richard. But I was talking it over with Mother yesterday evening, and she thinks you should know.'

'Know what?' Elizabeth asked, pardonably bewildered. It was not like Jack to be so hesitant. The music from upstairs ceased abruptly, leaving a deafening hush.

'Back in the summer,' Jack went on, apparently ignoring her question, 'Mother and I decided to sort out and get rid of Mary's clothes. We gave them to the W V S for refugees and people who have been bombed out and so on . . . Lizzie, do you recall a cream wool coat that you liked so much, and which Mary hardly ever wore?' Elizabeth nodded, still puzzled. 'Well, turning out the pockets, I came across a letter from Alan Davies.'

'A recent letter?' Elizabeth asked sharply.

'There was no date on it, but I imagine it had been written some time in 1939. There must have been others, and this was one she forgot to throw away. From its contents it's pretty obvious that Alan had been blackmailing Mary. At least, I thought so when I read it, so I checked with the bank. They looked up their records, and for quite a while before her death Mary had been drawing sums of fifty or a hundred pounds at various intervals; sums which I can't account for in any other way, unless she'd been giving them to Alan.'

'But you would have know that, at the time, surely?'

'No. When we married, I gave Mary her own account and made her a quarterly dress allowance. I never asked how she spent the money. I felt that was her business.'

'In any case, the thing's ridiculous!' Elizabeth expostulated. 'How could Alan possibly blackmail Mary? I mean, it doesn't make sense. Anything of that sort could only have worked the other way round. And how did he know where to find her? Where was he writing from? Where has he been all these years?'

'Calm down a minute and I'll do my best to explain.' Jack sat upright in his chair, clasping his hands between his knees. 'As far as I can gather from this one letter, Mary was paying him money to keep him quiet for your sake and for Richard's. I should guess that Alan was threatening to make the story of his bigamous marriage to her public unless she paid him to keep quiet. It wouldn't have done Richard's film career a lot of good if the newspapers had got hold of that particular item. Richard Davies's father arrested for bigamy, and, no doubt, some twisted sob-story about a man down on his luck, while his son lives in luxury with a rich wife ten years his senior; a wife, moreover, who lends money for a living. Mary knew that the reporters would have had a field-day.'

'But Alan would have gone to prison, for heaven's sake! A self-confessed bigamist who'd evaded punishment for his crime!'

'And you helped him evade that punishment,' Jack pointed out drily.

'Dear God, so I did. But I don't believe for a moment Alan would really have carried out his threat.'

'Neither do I. And if Mary had come to me, I'd have told her to call his bluff. But she evidently wasn't prepared to take the risk.'

Elizabeth was on her feet, pacing angrily around the room. 'The bastard! Oh, how I'd love to get my hands on him! I'd ring his blasted neck!' She paused by Jack's chair. 'I take it, however, that the blackmailing must have stopped. I imagine you've opened all letters addressed to her since her death, and obviously there's been nothing else since. I wonder why.'

Jack shrugged. 'There are two possible answers. Either he read about Mary's death in the local papers, which means he's come back to Bristol to live; or, more likely, I think, he was called up. Mary died at the beginning of last year. Alan would then have been — what? Forty-eight or thereabouts? And the new conscription limit for men is fifty-one. Do sit down, Lizzie. You're making me dizzy, prowling about in that fashion.'

Elizabeth did as she was bid, her brow furrowed. 'But how did he get in touch with her in the first place? He only knew the Springtime Grove address.'

'If he did return to Bristol, it wouldn't be too difficult, surely? He would only have to brush an acquaintance with one of the staff at Evans and Hennessey House to discover where Mary and I were living. And your wedding made most of the dailies, so he'd know from those accounts that Mary and I were married.'

'That she was the wife of a rich man, you mean. The sod!' Elizabeth's long, mobile lips had thinned to a vicious line. 'Why on earth did Mary do it, Jack? Why did she protect Richard and me? Especially at the cost of her own peace of mind. I wouldn't have said she was fond enough of either of us.'

Jack leaned back in his chair, and Trojan leapt, purring, on to his lap. Absently, Jack stroked the cat's head.

'I think,' he said slowly, 'that she felt guilty about you; felt that she hadn't treated you very kindly when you were younger; that she owed you various kindnesses and favours which she had never properly repaid. I think, from little things she said from time to time, that she felt she was in your debt. She was fond of you, you know, Lizzie, in her own peculiar, undemonstrative way. It was an affection which deepened as she grew older. And she always was fond of Richard. She spoke of him with great affection.'

'Jack, why have you waited so long to tell me all this? I think I had a right to know before.'

'I told you: I didn't want to burden you with other

worries while Richard was on ops. But now his tour of operational duty is nearly over, I felt you ought to know. Just in case Alan ever turned up again and tried to blackmail you.' Jack stood up, tipping the indignant Trojan off his knees. 'I must be going. Mother and I are expected at Bridget's for lunch, and I daren't not go. As the only man in the family not in the forces — ' his voice was bitter ' — I'm much in demand for all those little jobs about the house normally done by husbands.' He bent and kissed Elizabeth. 'Don't brood about it, my dear. I don't suppose we'll ever hear from Alan again.'

Elizabeth returned his brotherly peck on the cheek with a sisterly one of her own. 'I'm not brooding, and I'm grateful that you've told me. You see ... I never knew before that Mary cared for me all that much.'

'And it hurt.'

'Yes, it did. I tried to pretend it didn't, but I always wanted her to like me from when I was very small. I didn't admit it, naturally. I knew I was bossy, and that she resented me fighting her battles for her all the time. But I also knew she was incapable of standing up for herself.' Elizabeth smiled tremulously. 'Now I don't have to pretend any longer.'

'No. She must have though a lot of you to do what she did, misguided though it might have been.' Jack glanced at his wristwatch. 'I must go. Mother will never forgive me if I'm late.'

'Thank you for coming, Jack. What a day this has turned out to be!'

But the day was not over. The news of the Japanese attack on the United States' fleet, anchored off Pearl Harbour, broke like a thunder-clap during the course of the evening. The two girls from the second storey flat came down to know if Elizabeth had heard, and to speculate about the possible implications. The Americans were in the war now, whether they wanted to be or not, and the only doubt was if the United States government would declare war on the Axis powers as well as Japan. But with the attack only a few hours old, and Congress and the Senate still reeling from shock, it was too soon for the B B C pundits to offer an opinion.

When her unexpected visitors had returned upstairs, Elizabeth sat quietly, not attempting to read her book — Cronin's latest novel, *The Keys of the Kingdom* — and mulled over in her mind the events of the day. Not even the news of Pearl Harbour could supplant Jack's revelations; and it was with an unpleasant jolt of surprise that Elizabeth realized that she was, in fact, Alan Davies's daughter-in-law. Her relationship to him was something she had never seriously considered before, so completely had he dropped out of their lives and so little did he seem to be connected with Richard. In all these years, Richard had never once mentioned his father or speculated what might have happened to him. It was almost, for his son, as if Alan Davies had never existed. Elizabeth realized, for the first time, that Richard must always have hated his father.

She rose and stretched, suddenly hungry. She had had nothing to eat since breakfast. She went into the kitchen.

The doorbell rang again, and, with a sigh, Elizabeth put down the bowl in which she was blending her week's ration of margarine and butter. It really had been one of those days. Wondering who it could be this time, she opened the door.

A telegraph-boy stood outside, holding a War Office telegram.

'And so I came as soon as I heard the news from Jack. I just wish somebody had told me sooner.' Helen took in Elizabeth's haggard face and unkempt appearance. She continued matter-of-factly: 'I know you don't want me here. That you don't want anyone. But the fact is, you can't go on like this, Lizzie. Besides, I need you. Now, are you going to be polite and invite me in?'

Elizabeth stared stupidly at her cousin for a moment

or two, then tried to shut the door. 'Go away, Helen, please. I don't need anyone, least of all you.'

Helen put her foot quickly into the narrowing gap and winced with pain as Elizabeth jammed the door hard against it.

'It's no good, Lizzie, I'm coming in. You shouldn't be by yourself at such a time. I know. I was always far too much alone.'

Elizabeth suddenly capitulated, gave a shrug and turned away, leaving the front door of the flat swinging open.

'Come in, if you must,' she said indifferently. 'But don't expect me to be pleased.'

Helen followed her into the sitting-room. It was dusty and untidy, as though it had not been touched for weeks; which, thought Helen, was probably the case. Through the open bedroom door, she could see the unmade bed and items of clothing scattered anyhow about the floor. She went into the kitchen, which again told the same story of neglect. A pile of dirty crockery stood on the draining-board; mostly cups and saucers and empty milk bottles, Helen noted. Obviously Elizabeth had been eating very little. There was a blackened frying-pan on the gas stove, containing the charred contents of a meal which Elizabeth had evidently started to cook, then either forgotton or abandoned. Jack had been right this morning when Helen had talked to him among the ruins of what had once been Bridge Street.

She had met him quite by chance, on her way home from a special detachment demonstration on gases, where she had spent the morning in her respirator, crawling through a gas-filled hut, erected on a bomb-site, 'rescuing' and being 'rescued' by, other members of the team. She had been feeling tired, but happy, still faintly astonished by her own resource-fulness and ability, when she had heard someone calling her name. She had turned to see Jack

Hennessey on the other side of the street.

The news of Richard's death in action over Germany had plunged Helen into a whirlpool of emotions; horror, shock, compassion for Elizabeth, and a sudden, jolting sense of personal loss. It had taken several moments to adjust and listen properly to what Jack was saying.

'It's more than three weeks now since he was killed, and Lizzie hasn't stirred outside the flat. She won't answer the 'phone, or let anyone inside the door. All through Christmas, she was there on her own. I've called to see her every day since it happened. My mother wanted her to come to Eastwood and stay with us. But she won't even discuss it. I wondered if you'd had better luck?'

'I haven't called,' Helen said. 'I didn't even know Richard had been killed.'

Jack looked vaguely surprised. 'It was in most of the papers. "Film star shot down over enemy territory." That sort of thing.'

Helen shook her head. 'I missed it, then. I haven't been reading the papers much lately. The news has been so depressing.'

'Well, now you do know, would you go and see Lizzie?' Jack asked. 'There's just a chance she might talk to you.'

Helen looked directly at him. 'Richard's ex-mistress? Do you think that's a good idea?'

Jack was as startled as if a nice child had suddenly used a four-letter swear-word. He focused his attention properly on Helen for the first time since meeting her, and saw what so many others had seen lately, that she had changed. She exuded a quiet self-confidence. If anyone could take Elizabeth in hand and shake her out of her excessive grieving, it might be Helen.

'Please try,' he had urged her. 'Of course, what she really needs is someone with her all the time, or she'll just keep slipping back into this awful slough of despondency.'

During the journey home, Jack's parting words kept spinning round inside Helen's head, and the idea of leaving Ben, which had been fermenting there for a very long time, suddenly hardened into resolve. She had asked for her cousin's help once before, and been refused: this time she would not take 'no' for an answer. This time, there was a mutual need, if only she could make Elizabeth see it.

'I've come to stay,' she announced baldly, as she re-entered the sitting-room, 'whether you want me or not. My cases are outside in a taxi. I've left Ben and I need somewhere to live. And you need someone to stay with you. It's no good arguing! My mind's made up. When I've paid off the driver, I'm going to clean up. Then I shall cook us a meal, which you are going to eat. And while I'm doing all that, you can have a bath and do your face. You look a mess. Then, after we've eaten, we'll sit down and have a long talk about Richard. It's no good bottling grief up, Lizzie, believe me. We'll talk about him everyday, for as long as you want.'

'Helen isn't here, I'm afraid.' Elizabeth showed her visitor into the sitting-room. 'I hope this isn't going to take long, Ben. I have to get to work. We've been half expecting you to call any time these past two months.'

Ben removed his hat and sat down in one of the armchairs, which he remembered having seen at The Brass Mill. There was very little else he recognized. Presumably most of Elizabeth's furniture was in store. It had the air of a furnished flat.

'Helen left me a letter, but she didn't say where she was going.' Ben looked accusingly at Elizabeth. 'It never occurred to me, in the circumstances, that she'd come to you.'

'So how did you eventually find out?'

'An acquaintance mentioned that he'd seen her

going in and out of here, so I came round as soon as I could. I'm on my way to the factory,' he added.

'Helen told Mrs Bagot where she was going.'

Ben's eyes darkened. 'That woman! She was always on Helen's side. She handed in her notice the day after Helen left.'

Elizabeth's eyebrows shot up. 'You're on your own, then?'

'Completely, if you discount the daily woman, which is easy enough to do as she's never there when I'm at home. She has her own key. The maids, of course, have been called up for war work.'

There was a silence while they took stock of one another.

Elizabeth was looking her age, Ben thought. Never fat, she had shed even more weight, and her pale skin had lost its bloom, that peculiar, almost translucent glow which had given her such an appearance of health and vitality. The reddish-brown hair was salted with grey and there were lines of unhappiness pulling down the corners of her mouth. She was still a handsome woman, but grief had left its mark.

Elizabeth, for her part, thought that Ben looked more normal than Helen had described him. Listening to her cousin's account of her life since she married Ben, Elizabeth had begun to think of him as some kind of monster; a sort of Jekyll and Hyde, more and more unable to control the darker side of his nature. But regarding him now, she saw only an older version of the young man she had once been in love with; although that seemed to have happened in a different life and to another person. Then he spoke, and she was startled by the slightly glazed look which crept into his eyes, and by the faint slur of hysteria which marred his speech.

'She'll come back to me, you know. Crawling on her hands and knees.'

Elizabeth suddenly felt sorry for him. 'I don't think she will,' she told him gently.

'What's she going to live on?' His lips curled. 'This bloody Red Cross work is only voluntary.'

'She's found a job. A very responsible one. I think we've all of us tended to underestimate her all these years. She's been recruited by the Censorship Department, censoring the Irish mail. Apparently that's done here, in Bristol. And she still does her four evenings a week at the nursing home.'

Ben laughed, and again there was a hint of something abnormal in the sound.

'The war won't last forever,' he said, 'especially not now the Yanks have come in. Censorship will finish with the end of hostilities. You can't have that sort of thing in peace time.'

'Then Helen will find herself another job. After all she's done for me these past two months, I'd give her one, just out of gratitude. But in fact she'd be an asset to our, or to any, firm.' Elizabeth leaned forward. 'Ben, you must accept that Helen has changed.'

'People don't change,' was his truculent response.

'All right. Then the real Helen never had the chance to express herself before. Leave her alone, Ben. You've got what you wanted; Gordon's and all that goes with it. She won't get a brass farthing unless you die before she does. As for the war not lasting for ever, it's going to be a long time yet.' She pointed to the morning paper, where the news of the fall of Singapore to the Japanese made banner headlines, and had pushed even the siege of Leningrad off the front page.

Ben stood up, buttoning his overcoat, and picked up his hat.

'I told Helen once,' he said, in a pleasant, conversational tone which made Elizabeth's spine tingle in sudden fear, 'that I'd kill her if she ever left me.'

'That would be a stupid thing to do,' she answered quickly. 'You'd lose her for ever that way. You'd never get her back.'

'But you've just told me she isn't coming back, ever.'
Ben looked at her and smiled.

Elizabeth thought: 'Dear God, I believe he is mad. But you'd have the devil of a job to prove it.' Sympathy flooded through her once again. She could see that Ben was a product of his mother's over-indulgence, just as Helen had been of her father's determination to mould her in his image of the perfect woman. She rose in her turn, and put a hand on Ben's arm.

'Let Helen live her own life,' she pleaded. 'You can afford to be generous. You have part, at least, of what you wanted from life.'

He shook off her hand roughly and turned to leave. 'You always were an interfering woman, Elizabeth Evans, meddling in other people's affairs. But you're not going to meddle in mine.'

CHAPTER THIRTY-ONE

It was summer before Bristol saw its first American troops, but when they did come, they came with a rush. One day there was no sign of them, the next, they were swarming all over the place. From there on, it was like a friendly invasion.

The first to arrive were the Pioneer Corps, mainly negroes. If any of these black G Is remembered, or even knew, that past Bristolians had waxed fat on the slave trade, and that it had formed the basis of much of the city's enormous wealth, the warmth of their welcome rapidly dispelled all such uneasy recollections. Within weeks of their arrival, the Americans, not only in Bristol, but up and down the country, had left an indelible mark on the surface of British life. Even the privates and non-commissioned officers wore smart uniforms and shoes, instead of boots. They were the dispensers of such long-forgotten luxuries as chocolate and chewing-gum. They were unexpectedly polite and had charming manners. Above all, they had a line in romantic patter that soon had every woman between fourteen and forty swooning at their feet. They were a million Hollywood phantasies come to life; a million Hollywood characters who had strayed out of the silver screen.

Elizabeth and Helen, both nearing forty and able to

recall the American Doughboys of the First World War, were able, without too much difficulty, to keep their heads. For Elizabeth, after a mere seven months, Richard's death was still a raw wound which would not heal. A dozen times a day she was reminded of him; would start eagerly out of her chair each morning when the post arrived, only to sink back in tears as she remembered. Persuaded by Helen, she had got rid of his clothes, but his books and gramophone records remained. It was a constant temptation either to read or to play them; yet she knew that Helen was right when she said that grief was powerful enough in it's own right, without being artificially induced. Richard's presence was everywhere, and if Elizabeth could have moved away from the flat she would have done so, but accommodation was almost impossible to find. Apart from the influx of B B C personnel and members of various government ministries at the begining of the war, there was now the additional problem of rehousing those people who had lost everything in the blitz.

Helen's main preoccupation was with Ben. He had not called again since that February morning, but his absence seemed somehow more sinister than any harassment would have been. A little of her old uneasiness returned to haunt her, undermining her new self-confidence.

'I wish he'd come and have it out with me,' she said to Elizabeth. 'A good row would clear the air. At least I'd know where I stood.'

'I thought you knew that,' Elizabeth objected. 'I thought you'd made your mind up to get a divorce.'

'But Ben will have to divorce *me*, for desertion. And that takes such an age, even supposing he'll agree. *I've* no grounds for divorcing him.'

Elizabeth, who was going out for the evening, was busy fixing her make-up in the heavy, gilt-framed mirror which hung over the sitting-room mantelpiece.

She had been invited to an M A P staff fund-raising party for the St John Ambulance Brigade, which was to be held in the garden of The Brass Mill. She had felt obliged to accept, but had done so with the greatest misgivings. She had recruited Jack to accompany her, but even the reassurance of his comforting presence could not overcome her reluctance to see her beautiful home — the home, moreover, where she and Richard had spent their happiest times together — in the impersonal hands of clerks and officials. For the last few days, the prospect had depressed her, and now that the moment was almost upon her, she felt as nervous and jumpy as a cat.

As she dropped her lipstick and powder compact into her handbag, she said snappily: 'You could give Ben grounds other than desertion. You've done it before.' She stood aghast, listening to the echo of her words scoring the silence, then she sat down on the sofa and flung her arms around her cousin. 'Helen, darling, I'm sorry! I don't know what's got into me tonight. I didn't mean it, honestly. Say that you forgive me.'

'It's all right. I understand.' Helen hugged her in return. 'You're hating the thought of this evening. I think it's very brave of you to go.'

'I'm a bitch,' Elizabeth said, kissing Helen's cheek. She got up. 'Where did I put my hat?' She picked up the wide-brimmed straw with its band of black silk ribbon. 'Helen . . . ' She glanced down uncertainly at her cousin. 'You're not still afraid of Ben?'

Unconsciously, Helen began pleating the skirt of her blue cotton dress. 'Of course not. At least . . . I don't think so.'

'And what does that mean?'

'Nothing.' The front-doorbell rang. 'There's Jack. Now, try to pretend that The Brass Mill has nothing to do with you; that it's a strange house you've never seen before. Alternatively, keep reminding yourself that as soon as the war's over, you'll get it back.'

'But in what state?' Elizabeth demanded grimly, moving towards the door. 'Goodbye, darling. I shan't be late.'

Helen watched Elizabeth and Jack drive away. When the black Citröen had disappeared round the corner in the direction of the Suspension Bridge, she returned indoors. This evening, she would have welcomed the strains of Vera Lynn singing *We'll meet Again* or *The White Cliffs of Dover* played at full blast, but the two girls who lived above were away on some training course or other, and the flat upstairs was deserted.

For a while Helen tried to read, but her eyes were tired. Occasionally she wished that illiteracy would strike the entire Irish population of Eire and the British Isles. She got out her Red Cross manual and attempted some study for the advanced proficiency examination in Home Nursing, which she was due to sit on Friday, but she could not concentrate. In spite of the fact that it was a warm, sunny evening, she went round the flat making sure that all but the most inaccessible windows were closed and all the doors bolted. She checked particularly on the side door which led in from the garden.

She wished now that she had confided in Elizabeth about her meeting with Miss Beaumont. Helen had run into Ben's secretary during her lunch hour, while she was shopping in Queen's Road. Miss Beaumont, it seemed, had the day off, and Helen suggested that they have a quick sandwich together. During the brief meal, the secretary had at first appeared reticent and embarrassed; then, like someone who had suddenly determined to take the plunge, revealed that she was very concerned about Ben.

'Well, it's not just me, Mrs Sawyer, but quite a few of the senior staff, too. He seems . . . well . . . odd.'

'How do you mean, odd?' Helen had tried to speak calmly, but her nerves were jumping.

'Forgetful. Preoccupied. Sometimes he just sits, staring into space. It's not like him. He's always been so efficient, so absorbed in the business. Nowadays, though, he leaves a lot of the running of Gordon's to other people. It's as though he doesn't care any more. And he's brought in this huge photograph of you, which he keeps on his desk. I catch him looking at it from time to time a bit . . . well . . . queerly. There's no other way I can describe it. I . . . that is to say, we — ' the secretary did not specify who 'we' were, but hurried on ' — were wondering if you could possibly persuade Mr Sawyer to see a doctor?'

'I'm sorry, but it's nothing to do with me anymore, Miss Beaumont,' Helen had disclaimed. 'My husband and I, as you must very well know, are separated. His mother died a year or two ago, but he has an aunt still living, somewhere in Eastwood. If you really are that worried, you might try getting in touch with her . . . '

Helen closed her manual with a flick of the pages and got to her feet. It was ridiculous feeling like this again, after all this time; jumping at every sound, keeping away from the windows, as though she expected Ben to be lurking outside. Yet, she had been afraid of him once, conscious of some mental imbalance which, in those days, no one else had seemed to be aware of. She had convinced herself, until today, that it had largely been her own imagination; that she had used fear as an excuse for indecision and inaction. Now, she was not sure any more. Other people, including the prosaic Miss Beaumont were begining to find Ben's conduct strange. She thought of her photograph, which he kept on his desk, and shivered.

Stop being a fool, Helen told herself firmly. She would put on the wireless and listen to something; anything. She looked round for the *Radio Times*, and found it lying beside Elizabeth's chair. She picked it up and had just started turning the pages, when the doorbell rang.

Helen jumped, letting the magazine slip from her fingers. Her hands jerked out, pressing against the nearest chair back for support. Her mouth and throat felt dry, and she had difficulty breathing.

The bell sounded again, the ring longer and more loudly imperious than before. Helen moved, but only to flatten herself against the wall beside the chimney-breast, where she could not be seen from the window. She waited, her heart thumping, the blood seeming to freeze in her veins.

How long she stood there, Helen had no idea. Later, she realized it could have been no more than a few minutes, but at the time every dragging second felt like an age. Finally, with an enormous effort of will, she propelled herself away from the wall and forced herself into the tiny hallway. There had been no further ring, and the front door stood blank and unrevealing in its coat of dark brown paint.

Something moved against her legs and Helen screamed; a shrill sound which tore through the flat, ripping silence to shreds and sending Trojan, with an indignant squawk, hurtling for the safety of Elizabeth's bedroom. Helen sank on to the chair beside the telephone, one hand pressed to her heart, the breath rasping in her throat. She began to laugh, softly at first, then on a rising note of hysteria. She heard and recognized it, and pulled herself together. Trembling, she got up and managed, at the third attempt, to open the front door, her hands slipping on the metal catch.

There was no one there. Whoever had rung the bell had long since gone. It was still broad daylight, and people were walking up and down the narrow, mews-type street. From the direction of the Downs came the sound of children's voices. A barrage balloon kept its lonely vigil above the roof tops, the evening sun glinting along its silver fabric sides. Cautiously, Helen stepped outside into the tiny front garden and peered round the corner of the house. The patch of grass and shrubs was empty, as was the even tinier oblong of lawn at the back. There was nowhere that anyone could possibly hide, and the high garden wall, which separated them from the houses immediately at the rear, defied scaling without the help of a ladder.

Helen returned to the flat, closing the door behind her. She felt extremely foolish and thoroughly ashamed. This was the old Helen, the woman she thought she had put behind her once and for all. She went into the kitchen and made herself a cup of hot, sweet tea — 'treat for shock,' she told herself with a grim, inward smile — then went back to the sitting-room and forced herself to concentrate on her Home Nursing Manual.

'Have you been indoors?' Jack asked, handing Elizabeth a glass of rum punch. 'Here, try one of these vol-au-vents. They're filled with some fish called tuna, in a white sauce made with powdered milk. One of the typists told me. She made them.' He grinned. 'They're not at all bad, considering.'

Elizabeth shook her head. 'No thanks. I'm not hungry. Yes, I went indoors just now. A couple of the big-wigs from the M A P and the St John Ambulance Brigade insisted on escorting me round. I find I'm the guest of honour.'

'And so you should be. What did you think? They haven't treated the place too badly, have they?'

'No.' Elizabeth's tone was noncommittal. 'It could have been a lot worse. Strange, of course, to see desks and typewriters and notice-boards everywhere. But it could have been commandeered by the military, I suppose, and God knows what sort of state it would have been in by now. I've been very lucky, really.'

'Then just hang on to that thought,' Jack advised her. 'Hello! That redheaded female who took you inside is bearing down on you again. She looks purposeful. She has some Americans in tow. I saw a contingent of brass-

412

hats, with their acolytes, arriving a little while ago.'

'Oh damn.' Elizabeth took an unladylike gulp of her rum punch and tore her eyes away from the well-remembered vista of lawns and flower-beds and trees. She had a momentary vision of driving all this silly, chattering throng of people out of her garden, out of her house, and of pitching all their precious office equipment over the side of the Gorge, into the Avon's muddy waters. The phantasy was exhilarating, but brief. She arranged her features in a polite, company smile of welcome, and turned to face her hostess.

'My dear Mrs Davies!' The redhead was even more effusive than she had been earlier in the evening. 'Some of our American allies. Please let me introduce them. Gentlemen, this is the lady who owns these lovely gardens. And, of course, the house.' She gave an affected trill of laughter before adding, in a hissing aside, to the nearest soldier — a tall man with a quantity of stars and gold braid which, Elizabeth considered must make him a general at the very least — 'The widow of the film star, Richard Davies.'

Elizabeth felt Jack's steadying hand beneath her elbow and heard his softly breathed curse at the woman's callous stupidity; then she was shaking hands and murmuring platitudes in response to the polite, almost reverent, American greetings.

'Most kind of you to come. Delighted to see you. I think the party has already raised nearly five hundred pounds for the St John Ambulance people. Isn't that so, Miss — er — ?'

'It is indeed.' The redhead smiled coyly. 'And we shall be asking you for more, when we pass round the collecting boxes in a minute.' Another American joined the group and was immediately brought forward for introduction. 'And this is Major Morgan. He's been most insistent on meeting the lady of the house.'

Elizabeth took Chris Morgan's hand in a daze, unable

413

to say a word. It was Jack who exclaimed delightedly: 'Good God! Chris! What a marvellous surprise! How long have you been back in England?'

'A little over three weeks. We flew in towards the end of last month. Isn't it a piece of luck, my being stationed near Bristol?'

He spoke in answer to Jack, but his eyes never left Elizabeth's face. There was a query in them, as though he were uncertain of his welcome. As well he might be, Elizabeth thought angrily, the way he had treated Helen.

As though in answer to her unspoken reproaches, Chris asked abruptly: 'How is she? How's Helen?'

'Very well,' Elizabeth answered coldly, 'although no thanks to you, Major Morgan.' She added with a burst of suppressed fury: 'What a shit you turned out to be! You didn't even write to her!'

Jack, who was looking puzzled, whispered: 'Whatever this is about it would be better if you lowered your voice, Lizzie. Someone will hear you. This is a party, for goodness' sake!'

Chris was looking equally puzzled. 'I don't know what you're talking about, Mrs Davies. I did write to Helen, several times, to apologize. Grovel would, perhaps, be a more appropriate word. I behaved badly and I wanted to make amends. But she never replied.'

The silence stretched, while they stared at one another, the same thought taking shape in both their minds.

'Ben!' Elizabeth said.

Almost at the same instant, Chris swore and muttered: 'Sawyer!'

'I suppose she might have thought of that,' Elizabeth said slowly. She shifted her gaze impatiently to someone who was trying to attract her attention, glared, and looked back again at Chris. 'What did the letters say?'

Chris flushed. 'I told you. They said that I was sorry;

414

that I was wrong; that I blamed myself for losing my temper the way I did. I urged her to leave Ben, to get a passport and come to the States. To get a divorce.'

'Did you tell her that you still loved her?'

'Lizzie!' The little explosion of protest came from Jack, who had managed, more or less, to piece together the events which must lie behind this conversation. 'You mustn't ask questions like that.'

Elizabeth ignored him and took another sip of her rum punch. Her eyes were still fixed unwaveringly on Chris Morgan's face. 'Well?' she demanded. 'Did you?'

'Yes,' he answered steadily. 'As a matter of fact, I did.'

Elizabeth let out her breath on a long-drawn sigh of relief. 'Helen has left Ben,' she said, smiling for the first time since she met Chris. 'Since ... Since Richard's death, she lives with me. We have a flat in Clifton.' She gave him the address and telephone number. 'So the next time you have leave, Major Morgan, even if it's only a twenty-four hour pass, we shall expect to see you. Now, you'd better go and circulate, or I shall be accused of monopolizing the most handsome man at the party. By the way,' she called after him, as he obediently moved away, 'be prepared to find that Helen has changed.'

It was some weeks later, almost the end of August, before Chris turned up at the flat, late one evening, on a three-day pass. He came laden with chocolates, food and half-a-dozen pairs of precious nylon stockings for which most English women at that time would have sold their souls, and for which many were perfectly ready to surrender their virginity. In fact, it seemed to Elizabeth that there was scarcely one of the very young girls or elderly women, who were now the mainstay of Evans and Hennessey House, who could not sport at least one pair of American nylons. 'Overpaid, oversexed and over here!' had become the cry of the outraged British male, both military and civilian, as he helplessly watched his womenfolk succumb in droves to the friendly — the far too friendly — invaders.

If Chris had expected Helen to fall on his neck, he was disappointed. He knew that Elizabeth must have told her the truth about the letters, and had half-expected an emotional reconciliation. Instead, the woman in the blue-grey dress and white apron of a British V A D, who opened the door to him, seemed cool and rather remote. He had to look twice to convince himself that it really was Helen.

As for Helen herself, her feelings were mixed. When Elizabeth had told her of the meeting at The Brass Mill, she had experienced shock, anger, remorse, excitement in quick succession, but the final sensation had been one of emptiness; a feeling of anti-climax and a sense of everything having come too late. When Chris had telephoned, asking permission to spend his seventy-two hour pass with them, it was Elizabeth who had been most pleased. Helen had pretended, but underneath she had found it difficult to drum up any emotion.

Now he was finally there, however, standing in front of her — solid flesh-and-blood, not some half forgotten dream — her heart began to beat ridiculously fast. She could not speak, merely holding the front door wide for him to enter, and, consequently, her welcome seemed more dispassionate than it really was.

'I'm sorry,' she said stiffly, 'about the uniform, but I was on duty earlier this evening and I haven't had time to change. I only got in a few minutes ago.'

Elizabeth came to greet Chris at the door of the sitting-room, her eyes flickering from one embarrassed face to the other.

'Chris!' she exclaimed warmly. 'How lovely that you're here. We've put you in Helen's bedroom, and she's sleeping with me for the next two nights. As you see, we're rather cramped, but it's fine for just the two of us.' She was talking rather too fast and being rather too gushing in order to gloss over Helen's silence.

Chris indicated one of his bags. 'I've brought some coffee,' he said, 'and a tin of Spam and another of butter. I guess you can use them.'

Elizabeth laughed. 'I thought it was the British who were supposed to be the masters of understatement.' Her smile held, by now, a hint of desperation. 'Let's have some sherry,' she suggested, 'before I fetch in the casserole. Or would you prefer to unpack first?'

'No. Sherry would be fine.'

'I'll pour it,' Helen said, as though anxious to be doing something. 'Lizzie can tell you all about Evans and Hennessey's cinema chain.'

'Heavens! Chris doesn't want to hear about that!' Elizabeth protested. She took her glass of sherry and moved resolutely towards the kitchen. 'I'll dish up. Chris, the bathroom is on the other side of the hall. You can't miss it.'

The casserole, which had taken nearly all her and Helen's meat ration for the week, was delicious, the steak proving unexpectedly tender. With the help of a bottle of wine, which Elizabeth had bought earlier in the evening from the off-licence round the corner, the atmosphere began to thaw. By the time she brought in the coffee, made with part of Chris's plunder from the quartermaster's stores, she was happy to note that the other two were laughing and chatting like old friends. It was a start, she thought. Her mind leapt ahead. Ben really must be made to see sense and give Helen a divorce.

'Helen's taken the next two days off work,' Elizabeth announced as she sat down. 'Did she tell you?' She sipped her coffee. 'Dear, sweet heaven! That's good! Not like that ghastly coffee and chicory stuff we've been getting.'

Chris nodded. 'She told me. We're going to spend

tomorrow renewing my acquaintance with Bristol. Will it be OK if we take in Evans and Hennessey House on our itinerary? I'd rather like to see Jack again.'

But Jack was not there when Helen and Chris appeared in Elizabeth's office the following day. After nearly eighteen month's freedom from bombing, Bristol has been rocked, at twenty past nine that morning, by a single, enormous explosion. There had been no warning siren, but it was obvious that a bomb had been dropped somewhere. Elizabeth's secretary was sent to find out what she could, and returned, an hour later, with the news that a solitary German bomber, presumably off-course after a mission elsewhere, had shed his load over Bristol, dropping a massive, five hundred pound bomb on Broad Weir, near the junction with Philadelphia Street. It had set three buses, loaded with passengers, on fire, as well as causing extensive damage to surrounding property. It was feared that there had been considerable loss of life.

It was shortly before Helen and Chris arrived that Jack was sent for. Eileen Hennessey, who had gone into town early to do some shopping, had been one of those killed.

CHAPTER THIRTY-TWO

The last bombs to be dropped on Bristol, although no one could know it at the time, were ten high explosives, which fell on the night of May the fifteenth, 1944. Five were dropped at Abbot's Leigh on the Somerset side of the Avon Gorge, but The Brass Mill was untouched. The following morning, Elizabeth verified the house's safety with the police, replaced her telephone receiver on its cradle, and sank back in her chair, shaking with relief.

Jack came through the adjoining door from his office. 'Everything all right?' he enquired, but he could already see the answer in her face.

'Yes, thank God. Not even a pane of glass cracked. It's business as usual for the staff of the M A P.' She glanced at Jack. He did not look well. He seemed never to have fully recovered from the shock of his mother's death.

His sister Bridget, with her son and two daughters, had moved into the big Eastwood house to take care of him — 'Sponge off him, more like,' Elizabeth reflected indignantly — but he was not happy. Jack was fond of his nieces and nephew, but he was unused to the constant presence of children, and, at forty-four, was set in his ways. Moreover, the children were unruly, lacking the discipline of their father, who was now somewhere on the south coast of England, training for the invasion of Europe.

The past twenty-one months had seen the tide of war at last flow against Nazi Germany and turn everywhere in favour of the Allies. The victorious Russians were clamouring for a 'second front', and in this late spring of 1944 anticipation was high that, at last, France was about to be invaded. Helen and Elizabeth had not seen Chris Morgan for well over two months. He had moved right away from the Bristol area and his letters were heavily censored.

What the true state of affairs was between him and her cousin, Elizabeth had no idea. Chris came and went, using the Clifton flat as a base for all his furloughs, but although he and Helen seemed cheerful and content in one another's company, there was nothing lover-like about their relationship. When Elizabeth tackled Helen about approaching Ben for a divorce, her cousin replied maddeningly that there was plenty of time.

'Let's get the war over first, Lizzie, then see what happens. Once the invasion starts, there's going to be a lot of hard fighting. Chris might never come back.'

Elizabeth was horrified at this level-headed, detached point of view, and without saying a word to anyone, went to see Ben. But he was not there. The new housekeeper, who had replaced Mrs Bagot and the subsequent daily char-lady, seemed evasive, and would not even invite Elizabeth inside. No, the woman said coldly, Mr Sawyer was away from home and she could not say when he would return. It might be a month, it might be longer. He had been overworking, and had been advised to take a protracted rest. That was all she knew. She shut the door in Elizabeth's face.

Elizabeth telephoned Miss Beaumont at Gordon's, but received the same stonewall treatment. Her suspicions aroused, she began making further enquiries through her network of business contacts, and eventually discovered that Ben had suffered a mental breakdown and was a voluntary patient in an exclusive clinic near Bournemouth, where they specialized in psychiatric disorders. All that had happened a year ago.

Then three days earlier an acquaintance had told her that Ben was back at Gordon's, apparently completely recovered, adding, however, that there was a strong rumour that he had discharged himself. Elizabeth had mentioned nothing of this to Helen. She had not even confided in Jack.

She reached out now and took Jack's hand, squeezing it affectionally. 'You look fagged to death. Shall I treat you to the pictures tonight? Or what about the theatre? The Old Vic company's at the Royal. Flora Robson in *Thérèse Raquin*.'

Jack returned the pressure of her fingers. 'I'd love to, my dear, but unfortunately I have to work on. The Barndale contract. But why don't you go? Take Helen, if she's not on duty at the nursing home. It'll do you both good to have an evening out.'

So Elizabeth telephoned Helen, and they went to the newly restored Theatre Royal in King Street; Bristol's eighteenth-century gem, which had been rescued from years of neglect and dereliction, and the final indignity of being sold as a fruit and vegetable warehouse, largely by the interest, intervention and string-pulling assistance of that architect of Lend-Lease, John Maynard Keynes.

They emerged from the theatre on to the cobbles of King Street to find a clear, dry, starlit night.

'Let's walk,' Elizabeth suggested. 'I'm feeling energetic, and it won't take more than half an hour if we move briskly. And the 'buses will be full of drunks this time of night. Not to mention the licentious soldiery.'

Helen laughed and agreed. She, too, was feeling the need of exercise after sitting at a desk all day.

It did, in fact, take them a little longer than the

predicted half an hour, and it was nearly a quarter to eleven when Elizabeth finally, and thankfully, inserted her key in the front door lock. The windows of the flat above were curtained and silent. The girls, most untypically, were having an early night. Either that, or they were out on an all-night date. Half the allied forces seemed to have paraded up the stairs at one time or another during the past four years.

While she waited for Elizabeth to unlock the door, Helen eased one foot out of its shoe and gingerly flexed her toes.

'Won't it be lovely,' she murmured, 'when petrol isn't rationed any more, and we can drive our cars all day and every day, anywhere we like, if we want to?'

'When that happens — ' Elizabeth began, as she stepped into the darkened hallway, but did not finish her sentence.

'When that happens, what?' Helen asked, closing the front door behind her. Then she, too, stopped, her voice trailing on a terrified gasp.

The silhouette of a man was plainly visible, standing in the sitting-room doorway.

'Lizzie, don't be a fool!' Elizabeth had never seen Jack really, blazingly angry before. It was an unnerving experience. 'You can't shelter him! The man's a deserter. And a bloody blackmailer, into the bargain!'

Elizabeth glanced despairingly at the work piled on her desk, needing her urgent attention. It would have to wait. She couldn't tackle it. She felt like death. She said feebly: 'Alan Davies is my father-in-law, Jack.'

'He *was* your father-in-law,' Jack answered, adding brutally: 'Richard's dead.'

Elizabeth was too numb to feel resentment. She was still in shock from the traumatic events of the previous night.

'How did he get into the flat?' Jack asked.

422

'He'd broken a pane of glass in the garden door, and managed to turn the key in the lock.'

'You hadn't bolted it?'

'No . . . No, we never do, except when we go to bed.'

Jack swore under his breath. 'That's damnably stupid, for a start. How did Davies know where you were living?'

'Simple. He went to the Mill, told them he was an old friend of mine, and some clerk gave him my address.'

The telephone rang. Jack picked up the receiver, barked: 'Mrs Davies is taking no calls at the moment,' and slammed it into its rest again. 'How long has Alan been on the run?' he asked.

Elizabeth shrugged. 'A day, I should say, no more. He must have made a bee-line for me. You were right: he had been conscripted into the army. He was at Dunkirk, and the experience terrified him. It's fairly obvious that for the past few months, he's been in training for the invasion. From what he says, it's due fairly soon. He doesn't want anything to do with it. He managed to slip camp, God knows how, and run away.'

'Dear heaven!' Jack's face was grey. 'The man's a mine of information, don't you realize that? Every military and civil policeman from Land's End to John O'Groats will be on the look out for him. They'll dig up every known fact about him. And sooner, rather than later, those facts are going to lead them to you. Lizzie!' Jack bent over her chair, forcing her round to face him. 'You'll be arrested as an accessory. And you're dragging Helen into this mess, too.'

'He'll be gone by that time. He's promised he'll only stay a couple of nights, just while he gets some rest and food. While he decides what to do next. It stands to reason he won't stop longer than he has to. He knows the odds as well as you do on the military digging up his connection with me.'

Jack swore again. 'A couple of nights is forty-eight hours too long. And another thing.' Jack's eyes narrowed suspiciously. 'Why is he trusting you and Helen out of his sight? How does he know that one of you — Helen, in particular — won't go straight to the police? After all, you've told me.'

'I told you because I had to tell someone, in case . . . in case anything goes wrong. Because I've always told you everything. Because you're my friend.'

The telephone bell rang once more. And once more it was Jack who lifted the receiver and snapped furiously at the switchboard operator: 'Not now! I told you, Mrs Davies is taking no calls!' He turned to Elizabeth. 'What do you mean, "in case something goes wrong"?'

After a momentary hesitation, Elizabeth admitted: 'Helen hasn't gone to work today. I telephoned the censorship office when I got in, to say she's ill.' Elizabeth raised her eyes fleetingly to Jack's face, then hurriedly lowered them again. 'He — Alan — has a service revolver. He's keeping Helen in the flat with him. A . . . a hostage for my good behaviour.'

'And you came out and left her alone with him?' Jack's tone was so incredulous that the colour flooded into Elizabeth's face.

'I had to. I had no option. Alan insisted. He wanted everything as normal as possible.'

Jack expelled his breath on a long sigh. His features relaxed slightly.

'At least the gun exonerates you and Helen. You're not helping him voluntarily. Why on earth didn't you tell me that immediately? It changes the whole complexion of the thing. We must go to the police at once. They'll think of some way of surrounding the flat without Alan knowing.'

'No!' Elizabeth's voice was sharp. She got up from her desk and faced Jack defiantly. 'If I can get rid of Alan without fuss, I'm going to. Don't you realize that if I'm involved in his capture, everyone's going to connect me with Richard? It'll be in all the papers. "Richard Davies's Father Arrested for Desertion." No,

Jack! I won't have that sort of slur cast on Richard's memory if I can possibly help it.' She was shaking violently and began to cry.

Jack cursed, then walked round the desk and took her in his arms, comforting her as he would a child. He realized that it was no good arguing with her in her present irrational state.

'You're going back to the flat now,' he said, 'and I'm coming with you. It will give me the greatest pleasure to give that bastard a piece of my mind.'

'It won't do any good, Jack. He'll only have you at his mercy, as well.'

'There will be three of us,' Jack reminded her. 'Three to his one. Besides, I can't let you return to that flat alone, knowing you and Helen are at Alan's mercy. I should have no choice but to notify the police forthwith. Perhaps, at least, I shall be able to persuade the bastard to leave quietly and at once.'

Elizabeth shivered. 'He's desperate, Jack. He's a very frightened man.'

'All the more reason for me to come with you.' The telephone rang for the third time. 'Leave it,' Jack ordered her. 'Here are your jacket and gloves. Tell your secretary that you'll be unavailable for the rest of the day. I'll get my hat and cancel my appointments.'

Jack's first impression was that, apart from a day's growth of beard around his chin, Alan Davies had changed very little. A second, closer inspection revealed bags beneath the eyes, and lines deeply grooved into the cheeks.

'I'm too old for this sodding lark,' he told Jack. 'I figured I might just as well take a chance on being shot as a deserter as be mown down on those bloody French beaches the minute we land. This way, the odds are longer on staying alive. And anyway, they don't shoot deserters nowadays.'

'You could be in prison for years,' Jack said.

'Deserting from the army's a serious crime at any time. But now, knowing what you must know . . . '

'They haven't told us anything worth passing on to Adolf, boy-o! Still, as you say, they wouldn't take that into account.'

The Welsh lilt in his voice was more pronounced than Jack remembered it. He guessed that Alan, after leaving Bristol, must have returned to his native valleys.

Elizabeth, closely followed by Helen, came in from the kitchen, carrying a tray of coffee things. Both women looked pale, and were visibly clinging to the rags of their composure so as not to irritate Alan. Helen drew forward a small table on which Elizabeth placed the tray. Jack sat in an armchair and Alan on one end of the sofa. On another small table, drawn up near its padded arm, reposed his service revolver, where he could reach it with the slightest movement of his right hand. He grinned unpleasantly at Jack. 'Still playing the bloody lap-dog, are you? Still following your mistress around? Sorry, I don't suppose "mistress" is quite the right word. Never fancied you in that way, our Lizzie, did she?'

Elizabeth stood up, a cup of scalding hot coffee poised above Alan's head. 'Speak to Jack like that again,' she said quietly, 'and I'll pour this all over you.'

Alan laughed, but there was no warmth in the sound. 'God knows what Richie saw in a harpy like you, nearly old enough to be his mother.'

Elizabeth flushed. 'And God knows how he came to have a father such as you!' she exclaimed rancorously. 'Are you sure your wife didn't deceive you? Before she finally had enough of you and left, I mean!'

It was Alan's turn to grow red. Balancing his coffee cup in his left hand, his right strayed suggestively towards his gun.

'Stop it, Lizzie!' Jack spoke angrily. 'It's not safe to pick a fight with him.'

'That's right.' Alan grinned again. 'Just remember, I've got the revolver.'

'You can't keep us cooped up here for ever,' Jack pointed out. 'Someone's bound to come looking. And if you kill one of us, you'll be caught and hanged. Over a day now, isn't it, since you went absent without leave? It wouldn't surprise me if the M Ps were to bang on this door any minute. They'll check on everyone with whom you've ever had any contact. Lizzie'll be high on the list. If I were you, Alan, I'd get going.'

'Well, you're not me, you little fart!' Alan sneered. 'I had you beaten up once, Hennessey, for poking your nose into my affairs, and here you are doing it again. You're the sort who never learns. It's time someone taught you a lesson.'

Elizabeth sprang to her feet in an uncontrollable fury. 'You rotten little coward,' she stormed. 'You rotten, filthy bigamist! You blackmailer! You're not fit to lick Jack's boots! Go on shoot me! Add murder to your list of crimes!'

'Lizzie, stop it!' Jack urged her again. 'Sit down and have your coffee. Leave this to me. Let him insult me; words can't do any harm.' As Elizabeth subsided on to the other end of the sofa, dashing away hysterical tears, Jack turned back to Alan. Out of the corner of his eye, he could see Helen , as white as her blouse, sitting rigidly on the other armchair. 'I want you to leave, Davies. Now.'

'Oh, do you?' Alan's face was distorted and ugly with rage. 'I'll go when I'm ready, and not before. Get that into your stupid head.'

'Then, when I leave here, I shall go straight to the police.' Slowly, steadily, Jack rose from his chair. 'You can't hold me here indefinitely.'

For answer, Alan, without taking his eyes from Jack's face, reached for the revolver and levelled it at the other man's chest. 'I know how to use this thing,' he threatened.

'Use it then,' Jack replied calmly, and began to move towards the sitting-room door.

'Jack, no! For God's sake,' Elizabeth whispered. 'Don't be a fool. He means it.'

'And I mean it. I'm calling his bluff.' Jack kept moving, but he was not as confident as he sounded. He saw Alan's finger start to tighten on the trigger.

'Jack, please! For my sake — ' Elizabeth was beginning, but the sentence was never finished.

Loud and insistent, into the silence, came the harsh, high shrilling of the front doorbell.

Quick as a flash, Alan was across the room and had pulled Helen up, out of her chair, and pinioned her arms mercilessly behind her. Roughly, he propelled her in the direction of Elizabeth's bedroom.

'Whoever it is, get rid of them,' he snapped at Elizabeth. 'Whoever it is. Understand me?' He shoved his revolver against Helen's side, making her cry out. 'Or your cousin's dead.'

There was no longer any doubting Alan's intentions. He was terrified, and as dangerous as a cornered rattlesnake. Elizabeth passed her tongue across her lips and looked at Jack, who nodded.

'Do as he says, Lizzie. Do you want me to come with you?'

'Oh, no you don't, Hennessey. You stay here, where I can keep my eye on you.' Alan gestured with the revolver at Elizabeth. 'Go on. And make it snappy.'

There was a noise behind him, and he jerked round, wrenching Helen with him. She yelped with pain as her arm twisted in its socket. The door into the garden, with its broken pane of glass, was pulled open and Ben stepped inside. He had eyes for no one but Elizabeth.

'I've been trying to get you all morning,' he accused her. 'The operator at your office kept telling me you were otherwise engaged. Then she said you'd gone home. And now you won't even answer the doorbell.'

He stepped up to her, his eyes blazing, and seized her wrist. 'What the hell do you think you're playing at? You've been making enquiries about me, haven't you? Prying into what doesn't concern you again.'

'For pity's sake, Ben, not now.' Elizabeth tried to free herself. 'Can't you see we've got company?'

Frantically, she tried to reassess the situation; to work out how Ben's unexpected arrival could help them, now that they were four to one. Would it be possible to rush Alan and seize his revolver before he had time to harm Helen?

Jack evidently was thinking along the same lines. He said quietly: 'Sawyer, behind you.'

Ben stared blankly at him for a moment or two, as though suddenly aware that he and Elizabeth were not alone. Then he spun on his heel and looked at Alan and Helen. As he did so, Elizabeth realized how strange Ben's eyes were. A second before they had been snapping with anger; now they were bland and expressionless, as calm as the high snows and almost as remote.

'Ah,' he said, 'Davies, how are you? Haven't seen you for a long time, but I recall you quite well. How's Mary?' His brows came together in a sudden frown, and there was a rapid and disconcerting change of mood. 'What are you doing to my wife? Take your hands off her!' Helen moaned with pain. 'You're hurting her. Let her go!' His eyes widened in outrage. 'You have a gun!'

'And I'm bloody well going to use it if you don't shut up.' Alan, as Jack recognized with a growing sense of panic, was fast reaching the limits of reason. He had been angry when confronted with Jack, but not too alarmed. He remembered Jack's devotion to Elizabeth well enough to be certain that the younger man would do nothing contrary to her wishes if he could possibly avoid it. But now there was another player in the game; someone who knew him, and whose reactions were unpredictable. The situation was getting out of hand. Ben Sawyer had recognized him and was, presumably, capable of putting two and two together. Alan was wearing his army issue trousers and shirt. The battledress tunic lay flung across a chair in the corner. Once more, his finger tightened on the trigger. 'Keep back,' he rasped.

'Do as he says, Ben,' Elizabeth whispered. 'You don't want Helen to be hurt.'

At the mention of her name, Ben's gaze concentrated itself on his wife. 'It's you, isn't it?' he demanded, suddenly vicious. 'You've found another bloody man! Men! Men! That's all you ever thought about!' He was shouting now, yelling at the top of his voice. 'Whore! I was never good enough for you, was I? There always had to be someone else! First Richard Davies, then that blasted American. He's back, isn't he, that one? Oh, yes, I hear things, you know. I see things. Someone told me he'd been sniffing around here, like a dog after a bitch on heat. Well, you're not going to make a fool out of me again! I warned you! This time, I'll kill you!'

He lunged towards Helen, mouthing obscenities like a maniac. Simultaneously, Jack moved, with no very clear idea of what he intended to do, except that, somehow or other, he must prevent Ben from harming his wife. Elizabeth shrieked:'Jack! Be careful!' at the same time conscious that the front doorbell and the telephone were both ringing. Helen screamed as Ben's hands closed round her throat; and Trojan hurtled from beneath a chair, spitting with fear, the fur rising along his back. He brushed between Alan's feet in a bid for the garden door and freedom.

The crescendo of noise and movement ended abruptly, sliced cleanly through by the sound of a single shot. Ben staggered backwards, blood pouring from his head, his eyes wide with surprise, before he swayed and fell. His body jerked once, then lay still. The ringing of the front doorbell had stopped, but the telephone shrilled on and on, nerve-shatteringly, into the silence.

Helen was on her knees, fighting for breath, and Elizabeth, the first to gather her scattered wits, ran and helped her cousin into a chair. The telephone bell suddenly ceased its clamour as Jack moved towards Alan, holding out his hand for the gun. Alan himself stared stupidly at the smoking revolver and then at the dead body on the floor, as though unable to believe what had happened. But at Jack's approach, he seemed to regain his senses and backed up against the wall, ready to shoot.

'Stay away from me, Hennessey,' he said, speaking with difficulty. The breath kept catching in his throat. 'I've killed once. I might as well be hung for a sheep as a lamb.'

Jack made a grab for the gun and Elizabeth screamed, reading the murderous intent in Alan's eyes. As she tried to fling herself between the two men, the only thought in her head being that life without Jack would be intolerable, that she loved him and had probably always loved him in some remote corner of her mind, two military policemen, accompanied by a local constable, burst in through the garden door. She saw them out of the corner of her eye, as she clung to Jack, shielding him with her body.

Alan saw them, too. He hesitated for the fraction of a second as they closed on him; then he lifted the revolver, placed the muzzle inside his mouth and squeezed the trigger.

CHAPTER THIRTY-THREE

'It's not like it was in 1918,' Elizabeth said to Jack, watching the crowds below her office window, surging across the Tramways Centre, holding hands and singing. 'There's not the excitement. Oh, people are pleased enough, but their happiness somehow lacks fervour.'

Jack joined her at the window, slipping his arm about her waist. He smiled to himself as he felt the eager response of her body.

'You have to remember, my darling that we've already had one victory celebration, in May. And the ending of the war in the Far East doesn't mean as much to us Europeans as beating Hitler did. There's the way, too, that Japan was beaten. The atom bomb opens up vistas which make the imagination reel. And the "war to end wars" proved a bitter illusion. People are more cynical this time.'

Elizabeth nodded, turning away from the window and glancing at the calendar on her desk. August the fifteenth, 1945. V J Day. Victory over Japan. Three months after V E — Victory in Europe — Day, it was finally the end of the war. It was time to begin afresh; to pick up, wherever possible, the shattered pieces of people's lives; to build a new Britain with a new Labour Government, elected the previous month on a landslide vote.

'Have you sent everyone home?' she asked.

It was Jack's turn to nod. 'Those that bothered to come in. A few of the senior staff are in my office. I'm opening a bottle of champagne. Are you ready, Mrs Hennessey?'

'Just let me powder my nose.' Elizabeth searched in her handbag for the gold powder compact which Jack had given her last birthday, in celebration of the fact that, in spite of his previous marriage to her sister, they had been given permission to wed.

Elizabeth flicked open the lid and paused, studying her face in the tiny mirror. 'Forty-three,' she murmured. 'Or very nearly. Wrinkles and grey hairs. Oh dear.'

'You have extremely few of either,' Jack said. 'You look wonderful. Now, hurry up, woman, and stop prinking. What shall we do with ourselves for the rest of the day?'

Elizabeth grinned. 'Not what you have in mind,' she reproved him. 'I want to go to see how they're getting on with the renovation to the Mill. I'm hoping we can move in by Christmas.' She tilted her head to one side, regarding him doubtfully. 'You really and truly won't mind going to live there, Jack? You never cared much for it in the past.'

'I'd live in a mud hut at Severn Beach with you,' he assured her cheerfully. 'My objection to the Mill was that I always felt excluded, first by the ghost of Ben, and then by the very real presence of Richard. I can admit that now.'

Elizabeth's face clouded. 'Poor Ben. Yes, I suppose I had always envisaged him and The Brass Mill as going together. And then he jilted me for Helen . . . he must have been mentally sick for a long time before . . . before that awful day.'

'Probably for years,' Jack agreed sombrely. 'I suppose it crept up on him so slowly that no one understood what was happening to him. Not even Helen.'

'Especially not Helen. She was too close to him. She used to say he was mad, but without any conviction. She didn't really believe what she was saying. It was the same with me. Even after I found out that he'd been in that home near Bournemouth, I couldn't really accept that he was dangerous.'

'He always had delusions of grandeur,' Jack said, 'fostered by his mother and aunt.'

'Mmm. But I can't help wondering now if the reason they both indulged him so much was because, subconsciously, they recognized the instability in him. It was something they were afraid of disturbing.'

'You could be right. I think you probably are.'

Elizabeth shivered. 'I still dream about that horrible morning. I can see Ben and . . . and . . . Alan, so vividly.'

Jack took her in his arms, soothing her gently. 'I know. But the memory will fade in time.'

Elizabeth rested her cheek against his shoulder. 'You were wonderful. So calm and collected. You handled the situation so well. The police never suspected that I had any intention of helping Alan.'

'The gun and Ben's death convinced them of that, not me. The violence spoke for itself. You couldn't blame them for believing that Alan had been holding you and Helen hostage, and that I'd just blundered into the situation, like Ben.'

'The truth could have come out, all the same, if you hadn't kept your head. Helen and I were too shocked to think straight.' She sighed. 'What an idiot I was! And it never got into the papers, after all, that Alan was Richard's father.'

'You can thank D-Day for that. Nothing else was of any interest around that time. But it might have been. You weren't to know. Your instinct was to protect Richard's memory. It's called loyalty.'

'I wonder if the estate agents ever managed to let that flat again? I expect they did, after a while, when people had forgotten what happened.' Elizabeth snuggled closer. 'That's something else Helen and I have to be grateful to you for. Taking us in. We couldn't possibly have stayed there.'

Jack laughed. 'What's brought on this reminiscent mood? You don't have to convince me that you love me, you know. You've given me ample proof these last eighteen months.'

Elizabeth freed herself from his embrace and smoothed down her blue silk frock. 'I think I have to remind myself about that day, every now and then, to teach myself a lesson. To remind myself that I had to come to the brink of losing you — of seeing you killed in front of my eyes — before I could accept the truth: that you had always been the most important person in my life.'

He reached out and touched her hair. 'Better late than never,' he answered gently. 'But don't delude yourself that you weren't in love with Richard.'

'I don't. But it was a different kind of love. It was mad and passionate and wholly extraneous to my life. Whereas my love for you has always been at the very core of everything I've ever thought or done. You should have taken me by the scruff of the neck and shaken some sense into me, years ago.'

Jack grimaced. 'I'd like to see anyone try. You're still a very domineering woman, Lizzie.'

'No, I'm not!' She refuted the accusation hotly, then relented. 'Well, now and then, perhaps. But I do like people to be happy.'

'In your way, which isn't always theirs. You do interfere, my darling. Like inviting Chris Morgan to spend his next leave with us, at Eastwood, without consulting Helen. She may not want him there. It doesn't strike me that she's that interested in him any more. And now that she's running Gordon's . . . '

'Nonsense!' Elizabeth interrupted stoutly. 'She's in love with the man. Now, for heaven's sake, let's go and

435

open that champagne. The staff will think we've forgotten them and gone home.' She picked up her navy-blue handbag and tidied away a stray wisp of hair. 'Let's go and drink to Mr Churchill, Clem Attlee, Harry S. Truman, Dwight D. Eisenhower, old Uncle Tom Cobleigh and all.'

'It's strange,' Chris Morgan said, 'being back in Eastwood again. I passed the Tivoli on my way here. It looks thriving.'

'Just one of our chain,' Elizabeth smiled, handing him a dish of potatoes. 'The most important one, of course, because it was the first. Next time you come to see us, we hope to be settled in The Brass Mill. At present, it's being done up, after the depredations of the M A P.'

'Only the office staff,' Jack put in with a laugh. 'Don't let Lizzie fool you into thinking they actually assembled aircraft at the Mill. An impression you might well get, when you hear her carrying on. More salad?'

'Thank you. But I know about the Mill's wartime role. I was at the garden party, remember?'

'Of course. Silly of me to have forgotten.' Jack glanced at Helen, who, so far during supper, had not spoken.

Chris followed his gaze. 'Are you going to live at the Mill, too, Helen?' he enquired.

She jumped, as though her thoughts had been far away and his question had startled her. 'Oh ... No. I haven't made up my mind what I shall do yet. Now that Gordon's belongs to me, it might be convenient to live in Eastwood.'

'Ah! The factory. It came to you when ... after ... '

'After Ben died. Yes; those were the terms of my father's will. Of course, he never envisaged me running it. I suppose he thought that if Ben died before me, I'd either sell it or get someone to run it for me.'

'And you don't intend doing either of those things?'

'Not at the moment. I'm quite enjoying learning the ropes.'

'But you haven't shut your mind against either of those possibilities, have you, darling?' Elizabeth asked her quickly.

'Not yet,' Helen smiled serenely. 'Where are you stationed now, Chris? Germany, somewhere, isn't it? What are your chances of being demobbed and returning home?'

The conversation turned smoothly to Chris's affairs; his experiences during, and since the end of, the war; the cessation of hostilities and the opening of the Nuremberg War Crimes Tribunal.

'Honestly, I could shake the pair of them,' Elizabeth said to Jack when they were in bed that night. 'They're behaving like a couple of strangers.'

'Perhaps that's how they feel,' Jack murmured, drawing her down beside him and kissing her. 'Lizzie, mind your own business. Just concentrate on me.'

She giggled and returned his embrace, running her hands across his naked back.

'I'll try,' she said. 'I really will. But don't ask me to promise.'

In the next room, Helen stared at the ceiling. Unable to sleep, she lay rigid under her bedclothes, lowering her eyes to trace the outline of a dark patch on the opposite wall; a stain left when one of Jack's nieces had thrown her cocoa at the wallpaper. Jack's sister and her children were gone now, to join Bridget's husband, who was one of the British peace-keeping force in Germany. Which was just as well, Helen reflected: Elizabeth had never really got on with any of Jack's family.

Helen rolled on to her side. The knowledge that Chris was in the room across the landing disturbed and excited her, but not, she felt, as much as it ought to, considering what they had once been to one another.

There had been a time when Chris had been her world; but then, so had her father, Charlie, Ben and Richard Davies before him. She was able to admit that now, because she was no longer afraid to face up to the truth. And the truth was that she had always let herself be used by men. Her father had wanted her to be his ideal woman; a pretty, mindless little doll, whom he could indulge and parade in order to satisfy his own vanity. Charlie had wanted an extension of his childhood companion; someone to support and cherish him, take care of him when he was ill; a playmate and a mother. What she might need from marriage he had never thought it worthwhile to consider — so neither had she.

Ben had been different. He had used her first as a means to an end; power, and the style of living that went with it. Then, when, against all expectations, he had fallen in love with her, he had grown desperately possessive; the first overt manifestation, she realized that now, of his illness. Richard Davies, who had never pretended to be in love with her, had used her for experience; for the glamour and excitement of having an affair with an older, married woman. He, at least, had been honest. She supposed, even then, he must have been in love with Elizabeth.

And that left Chris, who, she believed, had genuinely loved her in his fashion, but who, in the end, had been unable to tolerate the ineptitude and blundering foolishness which had been the result of her upbringing and her former experience with men.

The war had proved a catalyst; her salvation. It had taught her that she was a capable woman, able to shoulder responsibility without making a mess of things, and without having to depend on drugs. She had not changed — people rarely changed — it was simply that she had learned to use and develop the ability she had always possessed. And now Gordon's was hers. She sat in the office where her father and Ben had sat, guiding the company back into its peacetime grooves. It was a difficult transition, but with help from the senior members of the firm she was handling it well. No one had expected her to tackle it. Everyone had assumed, after Ben's death, that Gordon's would be sold. Nowadays the most frequently expressed opinion was how like her cousin, Elizabeth, she had turned out to be.

And yet, ironically, Elizabeth had also turned out to be like Helen. She had needed to be loved just as much, and had probably found more romance in her two marriages than Helen had done in either of hers. Mary had been the odd one out; one of those victims staked out by life from the moment she was born; always denied the things she most wanted. Mary had never grasped the simple truth that women could be fighters just as well as men; that it was time for the age-old mores and misconceptions to be thrown on the dustheap. Two world wars in a little over thirty years had ensured that attitudes towards women could never be quite the same again.

Helen sat up, looking at the moonlight dappling the bedroom floor. A tree outside the window cast a delicate pattern of light and shade, tracing a design like a Japanese painting over the white silk coverlet. She slid silently out of bed, pulled on her dressing-gown and slippers, quietly opened her bedroom door and tiptoed across the landing. She paused for a moment, listening, but there was no sound from Elizabeth's and Jack's room.

Equally silently, she turned the handle of Chris's door and slipped inside. It was time to take the initiative and make some discoveries of her own.

It was on September the second, the day that Japan formally surrendered, that Elizabeth announced she was going to have a baby.

'I haven't quite taken it in yet,' she said, her face

radiant. 'The doctor only confirmed it yesterday evening. Here I am, forty-three years of age, and pregnant.'

It was the last morning of Chris's leave, and they were all three going with him to Temple Meads station to see him off on the first leg of his journey back to Germany. From there, in a few months' time, he would return to the States. As far as Elizabeth could make out, Helen had no plans to join him. She had hoped for some last minute announcement during this final breakfast; but instead, she had been the one with the news.

Helen and Chris, after the first, startled silence, during which they rapidly assessed Elizabeth's and Jack's own reactions, were warm in their congratulations.

'You'll have to take care, Lizzie,' Helen warned. 'You'll have to stop working.'

'For a while,' Elizabeth smiled, beatifically.

'You'll take care of yourself,' Jack ordered brusquely. 'For once, you'll do as you're told.'

Elizabeth grimaced, then laughed.

'She's enjoying herself,' Helen thought, amused. 'She's loving every minute of being cosseted and fussed over.' And she realized that her cousin had had very little of that in her life. Elizabeth had always been the strong one, on whom everyone else depended.

After breakfast, while Helen was upstairs, putting on her hat and coat, Elizabeth knocked and entered her bedroom.

'Look,' she said, sitting on the edge of the bed and swinging one leg in its sheer nylon stocking. 'I don't care if you do tell me to get out, mind my own business or whatever; I simply have to ask you or I shall die of curiosity. What's happening between you and Chris?'

Helen fixed her white straw hat, with its navy and white spotted ribbon, tilted at a ridiculous angle over one eye, and smiled at her cousin's reflection in the mirror.

'Nothing,' she answered. 'He's going back to the States to help run his father's grocery chain. I'm staying here to run Gordon's.'

'But Helen, darling!' Elizabeth looked as disappointed as a child who had just been deprived of a favourite treat. 'Don't . . . Don't you love one another any more? I know you've been sleeping with him this leave. Don't be cross. I wasn't prying. I happened to see you come out of his room early one morning.'

'Chris and I are very fond of each other,' Helen said quietly, 'but a great deal of water has run under a lot of bridges since those heady days when I thought I couldn't live without him.' She sat down on the opposite side of the bed. 'Yes, we've been sleeping together. That was my doing, I'm afraid. I wanted to be certain that there was a difference, for me, at least, between being in love and simply wanting to make love.'

'And was there?'

'Yes.' Helen leaned across the white silk coverlet and squeezed her cousin's hand. 'Don't look so stricken, Lizzie. I've discovered what I want out of life; at any rate, for the time being. I want to see if I can run Gordon's successfully. I want to prove people's estimate of me wrong. Above all, I need to convince myself, once and for all, that I'm not the silly, drug-dependent woman I once let people persuade me that I was. Does that make sense to you?' Elizabeth nodded reluctantly. 'Well, there you are.' Helen stood up. 'We'd better be going. We don't want Chris to miss his train. I can hear Jack calling us from downstairs.' She picked up her gloves and handbag. 'By the way, did Jack tell you that when you and he move to The Brass Mill at Christmas, I'm going to buy this house from him? It's a comfortable old place and it will be handy for the factory.'

Chris Morgan leant from the train window, clasping

Helen's hand. The guard was moving along the platform, purposefully slamming carriage doors. The engine sent coils of steam hissing into the station roof. Khaki, navy-blue and air-force blue were still the predominant colours, in spite of a brave show by the late summer suits, coats and dresses.

'You'll write,' he said. 'You've promised.'

'Of course. As often as I can. And you. You've promised too.'

'Naturally. We Morgans are men of our word.'

'That's all right, then.' Her smile wavered a little. 'I shall expect Morgan's to get even larger and more famous, now that you're going into the business with your father.'

'That's a foregone conclusion.' His eyes glinted down at her. 'We might even open up branches in the U K one of these fine days. So you could be seeing me again sooner than you think.'

'That would be nice,' Helen said, and found that she meant it. The guard blew his whistle and waved his green flag. Very slowly, the train began to move. Helen walked along the platform, keeping pace with it, still holding Chris's hand. 'You do understand?' she asked him. The train began to gather pace.

'I understand,' he answered gently. Their fingers clung for a second or two longer, before being forcibly separated by the widening gap between them.

'Goodbye!' she called, running now and waving.

'*Au revoir!*' he shouted back. 'So long!'

Helen stopped running, and stood, watching the train rattle and rock around the bend until the last carriage had disappeared from view, carrying Chris Morgan away and out of her life, as, once before, he had gone, putting the seemingly endless stretch of miles between them. Then, she had been devastated: now, although there were tears in her eyes and a lingering regret in her heart, she felt suddenly free; a prisoner who had been unexpectedly released after years of incarceration. She searched for, and found, her handkerchief in her handbag, blew her nose, dabbed her eyes and drew a deep breath, before walking briskly across the platform towards the exit, to rejoin Elizabeth and Jack, who were waiting outside, in the car.

How unpredictable life was, Helen reflected. There was Elizabeth, who had defied every convention to breach and enter that male holy of holies, the commercial world, and to make a success of it, now dewy-eyed with excitement at the prospect of becoming a mother; of being forced to retire, if only temporarily, from her precious office and desk. And on the other hand, here was she, Helen Gordon-Harrison-Sawyer, who had set so much store by loving and being loved, turning aside from marriage, affection, warmth, protection, to take on, in her turn, that male bastion almost single-handed. At the thought, she felt the blood race and tingle along her veins in anticipation. She might not make a go of it, but it wouldn't be for the want of trying. She nearly laughed out loud from the sheer exhilaration of living.

Helen came out of the station and saw Elizabeth, peering from the car window, her face anxious. Jack was out of the car, standing with elbows resting on its roof. He, too, looked worried. Helen caught their eye and raised her arm in greeting. Then, smiling broadly, her eyes shining, she crossed the road towards them.

THE END

SUSAN SALLIS

A SCATTERING OF DAISIES

THE DAFFODILS OF NEWENT

BLUEBELL WINDOWS

ROSEMARY FOR REMEMBRANCE

Will Rising had dragged himself from humble beginnings to his own small tailoring business in Gloucester – and on the way he'd fallen violently in love with Florence, refined, delicate, and wanting something better for her children.

March was the eldest girl, the least loved, the plain, unattractive one who, as the family grew, became more and more the household drudge. But March, a strange, intelligent, unhappy child, had inherited some of her mother's dreams. March Rising was determined to break out of the round of poverty and hard work, to find wealth, and love, and happiness.

The story of the Rising girls continues in The Daffodils of Newent and Bluebell Windows, finally reaching it's conclusion in Rosemary for Remembrance.

CORGI BOOKS

DIANE PEARSON

THE SUMMER OF THE BARSHINSKEYS

'Although the story of the Barshinskeys, which became our story too, stretched over many summers and winters, that golden time of 1902 was when our strange involved relationship began, when our youthful longing for the exotic took a solid and restless hold upon us . . .'

It is at this enchanted moment that *The Summer of the Barshinskeys* begins. A beautifully told, compelling story that moves from a small Kentish village to London, and from war-torn St Petersburg to a Quaker relief unit in the Volga provinces. It is the unforgettable story of two families, one English, the other Russian, who form a lifetime pattern of friendship, passion, hatred, and love.

'An engrossing saga . . . she evokes rural England at the turn of the century with her sure and skilful touch'
Barbara Taylor Bradford

'The Russian section is reminiscent of Pasternak's *Doctor Zhivago*, horrifying yet hauntingly beautiful'
New York Tribune

0 552 12641 1

CORGI BOOKS

Catherine Cookson
THE MOTH

When Robert Bradley gave up his job in the Jarrow
shipyards to work at his uncle's old-established
carpenter's shop in a small village, he found that life
with domineering Uncle John did not always prove
easy. As a diversion, he began exploring the Durham
countryside and it was there that he had his first
strange encounter with Millie, the ethereal girl-child
whose odd ways and nocturnal wanderings had led
her to be known locally as 'Thorman's Moth'.

The time came when a dramatic turn in Robert's
affairs brought him into a close involvement with the
Thormans of Foreshaw and especially with the eldest
daughter, Agnes, who alone of the family loved and
protected the frail, unworldly Millie. But this was
1913, and anything beyond the most formal
relationship had to face the barriers and injustices of a
rigid social hierarchy that was soon to perish in the
flames of war.

THE MOTH
is both a moving love story and a vivid evocation of a
vanished world, brilliantly created by one of the most
gifted storytellers of our time.
0 552 12524 5

MY FRIENDS THE MISS BOYDS
BY JANE DUNCAN

The My Friend books tell the story of Janet Sandison, of her Highland family, and of the fascinating and varied friends who shaped her life.

MY FRIENDS THE MISS BOYDS is the story of her family home, Reachfar, a Ross-shire farm run by her stern grandparents. It tells of life in a Highland village before the first World War and of the shocked consternation caused when the Miss Boyds, frivolous, men-mad old maids, bring their scandalous behaviour into the community.

This is the first of the My Friends books.

'An enchanting novel. It is a full, rich life that Miss Duncan describes, and her characterizations are sharp and sometimes poignant.'
The Times

'It grows on you uncannily. This is only the first of the happy saga.'
Manchester Guardian

0 552 12874 0

A SELECTED LIST OF TITLES
AVAILABLE FROM CORGI BOOKS

THE PRICES SHOWN BELOW WERE CORRECT AT THE TIME OF GOING TO PRESS. HOWEVER TRANSWORLD PUBLISHERS RESERVE THE RIGHT TO SHOW NEW RETAIL PRICES ON COVERS WHICH MAY DIFFER FROM THOSE PREVIOUSLY ADVERTISED IN THE TEXT OR ELSEWHERE.

☐	13016 8	BILL BAILEY		
☐	12524 5			
☐	12874 0	THE MOTH	Catherine Cookson	£2.50
☐	12875 9	MY FRIENDS THE MISS BOYDS	Catherine Cookson	£2.50
☐	12876 7	MY FRIEND MURIEL	Jane Duncan	£2.50
☐	12877 5	MY FRIEND MONICA	Jane Duncan	£2.50
☐	12878 3	MY FRIEND ANNIE	Jane Duncan	£2.50
☐	12387 0	MY FRIEND ROSE	Jane Duncan	£2.50
☐	12637 3	COPPER KINGDOM	Jane Duncan	£2.50
☐	12638 1	PROUD MARY	Iris Gower	£2.50
☐	13138 5	SPINNERS WHARF	Iris Gower	£2.50
☐	10249 0	MORGAN'S WOMEN	Iris Gower	£2.95
☐	10375 6	BRIDE OF TANCRED	Iris Gower	£2.95
☐	10271 7	CSARDAS	Diane Pearson	£1.95
☐	09140 5	THE MARIGOLD FIELD	Diane Pearson	£3.95
☐	12641 1	SARAH WHITMAN	Diane Pearson	£2.50
☐	12579 2	THE SUMMER OF THE BARSHINSKEYS	Diane Pearson	£2.50
☐	12375 7	THE DAFFODILS OF NEWENT	Susan Sallis	£1.95
☐	12880 5	A SCATTERING OF DAISIES	Susan Sallis	£2.50
☐	13136 9	BLUEBELL WINDOWS	Susan Sallis	£2.50
☐	12700 0	ROSEMARY FOR REMEMBRANCE	Susan Sallis	£2.50
☐	13097 4	LIGHT AND DARK	Margaret Thompson Davis	£2.95
		SCORPION IN THE FIRE	Margaret Thompson Davis	£2.95

All these books are available at your book shop or newsagent, or can be ordered direct from the publisher. Just tick the titles you want and fill in the form below.

TRANSWORLD PUBLISHERS, Cash Sales Department,
61-63 Uxbridge Road, Ealing, London W5 5SA

Plese send a cheque or postal order, not cash. All cheques and postal orders must be in £ sterling and made payable to Transworld Publishers Ltd.

Please allow cost of book(s) plus the following for postage and packing:

UK/Republic of Ireland Customers: Orders in excess of £5; no charge. Orders under £5; add 50p

Overseas Customers: All orders; add £1.50

NAME (Block Letters) . . . .

ADDRESS . . . .

. . . .